THE GREAT HAMSTER MASSACRE

The Great Critter Capers

THE GREAT HAMSTER MASSACRE

Katie Davies

Illustrated by Hannah Shaw

Beach Lane Books
New York London Toronto Sydney

BEACH LANE BOOKS
An imprint of Simon & Schuster Children's Publishing Division
1230 Avenue of the Americas, New York, New York 10020

Published by arrangement with Simon & Schuster UK Ltd
Originally published in Great Britain in 2010 by
Simon & Schuster UK Ltd, a CBS company.
First U.S. edition 2011

Manufactured in the United States of America
0412 FFG
4 6 8 10 9 7 5
Library of Congress Cataloging-in-Publication Data
Davies, Katie, 1978–
The great hamster massacre / Katie Davies ; illustrated by Hannah Shaw.—1st U.S. ed.
p. cm.
Summary: After a long pestering campaign, nine-year-old Anna and her younger brother Tom finally get a pair of hamsters, but when the pets are found mysteriously dead, the siblings and neighbor Suzanne launch an investigation throughout their neighborhood.
ISBN 978-1-4424-2062-5 (hardcover : alk. paper)
[1. Mystery and detective stories. 2. Hamsters—Fiction. 3. Brothers and sisters—Fiction. 4. Death—Fiction. 5. Grandmothers—Fiction. 6. Family life—England—Fiction. 7. England—Fiction. 8. Humorous stories.] I. Shaw, Hannah, ill II. Title.
PZ7.D283818Gre 2011
[Fic]—dc22
2011002046
ISBN 978-1-4424-2062-5 (paper-over-board)
ISBN 978-1-4424-3320-5 (eBook)

For Daniel

—K. D.

A big thank-you to my Mum and Dad, and my husband, Alan, and my agent, Clare Conville, for all their help. —K.D.

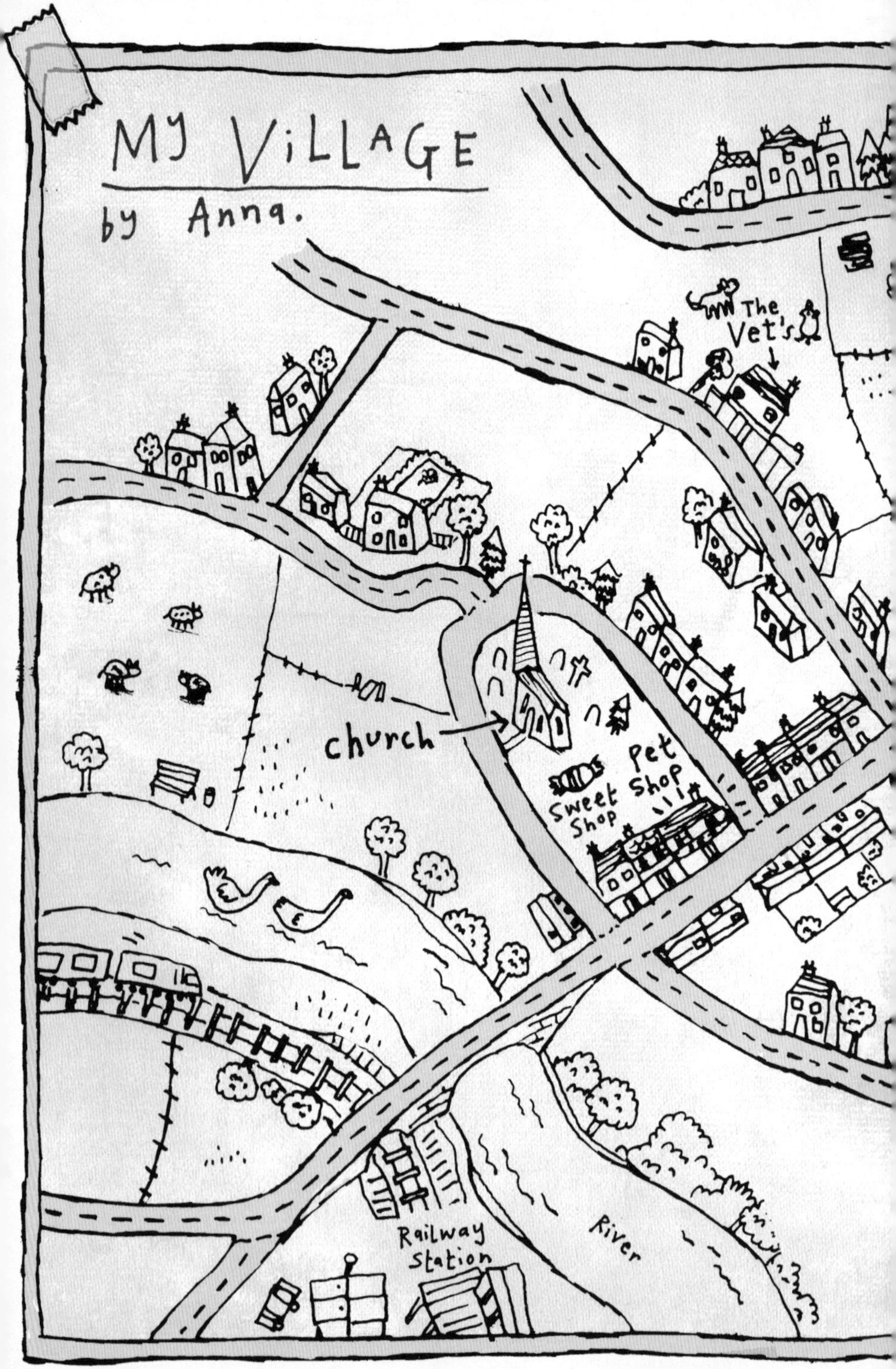
MY VILLAGE
by Anna.
The Vet's
church
Pet Shop
Sweet Shop
Railway Station
River

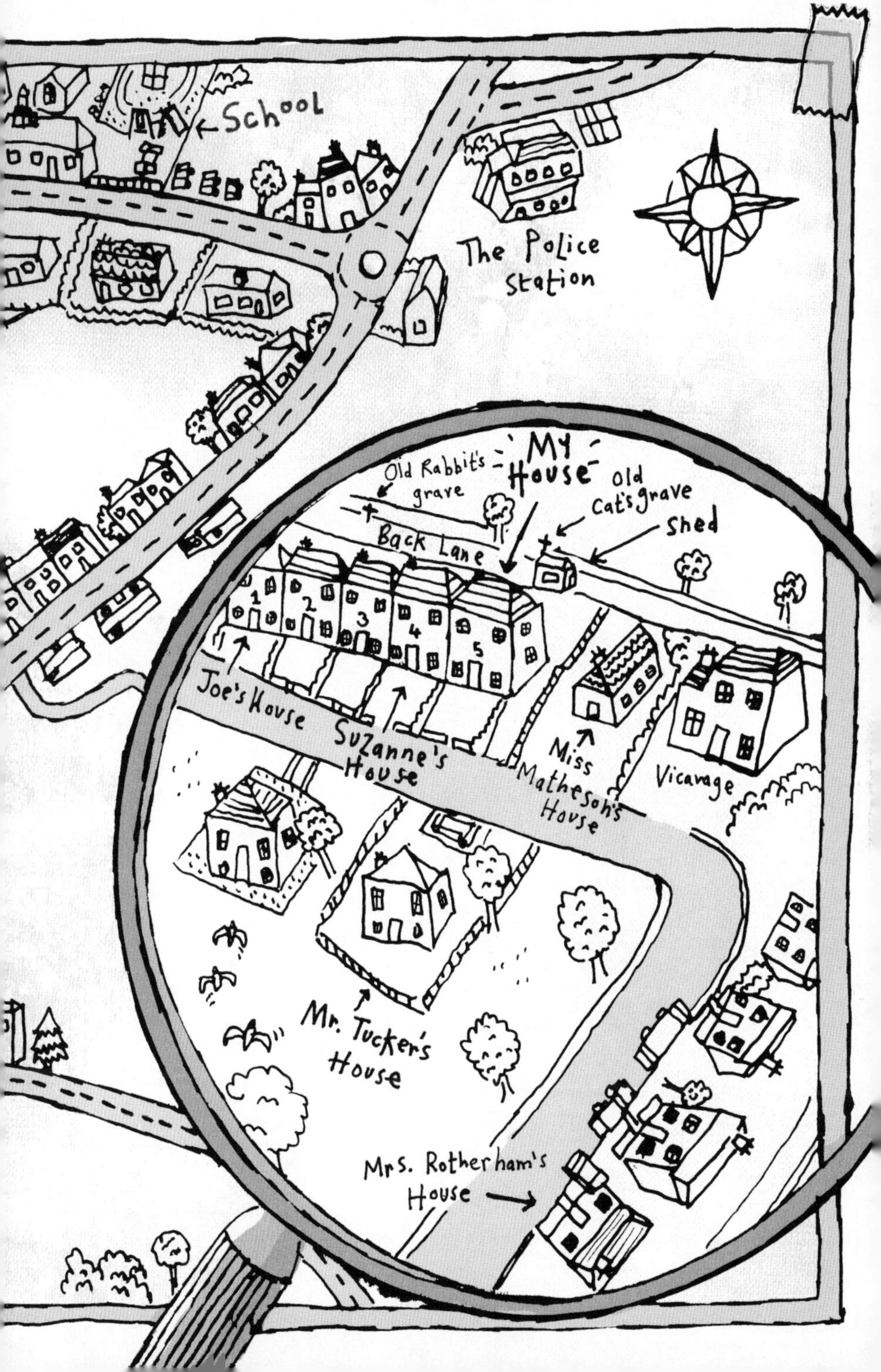
School
The Police Station
Old Rabbit's grave
My House
Old Cat's grave
Shed
Back Lane
1
2
3
4
5
Joe's House
Suzanne's House
Miss Matheson's House
Vicarage
Mr. Tucker's House
Mrs. Rotherham's House

THE GREAT HAMSTER MASSACRE

CHAPTER 1

What a Massacre Is

This is a story about me, and Tom, and our Investigation into the Hamster Massacre. I'm supposed to be writing my What-I-Did-On-My-Summer-Vacation story for school, but I'm going to write this story first because you should always write a Real Investigation up straight away. That's what my friend Suzanne says. And Suzanne knows everything about Real Investigations. Mom said she didn't think my teacher would like the story of my real summer vacation, and how the Hamster Massacre happened. She said, "Anna (that's my name), *some* nice things must have happened this summer and if you can't remember any, you can make some nice things up, and put them in your vacation report instead."

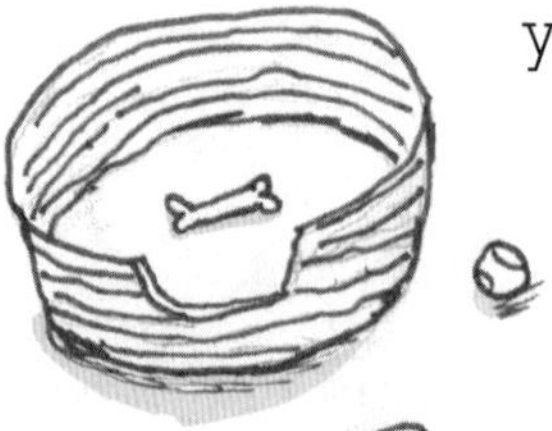

Mom doesn't think it matters if my Vacation Report isn't exactly true, but Graham

Roberts got in trouble last year when he put that he spent the whole vacation in the dog bed. His dog had died, so maybe he *did* stay in the dog bed all vacation, but Mrs. Peters said he must have come out to eat and go to the bathroom and things like that, and Joe-down-the-street told Tom he saw Graham at Scouts. And you can't be in a dog bed *there*.

Tom is my little brother. I've got another brother too, and a sister, but they're older than me and Tom and they don't really care about hamsters much, so they're not in this story. Tom is four years younger than me, except for a little while every year after he has his birthday, and before I have mine, when he is only *three* years younger. But most of the time he's four years younger, so it's best to say that.

Anyway, me and Tom are not supposed to talk about the hamsters and what happened to them anymore because it's best to try to forget about it all, and stop exaggerating, and making it worse than it actually was, and all that. But we couldn't do that anyway because massacres can't really get any worse than they are. That is the point of them. This is what it says about massacres in my dictionary. . . .

massacre [mass-a-ker] ✦ *noun*
a general slaughter of persons or animals: "the massacre of millions during the war"

The dictionary in Suzanne's house said you could have another kind of massacre. It said . . .

massacre [mass-a-ker] ✦ *informal*
a bad defeat, especially in sports: "England was massacred 5–0 by France in the semi-final"

But the Hamster Massacre was not that kind of massacre. The Hamster Massacre was definitely a *formal* kind of massacre.

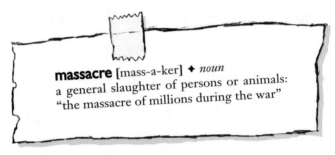

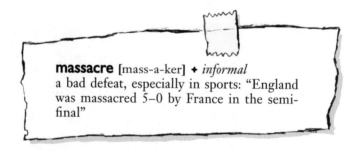

I will keep the story of the Hamster Massacre in the shed with the worms and the wasp trap and the pictures that we traced from Joe-down-the-street's Mom's book. Me and Suzanne have made a lock for the shed door, and we've got a new password. We are the only ones allowed in the shed, except when we let Tom in, but he gets bored when we are making the locks and deciding on the passwords and stuff, and he is too little for the pictures from Joe's Mom's book, so most of the time, when we go in the shed, Tom goes in the house and has a cookie.

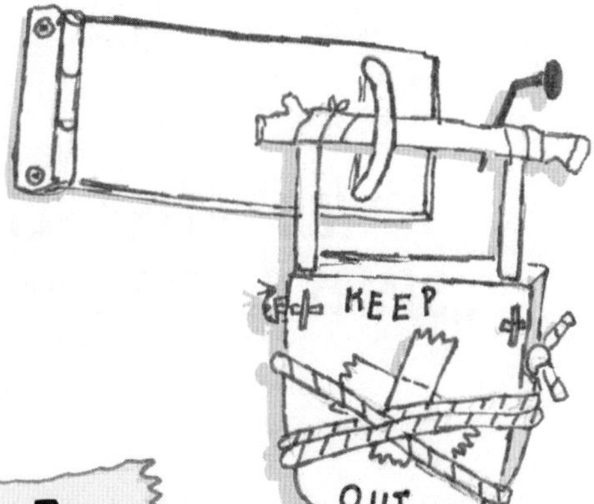

CHAPTER 2

The Wall and the Window

Suzanne lives next door. Her last name is Barry. The wall between our house and the Barrys' house is thin. We can hear the Barrys through the wall. We hear them when they scrape their plates, and when they flush the toilet, and we hear their Dad shout,

"YOU BETTER GET DOWN THESE STAIRS BEFORE I HAVE TO COME UP!"

Mom says, imagine what the Barrys can hear from our house. But none of the Barrys heard anything unusual the day the massacre happened.

Last summer, me and Suzanne made a plan for getting through the wall. Our bedrooms are right next to each other so, if I made a hole on my side of the wall, under my bed, and Suzanne made a hole in exactly the same place on her side of the wall, under her bed, the two holes would meet in the middle to make a tunnel. We wrote the plan on the back of a roll of wallpaper in the shed. Suzanne made a list of all the tools we needed, and I drew the diagrams with arrows.

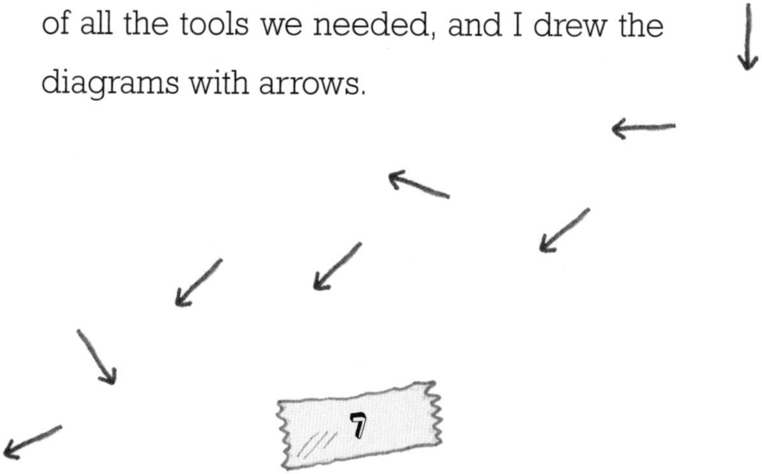

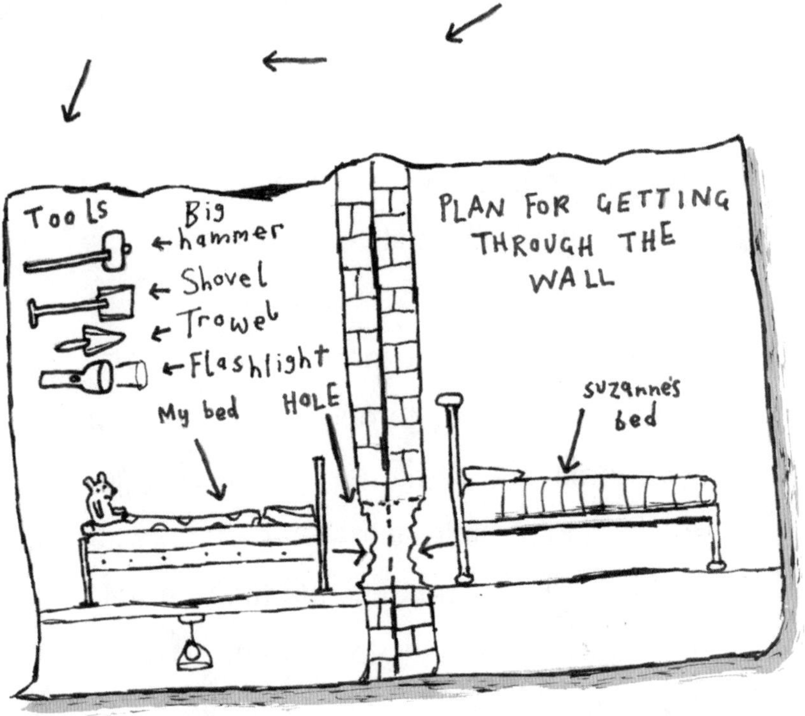

When we had finished, Suzanne wanted to do the diagrams again because she is a better drawer than I am, and then we had a fight, so I took all the tools and hid them, and then Suzanne took the plan and hid that.

And Suzanne's Dad found the plan, and he looked under Suzanne's bed, and he saw that the paint had been picked off the wall, and that a hole had been made in the plaster, and now me and Suzanne aren't allowed to play in Suzanne's room **"EVER AGAIN!"**

I don't ring the Barrys' doorbell now if Suzanne's Dad is at home.

Anyway, we don't need a tunnel anymore because we've got a Knocking Code. This is how it works: When I go to bed, I knock three times on my bedroom wall and, if the coast is clear, Suzanne knocks back three times, and then we both go to our windows and we open them and crawl out and sit outside on the ledge in the night.

Suzanne knows the names of all the stars like The Big Dipper and Orion's Belt, and how to spot them, but she always points to a different place, and I never see anything that looks like a dipper. I just say that I can.

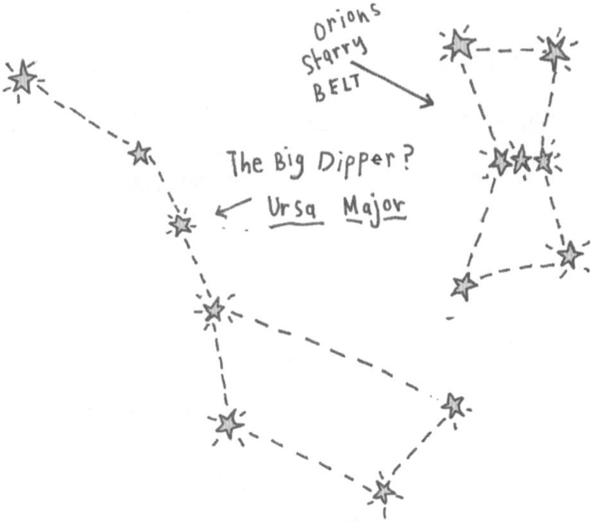

Sometimes we see Mr. Tucker across the street standing by his window too. Mr. Tucker's got a lot of medals from fighting for England in The Second World War. He is easier to spot than The Big Dipper. Normally, when Mr. Tucker's at his window, he's looking out for people doing things he doesn't like, like stealing, or fighting,

or littering. Then he comes out of his house and tells them to stop. Especially if they're littering.

Anyway, me and Suzanne have to be careful when we climb out on the window ledge now, especially if we spot Mr. Tucker, because he could tell Suzanne's Dad, and Suzanne's Dad says if he finds out she's been out there again she will have to swap bedrooms with her brother. His name is Carl but he isn't in this story because he's only a baby.

CHAPTER 3

The New Cat

Before me and Tom got the hamsters, there were a lot of reasons why we weren't allowed to have any. The first reason was the cat. Our cat is not an ordinary cat that sits by the fire and lets you stroke her, and that is because she is from a farm where she was a Wild Cat. We used to have another cat and it was a much better one. But it got run over by Miss Matheson in the back lane. Miss Matheson doesn't like it if you go in her bit of the back lane. She says, **"PRIVATE**

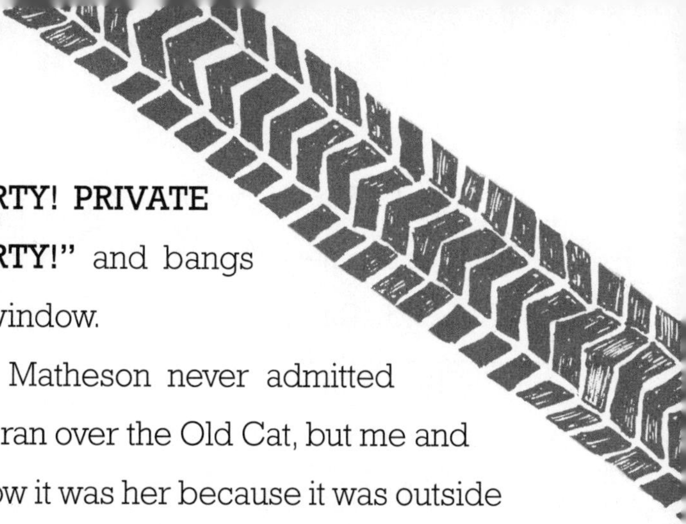

PROPERTY! PRIVATE PROPERTY!" and bangs on the window.

Miss Matheson never admitted that she ran over the Old Cat, but me and Tom know it was her because it was outside her house. And anyway, Suzanne saw cat blood on Miss Matheson's car tires.

Before she got run over, the Old Cat used to let you do anything. You could wrap her in a blanket, put a hat on her, put her in a stroller, and walk her down the road and she didn't even meow.

You couldn't put the New Cat in a stroller. You can't put the New Cat in anything, not even in its own basket, unless you've got gardening gloves on.

I bet Miss Matheson wishes she never killed the Old Cat because when it isn't hunting, or asleep with one eye open, the New Cat spends its time walking slowly up and down in front of Miss Matheson's gate. And it drives her dog mad.

Miss Matheson asked Mom if we could keep the cat inside, but you can't keep the New Cat anywhere.

The New Cat hunts. Its bowl is always full of cat food, *special* cat food from small silver tins that the Old Cat only used to get at Christmas, but it still hunts. It hunts birds, mice, and Joe-down-the-street's New Rabbit.

It tried to hunt Joe's Old Rabbit

too, but as soon as it saw our New Cat, Joe's Old Rabbit panicked and died.

Joe's Mom's Boyfriend looked at Joe's Old Rabbit and said, **"Heart attack. I'll get a trowel."**

And he did, and he dug a hole in the back lane and he put the Old Rabbit in the hole.

Joe didn't like seeing the soil go on the Old Rabbit's fur because when it was alive the Old Rabbit was very fussy about its fur, and it hated getting anything on it, and when it *did* get anything on it, like soil or bits of carrot, it cleaned it off right away.

I thought the Old Rabbit would rather have been put in a shoebox on some straw with a dandelion before it got put in the hole, but Joe's Mom's Boyfriend told me to be quiet.

Joe cried a lot because of the soil, and the fur, and because he wasn't allowed to even wipe it away from the Old Rabbit's eyes or mouth. And he knew the Old Rabbit would hate it.

Me and Suzanne told Joe that as soon as his Mom's Boyfriend went home, and stopped staying at his house, we would dig the Old Rabbit up, and clean its fur, and put it in a box, and make a cross to go in the ground behind it, like the Old Cat has.

But Joe kept on crying,

"GET THE SOIL OUT OF HIS EYES . . .
GET THE SOIL OUT OF HIS EYES . . ."

and his Mom's Boyfriend sent us home.

Anyway, when there aren't any birds or mice outside, and Joe is guarding his New Rabbit with a Super Soaker, and Miss Matheson won't let her dog in the garden, and the New Cat is sick of hunting spiders, and stones, and the wind, it sometimes wants to come in the house.

The New Cat doesn't stop hunting once it's inside the house and has finished fighting with the cat flap, either. Its favorite things to hunt inside the house are feet.

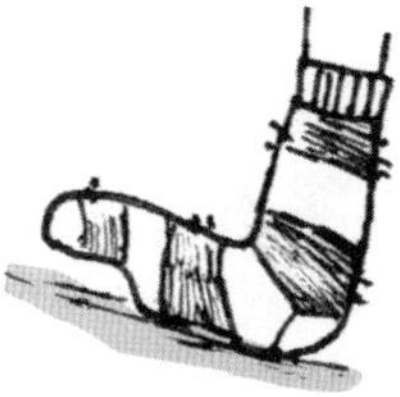

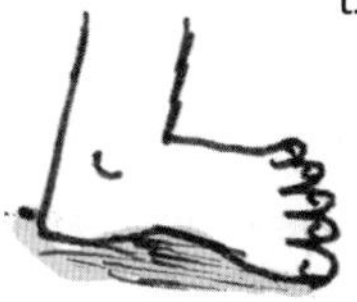

It likes bare feet best, then in socks, then in slippers. If all the feet in the house are in shoes, and it is raining

outside, it will also hunt the vacuum, the spider plants, and the sound of the Barrys' toilet flushing.

Mom said that wherever we might put a hamster, in whatever kind of a cage, with however many guards, if the New Cat couldn't scare it to death, the cat would hunt it and kill it in some other way.

She said, "You and your brother may as well kill a hamster yourselves as bring one within a mile of the New Cat."

I can't remember every single other

reason why we weren't allowed the hamsters before we got them, but I know that the New Cat was Reason Number One.

CHAPTER 4

Reasons and Real Reasons

A lot of times, when someone tells you a reason why you can't have something, the reason isn't really true. Like when Mom tells Tom he can't have a Two-Ball Screwball from the Ice Cream Man because the Ice Cream Man hasn't got any left. That reason isn't true. The *real* reason is that Two-Ball Screwballs have bubblegum in them, and Tom is too young for bubblegum. Last time he had some he squished it in the bath mat.

Out of all the reasons for why somebody

can't have something, being too young is the worst, so when "too young" is the real reason, Mom mostly makes another one up instead.

Other times, when someone tells you a reason why you can't have something, the reason might be true, but it still might not be the real reason why they don't want you to have it. Like when Suzanne's Dad told Suzanne that she couldn't have any pets because he was allergic to pet hair. That's true; Suzanne's Dad *is* allergic to pet hair. It makes his nose run and his eyes itch and his face go red. And that's why the Barrys had to send their dog Barney to live on a farm. But it isn't the *real* reason why he won't let Suzanne have any pets. The real reason is because he *hates* pets. It was Tom who found that out.

In our house, Tom gets told more

reasons for why he can't have things than anyone else. So all Tom does, whenever he gets told a reason, is think of something else he wants as fast as he can instead. So when me and Suzanne told Tom all about how Suzanne wasn't allowed any pets because her Dad was allergic to pet hair, Tom said, **"What about a tortoise? They don't have hairs on."**

Suzanne thought about all the pets she'd asked for. A dog, a cat, a rabbit, a guinea pig, a hamster, and a parakeet (a parakeet doesn't have hair exactly but her Dad said he is allergic to feathers, too) and she hadn't ever even *asked* for a pet without hair, like a tortoise.

So we thought of some pets that don't have hair on and we started to make a list.

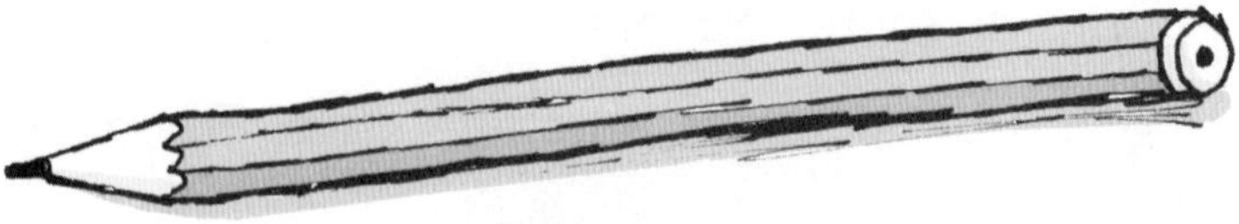

ANNA'S AND TOM'S AND SUZANNE'S LIST OF PETS WITH NO HAIRS ON THAT SUZANNE'S DAD WON'T BE ALLERGIC TO:

1. Tortoise
2. Frog
3. Snake
4. Stick Insect
5. Eel
6. Fish
7. Terrapin (a small turtle that likes water)
8. Lizard

We couldn't think of any more pets with no hair on, so we went on the computer and we put "pets with no hair" in, and guess what? You can get dogs and cats and rabbits and guinea pigs and rats and hamsters and every single kind of pet there is without any hair on if you want it. There was a cat with no hair on called a Sphinx, like the statues in Egypt that we learned about at school with Mrs. Peters, and there were five kinds of dogs with no hair on called Hairless Dogs, each with their own special name. Some of them are too hard to say, and they probably aren't even in English, but I'll write them down anyway.

HAIRLESS DOGS

1. Peruvian Inca Orchid
2. Hairless Chinese Crested
3. Hairless Khalla
4. American Hairless Terrier
5. Xoloitzcuintli

When Suzanne's Mom came to make her go home, we showed her the Hairless Dogs List and the pictures on the computer. When she saw the first ones she screamed and said, "Ugh! They look like aliens!" But when she saw the one called American Hairless Terrier, she said, "Oh," and she looked sad and put her head on one side and said, "That's the same kind of dog as Barney."

It didn't look like Barney to me. But Suzanne's Mom said it was "exactly like Barney. But bald." My Mom said a bald dog was better than no dog, and Suzanne's Mom said, "Same with men," and Suzanne's Mom and my Mom laughed a lot then, for ages, even though it isn't that funny. My Dad is bald. So is Suzanne's.

Suzanne's Mom said to Suzanne that if it was okay with her Dad, they could get a bald dog.

It wasn't okay with Suzanne's Dad, though, because we heard him shouting through the wall. He shouted louder than ever,

"I DON'T CARE ABOUT THE HAIR . . ."

He said,

"I JUST HATE PETS!"

And everyone went quiet because you can't ask, "What about a tortoise?" after a reason like that.

CHAPTER 5
Hamster Horror

Although the New Cat was always Reason Number One for us not being allowed a hamster, it turned out not to be the real reason after all.

One night after dinner, when me and Tom didn't eat our onions and we had go to our rooms until we were ready to say sorry to Mom for making sick noises, we got thinking about hamsters, and how it was all the New Cat's fault that we weren't allowed to have one. So we made a plan, and we went downstairs where Mom was watching TV with Nana.

And I said, **"We are sorry about the onions, Mom."**

Mom didn't say anything because *Coronation Street* was on and, even though she says she doesn't even like *Coronation Street*, and only puts it on for Nana, she never likes talking when it's on.

Anyway, Tom said, "Could we have a hamster if the New Cat was dead, or didn't live at our house for a different reason?"

Mom said, "Mmm . . . what?" and then she said, "No!"

And Tom said, "Why?" which is Tom's favorite question.

And Mom said, "Because. New Cat or no New Cat, hamsters are bad news."

And Tom said, "Why?" again.

And Mom said, "Because."

And then she said, "Bed."

And Tom said, "Why?"

And Mom said, "Okay!" And she stopped watching *Coronation Street* and she stood up and said, "Ten . . . nine . . . eight . . ."

And then Nana said, "Quick, go on up, Duck, and I'll come up too, and I'll tell you a story."

And Tom said, "Is it about hamsters?"

And Nana said, "Yes, it is. It's all about what happened to two little hamsters your Mom knew, and why they were both bad news."

Mom had never told us anything about knowing any hamsters, so we ran up and got ready as quickly as we could, and Tom let me brush his teeth because he takes ages when he does it himself, and he doesn't even brush really, he just eats the toothpaste, and we got in Tom's bed and we waited for Nana. Which took quite a long time because of Nana's hips, and the stairs, and because Mom had to help her.

CHAPTER 6

Geoff and the Sliding Doors

The first hamster Nana told us all about was named Geoff. Geoff was Mom's best friend Shirley's hamster, from when she and Shirley lived on the same street when they were girls. Shirley had six brothers in her house, and a hamster, and an extension, which was an extra room on the back of the house that Mom's house didn't have. The extension had sliding doors.

One day, Mom and Shirley and some of Shirley's brothers were playing with Geoff in the extension. Geoff was out of his cage, which Shirley's Mom didn't mind as long as Shirley and Mom picked up his poop after, and put it in the trash before Shirley's dinner was ready.

But Shirley's youngest brother kept picking up Geoff's poop too and chasing Mom and Shirley with it, and Mom and Shirley were screaming, and running in and out of the sliding doors to escape from him, and Shirley's youngest brother was chasing them, and Mom and Shirley were screaming even more, and sliding the doors shut on Shirley's youngest brother as quickly as they could. And Geoff was running around too, because that's what hamsters do when they're allowed out of their cages.

And Mom ran toward the sliding doors and screamed and slid them open, and

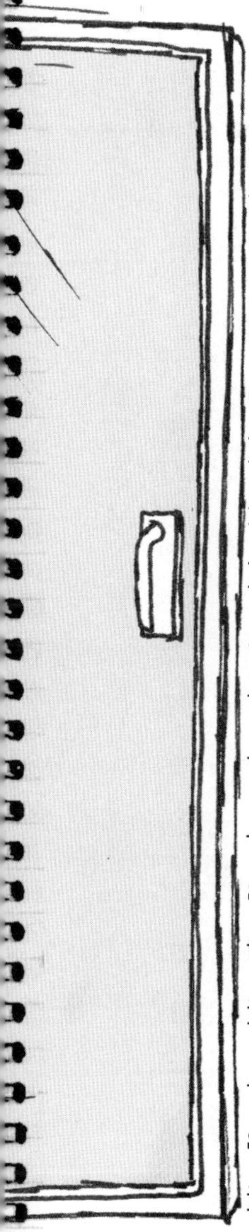

Shirley's brother ran after her. And Mom ran through the sliding doors into the garden and screamed, and slid them shut. And when she slid them shut she heard another little scream, from down low, and she looked to see what it was, and there, on *her* side of the door, in the garden, was the *front* half of Geoff. And she looked through the sliding doors, and there, on the *other* side of the door, in the extension, was the *back* half of Geoff. And the sliding doors were shut tight in-between.

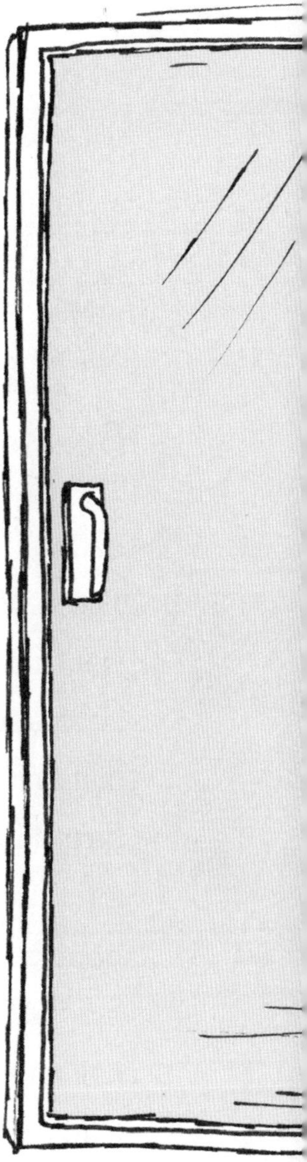

CHAPTER 7

Bernard and the Cashmere Coat

The second hamster Nana told us all about was named Bernard. Bernard was a big fat orange hamster with tiny black eyes that Dad bought Mom for her twenty-first birthday. Mom didn't really want a hamster for her twenty-first birthday, but Dad bought her one because Shirley had told him all about how Mom had cut Geoff in half with the sliding doors when they were little girls, and how sad she had been, and Dad thought that maybe now she was grown up it would be funny if he bought her a hamster of her own.

Anyway, what Mom *really* wanted for her birthday was a green cashmere coat. She had seen the coat in a shop when she was in town with Shirley. It was the most beautiful, and the most green, and the most expensive coat that Mom and Shirley had ever seen, and Mom showed it to Dad every time they went past it.

The night before Mom's birthday Dad told Mom that he had bought her a birthday present that was "lovely and soft and warm," and Mom was sure it was the cashmere coat.

In the morning, when Dad gave Mom a big fat orange hamster, Mom was not very pleased. But she thought that, seeing as Dad had given her a hamster, she had better call it something. So she named it Bernard. And she put its cage on the table in the kitchen, and she started doing lots of tidying and cleaning because she was having a birthday party that night.

When everything was nearly ready, Mom took Bernard's cage off the table because Bernard looked like the least clean and tidy thing in the house, and she put Bernard's cage on the shelf under the coat hooks in the closet under the stairs. She looked at Bernard and thought, *He's very nice really,* and she remembered how much she liked Geoff before she killed him by mistake, and she thought how nice it would be to have a hamster after all. She took Bernard out of his cage and she stroked him on his back, and he *was* very lovely, and very soft and very warm, and she kissed him on the head, and she put him back in the cage and she shut the closet door. And then the doorbell rang, and Mom went to answer it, and it was Shirley. She was wearing the green cashmere coat! She had walked past the shop that morning, and bought it on sale for half price. Shirley looked very nice in

the coat. And Mom thought how nice *she* would have looked in it if it was *her* coat. Dad and Shirley laughed when Mom told them how she had thought Dad was getting her the coat for her birthday, and then he had given her a hamster. And Mom laughed too, but only a bit, because she didn't think it was all that funny. And she took Shirley's beautiful green cashmere coat, and she hung it up in the closet on the hooks above Bernard's cage.

When the party was over and it was time for everyone to

go home, Mom went into the closet to get everyone's coats. She took down Shirley's green cashmere coat and was just thinking how beautiful, and how green, and how soft it was, when she noticed that in the back of the coat, just where Shirley's bottom would be if she were wearing it, there was a hole.

She didn't remember the hole being there when she hung the coat up, and she was just wondering how it might have gotten there, when she saw something in Bernard's cage. Right there, in the middle of the cage, was a very beautiful, very green, very soft-looking nest.

Mom lifted up the top of the nest, and she screamed,

"ARGHHHH, BERNARD!!!"

He was lying on his back in the middle

of the nest with his legs in the air, his little black eyes fixed and bulging, and his mouth, which was wide open, was full of very beautiful, very green, very expensive cashmere coat.

"And that," said Nana, "was the end of Bernard. And *that* is why your Mom said she would 'never, ever have another hamster.' Because hamsters are all Bad News."

And then Nana gave us a kiss. Her kiss smelled like her talcum powder. And she turned out the light. And I stayed in Tom's bed because, like Nana said, you don't have to stay in your own bed if it's summer vacation.

CHAPTER 8

Ask and It Shall Be Given

Most of the time, if you ask Mom for something a lot, especially if you follow her around and do it in a voice that goes, "**Oh PLeeEAse, Mom . . . PLeeEAse . . .**" in the end she will say, "Oh, for goodness' sake, all right."

But not this time. Not with the hamster. Even with Tom asking, "Why?"

And,

"What about if it's a very small hamster?"

Or,

"What about if we never let it out?"

Or,

"What about if we make it sleep in the garden?"

Mom just said, "No," and put the vacuum on and turned the radio right up. So we decided to ask Suzanne to make a plan with us for getting a hamster.

We knocked on the wall three times and then we waited for a bit. Suzanne didn't knock back so either the coast wasn't clear, or she didn't hear us knocking because she was asleep, or maybe she was downstairs having her breakfast. So we knocked another three times, and waited again, and she still didn't knock back, so we knocked as hard as we could for a long time, and then Suzanne's Dad opened the window very fast with his bathrobe on and he leaned out and shouted,

"FOR CRYING OUT LOUD, STOP BANGING ON THE WALL! AND RING THE DOORBELL LIKE A NORMAL HUMAN BEING!"

I didn't want to ring the doorbell like a normal human being, so Tom went over instead, and he told Suzanne we were making a plan.

Suzanne came round, and she brought all her pens, and we made a new password for the day for Shed Club. It took quite a long time because Tom wanted the password to be "Tom" and Suzanne said that was too easy.

And I wanted the password to be "Hamster Plan" and Suzanne said if anyone heard it they would know that we were making a plan about a hamster.

Suzanne wanted the password to be "Rabbit," and I said the plan was about hamsters, not rabbits, so why should that be the password? But Suzanne said if the password wasn't "Rabbit" she was going home, and she was taking her pens with her. So that was what it was.

After we decided on the password, Tom went into the house for a cookie, and Suzanne started thinking of all the things that I could do to get a hamster. And I started writing them all down. We made two lists. And this is what they said. . . .

ANNA'S AND SUZANNE'S TWO LISTS OF THINGS TO DO TO GET A HAMSTER

LIST NUMBER 1

Things to Do to Make Mom Let Us Have a Hamster

1. Jobs
2. Learn My Spelling Words
3. Cry
4. Go Back to Brownies and Say Sorry to Brown Owl
5. Stop Talking
6. Stop Eating

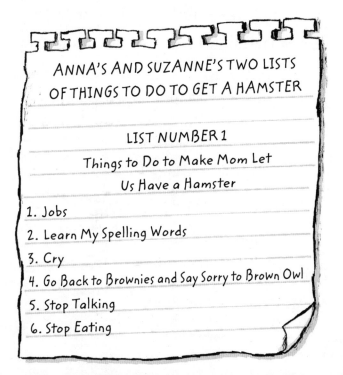

The thing was, I had already done most of the things that Suzanne thought of to put in List Number One. I had tried Jobs and I had tried Practicing My Spelling and I had tried Crying. Mom said I couldn't have a hamster but if I carried on crying she would give me an Oscar. And I was not going to go back to Brownies to say sorry to Brown Owl. I couldn't do that anyway, even if I wanted to, because Brown Owl said that I was Banned. And the only other things left on List Number One were Stop Eating, and Stop Talking, and I didn't think Mom would mind if I did either of those.

LIST NUMBER 2

Other Ways of Getting a Hamster
That Aren't to Do with Mom

1. Steal One
2. Ask Someone Else to Get Me One

The first thing on List Number Two was steal a hamster. I didn't really want to steal anything again if I could help it because the last time I stole something Mom made me take it back, and she said she had half a mind to tell Nana's friend Mrs. Rotherham up the road on me because Mrs. Rotherham used to be in the police. And then I would have to go to Juvenile Hall, which is a jail, but for children, and I definitely wouldn't be allowed to have a hamster there. Me and Tom always used to run when we went past Mrs. Rotherham's house.

The only other thing that was left on the list was to Ask Someone Else to Get Me One. Suzanne said I should ask my Dad. It's different with my Dad than Suzanne's Dad though, because if you ask my Dad something he never says yes or no, he only says, "Ask your mother. She's in charge."

And then Mom says she is not in charge, and if she *was* in charge, Dad would be clearing out all of his junk from the closet under the stairs, like she has been asking him to do for the last ten years, instead of drinking beer and watching football, and then she says, **"And NO. For the last time, you cannot have a hamster!"**

So we tried to think of someone else who was in charge of Mom to ask to get me a hamster. And the only person we could think of was Nana.

Nana stayed at our house a lot because of her hips, and needing help, and things like that. And some of the time when she came to our house she had to stay in bed. And then Nana really liked it if we went into her room to ask her if she wanted anything. Normally she only wanted you to sit on the bed with her, which Mom said we could, as long as Nana wasn't asleep. This time Nana was asleep, but I went in to ask her if she wanted anything anyway because then I could ask her if she would get me a hamster. It took ages trying to ask Nana because first she had to wake up, and then she had to put her hearing aid in, and then she couldn't turn it on, and it kept squeaking, and in the end she said I should just shout because she couldn't make the hearing aid work.

So I did. I tried shouting to ask if she wanted me to get her anything first, but she still couldn't hear, so in the end I just shouted as loud as I could, "CAN. I. HAVE. A. HAMSTER?"

Nana laughed. I didn't laugh because I didn't think it was funny.

And then Nana said, "Ah, I'm sorry, Duck, hop up." And she patted the bed. Nana's bed smelled like her talcum powder. Nana said, "If I was in charge, I'd let you have ten hamsters, Duck. But I'm not, I'm sorry."

And she cuddled me in, and stroked me on the head until she fell asleep again.

I went back to the shed and told Suzanne what Nana said about not being in charge. And I said that maybe we should go and dig up Joe-down-the-street's Old Rabbit instead, because none of the plans for getting a hamster were working. But Suzanne had thought of another person to ask for a hamster, someone who Mom wasn't in charge of, and that person was God.

CHAPTER 9

Our Father . . .

Sometimes, on Sundays, Mom and Nana go to Church, and me and Tom go to Sunday School in the cottage next door to the Church, because children aren't allowed to be in Church for long in case they start laughing or crying or needing to pee. You can't do those kinds of things in Church. The only things you *can* do in Church are kneeling on the cushions and saying the

Amens. Unless you are Confirmed, and then you can eat the Body of Christ and drink His Blood.

But me and Tom aren't old enough to do that, so we go to Sunday School instead and just go into Church for the last part at the end.

You can do most things in Sunday School, like coloring and singing and dressing up, as long as you don't dress up as Jesus on the cross, because Graham Roberts did that once, just in his underwear, and Mrs. Constantine didn't like it.

Mrs. Constantine is in charge of Sunday School, and she is the Vicar's Wife.

Anyway, when Sunday School is finished you do the Prayer, and have a cookie, and then everyone from Sunday School goes into Church for the last part and sits with their moms. Sometimes they sit with their dads, as well, but mostly they sit with their moms because not many dads go to Church.

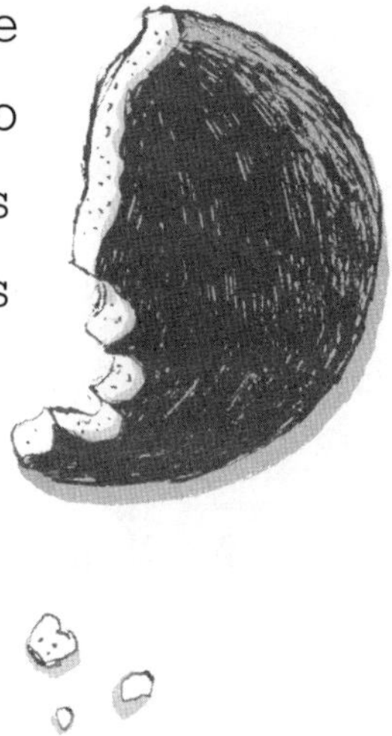

Our Dad doesn't go. He doesn't even believe in God. Graham Roberts said Dad will probably go to Hell. Nana said Dad won't go to Hell and Graham Roberts shouldn't say things like that because he doesn't know what he is talking about.

There aren't very many children in Sunday School. Sometimes it's ten, and sometimes it's six, and once it was only two, and that was when it was just me and Tom, and then Mrs. Constantine said there wasn't any point in even doing Sunday School that week, and she made me and Tom go into Church for the whole time with Mom and Nana. And that was when we got in Big Trouble because we had The Hysterics, because first everyone in Church had to shake hands with each other and say, "Peace be with you," and the lady who was sitting behind Tom kept saying "*Peath* be with you" instead. And then the Vicar said "Hymn 97" and that's the hymn that goes . . .

I was cold. I was naked.
Were you there?
Were you there?
I was cold. I was naked.
Were you there?

And me and Tom kept thinking about when Graham Roberts was Jesus, in his underwear. And then the lady who was sitting behind us who had said "Peath be with you" hit Tom hard on the head with her hymn book.

And then we *really* got The Hysterics. And we had to lie on the floor under the pew.

Nana asked the Peath Be With You lady if she would mind *not* hitting Tom on the head with her hymn book.

But the Peath Be With You lady said she would very much mind not hitting Tom on the head with her hymn book, because Tom was Out Of Control and children like us had "No buithneth being in Church."

And Nana said, "Suffer the little children," which is something from in the Bible that Jesus said, which means you can't really hit children on the head with your hymn book or anything, even if they *have* got The Hysterics.

Then the Peath Be With You lady said, "Thuffer nothing. They've ruined the thurvith."

And then Nana had to leave the Church because she said she had a bad cough, but really it was because she had The Hysterics a bit too.

And she took me and Tom with her and we went to get ice cream, even though it was raining, because Nana said ice cream is good for calming down.

• • •

But we didn't get The Hysterics when we went to Church to ask God about getting a hamster.

Mom didn't want to go to Church that day because Nana was staying in bed with her hips. But we promised we wouldn't get The Hysterics and, in the end, Mom said "All right then" because when you ask to go to Church, it's not really the kind of thing that a Mom can say no to. Not like when you ask to go to Disneyland or something like that.

And Suzanne said she wanted to come along too because she had never been to Church before.

In the morning, before we left, Mom said we should go and give Nana a kiss and tell her we were going to Church because she would like that. Maybe she did like it, but she didn't open her eyes. I gave Nana a kiss on the cheek, and so did Suzanne, and Tom gave her a kiss on the hand because he doesn't like kissing Nana on the cheek because he says she prickles, which she does, but only a little bit. Nana's cheek smelled like her talcum powder. Suzanne said our Nana looked very small in the bed, which she did, because she hardly made a shape under the covers, but the bed is quite big so that probably made her look smaller.

Mrs. Constantine was pleased that we had brought a new person to Sunday School, and she was even more pleased when she asked Suzanne what she would like to do and Suzanne said, "I need to ask God for something."

Mrs. Constantine told Suzanne that "asking God for something is called praying." Which Suzanne already knew, but she pretended she didn't. Mrs. Constantine gave Suzanne a Bible, and she showed her which page told you how to pray. It was quite hard to read, so Mrs. Constantine read it first. She said, "But thou, when thou prayest, enter into thy closet, and when thou hast shut thy door, pray to thy Father which is in secret; and thy Father which seeth in secret shall reward thee openly. . . . After this manner therefore pray ye:

Our Father which art in heaven,
hallowed be thy name.
Thy kingdom come.
Thy will be done, on earth, as it is in heaven.
Give us this day our daily bread.
And forgive us our trespasses,
as we forgive those who trespass against us.
Lead us not into temptation,
but deliver us from evil:
For thine is the kingdom,
the power and the glory,
forever and ever.
Amen."

Suzanne said thank you to Mrs. Constantine, and she took the Bible.

We waited until Mrs. Constantine wasn't looking, and then me and Tom and Suzanne snuck up the stairs, where you aren't supposed to go, into the store room where there is a big cupboard, which is almost a closet, where all the old Bibles are, and the hymn books, and the purple cloths, and the gold crosses and things like that, because that seemed like the best place to do it.

It was pretty dark inside the old cupboard, once you got right in. I wanted Suzanne and Tom to come into the cupboard with me, but Suzanne said I had to go in on my own and close the door, and pray in secret like Mrs. Constantine said.

I said the Prayer, the parts I could remember, because it was too dark to read, and then I said, "Amen," and then I waited for a bit. And then, just to make sure, I said, "Can I have a hamster?"

And then I said "Please."

And then I said "Amen" again.

When I was finished, and I tried to get out

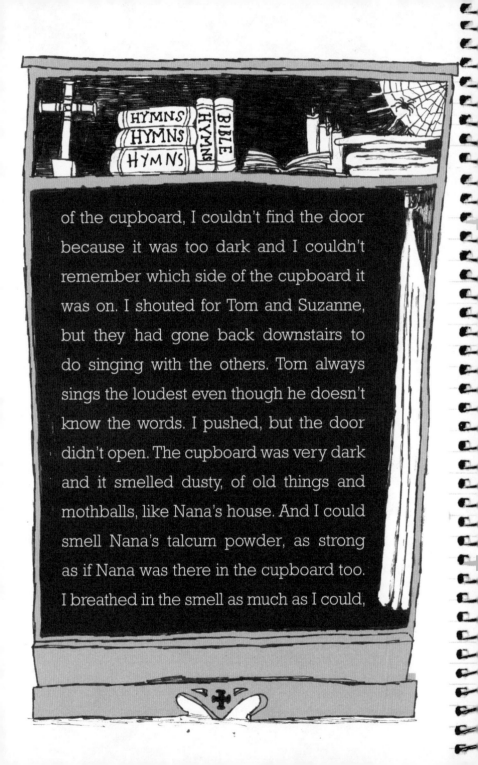

of the cupboard, I couldn't find the door because it was too dark and I couldn't remember which side of the cupboard it was on. I shouted for Tom and Suzanne, but they had gone back downstairs to do singing with the others. Tom always sings the loudest even though he doesn't know the words. I pushed, but the door didn't open. The cupboard was very dark and it smelled dusty, of old things and mothballs, like Nana's house. And I could smell Nana's talcum powder, as strong as if Nana was there in the cupboard too. I breathed in the smell as much as I could, until I thought I was going to sneeze, and I shouted,

"LET ME OUT!"

And then a spider, or a mouse, or a rat ran over my foot. So then I *really* wanted to get out of the cupboard. I am not scared of spiders and mice and rats and things because I quite like them, but I don't really like them running over my feet in a dark cupboard when I can't see. So I leaned on the door as hard as I could, and I screamed,

"HELP!"

And then the whole cupboard fell right over, and it crashed onto the floor with me inside.

Mrs. Constantine ran upstairs and said "Hello? Who's there?"

And I said "Me."

And she said "Who?"

And I said,

"ME! HELP! I'M IN THE CUPBOARD."

But Mrs. Constantine couldn't help because she couldn't lift the cupboard up, because it was quite a heavy cupboard, even when I wasn't inside it, and I weigh seventy-two pounds, so she had to get the caretaker.

When I got out we all had a cookie, and some juice, and looked for the rat, but we couldn't find it because it had got away, and then we went into Church for the last part. And we stood at the back. And the Vicar said, "Therefore I say unto you, what things soever ye desire, when ye pray, believe that ye receive them, and ye shall have them. For everyone that asketh receiveth; and he that seeketh findeth; and to him that knocketh it shall be opened. Or what man is there of you, whom if his son ask bread, will he give him a stone? Or if he ask a fish, will he give him a serpent?"

And Suzanne whispered, "Or, if she asks for a hamster, will he give a rat?"

And Mrs. Constantine said, "Shhh."

And then we went to sit with Mom.

When we got home, Dad told me and Tom to wait downstairs while Mom went upstairs to see Nana, but Tom went up anyway, and I followed after.

Mom was sitting on Nana's bed. And Nana was in it. Nana looked even smaller in the bed than before. And Mom was crying.

Tom asked Mom if she was sad. Mom nodded her head.

Tom said, "Why?" But Mom didn't answer because she put her hand over her mouth instead. And she patted the bed with her other hand.

And me and Tom got up. I could smell Nana's talcum powder again. And Mom said that Nana was dead. And she cried for a long time then, and she cuddled us in, and she stroked us on the head.

CHAPTER 10

The Hamsters Came In Two by Two

After Nana died, I decided I wouldn't ask Mom about a hamster again, and I wouldn't tell her how Nana said if she was in charge she would let me have ten hamsters, or how I asked God for one, because Mom was sad quite a lot.

Then, the day after

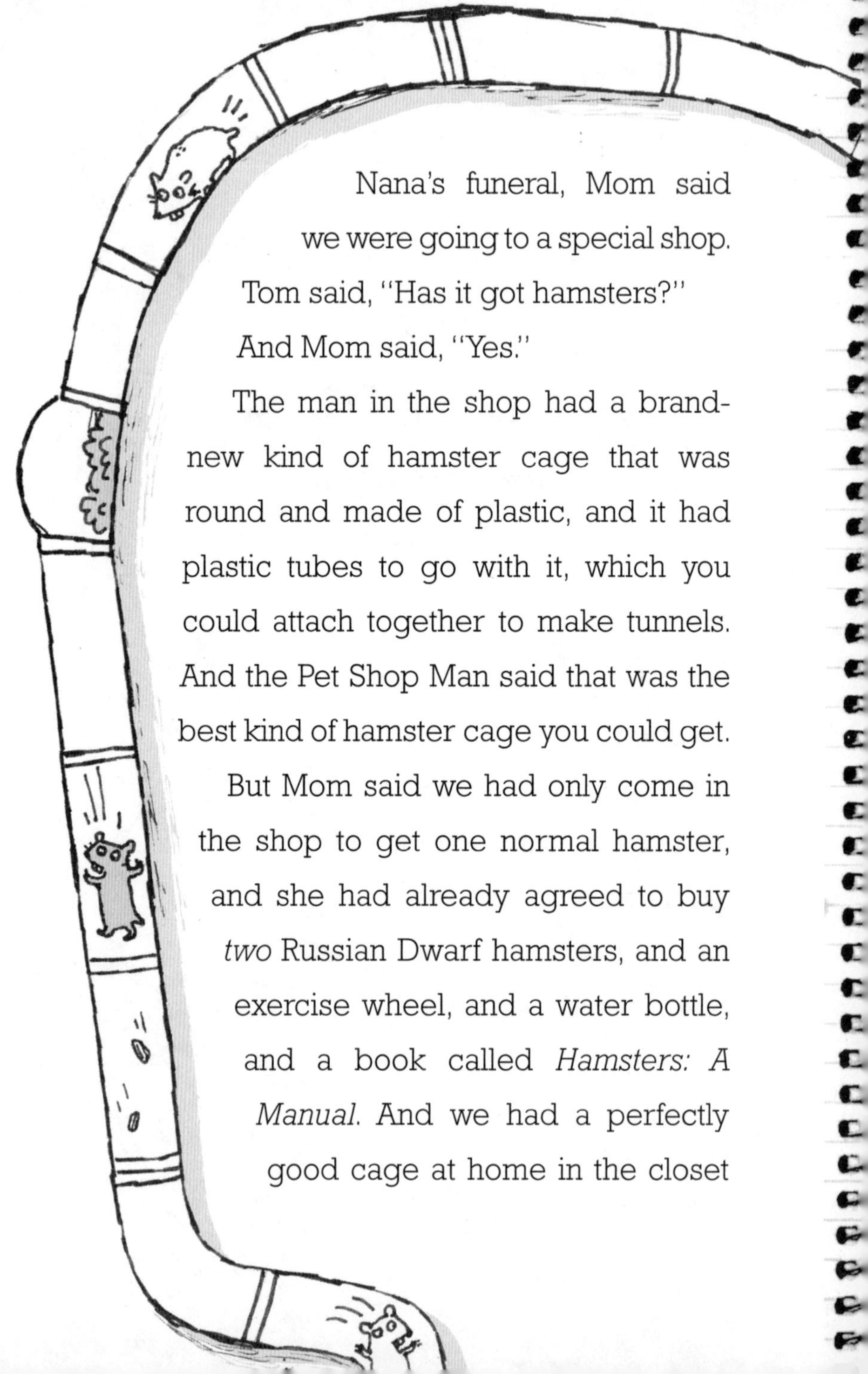

Nana's funeral, Mom said we were going to a special shop.

Tom said, "Has it got hamsters?"

And Mom said, "Yes."

The man in the shop had a brand-new kind of hamster cage that was round and made of plastic, and it had plastic tubes to go with it, which you could attach together to make tunnels. And the Pet Shop Man said that was the best kind of hamster cage you could get.

But Mom said we had only come in the shop to get one normal hamster, and she had already agreed to buy *two* Russian Dwarf hamsters, and an exercise wheel, and a water bottle, and a book called *Hamsters: A Manual*. And we had a perfectly good cage at home in the closet under the stairs and Dad would just have to find it.

So the Pet Shop Man put the hamsters in a brown box with some sawdust and some air holes and we took the hamsters home in that.

●⫶ ●⫶ ●⫶

When we got to the end of our street, Tom ran ahead to see if Dad had found the cage yet. Mr. Tucker was in the road picking up litter, which he always does. And Tom was running up the street, and Mr. Tucker was coming out of the hedge backward, and he had some toilet paper in one hand, and a bag full of litter in his other hand, and there were lots of

burrs and twigs and things stuck to his tie and his blazer. And Tom was running his fastest, and he probably had his eyes shut, and Mr. Tucker looked up and saw Tom coming and he said, "Hallo, look keen! Let up!"

But Tom ran right into Mr. Tucker, and Mr. Tucker dropped the toilet paper and the bag full of litter and said, "Oomph! Good God! What a belt!"

And Tom fell over on the gravel.

And Mr. Tucker said, "What's this arrival, eh? I could have done with an Arse-end Charlie there. I think that makes you an Ace, old chum." Mr. Tucker is quite hard to understand sometimes, what with being in The War and all.

And Tom started crying.

And Mr. Tucker said, "Aha, frozen on the stick, eh? Well, where's your salute,

Sir? You know the drill. On your feet. Look lively. Fling one up."

And Tom got up and gave Mr. Tucker the salute, even though he was crying, because it's one of Tom's favorite things to do when he sees Mr. Tucker, and Mr. Tucker gave him one back and he said, "Smashing job. Good show, me old sawn-off. Where's that knee? Better have a quick shufti. Ooh, a humdinger. Dicey do, that was. You'll live, I'd say, but will you have to have the leg off? What do you think?"

And Tom said No, because he had stopped crying, and his knee was only bleeding a bit.

And Mr. Tucker said, "No? Quite right. That's the spirit. Press on regardless. You're not washed out yet. Plane's a write-off but you'll just have to wear it. Be glad you didn't land in the drink. In a bad way myself, as it goes. Got me in the goolies."

And that made Tom laugh.

And Mr. Tucker said, "Hallo" to Mom.

And Mom said, "Hello" to Mr. Tucker.

And I didn't say anything because I didn't want to start talking to Mr. Tucker in case it was about litter.

And then Mr. Tucker said to Mom, "Black do, your mother hopping the twig. Heard a buzz the old girl was low on juice. Clocked the blood wagon outside a week gone Sunday, thought 'Hallo, look up,' and a couple of body-snatchers bringing her in. Bad show all round. Beautiful blond job like that. Doesn't do. Doesn't do."

And Mom said, "Thank you."

And then Mr. Tucker said, "What do

you say, Popsie? She was a fine woman, eh?"

And I said, "Yes."

And Mr. Tucker said, "A very fine woman." And then he said, "And she was flat-out for me plugging away at this litter situation. Took a dim view of it, very dim, I can tell you. Last time I saw her she said to me, 'Wing Commander,' she said, 'I think somebody, somewhere, is playing silly beggars with this litter.' 'Silly beggars,' she said."

And then Mr. Tucker stared at me until Tom said, "We've got hamsters."

Mr. Tucker pointed his finger at me, and closed one eye and said, "Mmmmm."

I didn't say anything to Mr. Tucker, but I don't believe Nana

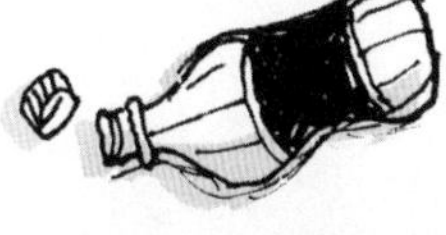

said anything about silly beggars because for one thing, that wasn't really the kind of thing that Nana ever said, and if she *was* going to say it, she probably wouldn't say it to Mr. Tucker because she didn't like talking about litter much either.

Mr. Tucker said, "Hamsters, Tom, is it? Where d'you get 'em?"

And Tom said, "The pet shop."

And Mr. Tucker said, "Pet shop, eh?"

And Tom said, "Yes."

And Mr. Tucker said, "How many?"

And Tom said, "Two."

Mr. Tucker said, "Two of 'em, eh?"

And Tom said, "Yes."

And Mr. Tucker said, "Smashing."

And Tom said, "Yes."

And I was getting bored of listening to Tom and Mr. Tucker so I said, "They're from Russia."

Mr. Tucker said, "Russia? Good God, girl! Have you lost your wool completely?"

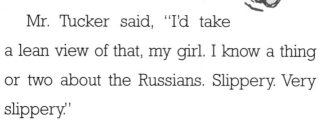

And I said how the man in the shop said that the Russian ones were the best.

Mr. Tucker said, "I'd take a lean view of that, my girl. I know a thing or two about the Russians. Slippery. Very slippery."

And then Mr. Tucker took the box with the hamsters from me, and took the lid off, and the hamsters could have gotten out in a second.

But they didn't.

And Mr. Tucker looked in the box and he said, "Just as I thought. Couple of gremlins. What are you calling them?"

Tom said, "Don't know."

And Mr. Tucker said, "Number One,

and Number Two, Basher. That's what I'd call 'em."

And Tom said, "I need to pee."

Which he did, because he was hopping from one foot to the other, and he had been doing it for ages, and that's what he does when he needs to pee.

So Mr. Tucker gave Tom the salute.

And Tom gave Mr. Tucker the salute back.

And Mr. Tucker said, "That's it. You've got the green, Old Chum. Chocks away."

And then he messed up Tom's hair.

And then he looked at me and said, "Silly beggars. . . . Mmmm."

And then he went back into the hedge.

And me and Tom and Mom went into the house.

CHAPTER 11

Housing the Hamsters

When we got in the house Dad had found the hamster cage and he'd cleaned it out and put it in my room, and put some sawdust in it and a food bowl. And Mom attached the water bottle and then she put the wheel in. The thing with the hamsters was, though, because of them being Russian Dwarf hamsters, when we put them in the cage, their legs were too small to make the wheel go round, and their mouths were too small

to get the water out of the bottle, and their bodies were too small to not be able to get out between the bars. And they did get out between the bars. And one of them peed on the carpet. And Mom started crying and left the room, even though it was only a little pee. But Dad said Mom wasn't really crying about the pee, and not to worry.

Tom said, "Is she crying about Nana?"

And Dad said, "Yes."

And then Mom and Dad went into Nana's room, and closed the door, and they changed Nana's bed, and put her things in boxes. And afterward it looked like nothing had ever happened.

Me and Tom cleaned up the pee on the carpet and we put the hamsters back in the brown box with the airholes. And after that Mom went to bed.

Then Dad went to see Mrs. Rotherham up the road because she has got a lot of fish in her house, and he said maybe she had an old fish tank that we could borrow, and we could use that for a hamster cage instead. And Tom stayed in the house because he didn't want to go to Mrs. Rotherham's because Mrs. Rotherham used to be in the police, and Mom sometimes said she had half a mind to tell Mrs. Rotherham on Tom when he was In Trouble, and Tom wasn't sure if she had or not.

And I stayed in the house too because I needed to find out some things about the hamsters.

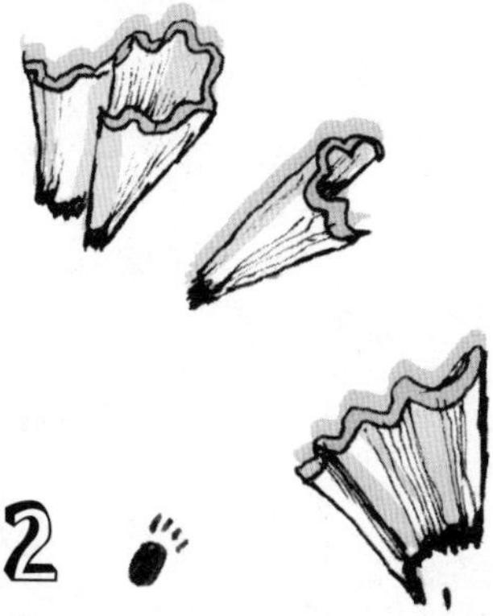

CHAPTER 12

From Russia with Love

This is what it said in my dictionary about Russians. . . .

Russian [rush-un] ✦ *noun*
someone or something from Russia

And this is what it said in my dictionary about dwarves. . . .

dwarf [dworf] ✦ *noun*
a person of abnormally small stature suffering from a bone-growth disorder

I didn't think that the hamsters were suffering from anything, except maybe being in the box, so I went and knocked on Suzanne's wall to see what the dictionary in her house said. Suzanne isn't allowed to take the dictionary out of her house anymore because last time she took it, when we needed to look up some words from Joe-down-the-street's Mom's book in the shed, she forgot to take it back. And that was when I thought it would be a good lid for the worms.

It wasn't a very good lid for the worms because the next day the worms weren't really moving anymore. And then the dictionary got some of the worms' mud on it. And then Suzanne got in Big Trouble with her Dad, because he said, **"WHERE ON EARTH IS MY DICTIONARY, SUZANNE?"**

And Suzanne came to my house to get it, and we tried to get the mud off but it just made it worse, and then Mom said I had to go with Suzanne to take the dictionary back.

And then Suzanne's Dad said, **"WHAT IN GOD'S NAME HAVE YOU BEEN DOING WITH IT?"**

And I said I had been using it for a worm lid.

And Suzanne's Dad said, **"DOES IT *LOOK* LIKE A WORM LID, FOR CRYING OUT LOUD?"**

And then Suzanne's Dad said Suzanne was never allowed to take the dictionary—or anything else—out of his house again, because of Suzanne being

". . . INCAPABLE OF BEHAVING LIKE A NORMAL HUMAN BEING!"

I said that maybe Suzanne could go and get the dictionary anyway, because her Dad wasn't at home, and she could stay in her room with the dictionary, which wouldn't be taking it out of the house, and I could go on the window ledge, and she could read what it says about dwarves through the window and I could write it down, and then she could put the dictionary straight back.

So that is what we did.

This is what it said about dwarves in the dictionary in Suzanne's house. . . .

dwarf [dworf] ✦ *noun*
a being in the form of a small mythical man, usually having magic powers

I didn't think the hamsters were men, because Mom asked the Pet Shop Man about ten times, and the Pet Shop Man said they were definitely both female. And I didn't think they had magic powers because I don't believe in that kind of thing anymore, because I am nine. Anyway, then the dictionary in Suzanne's house said . . .

dwarf [dworf] ✦ *noun*
of unusually small stature or size; diminutive. For example, dwarf star

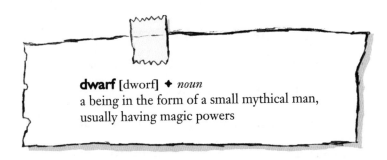

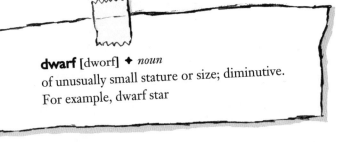

The hamsters *were* unusually small, because that was how they got through the bars in the cage. Suzanne said she knew how to spot Dwarf Stars, and she said she would tell me all about them if I liked. But I said I had to go and check on the hamsters. And then Suzanne said she had gotten a new bike that used to be her cousin's, and I should come to her house and see it. But Dad came back with a new wheel that was smaller, and a water bowl and a fish tank from Mrs. Rotherham. So I said, "I'll knock for you later," and I shut the window.

We put the sawdust in the fish tank, and the new wheel, and the water bowl, and the food bowl, and some tissue paper for a nest, and then we put the hamsters in. The hamsters stood very still in the middle of the fish tank. And then we looked in the book for what to do next. And Dad read it with us because it was quite hard to read.

"The Russian Dwarf, or Djungarian, Hamster, properly known as Phodopus Sungoris Campbelli and otherwise referred to as Campbell's Dwarf Hamster, or Hairy-Footed Dwarf Hamster, ought not to be confused with the Winter White, or Siberian, Hamster from the closely related sub-species, Phodopus Sungorus."

Tom said he didn't like the book and he wanted to go and see Mom.

But Dad said he couldn't, and he gave

Tom a whole packet of cookies, chocolate ones, and then Tom said he didn't mind staying. So Dad read some more.

"The Russian Dwarf Hamster is a diminutive rodent, compact of body, with an undersized tail and, in common with all Cricetinae, expandable cheek pouches. The range of normal length of the Russian Dwarf lies between 2.4 and 4.4 inches (tail inclusive)."

We got a tape measure, and we measured the hamsters, which was quite hard because they didn't really like being measured. Hamster Number One was about two inches long, and its tail was a quarter inch. And it was the Small One. Hamster Number Two was almost four and half inches long, and I couldn't measure its tail because it kept trying to bite me. But it was the Big One.

Anyway, then it said in the book . . .

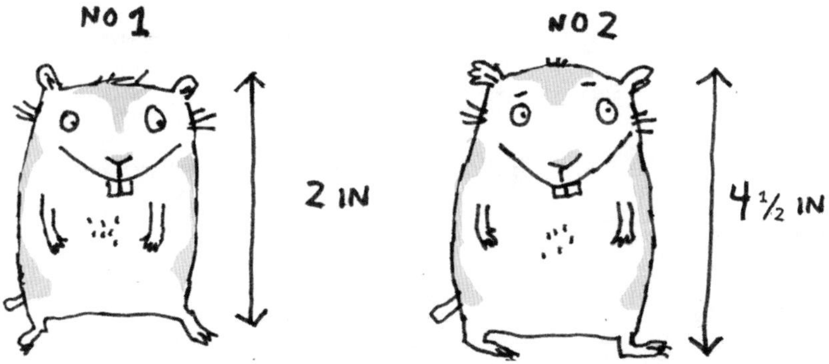

"There are numerous variants and hybrids in terms of coat and coloring. Most commonly, the fur of the upper body is short, flat, and grayish brown, with a white underside, and a dark brown stripe running the length of the spine. Such a variant is found in the wild, as well as domestically, and is properly referred to as the Agouti."

I didn't want to read the book anymore because it was hard to understand, and it didn't really help with what to do with hamsters, and Tom didn't want to read the book anymore either because he had finished the cookies. So Dad went to go and find something to make a lid for the fish tank. And me and Tom gave the hamsters some sunflower seeds instead.

You can feed hamsters sunflower seeds for ages because they just keep taking more and more and they stuff them in their cheeks until they look like they are going to burst and then (which is my favorite part) they go into a corner and they push all the seeds out of their cheeks, and they bury them in the sawdust for eating later.

If you want, you can collect up the old seeds that have been in their cheeks after they've emptied them out, and you can give them back to the hamsters to put them in their cheeks again, and that means you don't have to buy millions of seeds all the time. It's not very nice when you put the old seeds back in because they're normally pretty soggy, and sometimes they're mixed in with other things they've put in their cheeks, and sometimes that can be their poops.

I put some of the sunflower seeds on my hands and on my arms. And Hamster Number Two, which was the Big One, crawled along and put them in her cheeks. And then I put some sunflower seeds on Tom's arms, and on his shoulders, and some on the top of his head, and Hamster Number Two ran all over him.

Tom didn't really like that, because Hamster Number Two was too fast, and he didn't like its feet, and it emptied all the soggy sunflower seeds out of its cheeks into Tom's hair. Tom said he liked Hamster Number

One better because it was smaller and because it would sit still in your hand if you were very quiet, and it didn't mind being stroked if you gave it the crumbs from the cookies.

And then the doorbell rang and it was Suzanne. I knew it was Suzanne because she did three rings. So I put the hamsters back in the fish tank and I told Tom to watch them, and I went to the door.

Suzanne said, "Are you coming out?"

And I said, "No. I need to make an obstacle course for the hamsters. You could come in."

But Suzanne said, "No. I need to go on my bike. It's new."

And I said, "You can hold one of the hamsters."

But Suzanne said, "No. I don't want to. I'm probably allergic."

I said, "No, you're not."

And Suzanne said, "I could be. My Dad is. It might run in families."

And I said, "Your Dad's probably not allergic. He's probably lying."

And Suzanne said, "My Dad's not a liar. *You're* a liar. You said you were going to knock on the wall for me later and you didn't."

And then she said she was going to tell her Dad about how I made her get the dictionary. And she said she was going to go see Joe-down-the-street and ask him to come and ride bikes instead.

And I said, "Good." Because I said she probably loved Joe-down-the-street, and she was probably going to do all the things from Joe's Mom's book.

And Suzanne said, "No. You are, and you've probably done them already." And then she got on her bike and went away.

Sometimes I hate Suzanne.

I started doing the obstacle course and everything and then Suzanne came round to the back door. I knew it was Suzanne because she did three knocks.

When I opened the back door it was very loud because the garbage truck was there, collecting the trash. And Suzanne had to shout. She said,

"DO YOU WANT TO GO IN THE SHED AND MAKE A PLAN FOR DIGGING UP THE OLD RABBIT AND EVERYTHING, AND I CAN BRING ALL MY PENS OVER AND CARDS AND THINGS AND WE CAN MAKE A BOX?"

And I said, "NO." Because I was too busy with the hamsters.

And Suzanne said, "DO YOU WANT TO LOOK AT MY BIKE?"

And I said, "WHAT?" Because the garbage truck was getting louder because it was right by Suzanne's back door.

And Suzanne said, "MY BIKE!"

And I said, "WHERE IS IT?"

And Suzanne said, "THERE."

And I said, "WHERE?"

And Suzanne said, "THERE! BY THE TRASH CANS!"

And she turned round and pointed to

the cans. But her bike *wasn't* there because one of its wheels was sticking out of the garbage truck.

And Suzanne screamed and ran to the garbage man and said, "GET IT OUT! THAT'S MY NEW BIKE!"

But the teeth came down. There was a big crunch and a grinding noise.

And the garbage man said, **"TOO LATE, LOVE. I'M NOT PSYCHIC! IF IT'S NOT FOR**

THE GARBAGE TRUCK, DON'T PUT IT BY THE CANS!"

And he got in the garbage truck and drove off.

And Suzanne ran home.

And there was a lot of shouting in Suzanne's house because we heard it through the wall. And Suzanne cried a lot. Because of the bike. And the garbage man. And her Dad. And because it wasn't her fault, really.

And then, when it went quiet, she knocked on my wall three times.

And I opened my window.

And Suzanne opened her window and she said, "I hate you." And then she shut her window.

I didn't shut mine. I stayed on the window ledge for ages. There was a magpie in the garden, and I wanted to tell Suzanne because Nana once told me and Suzanne that whenever you see a magpie you should always say, "Hello, Mr. Magpie. How's your wife and children?" because that stops you from getting bad luck. And, since then, we always say it. So I knocked on Suzanne's window. But Suzanne closed her curtains.

When I came in from the window ledge the New Cat was in my bedroom. It was crouched down very low. And its eyes were very wide. And its mouth was very open. And it was staring right at the hamsters.

CHAPTER 13
The Birds and the Bees

Tom didn't look after the hamsters as much as me because sometimes he wanted to go outside and do other things, like hold the trash bag for Mr. Tucker, or walk in a straight line with his eyes closed, or collect gravel. But I didn't want to go out at all because I didn't feel like it, and because Suzanne didn't want to be my friend anymore, and because if Suzanne decided she *did* want to be my friend again I knew that she would knock on the wall and, if I went out, I wouldn't hear her. So I stayed in my room on my own with the hamsters. And that's probably why I didn't notice that anything was different about Number One. Because you don't really know that something is growing if you see it a lot. And that's why when you see a grown-up that you haven't seen for ages they say, "Ooh, you've grown," but people who see you every day, like your mom, don't say it because it happens too slowly for them to notice.

Tom said, "Number One is fat."

"No she isn't," I said.

"Yes she is," Tom said. "She's fat. She's more fatter than Number Two."

I looked at Number One, and I looked at Number Two. And Number One *was* fatter. A lot fatter.

"She used to be more skinnier," Tom said.

I measured Number Two's tummy. She bit me. It was three inches around. And then I measured Number One's tummy. It was four and a quarter inches around. I decided to put Number One on a diet.

It was quite hard putting Number One on a diet because Number One and Number Two shared the same food bowl. So I took Number One out of the fish tank when I fed Number Two. And I took Number Two out when I fed Number One. And I did that with gardening gloves on because of Number Two's biting. I gave Number One half the amount of food that I gave Number Two. And I didn't give Number One any sunflower seeds. And I made sure that Number Two didn't put her sunflower seeds in her cheeks to hide for later, in case Number One found them and ate them all. Because even though *I* wouldn't eat something that had been in someone else's cheeks and spat back out again, hamsters aren't very fussy about things like that.

I measured Number One every day. But she didn't get any smaller. She just kept on getting bigger.

One afternoon Mom came into my room and Tom said, "Number One is fat and she's getting even fatter. She's going to pop."

Mom looked at Number One and she

said, "Oh, please God, no." And she went downstairs to phone the Pet Shop Man.

Me and Tom picked up the other phone in Mom's room and listened in. We aren't allowed to listen in on the other phone, because Mom says it's rude, but sometimes we have to if it's very important.

Mom said, "I think one of the hamsters you sold us is pregnant."

Tom said, "Oh!"

Mom said, "Anna and Tom, I know you're there. Put the phone down."

We put the phone down. It was hard to be quiet, because if Number One *was* pregnant that meant we would get a baby hamster. In fact that meant we would get *lots* of baby hamsters, because hamsters don't just have one or two or even three babies at a time like people do. They have six, or seven, or eight or something like that. And one hamster, who lived in Louisiana, had twenty-six babies at a time, and that hamster got in the *Guinness Book of World Records*.

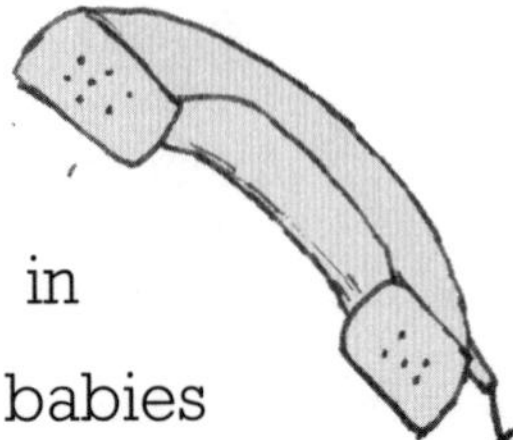

We picked the other phone up again to listen.

The Pet Shop Man said, "She can't be pregnant, because both the hamsters I sold you are female."

Mom said, "Maybe it was pregnant before it left the shop."

The Pet Shop Man said, "No. Impossible. It was only three weeks old, and every single hamster in this shop is female."

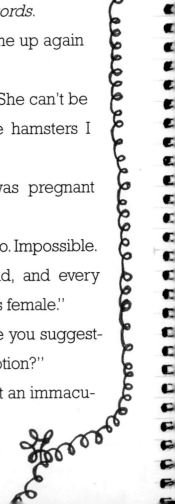

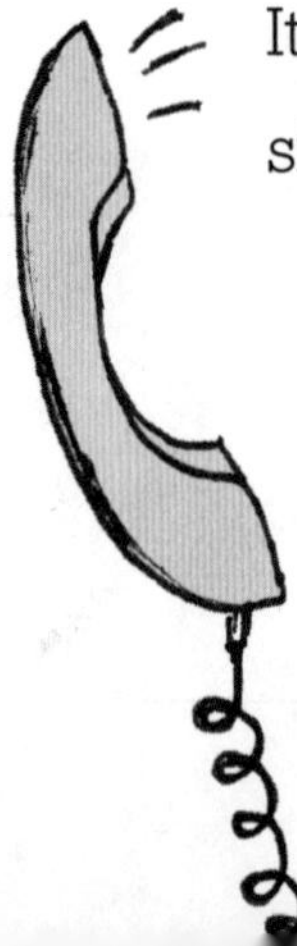

Mom said, "Well, what are you suggesting, an immaculate conception?"

I know all about what an immaculate conception is because I was the angel Gabriel in the Nativity at Church last year, and I had to visit Mary to tell her she was going to have a baby, and when Mary said to me, "How shall this be, seeing that I know not a man?" I had to say, "The Holy Ghost shall come upon thee, and the power of the Highest shall overshadow thee: therefore also that holy thing which shall be born of thee shall be called the Son of God. For with God nothing shall be impossible."

And that's what an immaculate conception is. But it doesn't happen with hamsters because I don't think it ever even happens with people, apart from Mary. Maybe.

Anyway, the Pet Shop Man said, "Maybe your hamster has just got gas."

And Mom said, "It's been getting fatter for weeks."

And the Pet Shop man said, "Or it could be a Phantom Pregnancy."

And I said, "What's a Phantom Pregnancy?"

And Mom said,

"PUT THE PHONE DOWN!"

And then she said, "How do I check if the other hamster is male?"

And the Pet Shop Man told her how.

Mom put the phone down. And me and Tom put the other phone down. And we ran back into my room and we sat on the bed.

Mom came in, and she picked Number Two up, and she turned Number Two on her back to look at her tummy. Number Two didn't like being on her back, and she bit Mom, and then Mom dropped Number Two, and she couldn't catch her for ages, and each time she did catch her, Number Two bit her again.

I got the gardening gloves and I put Number Two back in the fish tank. Mom said she would look at Number Two again tomorrow when she could take her by surprise.

I asked Mom what a Phantom Pregnancy was again.

Mom said, "It's nothing, Big Ears. It's time for bed."

It didn't sound like nothing to me. It didn't have "phantom pregnancy" in the dictionary in my house, but it did have "phantom," and it didn't sound very good.

This is what it said. . . .

phantom [fan-tum] ✦ *noun*
a spirit of a dead person believed by some to visit the living as a pale, almost transparent form of a person, animal, or other object; a ghost

I wanted to knock on the wall to ask

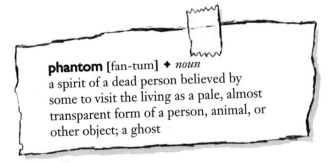

Suzanne what it said in the dictionary in her house about phantoms, in case the ones in my dictionary weren't the right kind. But I knew Suzanne wouldn't knock back. So I went to bed instead.

●ᵎ ●ᵎ ●ᵎ

I had a dream. A bad one. About Nana. She was in the back lane, and she was see-through, like a phantom, and she was digging in the ground trying to find the Old Rabbit. When I woke up it was still dark. I looked at my clock. It was two a.m. That means it was two o'clock in the morning. I've got a digital clock because I'm not very good at telling time.

Anyway, it was the middle of the night, and the hamster wheel was squeaking. I took the lid off the fish tank. Hamster Number Two was on the wheel. I pulled back some of the tissue paper from the top of the nest to see if Number One was in there. And she was. And next to Number One was a pale pink see-through thing that was moving. And when I looked closer it wasn't *one* pale pink see-through thing that was moving, it was *lots* of little pale pink see-through things.

They were tiny, like small prawns, and you could see all their veins, and you could even see their hearts beating through their skin. At first I thought they must be phantoms like the Pet Shop Man said, and like it said in the dictionary, but then I looked in the Hamster Manual.

I couldn't really understand what it said

about baby hamsters because of it using lots of hard words, but it had a picture of some babies, and they looked exactly like the Phantom Hamsters in the fish tank. So I decided they probably weren't Phantom Hamsters after all, even though they looked all pale and everything, because that's how they looked in the book too, and anyway when Tom was born he looked a bit pale and see-through too and *he* wasn't a phantom.

I went into Tom's room and woke him up and he came to see.

"Oh, look!" he said. "There's millions of them." And he laughed, and then he hopped about from one foot to the other like he does when he needs to pee, but faster. And I did it too because that's the dance that me and Tom do sometimes, when something we love happens.

Tom said, "Count them. Count them!"

I counted the babies and there were eight. And then me and Tom got The Hysterics a bit, and we had to put our heads under the duvet so we didn't wake Mom up. And we had The Hysterics for ages. Because now we had eight new baby hamsters, and soon their eyes would open, and they would stop looking like phantoms, and start growing and getting fur and running around. And we would have ten hamsters altogether, and they could all do the obstacle course. And because as soon as we could tell them apart we would have to think of eight names for the new ones. And because we

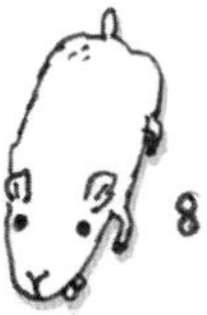

would never have been allowed eight more hamsters if we had asked, but now that we had them, no one could take them away because they would have to stay with their mom until they were all grown up.

I put the lid back on the fish tank. Or at least I meant to put the lid back on the fish tank. And I shut my bedroom door. Or at least I meant to shut my bedroom door. And Tom got in my bed, because I didn't feel like sleeping on my own very much. And we talked about the baby hamsters, and what we might call them. And then we fell asleep.

And when I woke up it was because Tom said, "Ugh!"

CHAPTER 14

The Hamster MASSACRE

"Look," Tom said. He pointed at the fish tank.

There were spots on the glass. And the sawdust near the nest was wet. I lifted up the tissue paper. It was sticky and red. And underneath, in the middle, were the eight baby hamsters. They were covered with blood. And all of them were dead. Number One was in the corner of the tank. She had blood around her mouth, and one of her back legs was gone. And the other thing that was gone was Hamster Number Two.

"There's only one hamster left," Tom said.

And I said, "MOOOOOOOOOOM!"

CHAPTER 15

In Shock

The vet put three stitches in the end of the stump where Number One's back leg used to be. Number One didn't move, and she didn't even squeak. The vet said she thought that Number One was in shock. And I said I thought Number One was in shock too, because I would be in shock if something bit my back leg off and killed all my babies and kidnapped my friend.

But the vet said, "I'm afraid to say this hamster probably killed the babies herself.

It's quite common. You see, the male hamster becomes more and more aggressive during the pregnancy, and the female feels threatened, and eliminates her dependents. You wouldn't have known, but it's a standard response. I'm very sorry."

I didn't really know what "eliminates" or "dependents" or "standard" was, but I said that one thing I *did* know was that Number One wouldn't kill her own babies, even if she did feel threatened, because she wasn't really that kind of hamster. And I also knew for another thing that Number Two wasn't a male hamster because the Pet Shop Man had said she was a female.

The vet said, "Mmm, the Pet Shop Man.

How long have you had the hamsters?"

And I said, "Five weeks."

And the vet said, "Well, there you are, you see. The gestation period of a hamster, which is to say the time from conception to birth, is around twenty-one days."

I didn't say anything.

The vet said, "How old are you?"

I didn't see what how old I was had to do with anything but I said "I am nine" anyway, and the vet said, "How can I put it? Urm . . . It's like this. A girl buys two hamsters. She has had the hamsters for five weeks when one of the hamsters gives birth. The length of time for which hamsters are pregnant is around three weeks. Did the hamster become pregnant before or after the girl bought it? And, if the hamster became pregnant *after* the girl bought it, what sex was the other hamster?"

I looked at my shoes because I hate math and I hate riddles, and I especially hate it when someone is staring at you and waiting for you to answer because it keeps you from being able to think, so I undid the laces on my shoes. And then I did them back up again.

And Mom said, "You see? Unless it *was* an immaculate conception."

I said, "No. It wasn't an immaculate conception because hamsters don't have immaculate conceptions because that only happened to Mary."

And then the vet laughed. Even though

it wasn't funny and even though vets aren't supposed to ask people math problems or riddles or laugh at jokes or anything like that because they're supposed to just look at the pets and do the stitches.

I said, "Even if Number Two *was* a male that doesn't mean it was him who bit Number One's leg off, because it could have been something else. Because anyone could have got in the fish tank and taken Number Two away and bitten Number One's leg off and killed the babies."

And Mom said, "Like who?"

And I said, "Like the New Cat."

And the vet said, "This wound is not consistent with something that might be inflicted by a cat, I'm afraid. Also, a cat would not leave Hamster Number One alive,

and it would not cover the baby hamsters over, and leave them dead in the nest. Cats take their kills away with them, you see."

I didn't say anything because the vet didn't know what the New Cat was like. Because the New Cat didn't just bite things; sometimes she killed things by scaring them to death and things like that. Like with the Old Rabbit. And foxes sometimes kill chickens and just leave them. Graham Roberts told me that, and his Dad is a farmer, and they know more about things killing things than vets do.

I said, "Well, where is Number Two now?"

And the vet said, "That is the question. It must have escaped."

But I didn't think that Number Two had escaped because, even though I might have forgotten to put the lid on the fish tank, and even though I might have left my bedroom door open, Number Two couldn't climb up the glass. Not unless it got on top of the wheel. And Number Two had only ever gotten on top of the wheel once before because it was a very hard thing to do.

Anyway, I didn't speak to the vet after that because she said that she didn't think that Number One would live very long without her leg. And I wanted to go home.

When we got back to the house I went upstairs to have a look at the dead baby hamsters. But the dead baby hamsters weren't there because Dad had cleaned the fish tank out, and he had put new sawdust in, and he had made it look like nothing had ever even happened. Just like in Nana's room. And he had got all the old sawdust, and the nest with the blood, and all the baby hamsters, and put them in a bag. And he had put the bag in the outside trash can.

I ran out the back. Dad shouted after me, and Mom grabbed me by my hood, but I wriggled out of my coat, and I got away, and I got the bag out of the trash can, and Dad said, "Put it back."

And I said,

"THEY DON'T GO IN THE GARBAGE!"

And I ran past Mom and Dad and upstairs to my room, and I shut the door and sat against it. And Mom and Dad and Tom wanted to come in but I didn't let them because Dad had put the hamsters in the trash, and Mom didn't even want the hamsters in the first place, and Tom said "ugh" about the babies.

And I sat against the door until they all went away. And then I looked inside the bag. I took out the nest, and I picked the eight baby hamsters out, one by one, and they were cold, and wet, and I put them on some tissue in my sandwich box. And then I put the lid on the box. And then I cried. And I couldn't stop crying. And I didn't want to.

After ages I heard three knocks on the wall. I stopped crying and I went to my window and I opened it. Suzanne opened her window too. She got out on the window ledge. "I heard about your hamsters," she said.

I said, "Number Two has gone missing and Number One has only got three legs left and she had to have stitches and she had eight babies and they're all dead and Dad put them in the trash and I got them out."

Suzanne said, "Can I see?"

So I lifted up the lid on the sandwich box and showed her the eight tiny hamsters in a row on the tissue.

Suzanne said, "They don't look like hamsters."

Because they didn't, really.

I said, "It's because they are a bit

mushed and they haven't got their fur yet."

And then I put the lid back on the hamsters and I started crying again because they never would get any fur because they were dead, and because they were so small, and because they hadn't even opened their eyes yet, and because Dad put them in the trash, and because I didn't want Number Two to have bitten Number One's leg off and escaped, and because I didn't want Number One to have killed all the babies.

But Suzanne said, "Maybe it wasn't Number Two who bit Number One's leg off, and maybe it wasn't Number One who killed the babies because maybe it was someone else, and maybe you are right about the New Cat, or the fox, and maybe we could find out what really happened and who really killed the hamsters because we could do an investigation!"

And then Suzanne said she would help me to do an investigation. And she would help me to bury the baby hamsters too, if I liked.

I said, "I haven't got anything little enough to bury them in."

But Suzanne said that she did. And she said she would bring all the things that we needed for burying the hamsters over to the shed.

And then she said, "You can choose the password."

I said, "The password should be 'Dead.'"

And Suzanne said, "Yes."

CHAPTER 16

Ashes to Ashes

Suzanne brought eight matchboxes. And she brought colored paper. And all her pens. And glue. And glitter. And her best shells from the beach to stick on the boxes. And she brought some twigs and some twine to make crosses. And a shoebox that she had covered in black paper with red ribbon to put around it.

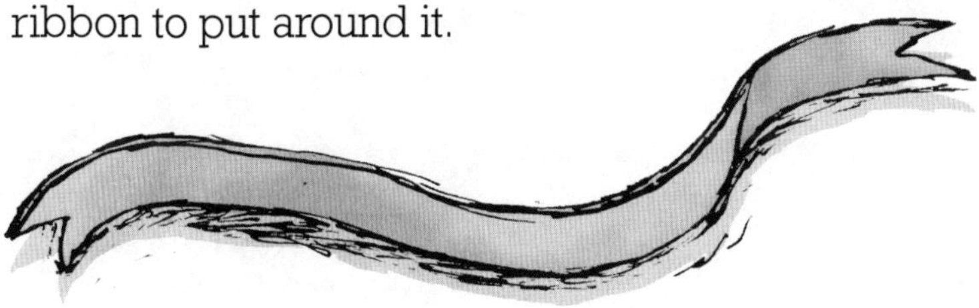

"It's for the Old Rabbit," she said. Because if I didn't mind, she said, we could dig the Old Rabbit up and bury it again at the same time as the hamsters. And I didn't mind. So that is what we decided to do.

We stayed in the shed making the boxes for the baby hamsters all day, and we did them in eight different colors, and Mom brought us some sandwiches, and we didn't even come out for lunch, and we stuck a shell on each one, and some glitter, and we put a little bit of grass in them to make it nice inside.

When they were all done, I opened the lid of the sandwich box with the dead baby hamsters in it, and I took the baby hamsters out one at a time, and I picked the sawdust off them, and the tissue paper, and Suzanne wiped the blood with her hankie. And I put each one in its own box. And I made eight holes in the ground next to where the Old Cat was buried, and Suzanne put the eight little stick crosses in the ground behind the holes. And then we went and got Tom, and then me and Suzanne and Tom went and got Joe-down-the-street.

The potato chip bag that Joe had put under a stone to show where the Old Rabbit was buried wasn't there anymore. But Joe said he knew exactly where it was anyway, and he pointed to the spot.

I started to dig. I didn't dig with the trowel like I did for the eight hamster holes because Joe said I might dig through the Old Rabbit. So I dug with my hands, and after a while I could feel something hard. I flicked all the mud off the hard thing, and I could feel that the hard thing had fur. The Old Rabbit looked very old in the ground. And it smelled.

Joe said he hoped there weren't any worms, and there weren't, but there were some maggots because some of them fell out of the Old Rabbit's mouth when I got it out of the ground. But Joe didn't see, and I brushed the mud away from the Old Rabbit's face and out of its eyes before I showed it to him. And I showed him the side with the closed eye because on the other side the eye was still open, and it had gone a bit funny, and I didn't think Joe would like it.

Joe stroked the Old Rabbit on its nose, and he wiped its body with Suzanne's hankie, and made its fur all smooth, and then he held the Old Rabbit to his cheek, and after that he put the Old Rabbit in the box, on the straw, and Suzanne put a dandelion in, and I put the lid on, and I put the box in the ground, and I covered it over, and Suzanne put a cross in the ground behind it.

And then Joe said he had to go because even though he liked the Old Rabbit best, the New Cat might be hunting the New Rabbit for all he knew, and he had to go back to sit on the hutch with his Super Soaker, just in case.

Suzanne put the eight baby hamsters in the ground and I covered them. Suzanne said we should all say something about the baby hamsters. I didn't want to say anything about them because I couldn't really think of anything except that they looked a bit like prawns, and I didn't want to say that. But Suzanne said it wasn't really a proper funeral if no one said anything.

So Suzanne said, "They didn't look like hamsters but they were. They just hadn't got their fur yet."

Which was true.

And I said, "They were born in the night and in the morning they were dead."

Which was also true.

And Tom said, "They are under the mud."

Which was true as well. And which was better than at Nana's funeral because there the Vicar kept saying how Nana never had a bad word to say about anyone. And that wasn't true because Nana did have a bad word to say about some people sometimes. Like Suzanne's Dad, and Miss Matheson, and Joe-down-the-street's Mom's Boyfriend. But she never said a bad word about me, or Tom, or *Coronation Street*.

CHAPTER 17
A Real Investigation

In the morning, when Suzanne knocked on the wall three times, me and Tom were ready. We met at the shed at eight o'clock and Suzanne said we should call it "Oh, Eight Hundred Hours," so we did. Suzanne's Mom watches all the police dramas on TV, and Suzanne does too, even the late ones that I'm not allowed to watch, and that's how Suzanne knows all about exactly what you should call things in a Real Investigation.

Suzanne said the first thing we should

do was have a meeting. The password was "Investigation." Tom didn't like the password being "Investigation" at first because it's quite a hard word, because he's only five, and he kept calling it "In-ges-tiv-ation."

I said it didn't matter if Tom got the password a little bit wrong, as long as it was nearly right.

And Suzanne said it didn't really even matter if he couldn't remember it at all, because he could just say, "Hello, it's me, Tom," like he always does, because he always ends up forgetting what the password is anyway.

After we had the meeting and decided on the password, I said I thought we should go and see Mrs. Rotherham up the road because she would know what to do because she used to be in the police.

Tom didn't want to go because he is scared of Mrs. Rotherham. He thought we should go in the house and see Mom and have a cookie instead. But Suzanne said that having a cookie definitely wasn't the next thing to do.

I'm not scared of Mrs. Rotherham. I wasn't that scared of her in the first place but I'm really not scared of her now because at Nana's funeral, Mrs. Rotherham gave me her hankie and, after I'd blown my nose on it, she said I could keep it. It's a really old hankie, probably about a hundred years old or something, and it's got lace on it. Mrs. Rotherham made it herself.

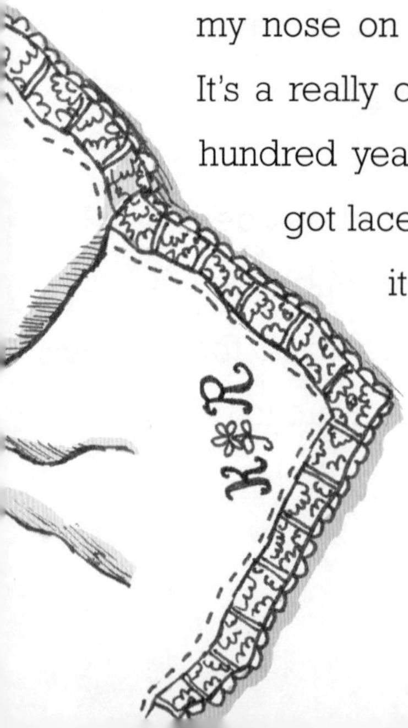

Anyway, Mom hadn't told Mrs. Rotherham any of the bad things about me and Tom that she always said she had half a mind to. Or, if she had, Mrs. Rotherham didn't seem to care. Mrs. Rotherham winked at me when the Vicar was saying how Nana never said a bad word about anyone. And afterward she showed me how to wink. I can only do it with one eye. I'm practicing with the other one. Mrs. Rotherham said I could come to her house whenever I liked.

Tom said he would come up the road with me and Suzanne as long as he could wait outside. So that is what we did.

Mrs. Rotherham's house smells of old things, and mothballs, the same as Nana's used to. Most old ladies' houses smell a bit the same when they are really old. It's a funny smell, a bit like the old cupboard upstairs at Sunday School. Our house will probably smell like that soon because Mom keeps finding gray hairs on her head and that means she must be nearly old too.

Anyway, I told Mrs. Rotherham all about what happened to the hamsters. Mrs. Rotherham said, "Well, well, well." And then she said, "Oh dear, oh dear, oh dear." Which Suzanne said afterward is what police people used to say in the olden days. And then she said, "A *massacre*!"

I told Mrs. Rotherham all about what the vet had said about how she thought that Number Two had bitten Number One's leg off, and how she thought Number One had killed all the babies, and how she thought Number Two had escaped.

Mrs. Rotherham said, "The vet is probably right."

And I said "Oh," because for one thing that wasn't really what I wanted Mrs. Rotherham to say, and for another thing it didn't really help us with our investigation.

Suzanne told Mrs. Rotherham how we were doing an investigation, and how we thought Mrs. Rotherham might be able to help because, she said, "Maybe the vet *wasn't* right, and maybe someone else killed the hamsters, and maybe seeing as how you used to be in the police, you could help us catch whoever it was by telling us what to do in a Real Investigation."

Mrs. Rotherham said, "I see. The vet probably is right. But, in a Real Investigation, probably is not good enough. *Probably* doesn't come into it."

And then she winked.

"The first thing to do in a Real Investigation—particularly a murder investigation—

and particularly a mass-murder investigation, such as this one, is to get yourself a nice cup of tea and a cookie."

And she went into the kitchen. After a while she came back with the tea, and with some cookies, and she poured the tea out, and she put the milk in, and the sugars, because she said sweet tea was best for this sort of thing. And she drank her tea, and we drank our tea.

And then she said, "Is your brother going to come in?"

I said he wasn't.

Mrs. Rotherham said, "But it's raining."

And I said, "Tom doesn't mind if it's raining."

Which he didn't.

"Because," I said, "once me and Tom went out and stood in the rain for ages on purpose to see how wet we could get and we got really, really wet and that was about the best thing Tom said he had ever done. . . ."

Suzanne said we didn't have time to talk about Tom and the rain, and we had to get on with the investigation.

Mrs. Rotherham said, "Quite right." And she looked very serious. And then she said, "You will need these." And she gave us a small notepad and a pencil. And then she said, "And you might need this." And she gave us a magnifying glass. And then she said, "And this." And she gave us a Dictaphone, which is a thing for recording what people say, and it's got a little tape inside. And then she said,

"And you will definitely need this," and she gave us a real police badge. And then Mrs. Rotherham wrote on a piece of paper for quite a long time. And she put the piece of paper in an envelope. And she wrote "Investigation Instructions" on the envelope and she gave the envelope to Suzanne. And she gave me three cookies to give to Tom.

And then she said, "I'll expect you back before dinner."

Tom was still waiting outside, and he was quite wet, especially his feet because he was waiting in a puddle. But he didn't mind, and he was very pleased about the cookies, especially when we told him that Mrs. Rotherham said that tea and cookies were the first things that you should do in a Real Investigation. Because Tom said he thought that they might be.

And then me and Suzanne and Tom went back to the shed.

CHAPTER 18
Who Done It?

Suzanne opened the envelope and she read out what it said on the piece of paper. And then I read out what it said on the piece of paper again because Suzanne isn't all that good at reading sometimes, and Mrs. Rotherham's handwriting was quite curly like Nana's used to be, like old people always write, and it was quite shaky too, and Suzanne kept getting the words wrong.

The first thing it said on Mrs. Rotherham's piece of paper was . . .

MAKE A LIST OF SUSPECTS

To do this you will need:

a) Your notepad and pencil

b) Your brain

You must ask yourself the following questions:

1. Who do you think might have murdered the hamsters?

2. Have they done or said anything that makes you suspect them?

3. Do they have any prior record of violence or murder? (This means have they done something like it before)

(Tip: A hunch is as good a reason as any to make someone a suspect.)

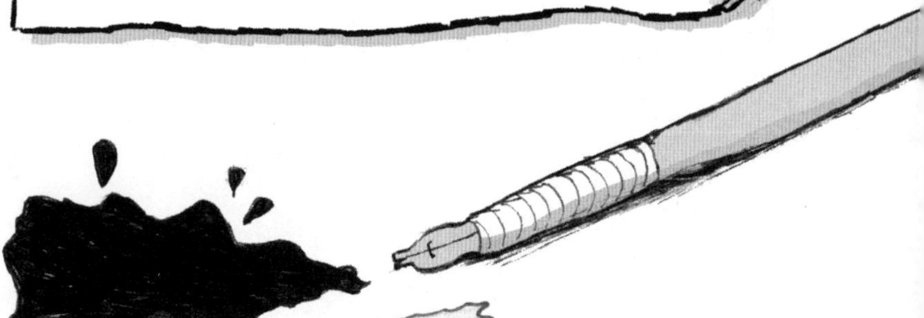

We thought of some suspects and I wrote them down. We had eight suspects altogether. We did have nine but then Suzanne said she thought we should take one of them off, which was the fox, because she said, "No one has seen a fox in the street, and a fox would be too big to get in through the cat flap, and it wouldn't be able to get in the house any other way."

I said, "I think a fox might be able to get through the cat flap, if it was a very skinny one."

But Tom said, "I am smaller than a fox, and *I* can't get through the cat flap because I have tried lots of times and I always get stuck."

So this is what it said on our suspects list. . . .

ANNA'S AND SUZANNE'S AND TOM'S LIST OF SUSPECTS FOR THE HAMSTER MASSACRE INVESTIGATION

1. Mr. Tucker

Because . . .

a) He doesn't like Russians

b) He called the hamsters "gremlins"

2. Joe-down-the-street's Mom's Boyfriend

Because . . .

a) We have got a hunch

b) ?

3. Hamster Number Two

Because . . .

a) He used to bite a lot and he could have bitten Number One's leg off and killed the babies and escaped

4. The New Cat

Because . . .

a) She is always crouching near my bedroom door in a hunting kind of way

b) She has already killed four sparrows, three field mice, five moths, eight spiders, one bumblebee and scared the Old Rabbit to death

5. Mom

Because . . .

a) She didn't want the hamsters in the first place

b) She has already killed two hamsters named Geoff and Bernard

6. Suzanne's Dad

Because . . .

a) He "HATES PETS"

7. Hamster Number One

Because . . .

a) She was in the cage at the time

b) The vet said so

c) Mom said so

d) Dad said so

e) The Internet said so

f) The chapter called "Severely Stressed Hamsters" in the *Hamsters: A Manual* book said so

8. Miss Matheson

Because . . .

a) She killed the Old Cat

b) She doesn't like people on her private property

The next thing it said to do on Mrs. Rotherham's piece of paper after making a list of suspects was . . .

INTERVIEW YOUR SUSPECTS
To do this you will need . . .
1) Your police badge
2) Your notepad and pencil
3) Your Dictaphone to record the interviews
4) Your magnifying glass to look for clues

You should . . .

1. Ask the suspects where they were when the massacre was committed.
2. Ask them to prove that they were where they say they were. (Do they have an alibi? Was someone with them at the time?)
3. If they have a solid alibi you must eliminate them from your investigation (cross them off the suspect list).

This is what it says an alibi is in my dictionary . . .

alibi [al-uh-by] ✦ *noun*
proof that someone who is thought to have committed a crime could not have done it, especially the fact or claim that they were in another place at the time it happened.

We didn't check what it said in the dictionary in Suzanne's house because for one thing the dictionary in Suzanne's house always ends up getting us into trouble, and for another thing my dictionary sounded like it had the right kind of alibi in it. We decided I would be the one to tell people what had happened with the hamsters, and to press record on the Dictaphone when people started talking, because I was the only one with pockets big enough to fit the Dictaphone in, and if people knew they were being recorded they might not like it. And Suzanne would be the one to hold the real police badge and ask the questions and write in the notepad. And Tom would be the one to hold the magnifying glass and look for clues.

The first suspect on our list was Mr.

Tucker. I didn't really want to go to Mr. Tucker's house first because I thought we might get stuck talking about litter and everything, but Tom said he wanted to see Mr. Tucker anyway and Suzanne said that she would hold up the police badge and tell Mr. Tucker that we didn't have time to talk about litter.

So we went and knocked on Mr. Tucker's door.

I told Mr. Tucker how the eight baby hamsters were dead and how Number Two was missing and how Number One only had three legs left.

Mr. Tucker said, "Good God! A wilding! You had better come in. If you ask me—"

But Suzanne got the police badge out. And she said, "Mr. Tucker. Where were your whereabouts between the hours of two a.m. and seven a.m. on Thursday morning?"

Mr. Tucker said, "So, that's how it is, eh?"

And he sat down and said, "In bed. Civvy kip. Where else should an old lag be?"

Tom put the magnifying glass up close to Mr. Tucker's face and looked him up and down. Mr. Tucker's eye bulged through the glass.

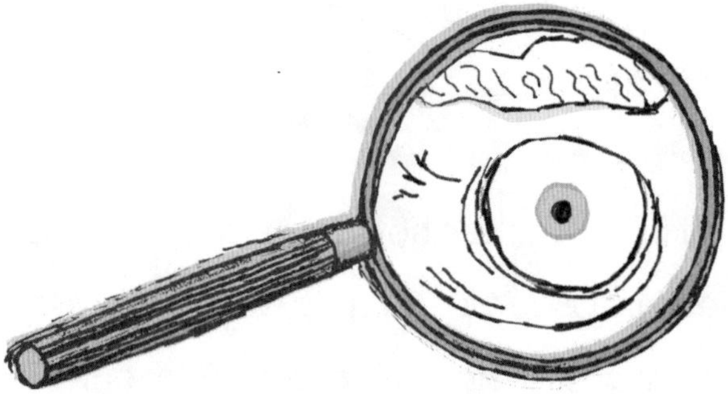

Mr. Tucker said, "A snoop! Tom! I didn't have you down for that, Old Chum."

Suzanne said, "Was anyone else in bed with you?"

And Mr. Tucker said, "Mrs. Tucker, of course. Upstart!"

And then he shouted up the stairs, **"DICKEY. COME DOWN, WILL YOU!"**

And Mrs. Tucker came down.

Mr. Tucker said, "Now, Dickey, don't fold up. Give 'em a good show, and for God's sake keep doggo about the bodies out the back." And then he made faces at Tom through the magnifying glass.

Suzanne said, "Name?" to Mrs. Tucker.

And Mrs. Tucker said, "Dickey Tucker."

And then we had to stop for a bit because Suzanne had to go to the bathroom.

When Suzanne came back from the toilet, Mrs. Tucker said that Mr. Tucker was definitely in bed asleep between two a.m. and seven a.m. on Thursday, because she was there too, and she is a very light sleeper, and she said, "Mr. Tucker snores a lot, and thrashes about, and shouts out, and I was wide awake, reading. I haven't slept more than four hours a night since 1945."

I was not sure Mrs. Tucker was telling the truth but she took her glasses off and pointed to the bags under her eyes, and Tom looked at them with the magnifying glass, and they were very big. And then Mr. Tucker pretended to fall asleep in the chair and he did lots of snoring and he shouted, "We're hit! We're hit! One engine down! Come in, Charlie!"

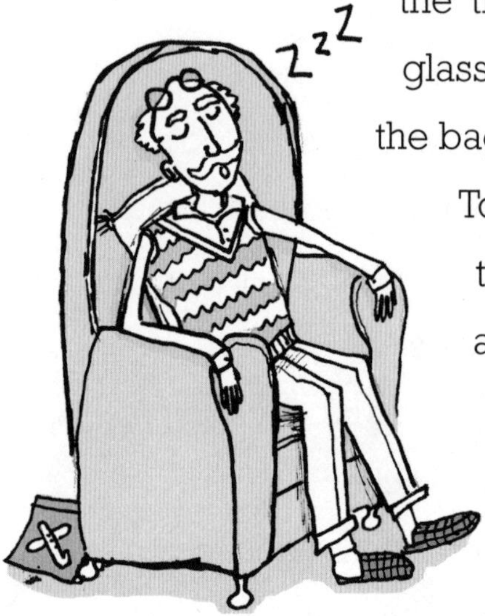

And Tom thought that was the best thing ever and he laughed a lot.

And then Mr. Tucker picked Tom up, and flew him round the room.

And then he sat down because Mrs. Tucker said, "Stop it, Raymond! You'll give yourself a heart attack."

And then she went to get some lemonade.

We drank the lemonade and said thank you to Mrs. Tucker. And then we crossed Mr. Tucker off the Suspect List.

The next person on our list was Joe-down-the-street's Mom's Boyfriend. Because we had a hunch about him. And Mrs. Rotherham had said that a hunch was as good a reason as any.

Joe was sitting on the New Rabbit's hutch in the backyard with the Super Soaker. We asked Joe if his Mom's Boyfriend was there. But Joe didn't answer. Joe never answers if he doesn't want to.

Joe's Mom was standing, looking out of the back window.

I told Joe's Mom about what had happened with the hamsters and how we were asking people if they had seen anything unusual and Suzanne said, "Can you tell us where your boyfriend's whereabouts were between two a.m. and seven a.m. on Thursday?"

And Joe's Mom said, "I can tell you *exactly* where his whereabouts were between two a.m. and seven a.m. on Thursday. His whereabouts were in Kuala bloomin' Lumpur. In the Mandarin Oriental Hotel. And the babysitter's whereabouts were there as well!"

And she showed us Kuala Lumpur on Joe's globe. It's a long way away.

And then she showed us her boyfriend's bank statement. And Tom looked at it through the magnifying glass. It said,

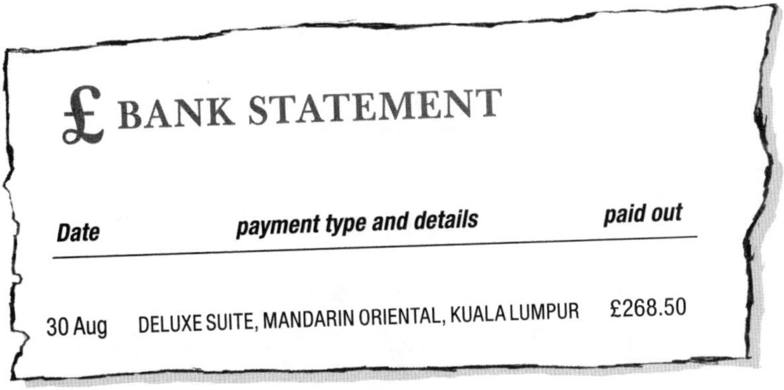
£ BANK STATEMENT

Date	payment type and details	paid out
30 Aug	DELUXE SUITE, MANDARIN ORIENTAL, KUALA LUMPUR	£268.50

We said thank you to Joe's Mom, and she gave Tom a cookie, because he asked for one. And we crossed her Boyfriend off the list.

The next suspect on the list was Hamster Number Two. We couldn't interview Number Two because he was still missing. And even though we had put trails of food out every night, he hadn't come back yet.

So Suzanne wrote "missing" next to Number Two's name on the Suspect List. And we went to find the New Cat.

It was a bit difficult to interview the New Cat because of her being a cat, and because she couldn't answer the questions, but Tom said he just wanted to look the New Cat in the eye with the magnifying glass to see if he could tell anything by that.

The New Cat looked even angrier than ever through the magnifying glass. She hissed at Tom and made her fur go big. And then Tom tried to pick the New Cat up. And the New Cat bit Tom really hard. And then Tom bit the New Cat back, even harder. And the New Cat looked very surprised because no one had ever bitten her back before. And Tom looked quite surprised too, because he had never bitten a cat before either. And also because he had quite a lot of the New Cat's fur in his mouth.

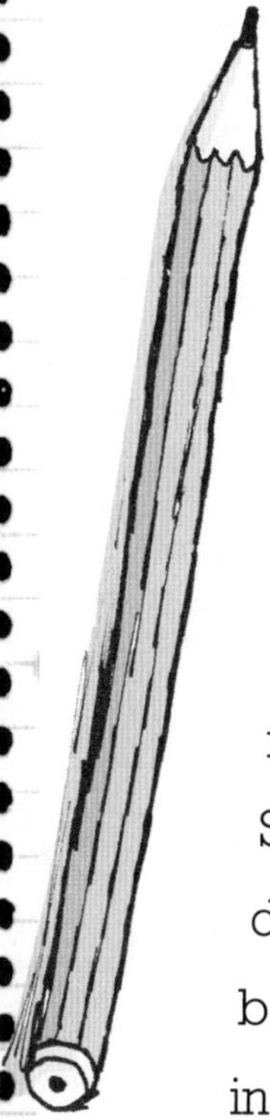

Tom said he wanted to go and see Mom to get the fur out of his mouth. And Mom was the next person on our list anyway. So that is what we did.

Mom didn't really like being questioned. She made Tom put the magnifying glass down, and she made Suzanne put the notepad down. But she didn't make me turn the Dictaphone off because she didn't know it was on record in my pocket.

Mom said, "We've been through all this already. You know perfectly well that I was in bed. And that I didn't hear anything. This is getting beyond a joke."

I said, "It never was a joke," because it wasn't.

I said, "It's an investigation."

But Mom said, "It's not healthy. All this digging about death. And you shouldn't be dragging poor Suzanne into it."

Suzanne said how she wasn't being dragged into it because she was in charge, actually.

But Mom said, "The *investigation* is *over*. If you don't drop it, right now, and accept that Number One killed the babies, and Number Two bit her leg off and escaped, then I am sending Suzanne home. And I'm going to phone Mrs. Rotherham because I'm annoyed that she is encouraging all of this."

So we promised that we would drop it, and that we wouldn't investigate anyone else, and we crossed Mom off the list.

And we just went to investigate Suzanne's Dad and Number One and Miss Matheson very quickly because they were the only suspects left.

When we got to Suzanne's house, Suzanne's Dad was in the bathroom. Suzanne banged on the door.

Suzanne's Dad shouted, **"I'M ON THE TOILET, FOR CRYING OUT LOUD!"**

Suzanne said that her Dad sometimes sits on the toilet for hours. We didn't have time to wait for him to get off the toilet, especially because Suzanne said she didn't think her Dad was in a very good mood anyway, not enough to be asked about his whereabouts, so we asked Suzanne's Mom instead.

I told Suzanne's Mom all about what had happened with the hamsters and everything.

Suzanne's Mom said my Mom had already told her.

Suzanne said, "Yes, but can you tell us about where Dad's whereabouts were between two a.m. and seven a.m. on Thursday morning?"

Suzanne's Mom said, "Yes. He was here. Up and down with his piles all night."

I said, "What are piles?"

Suzanne's Mom said, "I haven't got time to stand around talking about piles all day. You get them in your bottom. They aren't very nice."

This is what it says about piles in the dictionary in Suzanne's house . . .

piles ✦ *noun*
swollen and painful varicose veins in the canal of the anus also known as hemorrhoids

We crossed Suzanne's Dad off the list and we went to see Hamster Number One.

Number One was in the nest. I peeled back the top of the nest and picked Number One up and stroked her on the head. I could feel the stitches where her leg used to be. Number One looked very thin, and her fur was all matted, and she didn't even open her eyes.

I said, "I think Number One is too sick to be interviewed."

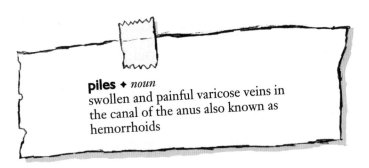

Tom looked at Number One through the magnifying glass. And he said that he thought so too.

I gave Number One a kiss on the head, and put her back in the nest, and Suzanne wrote "Sick" next to her name on the Suspect List, and said we should come back when Number One was better.

And then we went to see Miss Matheson.

Miss Matheson didn't take the chain off when she answered the door. I told her what had happened to the hamsters through the crack.

Suzanne showed Miss Matheson the real police badge and said, "We need to know where your whereabouts were between two a.m. and seven a.m. on Thursday, Miss Matheson."

Miss Matheson took the chain off the door and said, **"GET OFF MY PROPERTY BEFORE I CALL THE POLICE! I WARNED YOU ABOUT ALL THIS LAST TIME WITH THAT AWFUL OLD CAT. THIS IS TRESPASSING. I'VE KEPT A RECORD!"**

So we ran up the road to Mrs. Rotherham's because we were already late and because it was seventeen hundred and a half hours and that is after dinnertime.

And Tom said he would come into Mrs. Rotherham's house with us because he wasn't scared of her anymore and because he liked her cookies.

CHAPTER 19
The Hysterics

Mrs. Rotherham loved it when we played her all the interviews on the Dictaphone. She said it was the best thing she had ever heard in her life. Mrs. Rotherham got The Hysterics.

Me and Tom and Suzanne got The Hysterics a bit too, but not as much as Mrs. Rotherham.

Mrs. Rotherham got The Hysterics all the way through. She got them so badly she had to lie on the floor. She said it was a shame that Nana wasn't there because Nana would have got The Hysterics as well. And she would. Because it was almost as funny as when Graham Roberts was Jesus in his underwear.

Tom said, "Nana said ice cream is good when you need to calm down."

And Mrs. Rotherham went and got some out of the freezer.

After we ate the ice cream, and Mrs. Rotherham calmed down, Suzanne showed Mrs. Rotherham the Suspect List.

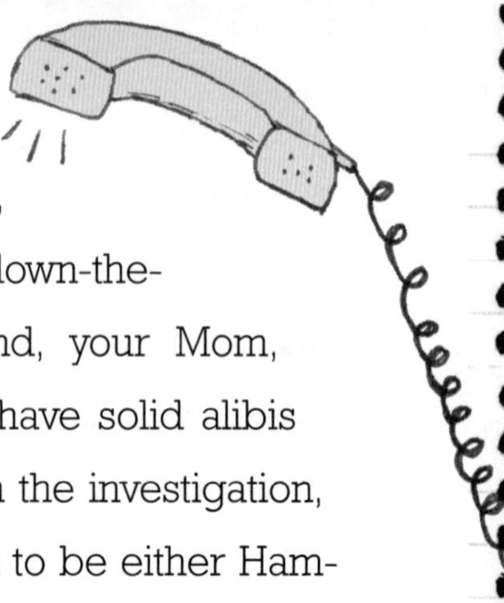

Mrs. Rotherham said, "So, Mr. Tucker, Joe-down-the-street's Mom's Boyfriend, your Mom, and Suzanne's Dad all have solid alibis and are eliminated from the investigation, which means that it had to be either Hamster Number One, or Hamster Number Two, or the New Cat, or Miss Matheson who committed the massacre."

Mrs. Rotherham's phone rang.

Mrs. Rotherham answered the phone and said, "Hello." And then she said, "It's your Mom." And then she winked.

And then she spoke into the phone and said, "Ah. I see. Leave it to me. Good-bye."

Mrs. Rotherham put the phone down. She looked very serious.

And she said, "I must inform you that the Investigation into the Hamster Massacre, although unsolved, is now, and

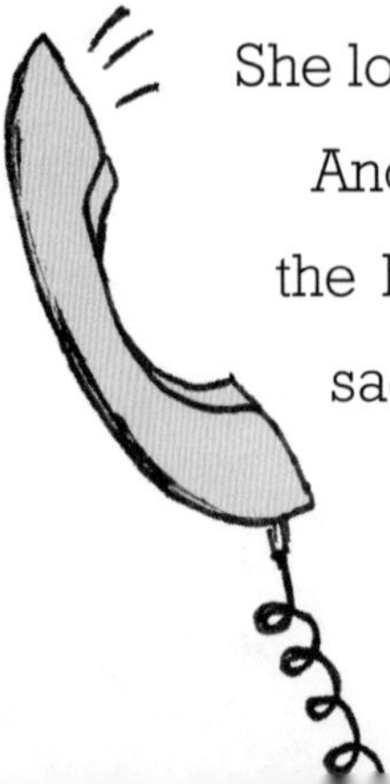

until further notice, officially closed."

I said, "Why?"

Mrs. Rotherham said, "The usual reasons: lack of funding and manpower and evidence, and missing and uncooperative suspects and witnesses. And because it's unlikely that new evidence will come to light at this late stage. Those are the main reasons.

"And also because Miss Matheson has called your Mom to complain, and also because your dinner is ready."

Tom said, "Let's go home," because he didn't want to do an investigation anymore because he was hungry, and he needed to pee, and because, he said, "It's probably Miss Matheson that did the murder anyway. It was her the last time."

I said, "Suzanne found cat blood on her tires."

And Mrs. Rotherham said, "Well done."

Suzanne said, "It was red."

Tom said, "Have you got any cookies?"

Mrs. Rotherham said she did. And she gave Tom a cookie, and Tom gave her back the magnifying glass, and I gave her the Dictaphone, and Suzanne gave her the police badge but Mrs. Rotherham said we could keep the notebook. And she said we should come back whenever we wanted, and especially if there was ever another investigation.

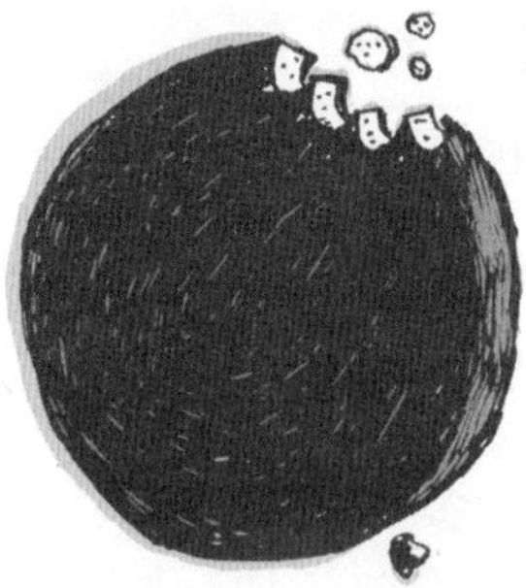

And Suzanne said, "There probably will be."

Because there quite often is. And we went back to the shed and we put the investigation notebook next to the worm box and the wasp trap and the pictures that we traced from Joe-down-the-street's Mom's book.

CHAPTER 20
What I Did On My Summer Vacation

So that's pretty much everything that has happened with the hamsters and everything. Except that Number One died. It was three days after Mrs. Rotherham closed the Real Investigation.

We didn't really do a funeral for Number One because for one thing Tom said he was sick of doing funerals, and for another thing I couldn't think of anything to say.

Suzanne says if you don't say

something it isn't really a funeral at all, which is true.

I buried Number One on my own. I dug a hole next to the eight baby hamsters and I put her in there. I put her in a box but I didn't decorate it. And I didn't put a cross in the ground either.

Mom said I could get another hamster if I wanted to. Just one. On its own. But I don't really want to. Tom says he doesn't want to either because he said the New Cat wouldn't like it. I don't really care about the New Cat but ever since Tom bit the New Cat back, Tom does.

That's when the New Cat started following Tom around. The New Cat follows Tom everywhere now. Even when Tom's busy holding the trash bag for Mr. Tucker, or walking in a straight line with his eyes closed, or collecting gravel, the New Cat goes too. I don't think I would like it if the New Cat followed *me* around. But Tom does. Sometimes the New Cat sleeps on Tom's bed. And sometimes it puts dead things on his pillow. I won't sleep in Tom's bed anymore because for one thing I don't like it that the New Cat might put a dead thing in it, and for another thing I'm too old

to sleep in Tom's bed really, because I'm nine, and for an even other thing it's school again tomorrow. And you have to sleep in your own bed when it's school again.

I really am supposed to be doing my What-I-Did-On-My-Summer-Vacation story for school now. I still can't remember any nice things to put in it. But, like Mom says, I can just make some nice things up because it's only a vacation story. So it doesn't really matter if it's not exactly true. Not like when you're writing up a Real Investigation. You can't make anything up at all when you're writing one of those. With a Real Investigation you have to write everything exactly right. And you have to write it right away. That's what Suzanne says.

So that's what I did.

The End

If you enjoyed **THE GREAT HAMSTER MASSACRE,**
look out for the next book about Anna,
Suzanne, Tom, and Joe-down-the-street . . .
Here's an excerpt from
THE GREAT RABBIT RESCUE,
coming soon!

Me and Suzanne peered into the hutch to have a look at the New Rabbit. There was a lot of hay in the way, all piled up against the wire mesh at the front. Suzanne reached her hand in through the hay and felt around.

"Oh," she said, "I can feel it. It's all soft and fluffy and warm."

And then she screamed, "AGH!" and she pulled her hand back. Her finger was bleeding. She put it in her mouth.

"It bit me!" she said.

I said, "Maybe it was asleep, and it got frightened when you put your hand in." Because when me and Tom had hamsters, we had this book, called *Hamsters: A Manual*, which said that hamsters only bite when they're frightened. Which you would be if a giant hand was coming at you from above. And it's probably the same with rabbits.

So I said, "Things only bite when they're frightened."

And Suzanne said, "No, they don't. Some things bite because they like it."

And I said, "Like what?"

And Suzanne said, "Like the New Cat!"

I said, "The New Cat is different. You

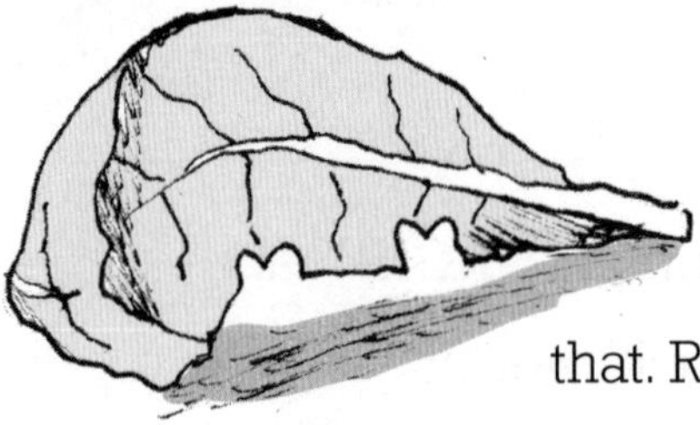

don't get rabbits like that. Rabbits just hop around, and eat lettuce, and fall asleep, and wear yellow ribbons on Easter cards and things."

Suzanne took her finger out of her mouth. It was still bleeding.

She said, "You put *your* hand in its hutch, then."

And I said, "I will."

I undid the latch and opened the hutch door a crack and put my hand in very slowly and lay it flat on the bottom of the hutch, like the hamster manual said you should. So that the rabbit would be curious and come and smell my hand, instead of being frightened and biting, like it did with Suzanne. We heard something rustle, but we couldn't see the rabbit through the hay. And then I felt the rabbit's fur against my hand, and its whiskers. I kept my hand

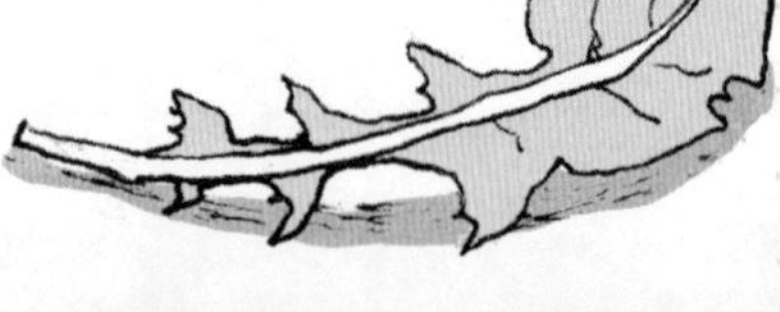

very still. And I said, "It's sniffing my hand. It tickles."

And then I said, "*Nice* New Rabbit."

And then I said, "AGH!"

And I jumped, and pulled my hand out. And put my finger in my mouth. And then I said, "It bit me!"

And Suzanne said, "*See*."

And she put the latch back on.

The New Rabbit rustled in the hay. And it pushed its way through it to the front of the hutch. It was white. And it had pink eyes. And it was *Absolutely Enormous*. The New Rabbit stared out at us through the wire mesh.

Suzanne said, "Look at its *eyes*!"

And I said, "Look at its *ears*!"

And Suzanne said, "Look at its *teeth*!"

And I said, "Look at its *claws*!"

And Suzanne said, "When did it get so *big*?"

Because the last time me and Suzanne had seen the New Rabbit, it was tiny. And its eyes were closed. And it fit in Joe's hands.

But me and Suzanne hadn't seen the New Rabbit for ages. Because even when we used to help Joe-down-the-street guard the New Rabbit, we hardly ever saw it, because it was always in its hutch, hiding behind the hay.

The New Rabbit gnawed on the wire on the front of the hutch. It had long yellow teeth.

Suzanne said, "It's not like Joe's *Old* Rabbit, is it?"

And it wasn't, because if you put your hand in the Old Rabbit's hutch, the Old Rabbit would rub its head against you, and hop onto your hand to be taken out. And then, if you let it, it would go up your sweater and nuzzle your neck, which was what it liked best. You couldn't fit the New Rabbit up your sweater. Not even if you wanted to. And you wouldn't want to anyway because the New Rabbit looked very angry.

We looked at the New Rabbit. And the New Rabbit looked back at us. Suzanne said, "It's too big for the hutch."

And it was, because it was almost as big as the hutch itself.

I said, "Maybe that's why it's angry."

Because the Old Rabbit had lots of room to hop around in the hutch. But if the New Rabbit stretched out, its feet would touch both ends.

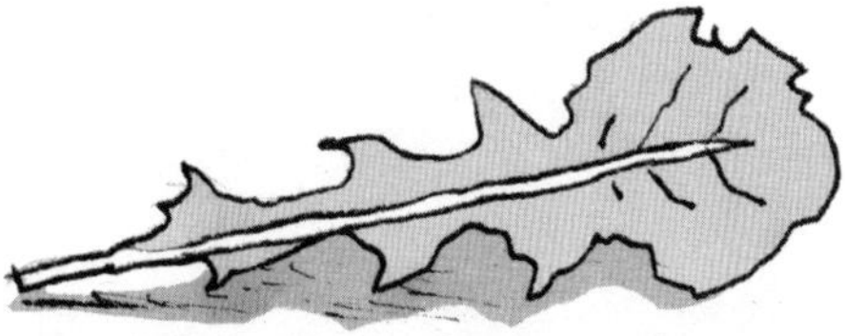

I said, "We could let it out for a bit."

And Suzanne said, "How will we get it back in?"

And I said, "We won't let it *out* out. We'll just let it out in the run. Only for a minute. And then we'll shoo it back in."

And Suzanne said, "Good idea."

Which Suzanne hardly ever says, so that means it was.

We picked up the run from the corner of the garden. And we put it on the front of the hutch. And it fit just right. Because that's how Joe's Dad had made it, ages ago, for the Old Rabbit, when he still lived with Joe and Joe's Mom.

There was a small hole in the wire mesh, in one corner of the run. We looked at the hole, and we looked at the rabbit. The hole was about the size of a jam jar. And the rabbit was about the size of a dog.

In fact, it was bigger than a dog. It was bigger than Miss Matheson's dog anyway, much bigger, because that's only the same size as a guinea pig. Anyway, the rabbit was definitely bigger than the hole. So we opened the door of the hutch. And the rabbit hopped out into the run. And it stood very still in the middle of the run, and it sniffed the air, and it put its ears right up. And then it hopped over to the corner with the hole. And it looked at the hole. And then, in a second, it squeezed through.

Suzanne said, "It's out!"

And I said, "The gate!"

And I ran to the gate and got there just before the rabbit did. And I slammed it shut. The rabbit looked angrier than ever. And it thumped its back leg on the ground. I tried to grab the rabbit. And Suzanne tried to grab the rabbit. But whenever we got near it, the New Rabbit ran at us and bit and scrabbled and scratched.

I said, "We need gardening gloves." Like Mom uses to put the New Cat in its carrying case when it has to go to the vet.

And I ran up the road to the shed, and got the gardening gloves, and put them on, and ran back down.

When I got back, Suzanne was running around Joe's garden in circles, and the New Rabbit was running after her. I told Suzanne to turn around and run at the rabbit, to shoo it toward me, so I could pick it up with the gardening gloves. And she did.

I grabbed hold of the rabbit. And it scrabbled and scratched and clawed and kicked. But I held on to it, tight. And then it bit me, hard, right through the gloves. And I dropped it.

I said, "It bit me! Right through the gardening gloves."

I could see a patch of blood. So I ran back up the road, and I got some Band-Aids, and my big brother Andy's football pads, and the helmet for his bike, and I put them on. And I got his shin guards, and his mouth guard, and some old oven mitts, and a balaclava for Suzanne. And I also got two fishing nets.

When I got back, Suzanne was in the corner of Joe's garden, pressed against the fence, and the New Rabbit was in front of her, and it was making a growling sound, and there were scratches all over her legs.

I said, "I didn't know rabbits growled."

And Suzanne said, "HELP!"

Katie Davies

Katie Davies was born in Newcastle upon Tyne in 1978. In 1989, after a relentless begging campaign, she was given two Russian Dwarf hamsters by her mom for Christmas. She is yet to recover from what happened to those hamsters. THE GREAT HAMSTER MASSACRE is Katie's first novel. She is currently working on its sequel, THE GREAT RABBIT RESCUE. Katie now lives in North London with her husband, the comedian Alan Davies. She does not have any hamsters.

Hannah Shaw

Hannah Shaw was born into a large family of sprout-munching vegetarians. She spent her formative years trying to be good at everything, from roller-skating to gymnastics, but she soon realized there wasn't much chance of her becoming a gold-medal-winning gymnast, so she resigned herself to writing stories and drawing pictures instead!

Hannah currently lives in a little cottage in the Cotswolds with her husband, Ben the blacksmith, and her rescue dog, Ren. She finds her overactive imagination fuels new ideas but unfortunately keeps her awake at night!

The Great Critter Capers

THE GREAT DOG Disaster

Katie Davies

Illustrated by Hannah Shaw

Beach Lane Books
New York London Toronto Sydney New Delhi

Thanks to Alan, and my Mum and Dad, and to Clare at Conville and Walsh, and Venetia at Simon and Schuster.

BEACH LANE BOOKS
An imprint of Simon & Schuster Children's Publishing Division
1230 Avenue of the Americas, New York, New York 10020

Originally published in Great Britain in 2012 by Simon & Schuster UK Ltd, a CBS company.
First U.S. edition 2013

Manufactured in the United States of America
0313 FFG
2 4 6 8 10 9 7 5 3 1
Library of Congress Cataloging-in-Publication Data
Davies, Katie, 1978–
The great dog disaster / Katie Davies ; illustrated by Hannah Shaw.—1st U.S. ed.
p. cm.
Sequel to: The great cat conspiracy.
Summary: Suzanne is delighted when her Great-Aunt Deidra leaves her Newfoundland, Beatrice, to Suzanne's mother, but Beatrice is old, slow, and has serious stomach issues that Suzanne and Anna must try to fix before Dad sends another dog away.
ISBN 978-1-4424-4517-8 (hardcover)
ISBN 978-1-4424-4519-2 (eBook)
[1. Brothers and sisters—Fiction. 2. Family life—England—Fiction. 3. Newfoundland dog—Fiction. 4. Dogs—Fiction. 5. England—Fiction. 6. Humorous stories.] I. Shaw, Hannah, ill. II. Title.
PZ7.D283818Gpm 2013
[Fic]—dc23
2012041868

For the Davis boys,
before you're all too big

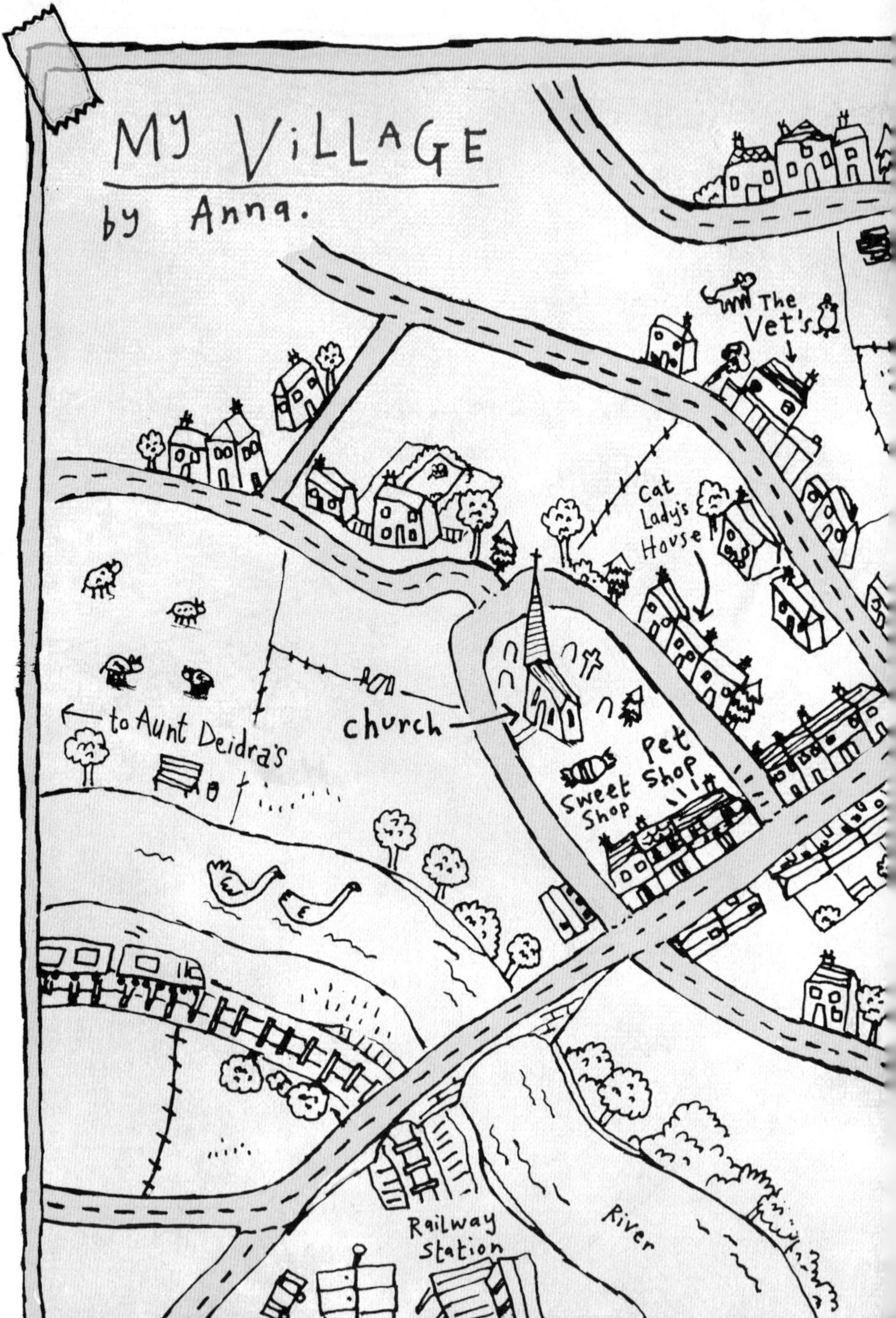
MY VILLAGE
by Anna.
The Vet's
Cat Lady's House
church
to Aunt Deidra's
Pet Shop
Sweet Shop
Railway Station
River

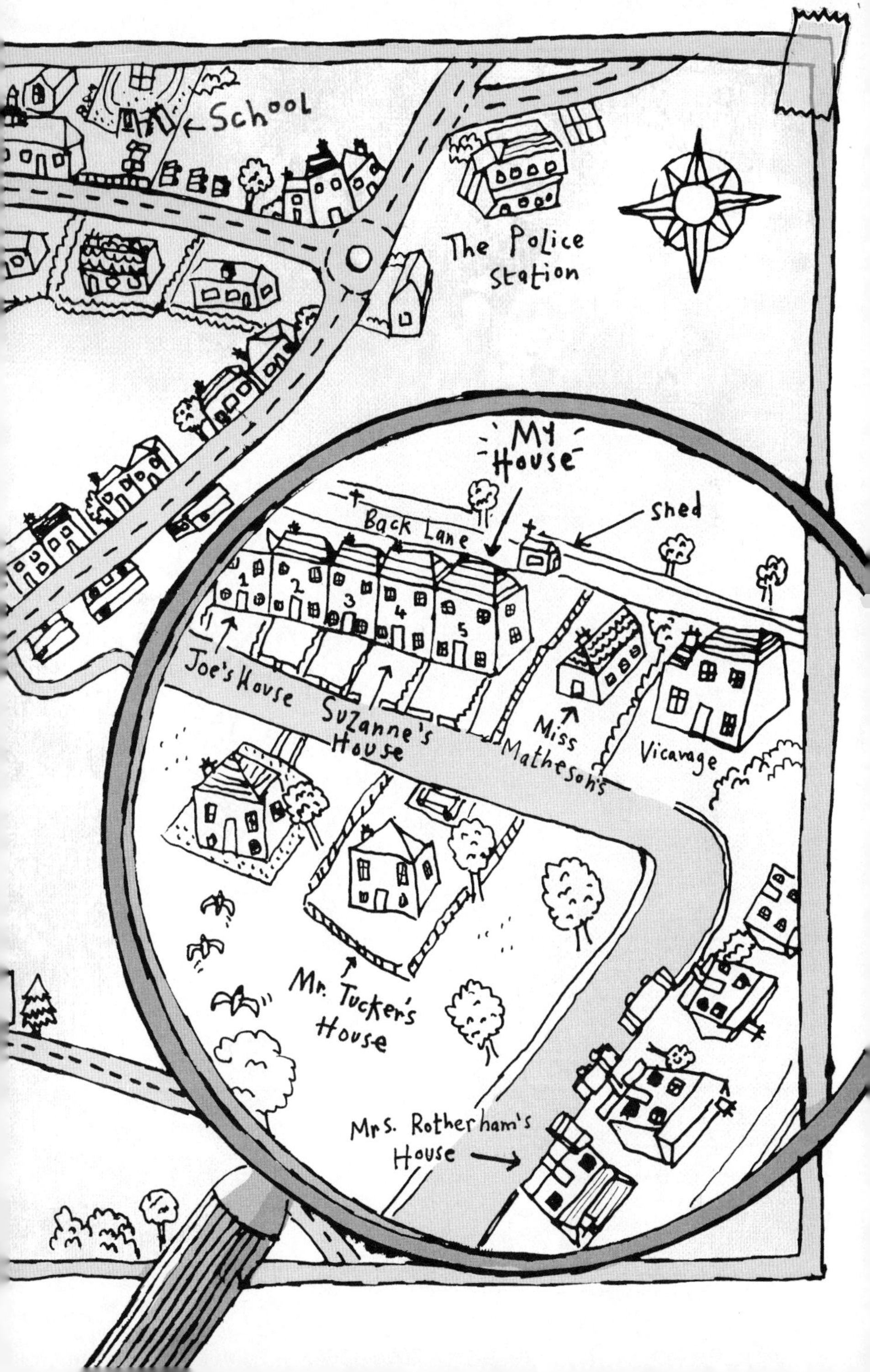

School
The Police Station
My House
Back Lane
Shed
1
2
3
4
5
Joe's House
Suzanne's House
Miss Matheson's
Vicarage
Mr. Tucker's House
Mrs. Rotherham's House

CHAPTER 1
An Actual Disaster

This is a story about my friend Suzanne, and her dog, and me, and Tom, and the Great Dog Disaster. Most of the time, when people say, "Oh, it's a disaster!" it probably isn't. Like when Dad's watching soccer, and they're up one to zero, and the whistle's going to go, and the keeper gets an own goal. Or when Mom's been to the shops, and

put the bags in the trunk, and slammed it shut, and locked the car keys inside it. Or when it's Mrs. Constantine's Sunday School Concert, and Emma Hendry starts her solo, and her hair gets set on fire by Graham Roberts's Christingle candle. Those things might be bad (especially for Emma Hendry, because her hair had never been cut before and she had to have a bob), but they aren't actual disasters. Because I looked "disaster" up in my dictionary, and this is what it said:

disaster [di-zas-ter] ✦ *noun*
a calamitous event, occurring suddenly
and causing great harm or death

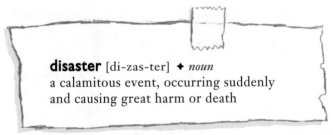

The Great Dog Disaster *was* an Actual Disaster though. It got on the news, and in the paper, and me and Tom and Suzanne had our photos taken and everything.

Tom is my brother. He's five. He's four years younger than me. I'm nine. My name is Anna. I've got another brother and a sister too, but they're not in this story because they're older than me and Tom and they don't really care about dogs, and disasters, and things that me and Suzanne do. Anyway, even though lots of people have heard about the Great Dog Disaster, it's only me who knows exactly what happened. Because there are some things about it that I have never told anyone. And I'm going to put those in this story as well. And when it's finished, I'll put my notebook in the shed, on the shelf, where no one will see it, behind the worms, and the wasp trap, and the piccalilli jar that's got all Suzanne's stitches in it.

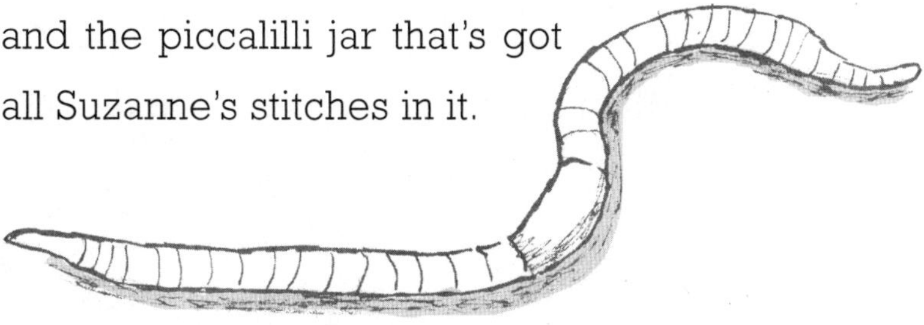

CHAPTER 2

The Guillotine

Suzanne lives next door. Her surname is Barry. Mine and Suzanne's bedrooms are right next to each other. The wall between our house and the Barrys' house is so thin that if you put your ear against the wall in our house, you can hear all the things the Barrys are doing on their side. When Mom sees me with my ear against the wall, she says, "For goodness' sake, Anna, can't you think of anything better to do than eavesdropping on next door?"

And I say, "No." Because if I *could* think of something better to do, I would have done that in the first place. Listening in on the Barrys is pretty good because you hear lots of things, like when it's time for lunch, and whether it's lentil soup,

and how afterward Suzanne's Dad can't come out of the toilet, and if Suzanne's that desperate she'll have to **"GO IN THE GARDEN!"**

Anyway, like I told Mom, I'm not the only one who eavesdrops. Because Suzanne listens in on *us* from her side of the wall as well. And in the morning, when we're walking to school, we tell each other all the things we heard happen through the wall the night before.

Me and Suzanne don't just listen

through the wall. We talk through it too. It's not that easy talking through a wall, unless you shout, but me and Suzanne can't do that because most of the things we need to say are secrets. We've tried millions of ways of talking through the wall. We put them on a list and pinned it up in the shed. The shed is out the back, in the lane, and only me and Suzanne are allowed to go in it. Except Tom, when he wants to, but most of the time he's busy doing other things, like talking to Mr. Tucker, or collecting gravel, or trying to walk in a straight line with his eyes closed.

ANNA'S AND SUZANNE'S LIST OF ALL THE WAYS WE HAVE TRIED FOR TALKING THROUGH THE WALL AND WHY WE HAD TO STOP AND TRY SOMETHING ELSE INSTEAD

WAY FOR TALKING THROUGH THE WALL:	WHY IT DIDN'T WORK:
Dig a tunnel through the wall to join our bedrooms together.	Suzanne's Dad looked under her bed, and saw where we had started digging, and banned us from Suzanne's bedroom.
Climb out of our bedroom windows and sit on our window ledges and talk out there.	Mom got bolts put into our window frames, and now we can't open them wide enough to climb out.

WAY FOR TALKING THROUGH THE WALL:	WHY IT DIDN'T WORK:
Talk on the walkie-talkies that Mrs. Rotherham gave us.	Suzanne's Dad confiscated them to stop us from talking on them at night.
Get the wall knocked down by doing a petition.	Only me, Suzanne, and Mrs. Rotherham signed it, so Suzanne's Mom said it didn't count.

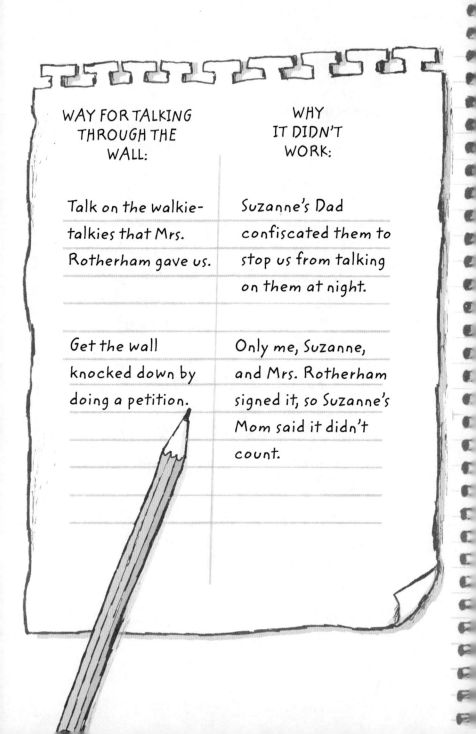

WAY FOR TALKING THROUGH THE WALL:	WHY IT DIDN'T WORK:
Climb up in the loft and talk through the hole where the bricks are missing.	Mom put a lock on the loft hatch after we made the ceiling fall in.

After all the ways on the list stopped working, me and Suzanne had to find a new way to talk through the wall. What we do now is knock three times to check if the coast is clear, and then we open our bedroom windows as far as they will go, up to the bolts, and stick our heads out. It's not that good talking with your head hanging out the window. Because you have to bend right over, and the window frame digs into your neck, and if it's raining, your head gets wet. When Mrs. Rotherham walked past and saw me and Suzanne with our heads sticking out, she said, "Hello, up there. You girls look as though you're about to be guillotined. Beautiful morning for it!"

I know all about guillotines because we did them at school with Mrs. Peters. This is what it says a "guillotine" is in my dictionary:

guillotine [gil-uh-teen] ♦ *noun*
a device for beheading a person by means of a heavy blade dropped between two posts: widely used during the French Revolution, particularly the Reign of Terror, between 1793 and 1794

Mrs. Rotherham is really old. If she were French, she would probably have seen people getting guillotined herself. Because everyone in France went to watch. Especially the old ladies. They did their knitting while they waited for the heads to get chopped off.

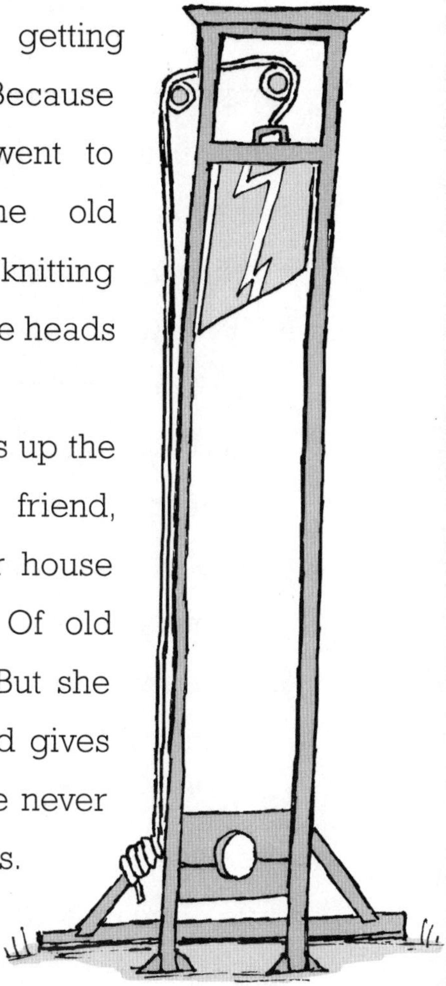

Mrs. Rotherham lives up the road. She was Nana's friend, before Nana died. Her house smells a bit strange. Of old things and mothballs. But she always asks you in, and gives you ice cream, and she never tells you not to do things.

Anyway, after Mrs. Rotherham said we

looked like we were in a guillotine, me and Suzanne started pretending that we were, and saying things in French, like "*bonjour*" and "*zut alors*" and "OFF WIZ ZER 'EADS!" And making the sound of the blades dropping down. And Suzanne pulls her head inside so it looks like it's been sliced off. And I scream, and make choking sounds, and pretend my guillotine's gone wrong and my head's still hanging on. Only I have to do it quietly, because if Mom hears, she comes in and says, "Don't play guillotines please, girls. It's not a good game." (Which isn't actually true, because it *is* a good game and, like Suzanne said, Mom wouldn't know

because she's probably never played it.)

Sometimes, when we're in the guillotine, me and Suzanne can see Mr. Tucker across the street. Mr. Tucker is old as well. Even older than Mrs. Rotherham. He was in The War. Flying planes, and fighting, and blowing stuff up and all that. Mr. Tucker doesn't fly planes anymore. Apart from pretend ones with Tom. Most of the time he just goes up and down the road, picking up the litter and checking how much rain there is in his rain gauge and spotting what kind the clouds are.

CHAPTER 3
A Hairy Heirloom

The day before Suzanne got her dog, I listened in on the Barrys a lot. Normally, when I wake up on weekends, I do stuff with Tom. Like helping him line up his stones, or finding him things to fix with his Bob the Builder tool kit, or counting how long he can hold his breath before he falls over. Because if you knock on Suzanne's wall, and ring the bell, and shout, "IS ANYBODY THERE?" through the letter box, before the Barrys' curtains are open, Suzanne's Dad runs down in his underpants, and opens the letter box from the inside, and says, **"IT'S six forty-five ON A SUNDAY! ARE YOU OUT OF YOUR MIND?"** Suzanne's Dad always shouts. You don't need to put your ear against the wall to hear *him*.

Anyway, this Sunday, Suzanne's Dad was up early, and he wasn't happy, because I could hear him through the wall, saying, **"WHAT?"** and **"YOU MUST BE JOKING!"** and **"I CAN'T BELIEVE WHAT I'M HEARING HERE!"**

So I left Tom in the hall, holding his breath, and I went to the kitchen, where the shouting was loudest. Mom was there, standing still, staring at the wall.

"Are you listening in on the Barrys?"

Mom jumped. "No."

"Oh."

"I'm making a cup of tea actually."

I didn't think Mom *was* making a cup of tea, because the kettle wasn't on, and she hadn't got a tea bag out, or a cup, but I didn't say anything, because I needed to listen in.

"NO, NO, NO!" Suzanne's Dad said, **"I DON'T NEED TO DISCUSS IT, BRIDGET."** Bridget is Suzanne's Mom's name. **"WE ARE DEFINITELY NOT GETTING A DOG!"**

But Mom turned the tap on, and filled the kettle, and started clanking about in the cup cupboard. "That's enough eavesdropping. Find something else to do, please, Big Ears."

So I went upstairs to knock for Suzanne. On the way I saw Tom. He was leaning against the wall in the hall, making a moaning sound. His head was bright red, like it was about to burst. "And . . . stop!" I said.

Tom breathed out, and fell down. "Phew! How long did I do?"

"Urm . . . a hundred and twenty seconds," I told him, which it probably wasn't, because I'd forgotten to keep count, and that's how long most grown-ups can hold their breath, and Tom's only five and he's the smallest in his class.

Tom was pretty pleased. "That's the best ever," he said. "I'd better get a cookie." After holding his breath, and spotting what kind the clouds are with Mr. Tucker, eating cookies is Tom's best thing.

I went upstairs to my bedroom and knocked three times on the wall. Suzanne knocked back. We stuck our heads out of our windows. *"Bonjour,"* I said.

"Bonjour."

"What was your Dad shouting about before?"

"I'm not supposed to say."

"Oh," I said. And I didn't ask again, because whenever Suzanne says she's not supposed to tell you something, she really just wants you to ask "Why?" a million times, and say, "Oh *please*, go *on*, I won't tell anyone. . . ." And the more you ask, the longer she makes you wait. So I just coughed, and made a clicking noise with my tongue, and picked a bit of paint off the window ledge.

And after ages, Suzanne said, "All right then, I'll tell you. Meet me at the shed. Zey 'ave pardoned us from ze guillotine zis time."

Suzanne's good at French. She's got a dictionary that says "French–English, English–French" on the front.

We put the lock on the shed door. And made up a password. And Suzanne told me all about what was happening in her house. And how her Mom had an aunt, called Deidra, who she hadn't seen in ages, even though she lived nearby, because of Aunt Deidra being on the side of the family that Suzanne's Gran didn't speak to. And how Aunt Deidra's Nephew, Mick, had left a message on their machine, saying that Aunt Deidra had died, and had left something behind for Suzanne's Mom in her will.

This is what it says a "will" is in my dictionary.

will [wil] ◆ *noun (DOCUMENT)*
an official statement of what a person has decided should be done with their money and property after their death

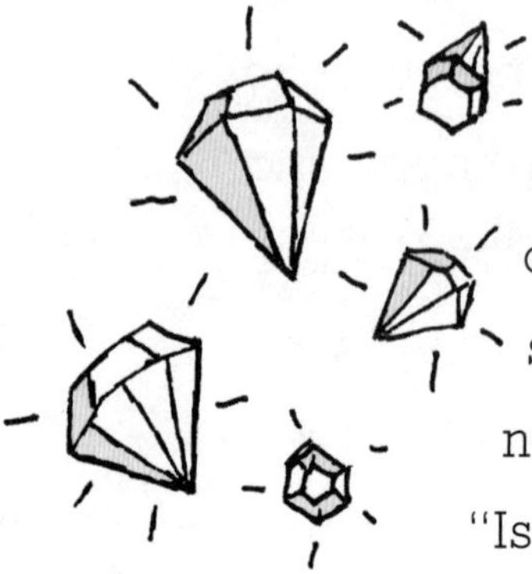

"Anyway," Suzanne said, "Dad hoped Great-Aunt Deidra had left Mom some diamonds. But she hadn't. It's something much better. You'll never guess what it is."

"Is it her dog?"

"Oh," Suzanne said. "Yes. It is." And she didn't look very pleased. Because she probably wanted to make me guess the answer for ages. And say, "Nope. Guess again." Like she normally does.

Anyway, Suzanne's Dad wasn't happy about the dog. He said he wouldn't have it in the house.

"We need to do something to make Dad change his mind."

I didn't think there was much point in trying to make Suzanne's Dad change his mind. Because for one thing

Suzanne's Dad is allergic to dogs. They make his nose run and his eyes itch and his face puff right up. And that's why he sent Suzanne's old dog, Barney, to live on a farm, where he can roam free in the fields and is much better off.

And for another thing he had already said, **"NO."** Three times. In a row. Really loud. Because I heard him through the wall. And for an even other thing Suzanne's Dad's not the kind of person who does change his mind. Especially not about dogs. Because Suzanne has tried to make him get another dog before. About a million times.

"But this time is different, because we have been *given* a dog," Suzanne said, "by a *dead* person." And she said we should do a list of reasons why getting Great-Aunt Deidra's Dog was a good idea. And give it to her Dad. So that's what we did. Because Suzanne's not the sort of person who changes her mind, either.

ANNA'S AND SUZANNE'S LIST OF REASONS WHY THE BARRYS SHOULD GET DEAD AUNT DEIDRA'S DOG

1. The dog can live in the garage, and never even come in the house at all. (Except on its birthday. And at Christmas. And then Suzanne's Dad can take tablets called anti-histamines, like Emma Hendry has at school, for when she goes too near the guinea pig.)

2. The dog can guard against burglars.

3. The dog can stop the New Cat from coming into the garden and hiding by the bird table, and killing all the Blue Tits. (The New Cat is our cat. It's not that new anymore, but that's still what it's called. We got it wild, off a farm, after the Old Cat died. Nobody likes it. Except Tom.)

4. Suzanne will take the dog for <u>two</u> walks every day, and feed it, and train it, and pick up all its poos. And no one else will have to do anything.

5. If she is allowed the dog, Suzanne will never ask for anything else again. Ever. And especially not any more dogs. And if she does, the dog can go back to Aunt Deidra's Nephew, Mick.

When the list was finished, Suzanne took it home to read to her Dad. I went into our kitchen and put my ear against the wall.

"I'm not interested," Suzanne's Dad said, before Suzanne had even started.

Suzanne read the list anyway. Then she waited. "Well?"

"Well *what*?"

"*Now* do you think it's a good idea to get the dog?"

"NO!"

"Oh."

"I'M GOING TO COUNT TO THREE, SUZANNE, AND IF YOU'RE STILL HERE . . . *ONE, TWO* . . ."

Suzanne ran upstairs.

I kept my ear against the wall. Suzanne's Mom came into their kitchen.

"DON'T START, BRIDGET!"

"I wasn't going to."

"GOOD."

"It's just it was poor Aunt Deidra's *dying wish*. . . ."

"YOU HADN'T SEEN YOUR AUNT DEIDRA IN YEARS!"

"All the more reason to have her dog now that she's dead."

And then Mom came into the kitchen and started going on about not eavesdropping again. And about last week's swimming things. And how I had to take them out of the bag, because if my suit went moldy again, I wasn't getting another one.

"Shh," I said. "You're making me miss what's happening in Suzanne's house."

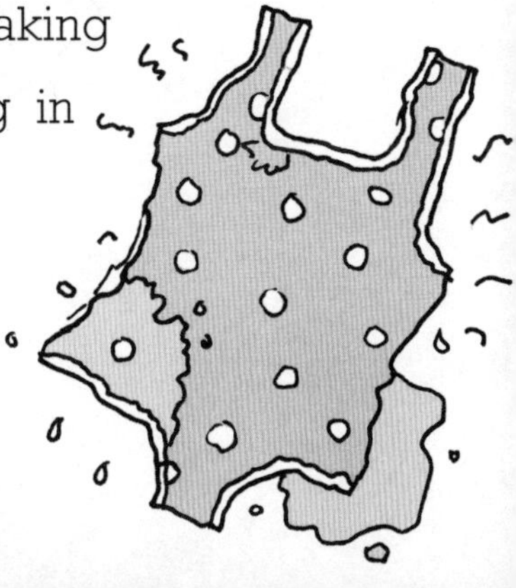

Then Suzanne's Dad said, **"IT'S MY HEALTH AND HAPPINESS OR THIS DAMN DOG'S. YOU DECIDE!"**

And the Barrys' front door slammed. And their car started. And went off down the road. And everything went quiet.

And Suzanne shouted through the wall, "*WE'RE GETTING DEAD AUNT DEIDRA'S DOG!*"

CHAPTER 4

Lifesavers

The next day was Monday. And apart from being the day that Suzanne's Great-Aunt Deidra's Dog was coming, nothing was different. Me and Suzanne woke up like normal. And walked to school together like normal. And sat at our desks like normal. And everything was just like it always is. Except longer. Because that's what happens when you're waiting for something. After school, me and Suzanne went swimming like we normally do on a

Monday. The swimming lesson we go to isn't a normal swimming lesson, though. Because, like Sandra, who's in charge, says, "You want to splash about, drift up and down, play around with floats? You've come to the wrong class, my friend. Try Water Wingers on Wednesdays. This is Lifesavers. Where swimming gets serious. There's nothing funny about subaqueous asphyxiation."

Which is true. This is what it says "subaqueous" is in my dictionary:

subaqueous [sub-ak-wee-us] ◆ *adjective*
taking place underwater

This is what it says about "asphyxiation":

asphyxiate [ass-fix-ee-ate] ◆ *verb*
to cause to die or lose consciousness by impairing normal breathing

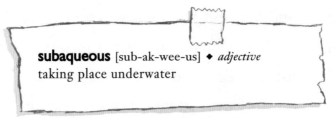

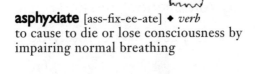

Suzanne didn't used to be allowed to go swimming. Because of her ear tubes. But now that she's had them taken out, she can. Suzanne keeps her ear tubes in the old piccalilli jar, with her adenoids and her stitches, on the shelf in the shed. She used to keep them on the shelf in her kitchen, until her Dad tried to put them in his cheese sandwich.

"Hey!" Suzanne said. "My adenoids!"

Suzanne's Dad threw them in the bin.

"WHO KEEPS OLD BODY PARTS IN WITH THE CONDIMENTS, FOR CRYING OUT LOUD?!"

And Suzanne had to fish them out.

Anyway, it's pretty good at Lifesavers, better than Brownies, because you don't have to do a sewing badge, or skip three times round a toadstool, or promise to serve the Queen. You dive to the bottom of the pool in your pajamas to get bricks

back, and throw ropes out into the water, and do Real-Life Rescues on Darren the Resuscitation Dummy. And sometimes Sandra says, "It's bad weather," and she puts the wave machine on, and the freezing cold hose, and runs up and down the side of the pool, blowing her whistle and shouting through the loudspeaker **"QUICK!"** and **"HE'S GOING UNDER!"** and **"TEN MORE SECONDS AND HE'LL BE BRAIN-DEAD!"** Which makes it even better.

Anyway, the day Great-Aunt Deidra's Dog was coming, after we had practiced speed swimming, and taken turns pumping water out of Darren the Resuscitation Dummy's

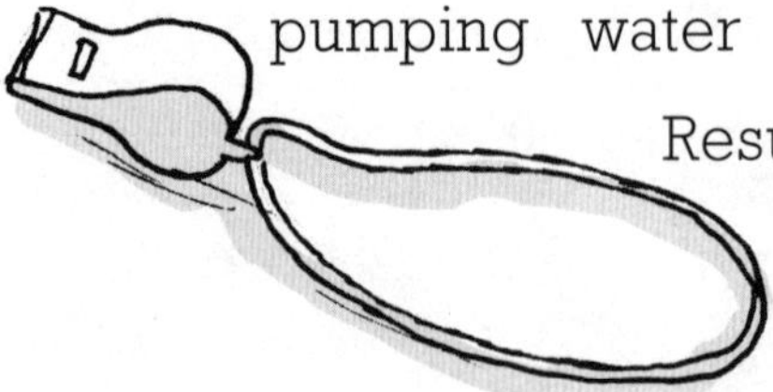

lungs, it was time to try Real-Life Rescues.

Sandra blew her whistle.

Fweeeeeeet!

"Everyone out, on the side. Let's see these Open-Water Rescue Skills in action. The situation is this: Emma

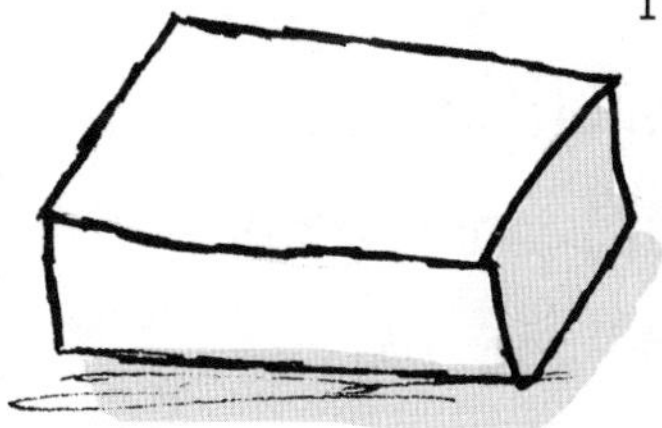

Hendry and Darren are having a picnic by a lake. The sun is shining. The birds are singing. What could possibly go wrong? But wait . . ." She pointed to the deep end. "The ground around the lake is wet, slippery still from last night's rain. Darren's a nonswimmer. Isn't he dangerously close to the edge? What about

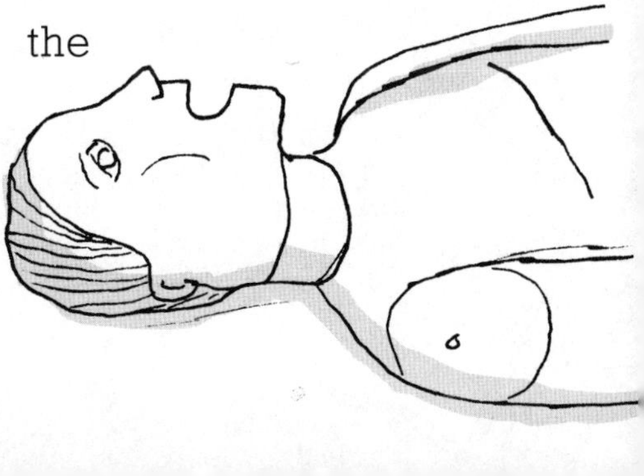

Emma's footwear? Is it appropriate?

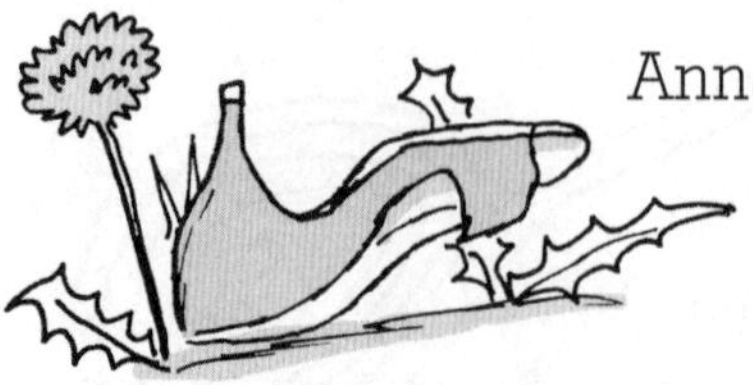

Anna Morris and Suzanne Barry, you're out walking nearby. Is that a splash you hear?" She blew her whistle again. **Fweeeeeet!** "Positions, people!"

Me and Suzanne went round the corner, into the changing room, and waited. And Emma spread an imaginary blanket on the ground, and sat Darren the Resuscitation Dummy down on it, and started putting out the picnic and saying, "Well, this is nice . . . ," and "Just the two of us, Darren . . . ," and "Cheese sandwich?" Which was taking ages. (It always takes ages with Emma. She's in the school Drama Group. And that's

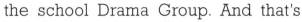

why sometimes Sandra shouts, **"MOVE IT ALONG, HENDRY. THIS IS AN *EMERGENCY*, NOT AN EPISODE OF *EASTENDERS*!"**)

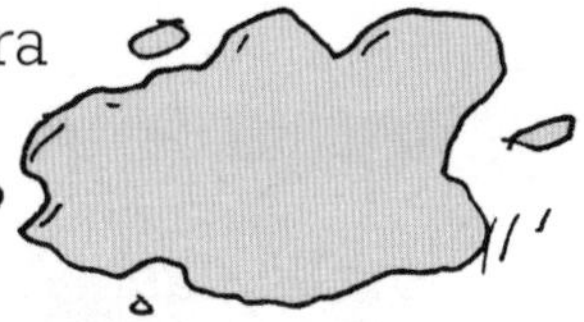

Anyway, while we were waiting for Emma to fall in the water, me and Suzanne started talking about Great-Aunt Deidra's Dog, and all the things we were going to do with it. Like race it up the road, and teach it tricks, and put it on an obstacle course, with cones and hoops and jumps, and all that. And Suzanne said we needed to decide on a name. And she told me the ones at the top of her list, like Cheetah, and Blaze, and Ace, and Bullet. And we forgot about the lake, for a bit, and listening out

for a splash. And then we heard, "HELP!"

We ran out of the changing room. Emma was thrashing around in the deep end. Suzanne grabbed the rescue rope from the hook on the wall. "Stand back!" She threw it out, across the water, to the other side of the pool. "Grab hold!" The rope landed right next to Emma's hand. Suzanne pulled her into the side, and we dragged her out of the water, and I wrapped her in the imaginary picnic blanket and put her in the recovery position.

Emma shivered, "D-D-D-Darren, help Darren . . ."

Suzanne dived in. I went after her. Darren was lying on his back at the bottom of the pool. We tried to pull him up, but he'd already filled with water.

Fweeeet! Sandra blew her whistle.

I came back up. "He's too heavy."

Suzanne came up for air. "We need more time."

"You're too late, ladies. Darren has been submerged for sixteen minutes."

"He might still be alive," I said. "Because Peter Colat from Switzerland is. And he once held his breath underwater for nineteen minutes and twenty-one seconds."

"Peter Colat is a professional free diver and world record holder, Anna. Darren's never even made it across the pool."

"If only he'd told me he couldn't swim," Emma said. "I wouldn't have sat him so close to the edge. . . ."

Sandra fished Darren out with the long pole with the hook on the end, and laid him facedown on the side. "Darren has *had it*."

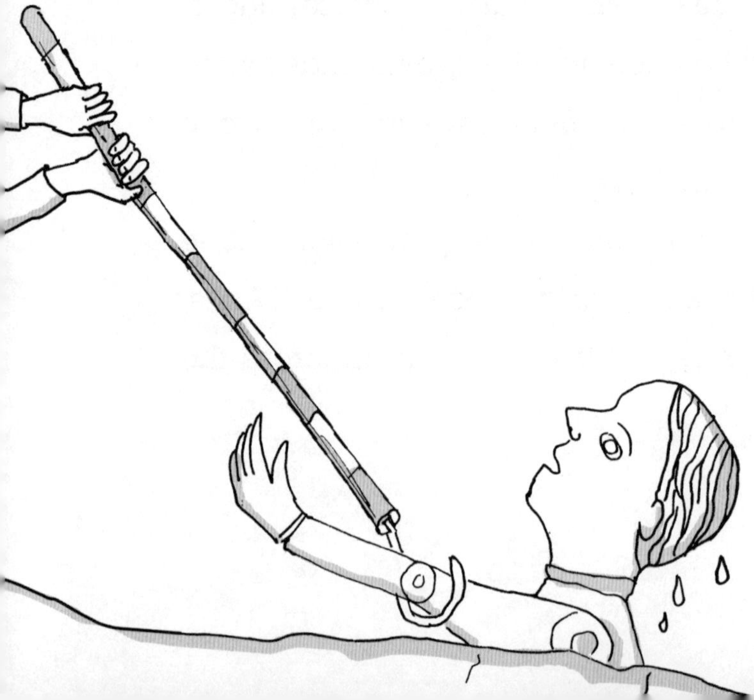

CHAPTER 5
The Rain Gauge

After we got back from Lifesavers, and had our dinner, me and Suzanne sat down on the path outside Suzanne's house and waited for Great-Aunt Deidra's Nephew to bring the dog. Mr. Tucker was in his front garden across the road, looking in the rain gauge with Tom. Tom and Mr. Tucker measure the rain gauge every day. Even on days when there hasn't been any rain. Because measuring the rain is one

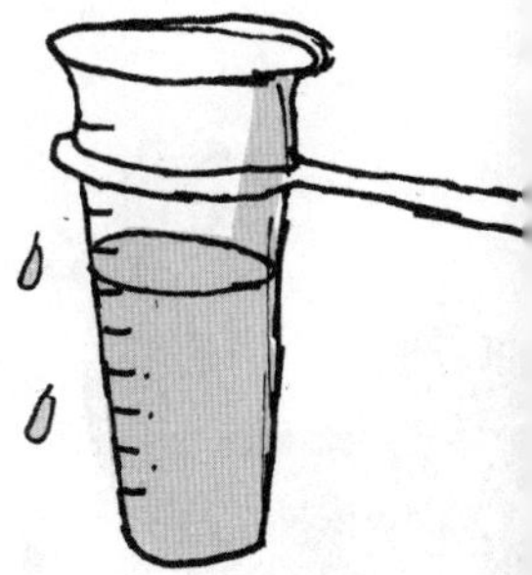

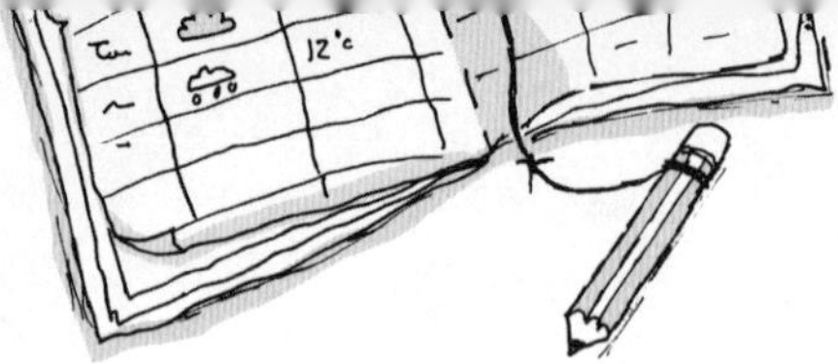

of Tom's best things. And they check the weathercock as well, to see which way the wind's blowing. And the thermometer, to see how hot it is. "Two inches of the old wet stuff today, Basher. What do you say, eh, Popsie?"

Mr. Tucker always calls me Popsie, even though, like I've told him, it's not my name. I didn't say anything, because I don't like talking to Mr. Tucker about the weather much, because it always takes ages, and sometimes he gets his logbook out, and that's got graphs in it.

"We're waiting for a dog," Suzanne said. And she told Mr. Tucker about her Mom's Aunt Deidra, and how she had died and left her dog behind.

"Sounds like a fine woman, this Deidra," Mr. Tucker said. "Black do, her dying. Great-aunts have a habit of it. Damned nasty business. Used to have one myself. Great-Aunt Eida. Six sons, until four of them went in The War. Crippled with arthritis but walked Hadrian's Wall in a one-piece for multiple sclerosis, and made marvelous mince pies. Still, a dog, eh, Blondie?"

Mr. Tucker always calls Suzanne Blondie, even though her hair is brown.

"What do you say, Basher?"

Tom said he hoped this dog didn't jump up, like Barney used to. Or lick. Or chase after the New Cat.

"It probably will," Suzanne said. "Because that's what dogs *do*."

"You have to be careful with cats," Tom said. Which is true. Apart from with the New Cat. Because it was a wild cat, off a farm. And it's not scared of anything. Especially not dogs. It's not scared of Miss Matheson's dog anyway. Miss Matheson lives next door to us, on the other side of Suzanne. Her dog is the same size as a guinea pig. It fits in her handbag. It runs up and down all day on the other side of Miss Matheson's fence and yaps and snaps, and if anyone comes close, it attacks.

"I shall take a shufti at this dog myself, of course, give it the old once-over. Debrief the animal, eh, Basher, that make you feel better?" And Tom said that would make him feel better, and *another* thing that would make him feel better was a cookie.

Mr. Tucker took Tom indoors, to see if he could find one.

CHAPTER 6

Dead Aunt Deidra's Dog

The car stopped outside Suzanne's house. A big man with a small T-shirt on opened the door and got out. Suzanne's Mom came out of the house to meet him.

"Mick?"

"Bridget."

"It must be ten years. You haven't changed a bit."

"Humph."

"I hope you won't find

the dog too hard to part with."

"Not *too* hard."

Mick went to the back door. Where me and Suzanne were looking through the window. There was something black and furry lying across the backseat. It looked like the black sheepskin rug Mrs. Rotherham has in front of her fire. Mick opened the door. And stepped back to let us see. The furry thing stayed still.

"Is it asleep?" Suzanne asked.

Suzanne's Mom opened the door opposite and stuck her head inside. "Well, hello . . . *oh*." She covered her mouth. "What on *earth* is that smell?"

"Dog doesn't like cars," Mick said.

"Phew. I've never smelled anything *like* it."

I stuck my head in the car and sniffed. "I have," I said. Which was true. Because it smelled like Mrs. Peters's class, the time Graham Roberts brought a dead vole in, in his PE bag, and left it all week on his peg.

Mick leaned in and gave the fur a shake. "We're here. Wake up!"

Two small brown eyes opened. They were bloodshot and a bit misty, like Nana's used to be, before she had her operation. The eyes looked up at Great-Aunt Deidra's Nephew, and blinked, then they closed again.

"It's gone back to sleep," I said.

"Come on, dog, jump down." Suzanne's Mom patted her knees. "You'll feel better out in the air." The dog stayed still.

"Doesn't like to move much, either," Mick said. "That's why I came in the car. Would've taken all week walking."

Suzanne's Mom clapped her hands. "That's it, down you come." The dog still didn't budge.

Mr. Tucker came out of his house with Tom, and crossed over to the car. He gave Great-Aunt Deidra's Nephew the salute. "Wing Commander Raymond Tucker, six-one-seven squadron."

Aunt Deidra's Nephew kept his hand in his pocket. "Mick."

"Black do about your Aunt. I had an Aunt myself. Wonderful woman—"And he started telling Suzanne's Great-Aunt Deidra's Nephew about his Aunt Eida's six sons, and the four that died, and her mince pies and all that.

"Where's the dog?" Tom asked.

Aunt Deidra's Nephew pointed to the backseat. The dog was lying flat on its back with its head hanging over the edge.

"Is it dead?"

"No," Suzanne said. "It's not."

"It won't come out," I said.

"It will. You just have to ask it right." Suzanne knows a lot about dogs because of Barney, and his training classes, and from her book called *You and Your Dog: Training and Tricks*. She held up her finger, and looked the dog in the eye, and said, "Come!" in her special dog-training voice. The dog didn't do anything. She said it again, slow, like a warning, *"Come . . ."* The dog looked back at Suzanne and blinked.

"Maybe it's deaf," I said.

"It's not deaf," Suzanne said.

"Frozen on the stick, eh?" Mr. Tucker stuck his head inside the car too. "Ahem, bit ripe in here, harrumph . . ." One of the dog's ears went up. "Now then, look lively, it's a simple op, dog. On three, my count, think of Aunt Deidra and bail out. One, two, three . . ." The dog didn't move. "That's it. You've got the green. Chocks away . . ." The dog

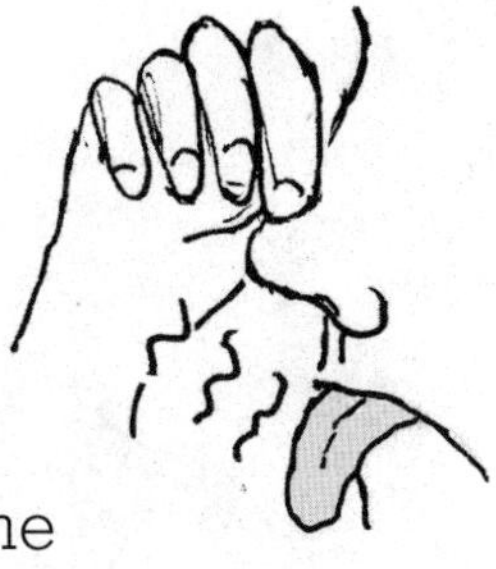

stayed still. "Now, that's a direct order, dog. Let's not play silly beggars."

"The only way to shift it is to give it a swift kick," Mick said.

"No need for roughhouse. Must be some other way to clear it out of the old land creeper here, eh?"

"We could get in a long line and pull it out, like in *The Enormous Turnip*," Tom said. *The Enormous Turnip* is one of Tom's best books.

Suzanne made her eyes go up, like

she does when she thinks you've said something stupid, and she started telling Tom how getting a dog out of a car isn't the same as getting a turnip out of the ground, because of dogs being different from turnips and all that.

But Mr. Tucker butted in. "Spot on, Basher. *Enormous Turnip* it is. Righto, wing, get weaving."

And he got us all in a line, in order of height. Apart from Great-Aunt Deidra's Nephew, because he said he had a bad back.

Mr. Tucker held on to the dog's collar, and Suzanne's Mom held on to Mr. Tucker, and I held on to Suzanne's Mom. And Suzanne held on to me, and Tom held on to Suzanne.

"That's it, wing. Stand to. Take the

strain . . . ," Mr. Tucker said. "Steady . . . *Pull* . . ." The dog slid out of the car and slopped onto the street.

And Great-Aunt Deidra's Nephew got back in the car and said good-bye, and drove off, quick.

CHAPTER 7

The New Cat

The dog got up on its feet.

"It's big," Tom said. And it was. It had a big head, and big legs, and a big body. It was the biggest dog I had ever seen.

"It could be a *bear*."

"It isn't a bear," Suzanne said.

"It *looks* like one," said Tom.

Which was true. It did. And not a very happy one.

"Like one of those dancing bears that have to stand on hot coals in Siberia, and get kept in cages," I said.

"No, it doesn't," Suzanne said. But it did. Because I've seen them. On TV.

"Maybe we should keep *this* one in a cage," Tom said, "in case it's the kind of *bear-dog* that jumps up, and licks, and goes after the New Cat."

"It's not going in a cage," Suzanne said.

Mr. Tucker pointed up the road. "Speak of the devil . . ."

The New Cat was sitting on Miss Matheson's wall, with its eyes all wide, and its fur all up, staring down at the dog.

Suzanne grabbed the dog's collar. "*Staaay* . . . ," she said, and pulled against it, like it was trying to get away.

The New Cat jumped down

and started walking toward it, all low down to the ground, like it does when it's hunting. And when it got close, it arched its back and hissed. "*Tssss.*"

Great-Aunt Deidra's Dog breathed in, and opened its jaws, wider and wider, showing its great big teeth.

"It's going to eat the New Cat!" Tom said. The New Cat's whiskers twitched. The dog's teeth snapped shut in front of the New Cat's nose. It stretched.

"What a *yawn*," said Mr. Tucker.

The dog turned round, in a circle, and lay down, and closed its eyes. The New Cat sat still for a bit and waited. Then it turned around, and put its tail in the air, and walked off up the road.

"It's not the kind of bear-dog that goes after cats," said Tom.

Suzanne's Mom laughed. "This dog's cat-catching days are over."

"Is it old?" Tom asked.

"Ooh, yes."

"It could catch cats," said Suzanne. "If it wanted." The dog started to snore.

"Quite right," said Mr. Tucker. "Dog's in its prime. Just like I am." He stretched. And rubbed his back. "What are we calling her when she's at home?"

"I thought Cheetah," Suzanne said, "or Blaze, or Bullet."

Suzanne's Mom felt around the dog's collar. "I think she already has a name." She showed Suzanne a tag.

Suzanne read it. "Sorrel Cottage."

"No, that's where Aunt Deidra lived. Turn it around. What does the other side say?"

"It says *Beatrice*," Suzanne said. And she didn't look very pleased.

CHAPTER 8

Walkies

After Mr. Tucker went home for his dinner, and Suzanne's Mom went in to give baby Carl his bath, and Tom went to ask Mom for a cookie, Suzanne decided it was time to take Beatrice for a walk.

"I don't think Beatrice is *that* old, do you, Anna?"

I looked at Beatrice. She was still asleep in the road. Her eyes were all droopy, and runny, with crusty stuff in the corners, and there were lumps, like warts, in her eyebrows, and her mouth sagged down, and her tongue hung out, and her teeth were brown, and there was a line of dribble from her lips, and her fur had matted patches, and there were other places where it was missing, and she smelled like Graham Roberts's PE bag with the dead vole at her back

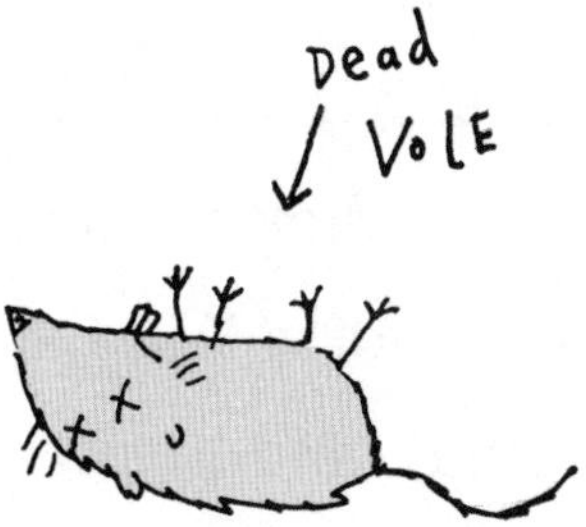

end. And at the front she smelled like Mrs. Constantine's pond, the time it went green with slime and the fish all floated to the top.

"It's hard to tell with dogs," I said. Because people have lots of things to show how old they are, like Mrs. Rotherham's got a walking stick, and two pairs of glasses on a chain around her neck that she swaps over all the time, and enormous underpants like cycling shorts that she hangs on the line. But dogs don't have any of those things.

"Beatrice might not even be old at all," Suzanne said. "She might just be tired because she probably hasn't been sleeping well, staying at Mick's house. And once she's been out for a W.A.L.K., she'll start sniffing around, and jumping up, and chasing after cats when they come near like proper dogs do."

I said I thought that Suzanne was right, because she normally is, about most things, and especially about dogs.

"I'll go and get the L.E.A.S.H. and some S.N.A.C.K.S."

Suzanne always spells out "leash" instead of saying it, and "walk" and "snacks" as well, because when she had Barney (before he went to live on the farm, to roam free, where he's better off), if he heard those words, he went mad, and ran round in circles, and jumped up and sent Suzanne flying.

Suzanne came back out, jangling the leash. "*Beatrice* . . ." Beatrice carried on snoring. Suzanne bent down and lifted up one of the dog's ears, "Beatrice?" Beatrice opened one eye. She looked at Suzanne, and she looked at the leash. "Walkies." Beatrice put her chin

on her paws and closed her eye again.

"Maybe Beatrice doesn't like walks."

Suzanne made her eyes go up. "*All* dogs like walks, Anna." She clipped the leash to Beatrice's collar and gave it a little tug. Then she gave it a bigger tug. Then she put it over her shoulder. "*Uungh* . . . you'll like it once you get going, Beatrice." And pulled as hard as she could. Beatrice didn't budge. "You'll have to push, Anna."

I wasn't sure Beatrice *would* like it once she got going, because that's what Mom always used to tell me about Brownies. And I never did. Apart from once, when she brought Tom with her to pick me up. And he ran in, in the middle of Shelly Wainwright's Promise Ceremony, and skipped around the toadstool and said his name was Rumpelstiltskin.

I went behind Beatrice and pushed anyway. Her fur was greasy and matted, and underneath it I could feel her bones.

"And *again*," Suzanne said.

I pushed harder.

"What if you got right underneath her, with your shoulder, and leaned in close, and pushed forward and up like a lever . . ."

I didn't really want to get underneath Beatrice with my shoulder and push up like a lever, because that would mean my face would be right in Beatrice's bum. And I don't like putting my face in dogs' bums much, and especially not in old dogs' bums, like Beatrice's, which have greasy hair, and bald bits, and matted lumps, and smell of a dead vole that's been in a PE bag for a week.

"What about if we swap places, and *I*

hold the leash and pull and *you* get down under Beatrice's bum and lever her up?"

"No," Suzanne said. "Because I'm the one who knows all about dogs and training, and what to say, and how to say it, like 'sit' and 'stay' and 'heel' and all that. And if we start swapping around, Beatrice will get confused."

So I got down on the ground, and took a deep breath, and held it, and wriggled my shoulder underneath Beatrice's bum.

"Ready?" Suzanne asked.

I nodded.

"Three, two, one . . . *Liftoff*."

I closed my eyes and pushed forward and up as hard as I could, and tried to think about something else. My arms shook.

"Push, Anna."

"Nngnngya!"

"That's it."

Beatrice's back end wobbled a bit, and lifted, until she was up on her feet.

"There," Suzanne said. "Easy." I didn't say anything. Because I was lying on the ground, in the gravel, getting Beatrice's hairs out of my mouth.

We started off down the road on our walk. It was slow. Even slower than when you go for a walk with Tom and he has to collect every stone. Because Beatrice stopped every few steps. And sometimes she tried to sit down. And at the bottom of the road she went solid, like a statue, and refused to turn right, so we had to go left instead. And Suzanne pulled at the *front* end of Beatrice, and I pushed at the *back*

end, all the way down the hill and into the village. It wasn't much fun, not like when we used to go with Barney, and you had to run to keep up, and he sniffed every lamppost, and barked at cars, and people waved, or gave him a pat and said, "Looks like the dog's taking *you* for a walk," and things like that. Because no one said anything about Beatrice. Except a man at the bottom bus stop, who shook his head and said, "Tut, tut, tut, shame."

When we got to the bridge, Beatrice went solid like a statue, again, just like she had at the bottom of our road, and we couldn't get her to go over.

"Let's turn around and go home," I said.

Suzanne pulled and I pushed. But Beatrice wouldn't turn around.

"She doesn't *want* to go home," Suzanne said. "I told you she'd like it once she got going. We'll have to turn right, and go along the river."

I didn't want to go along the river because for one thing it was cold, and for another thing it was getting dark, and for an even other thing I don't like the ducks.

"Unless you're scared of the *ducks*?" Suzanne asked.

"No," I said. Because I'm not scared of *most* ducks. Because most ducks just bob along on the water, and waddle about, and wait for bits of bread. But the ducks down by the river are different. Because there are millions of them. They live on the island in the middle. And they go around in gangs. And there's one that's the leader, who is bigger, with an extra-long neck and a white eye that looks off in the wrong direction. And Graham Roberts said it got crossed with a *swan*. And it could break your arm. Which is probably true. Because Graham lives on a farm.

"The ducks won't bother us when they see Beatrice," Suzanne said. "I'll let her off the leash and she can charge, like Barney used to, and send them all scattering."

We started down the path that leads to the riverbank. When we got to the bit where the grass opens out, Suzanne unclipped Beatrice's leash. "You're off the leash, Beatrice."

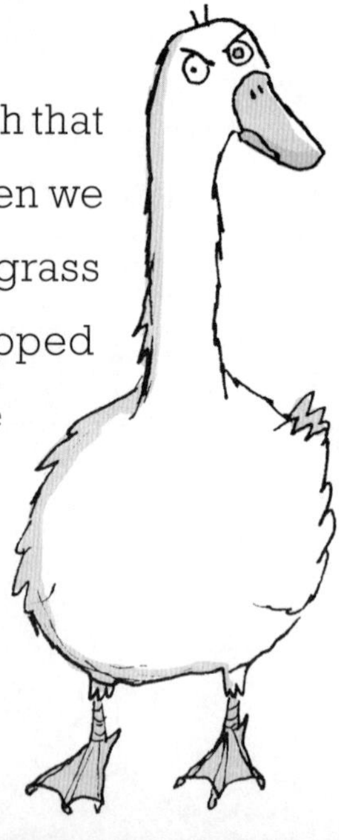

She patted her side, "You're *free*!"

Beatrice stood still.

"*Run*, Beatrice!"

Beatrice started walking slowly forward.

"Maybe if we ran around ourselves," said Suzanne, "that might get Beatrice going." So me and Suzanne chased each other, and jumped up and down, and clapped our hands. And threw sticks, and said, "*Come on*, Beatrice," and "Good dog," and "Off you go!" And we ran ahead, past the bin, and the gorse bushes, and up to the bench where the old people always sit.

And then we sat down and waited for Beatrice to catch up. And we walked on, to the row of cottages whose gardens go down to the riverbank.

When we came to the last cottage, Beatrice stopped. And sat down in front of it. The gate to the cottage was covered in ivy. There was a FOR SALE sign next to it. Beatrice pushed at the gate with her nose.

"What's she *doing*?" I asked.

Beatrice rubbed her head against the gate and whimpered.

"She wants to go *in*," Suzanne said. We leaned on the gate and looked over. There was a big kennel at the top of the garden. Suzanne looked at the kennel. And then she looked at the gate. And she pulled some of the ivy away from the nameplate. And she read it. "Sorrel Cottage. It says *Sorrel Cottage*, Anna."

"So?"

"So," Suzanne said, "look at what it says on the *kennel*."

Above the arch of the door, there was a name. "It says *Beatrice*!"

"This is Aunt *Deidra's* house, where Beatrice *lived*."

Beatrice put her nose in the air and made a strange howling noise. Like the whale music that Mrs. Peters puts on in PE for Free Movement.

Suzanne tried the gate. It was locked.

"Let's go home," I said. Because it was cold and was starting to get dark and the ducks were probably coming.

Suzanne held her finger up, and looked Beatrice in the eye, and started talking in her special dog-training voice again. "*Beatrice*, come . . ." Beatrice didn't budge. Suzanne clipped the leash to Beatrice's collar and gave

it a little tug. Then she gave it a bigger tug. Then she put it over her shoulder, and pulled as hard as she could. "Uungh . . ."

"Try giving her one of the S.N.A.C.K.S.," I said. Because when Suzanne had Barney, she could make him do anything for a snack, especially for one of baby Carl's rice cakes.

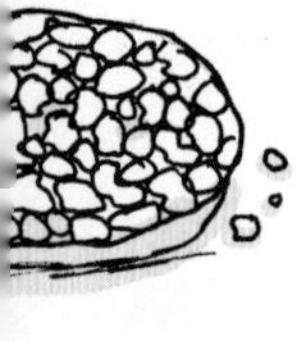

"You're only supposed to give S.N.A.C.K.S. for *good* behavior," Suzanne said. But she got the packet out of her pocket. Beatrice looked at them. Then she looked back at the gate and made the whale noises louder than ever. And then I heard *another* noise, nearby.

"Quack."

"What was that?"

"What?"

"I heard something."

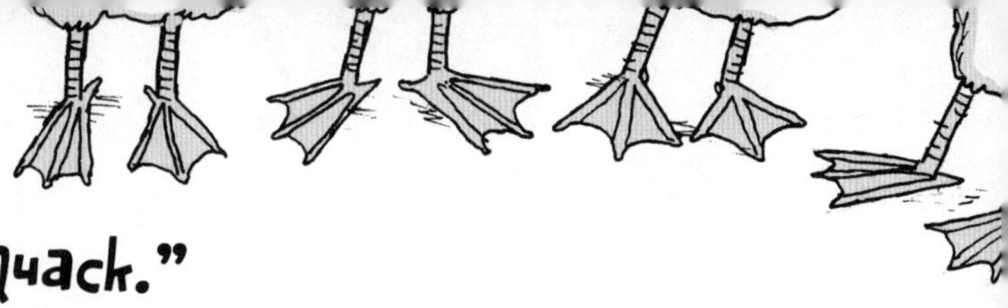

"Quack."

"Over there."

"Quack."

I turned around.

"Quack. Quack."

Three ducks waddled out of the water and up the bank toward us.

"Ducks," Suzanne said. "Ducks, Beatrice, *charge!*" But Beatrice didn't even turn around.

I clapped my hands at them. "Shoo." The ducks stopped.

Then, **"Quack."**

"On your left, Anna." Four more ducks came waddling out from in the gorse bushes. I turned around and ran at them and waved my arms.

"Quack." Four more ducks appeared on the right, from in the long grass.

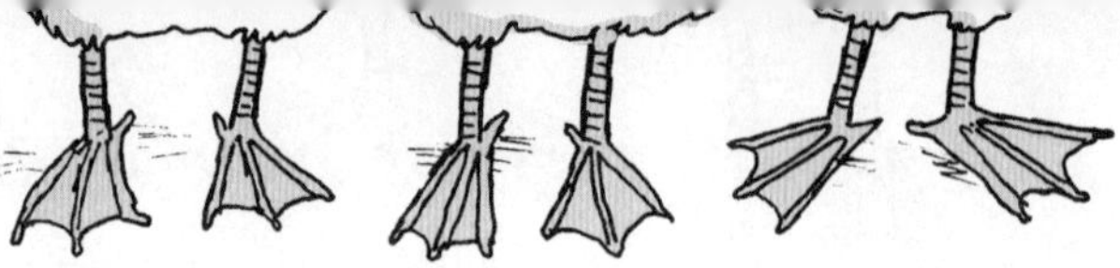

"Let's *go*," I said, "before they get us *surrounded*."

Suzanne pulled at Beatrice's leash. "I'll get Beatrice up, Anna. You fend off the ducks." Suzanne got a rice cake out of the packet and held it up in front of Beatrice. The ducks started flapping their wings, and quacking like mad, and waddling forward together.

Then, **"HONK."** The Swan Duck leader with the long neck, and the white eye that looks off the wrong way, shoved its way to the front. It stuck its neck forward, with its head on the side. And its good eye looked at Beatrice, and Suzanne, and the snacks. And the white eye, which looks off the wrong way, was watching *me*.

"HONK!" Suzanne jumped. Some of the rice cakes went up in the air and

fell on the ground around Beatrice. The Swan Duck stuck out its chest, and reared up, and opened its wings. It hissed, **"TSSSSS!"** And rushed forward. And the other ducks came behind it. All flapping and pecking and quacking like mad. At the rice cakes, and the ground, and Beatrice.

Beatrice put her nose farther in the air and made the whale noises louder than ever.

"DO SOMETHING, SUZANNE!"

Suzanne threw the bag of rice cakes as far as she could. The ducks ran after them, the Swan Duck first, all quacking and flapping and pecking at the snacks and one another. Suzanne grabbed the end of Beatrice's leash, and pulled as hard as she could. I got down on the

ground and wriggled my shoulder right under Beatrice. "Three, two, one . . ." I closed my eyes and pushed forward and up. Beatrice's back end wobbled a bit. "**Nngnngya!**"

Beatrice was on her feet. And we set off up over the fields, so we didn't have to go back past the ducks, and turned right onto the road that leads back into the village, pushing and pulling Beatrice, and stopping and starting, all the way home.

CHAPTER 9

"That Damn Dog!"

Me and Suzanne took Beatrice for another walk the next morning, before school. And when we got back from school, we took her out again. And the next day we did the same, and the day after that. And Suzanne said how when Beatrice was settled in, she would walk faster, and wag her tail, and she wouldn't always only go left at the bottom of the road, and right at the river, and stop outside Sorrel Cottage to make whale noises. Because Suzanne was going to start training Beatrice, and soon she would be fetching sticks, and doing tricks, and charging at the ducks and sending them all scattering, like Barney used to. And we could do races with her up the road, and go out on our bikes, and set up obstacle courses and all that. Instead of levering her up, and pulling and pushing and stopping and starting, and defending her from ducks, and picking up her poos in the garage when we got back.

But when the weekend came, Beatrice was still the same, and then another week went past, and she still wasn't better. And, if anything, she'd got worse. Because she was walking round and round in circles, in the garage, and refusing to eat her food, and making whale noises all night. Until one night Suzanne's Dad pulled his earplugs out and said,

"SOMETHING HAS TO BE DONE ABOUT THAT DAMN DOG!"

So Suzanne's Mom made an appointment for Beatrice at the vet's.

The vet looked with a little flashlight in Beatrice's ears, and her eyes. And she checked all the way down her back, and felt up and down her legs and lifted up each paw. And she listened to Beatrice's heart. And she looked serious and said, "*Hmmm* . . . ," and "Oh *dear,*" and "*That's* not good." And when she was finished, she said, "Beatrice has a few issues, I'm afraid. Starting at the top and working our way down . . ."

She pointed to different bits of Beatrice. "She has a septic wound on the top of her head; numerous small tumors above her eyes; a nasty nasal infection leading to secondary inflammation in the ear, just here, behind this buildup of wax; abscesses on two teeth; serious cavities in three; general buildup of tartar, and, judging by her breath, some kind of serious gastric problem. Moving down, possible arthritis of the spine, and almost certainly in the hips; limber tail syndrome; worms, I suspect; some rather inflamed fleabites . . ."

A pool of pee appeared on the floor, between Beatrice's back legs.

"Oh, and she's incontinent."

This is what it says about "incontinent" in my dictionary:

incontinent (in-kon-tin-unt] ◆ *adjective*
unable to restrain natural discharges or evacuations of urine or feces

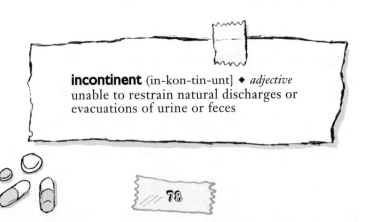

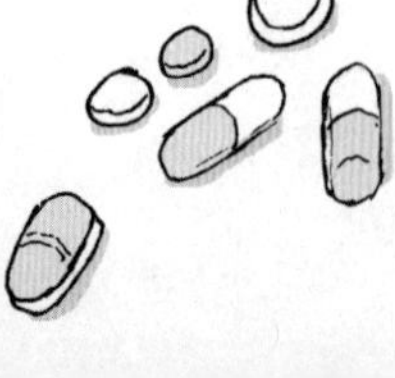

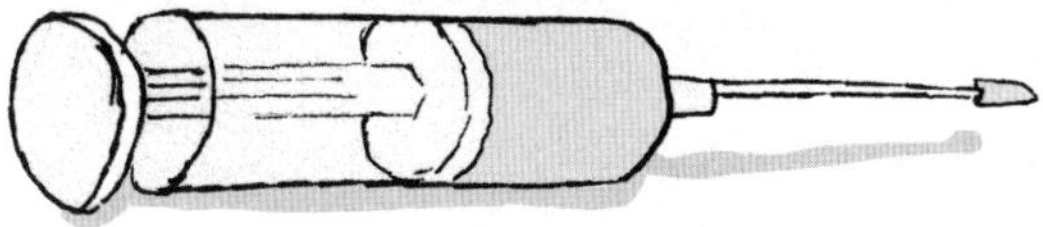

"I can treat some of the more minor issues now, while you wait: lancing the abscesses, putting a couple of stitches in, addressing the earwax buildup, an injection of antibiotics for the nasal infection, and a worming pill. The rest will require further investigation, longer appointments, and, of course, with her age, you'll want to consider the *cost*."

The vet pulled a pair of rubber gloves on. "The pointed scalpel, please, Patricia," she said, and put a white mask over her mouth. "It's probably best if you wait outside."

Me and Suzanne and Suzanne's Mom went back into the waiting room and sat down. We could hear Beatrice making whale noises behind the door.

"Do you think Beatrice is all right?"

"She will be," Suzanne said, "once the vet has finished, won't she, Mom?"

"Beatrice has lots of things wrong with her, Suzanne."

"Yes, but once the vet's fixed them, she'll be fine."

After ages the nurse brought Beatrice out into the waiting room. She had a bandage on her left front leg, a shaved patch on her back, and a white plastic cone around her head. She looked worse than ever.

Suzanne's Mom went to the reception desk.

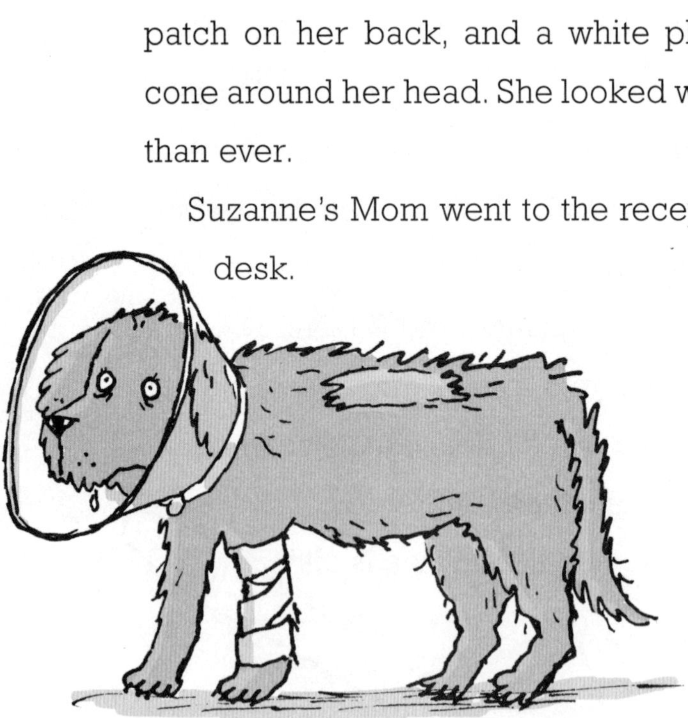

"This is the bill for today's procedures," the nurse said.

Suzanne's Mom looked at it. Her eyebrows went up.

"And these, here, are some of the more complicated treatments that Beatrice needs, along with the estimated costs."

Suzanne's Mom's eyebrows went up even higher. "How long does she have to keep the cone on?"

"At least a week," the nurse said, "to stop her from scratching her stitches."

Suzanne took Beatrice's leash from the nurse.

"Come, Beatrice." She gave the leash a little tug. Then she gave it a bigger tug. Then she put it over her shoulder and pulled as hard as she could. "Uungh . . ." Beatrice stood still.

I got down on the ground, and wriggled my shoulder right under Beatrice, and held my breath.

"Three, two, one . . . *Liftoff.*"

I pushed forward and up as hard as I could. Beatrice's back end wobbled a bit.

"That's it, Anna, *push.*"

"Nngnngya!"

CHAPTER 10
A Dog's Life

This is a list of all the things I do on school days since Suzanne got Beatrice.

6:00: Alarm goes off. Press snooze.

6:05: Alarm goes off. Press snooze.

6:10: Alarm goes off. Mom comes in: "Anna, stop pressing snooze and turn

off that alarm!" Turn off alarm. Get out of bed. Put coat and wellies on over pajamas. Meet Suzanne out front.

6:15: Lever Beatrice up and push her all the way to the river.

7:00: Wait while Beatrice makes whale noises at Great-Aunt Deidra's gate. Defend Beatrice from ducks. Throw rice cakes to keep ducks busy.

7:30: Lever Beatrice up while ducks eat rice cakes and attack one another. Push Beatrice all the way home.

8:15: Pick up Beatrice's poos in Suzanne's garage.

8:30: Wash dead vole smell off in shower. Eat cornflakes.

8:45: Go to school. Try not to fall asleep at desk.

3:30: School bell goes. Walk home.

3:45: Put wellies on over uniform and coat, and meet Suzanne out front.

4:00: Lever Beatrice up. Push her all the way to the river.

4:45: Wait while Beatrice makes whale noises at Great-Aunt Deidra's gate.

5:00: Defend Beatrice from ducks. Throw rice cakes to keep ducks busy.

5:15: Lever Beatrice up while ducks eat rice cakes and attack one another. Push Beatrice all the way back home.

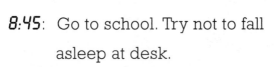

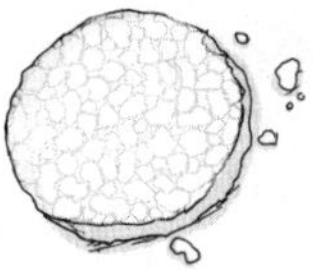

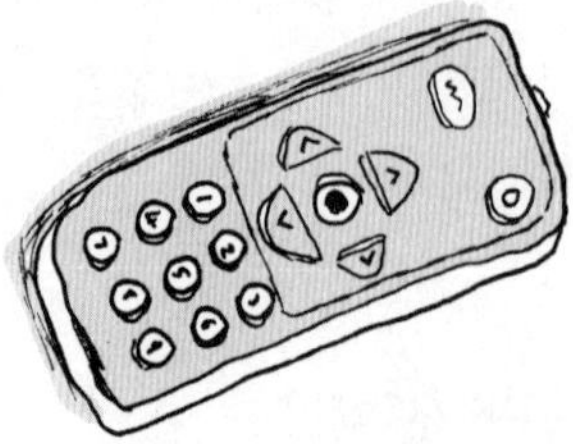

6:00: Pick up poos in Suzanne's garage.

6:15: Go home and wash dead vole smell off in shower.

6:30: Eat dinner. Wash up.

7:00: Do homework.

7:45: Watch TV.

8:00: Go to bed.

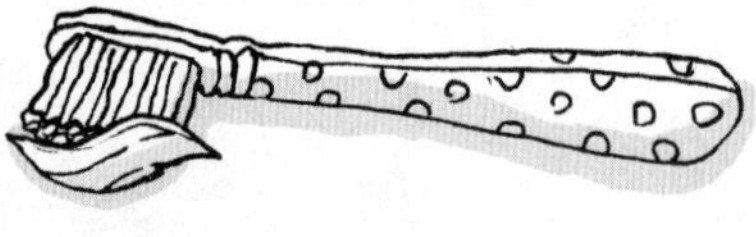

And weekends weren't much better. Because as well as taking Beatrice for two walks a day, there were other jobs to do for her, like sweeping up all her hair in the garage, and mopping the floor with disinfectant because of all the pees and poos during the week, and washing her bedding, and going shopping for dog food. And I was getting sick of doing things for Beatrice, because it had been better before, when me and Suzanne could do other stuff on Saturdays, like throwing the practice rope from Lifesavers to each other in the back lane, and going into the shed, and making up passwords, and plans, and doing spy clubs and all that.

So that Saturday I asked Suzanne, "Do we *have* to take Beatrice for a walk today?"

"Yes."

"Why?"

"Because walks are on the list we made of Reasons to Get Great-Aunt Deidra's Dog."

"What about if we just took her for *one* walk, then?"

"The list says 'two' and it's underlined. And it's on the fridge. Where Dad can see it. And if I miss anything, he can send Beatrice back to Aunt Deidra's Nephew, Mick."

Suzanne clipped Beatrice's leash onto her collar. "Come."

Beatrice didn't come.

"Heel." Beatrice didn't budge.

"You'll have to lever her up, Anna."

"Maybe *you* could be in charge of the back end of Beatrice today, and lever her up, and hold the plastic bags and all that. And pick up the poos in the garage after, and I'll be in charge of the *front* for once?"

But Suzanne said how Beatrice would

get confused, and it might set her back in her training and all that.

So I got down on the ground and wriggled my shoulder right under Beatrice, and tried not to think about where my nose was. Which was hard, with the dead vole smell and all that.

And we walked down to the river, pushing and pulling Beatrice, and stopping and starting. And we waited while Beatrice made whale noises. And we defended her from the ducks. And threw the rice cakes to distract them. And I got underneath Beatrice again, and levered her back up. And we went home over the fields. Pushing and pulling Beatrice, and stopping and starting. And into Suzanne's garage. And Suzanne tipped the old food and

water out, and put new in. And I picked up Beatrice's poos, and put them in plastic bags. And then we swept the floor to get all the hairs up, and mopped it with disinfectant. And Beatrice sat in the back lane, between the bins.

"Can we *please* go in the shed now, and make up a password, and put the lock on, and do some plans and all that?" I asked.

"I need to train Beatrice to fetch a stick first," Suzanne said, and she went out into the back lane.

"Beatrice *can't* fetch," I said.

"She can," Suzanne said. "She just doesn't know what 'fetch' means yet. I have to keep on training her so she doesn't forget the parts of the trick she's already learned."

"She hasn't learned *any* parts of it," I said. Which was true. Because there's only two parts to fetching a stick, the getting it part, and the bringing it back part, and Beatrice had never done either of them.

Suzanne looked the other way, like she always does when she doesn't like what you say, and she threw the stick anyway. "Fetch."

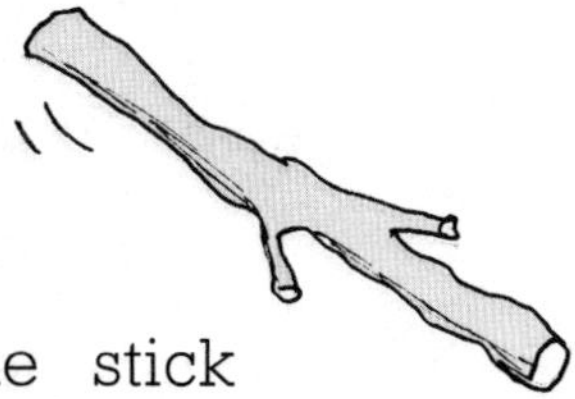

Beatrice stayed where she was.

"Fetch." Suzanne pointed to the stick. "Fetch the stick, Beatrice."

Beatrice yawned.

"Maybe if *you* went and got the stick, Anna, and brought it back, that

I would show Beatrice what fetching *is*."

So I ran down the lane and got the stick and brought it back to Suzanne.

"Beatrice is definitely watching you," Suzanne said. She threw the stick again. "Fetch!" And again. "Try running a bit faster, Anna."

And after about a million times of Suzanne telling me to "fetch," I stopped and said, "No." Because for one thing it's not much fun fetching a stick, and that's probably why Beatrice didn't want to do it. And for another thing Beatrice wasn't watching, because her eyes were closed and she had fallen asleep.

"Let's go in the shed."

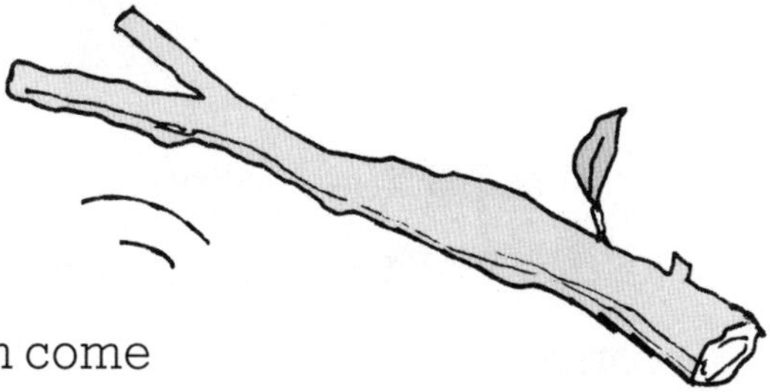

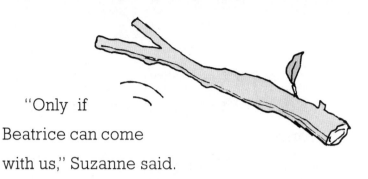

"Only if Beatrice can come with us," Suzanne said.

"Beatrice is too big to fit."

"We could take out the deck chairs and the bikes and deflate the dinghy."

"It's only supposed to be me and you allowed in the shed."

"Tom sometimes comes in."

"That's different."

"How?"

"Because Tom's smaller than Beatrice," I said, "and he doesn't pee on the floor."

"Yes, he does."

"Only once," I said. And it didn't count because it was hide-and-seek, and he had been there for ages, and he didn't want to come out, in case Suzanne saw him.

"Well, it does count, actually," Suzanne said, "because it still smells in that corner."

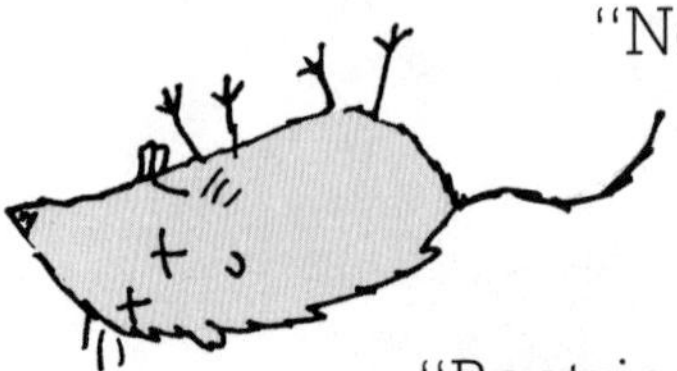

"No, it doesn't."

"It does. It *stinks*."

"Not as much as Beatrice."

"Beatrice doesn't stink."

"She does," I said, "because her front end stinks like Mrs. Constantine's pond, the time it went slimy and the fish floated to the top, and her back end stinks like Graham Roberts's dead vole. And she probably stinks in the *middle* as well."

And Suzanne went quiet and didn't say anything. And then she said that Beatrice didn't *want* to go in the shed and do Shed Club anyway, and neither did *she*. And she was going to set up her *own* club, in the garage, called Garage Club, which only her and Beatrice were allowed in.

And I said, "Good." And I went to the shed by myself and I put the lock on the door and made up a password, which was "I Hate Beatrice."

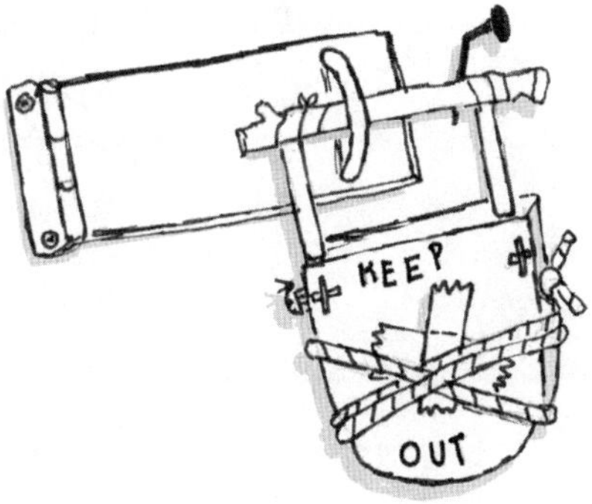

CHAPTER 11

Spy Club

After Suzanne left Shed Club and started up Garage Club with Beatrice, I got all of Suzanne's things off the shelf, like the piccalilli jar with her adenoids in, and her Dad's French–English, English–French dictionary, and I put them outside in the lane. And then I took her name off the KEEP OUT! BY ORDER OF ANNA & SUZANNE sign on the shed door. So it just said, KEEP OUT! BY

ORDER OF ANNA.
And off ANNA'S AND SUZANNE'S CLUB RULES AND REGULATIONS.
And off the Spy Club Notebook.

And I opened the notebook up and I flicked past the pages for all the people that me and Suzanne had spied on, like Miss Matheson and Suzanne's Dad and Joe-down-the-street's Mom's Old Boyfriend. And I got the binoculars Mrs. Rotherham gave us down off the shelf, and looked through the spy hole.

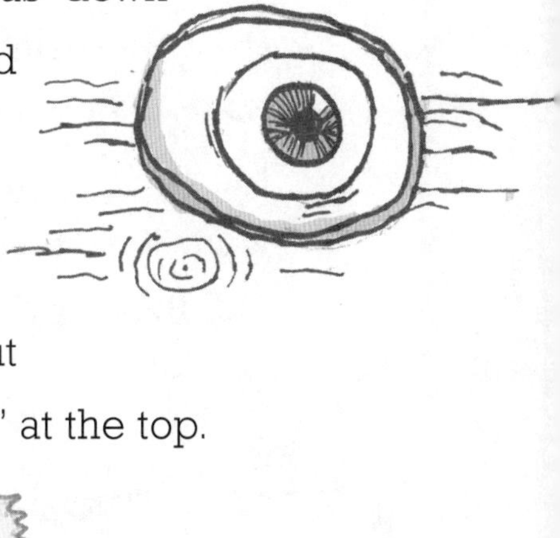

And I started a new page in the Spy Club Notebook. And I put "Suzanne and Beatrice" at the top.

10:45 a.m. - Suzanne tells Beatrice to "fetch" the stick.
Beatrice sits by bins.

10:51 a.m. - Suzanne goes inside, gets rice cake, puts it next to the stick, tells Beatrice to "fetch." Beatrice sits by bins.

11:03 a.m. - Suzanne goes back inside, gets piece of raw meat, puts the meat next to the stick, and tells Beatrice to "fetch." Beatrice sits by bins.

11:27 a.m. - Suzanne breaks the meat up into little pieces to make a trail, going all the way from Beatrice to the stick, and tells Beatrice to "fetch." Beatrice sits by bins. Suzanne breaks the stick, then shouts, "OH, WHY WON'T YOU JUST FETCH THE STICK LIKE BARNEY USED TO, BEATRICE?"

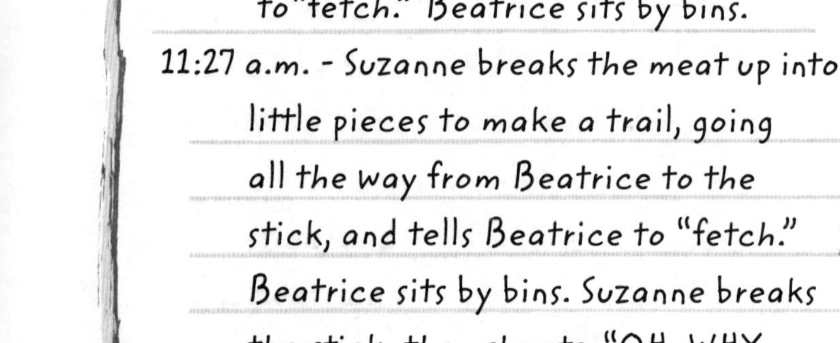

11:28 a.m. - Suzanne's Dad comes out, sees the trail of meat and goes mad, "THAT'S A TEN POUND PIECE OF PRIME FILLET, FOR CRYING OUT LOUD!" Suzanne's Dad goes back inside. Suzanne sits by Beatrice, by the bins.

After a while I got sick of Spy Club, because it's better when there's two of you doing it, like when it's me and Suzanne, and we take turns looking through the binoculars. And one of us says what's happening, and the other one checks the times and writes it all down. So I went to find Tom.

Tom was out front with Mr. Tucker. "Aha, Popsie, come to help me and

Basher check the old weather-measuring apparatus, eh?"

"No," I said. Because I hadn't. "I've come to ask Tom something."

"Fire away."

"It's *secret*."

Mr. Tucker covered his ears.

"Do you want to come and do Spy Club?" I whispered. And I put my hand in front of my mouth because Mr. Tucker didn't look like he was covering his ears properly, and he was in The War and all that, and he probably knows how to lip-read.

"Who are you spying on?" Tom asked.

"Suzanne," I said, "and Beatrice."

"No thanks," Tom said. "Beatrice is too big. Me and Mr. Tucker are spotting clouds."

"What do you say, Popsie? We could

do with another pair of eyes. See that one, shaped like a dog? That's a cirrus. Perfectly harmless more often than not but *could* indicate an approaching storm. . . ."

"No thanks," I said. Because I didn't want to spot clouds.

I went inside to see Mom. Mom was getting dirty washing out of the basket. "There's no one to do clubs with."

"Where's Suzanne?"

"We're not friends. She's in her own club, with Beatrice."

"You can be in my club if you like."

"What's it called?"

"Washing Club. We sort the washing into three piles. Whites, darks, and lights, and take the *biggest* pile to the *machine* and . . ."

I turned round. "No. I don't want to be in Washing Club."

Because it didn't sound very good.

Mom called after me, "Neither do *I*."

And I went up the road to see Mrs. Rotherham instead.

Mrs. Rotherham put the kettle on and made some tea and brought out the cookies. I told her how Suzanne had left Shed Club. And started up Garage Club, with Beatrice. And how we weren't friends anymore. Because all Suzanne wanted to do was train Beatrice to fetch a stick, and take her for walks, instead of going in the shed and doing plans and clubs and all that. And how I always had to be in charge of the back end of Beatrice, and lever her up and pick up the poos. And how Beatrice was the worst dog anyone ever had, because she never wagged her tail, or jumped up, or ran, and she hardly ate any food, and she peed everywhere all the time, even in her own bed, and pooed in the garage, and walked round in circles and made whale noises all night.

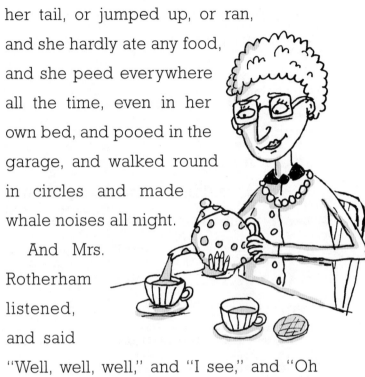

And Mrs. Rotherham listened, and said "Well, well, well," and "I see," and "Oh dear, oh dear, oh dear."

And she told me about how when she was in the police they had a police dog, called Colin, who had a handler called Stan. And Colin and Stan did everything together. And when Stan retired, Colin sat in Stan's parking space, for a week, and whined. And the vet said Colin was depressed, which meant he was sad all the time. "It sounds to me like Beatrice might be depressed as well," Mrs. Rotherham said.

And I said how Beatrice probably *was*. Because I would be sad all the time if *I* was Beatrice. Especially if I had to be in Garage Club with Suzanne and she kept trying to make me get a stick.

When I got back to the shed, I found "depression" in my dictionary. This is what it said:

depression [di-presh-un] ♦ *noun*
a condition of general emotional dejection and withdrawal; sadness greater and more prolonged than that warranted by any objective reason

And then I went on the computer and I put "depressed dog" in. And I found a page all about what makes dogs depressed. And it said the top three things were:

1. A change in environment, such as moving house.
2. A bereavement: the loss of a good doggie or human friend.
3. Physical problems: aches, pains, or illness.

And *Beatrice* had moved house, *and* she had lost Aunt Deidra, and she *definitely* had aches and pains and illnesses, because she still hadn't been back to the vet.

And there was an "Is Your Dog

Depressed?" questionnaire, to find out whether or not your dog has got it. And "Advice on Helping a Depressed Dog" as well. So I went and got the printer cable from on top of the kitchen cupboard, which is where Mom hides it to stop me printing things that she says I don't need, like 243 pages for Tom about Batman and Bob the Builder. And I printed all the pages about dogs and being depressed.

And then I went out to the shed, and I got all Suzanne's things, which I'd put outside, in the lane, like her piccalilli jar and her French–English, English–French dictionary, and I put them back in the shed, on the shelf. And I wrote Suzanne's name back on the KEEP OUT! BY ORDER OF ANNA sign on the shed door, so it said ANNA & SUZANNE again. And on the Club Rules and Regulations. And in the Spy Club Notebook. And I got a piece of paper, and a pen, and I put:

You are hereby invited to join
Shed Club
VID
(which means "Very Important Dog")
Lifelong Membership
You are bound by the rules and regulations
of Shed Club, available on request.

And I put the invitation in an envelope. And wrote "Beatrice" on the front of it. And went round to Suzanne's. And I rang the bell three times, because me and Suzanne always do things in threes if it's something important, and I posted the invitation through the Barrys' letter box. And then I ran away because it was Saturday and Suzanne's Dad was home, and he was already annoyed about his piece of prime fillet.

I went back to the shed, and waited.

And after ages I saw Suzanne, through the spy hole, coming up the back lane, moving Beatrice's feet forward, one at a time.

So I went and pushed the back end of Beatrice. And Suzanne pulled the front. And we didn't say anything. And we took the bikes out of the shed, and the deck chairs, and the dinghy, to make more room inside. And we both got underneath Beatrice, to lever her up into the shed.

"There," Suzanne said. "She does fit."

"Yes. And she doesn't stink." Which wasn't exactly true, especially once the door was closed. Because it's very small inside the shed. And it was quite hard to breathe.

Suzanne got two dust masks down off one of the shelves in the shed, which Dad uses when he's painting.

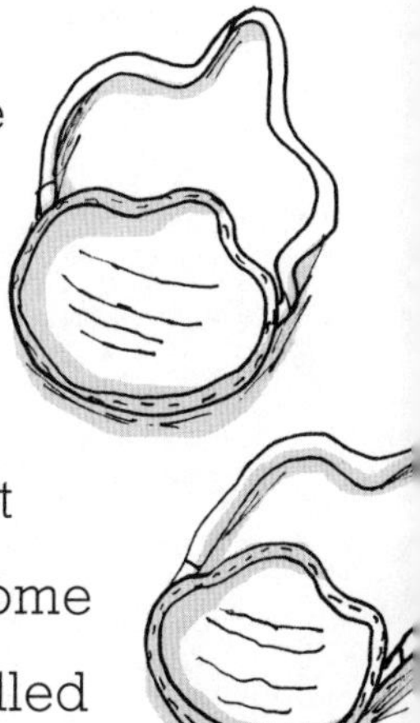

"Gas masks," she said. And we put them on. And closed the door again. And it still smelled pretty bad, because even though the masks can stop dust, they couldn't block out Beatrice. Suzanne got some Blu Tack down off the shelf. She pulled

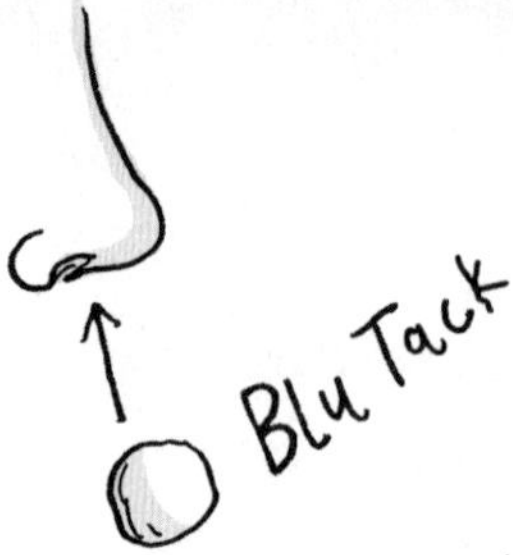

two bits off and rolled them into balls, and put one in each nostril. And I did the same. And we put the gas masks back on again. Which was much better. And I told Suzanne all about what Mrs. Rotherham said about Colin the police dog, and Stan, and how Colin got depressed when Stan left. And I had to say it quite loud and clear because the Blu Tack made me sound stuffed up, and the dust mask muffled my mouth, and because Beatrice had started snoring.

I showed Suzanne the "Is Your Dog Depressed?" questionnaire. And Suzanne said I should read out the questions. And she would answer them. So that's what we did.

"Does your dog look sad and mopey?"

"Yes."

"Does your dog sleep most of the time?"

"Yes."

"Does your dog have no interest in toys or games?"

"Yes."

"Does your dog have a poor appetite?"

"Yes."

"Does your dog prefer to be alone?"

"Yes."

"If you have ticked 'yes' for three or more of the above questions, your dog is depressed."

Suzanne counted the ticks. "Five. That's all of them." And we read the page called "Advice on Helping a Depressed Dog," and Suzanne said we should make a list of all the things it said we could do to help Beatrice get better. So we did.

ANNA'S AND SUZANNE'S LIST OF THINGS TO DO TO HELP STOP BEATRICE FROM BEING DEPRESSED

1. Increase your dog's self-esteem by frequent shows of affection (both verbal and physical). Encourage friends and family to do the same.
2. Make arrangements so that your dog is not left alone.
3. Take your dog to places that will lift its spirits.
4. Get another dog to keep your depressed dog company.
5. Have your dog assessed by a vet and carry out any recommended treatments.

CHAPTER 12

Making Beatrice Better

The first thing on the list was to give Beatrice verbal and physical affection. This is what it says about "verbal" in my dictionary:

verbal [vur-bul] ♦ *adjective*
consisting of or expressed in words
(as opposed to actions): e.g., a verbal protest

And this is what it says "physical" is:

physical (fizz-i-cul) ♦ *adjective*
Pertaining to or connected with the body

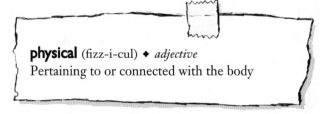

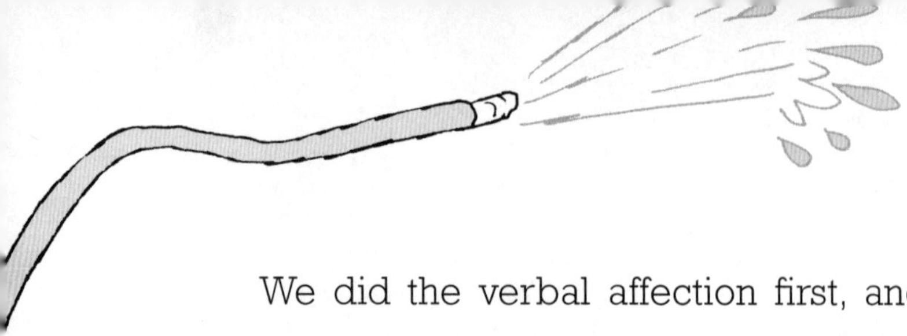

We did the verbal affection first, and told Beatrice what a good dog she was, and said how nice it was to see her, and told her how lovely she looked (which wasn't exactly true, because she still had the cone on, and the bald patch, and the bandage and all that). And then it was time for the physical affection. It wasn't easy to give Beatrice physical affection, because of the vole smell at the back and the fishpond smell at the front. So we decided before we gave Beatrice physical affection, we'd better give her a bath. So Suzanne went into her house, and I went into mine. And Suzanne brought out Carl's baby bath, and some shampoo and conditioner and her Mom's hairdressing kit. And I got a towel and Dad's washcloth, and a pair of rubber gloves and Mom's perfume.

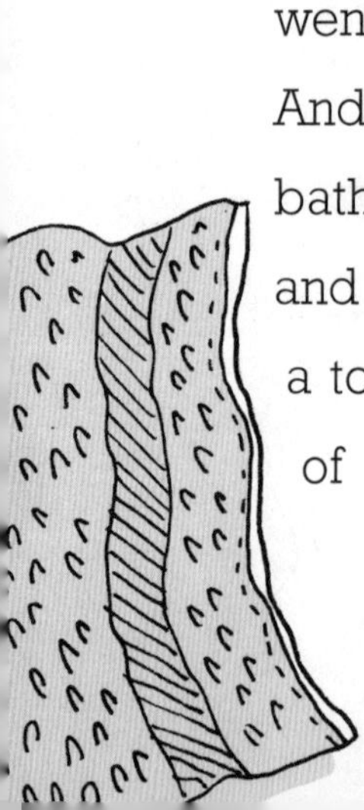

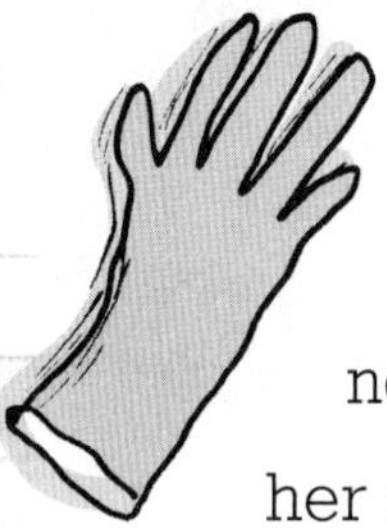

And we took the cone off Beatrice's neck carefully, and the bandage from her front leg. And we attached the hose to the tap in Suzanne's kitchen, and made sure the water came through nice and warm, and not too fast, and we filled up Carl's bath, and lifted up Beatrice's front paws, one at a time, and put them in. And as soon as she felt her paws in the water, Beatrice's tail came out from between her legs, and she stopped staring at the floor and looked up. And she moved her front paws up and down in the baby bath, and put her whole head in the water and moved it from side to side.

"She *loves* it," Suzanne said.

Me and Suzanne picked the baby bath up and tipped it over Beatrice. And Beatrice wagged her tail like mad, and then she lay down in

the water, in the lane, and rolled over and over. And I ran in and turned the hose on again, and Suzanne held it over Beatrice. And we shampooed her head, and all down her back, and each side. And I did her face with Dad's washcloth, and got the sleep out of her eyes. And I put the gloves on to do the matted bits round her bum. And we went down each leg to her paws and right to the tip of her tail. And then we rinsed it off, and shampooed her again, because it said on the bottle, "Repeat if necessary." And it was necessary with Beatrice. Because the water that was running off into the gutter was black. And then we put conditioner on, and combed it through, and massaged the ends. And let it soak in for deep conditioning, like it said. And Beatrice stood very still, and half closed

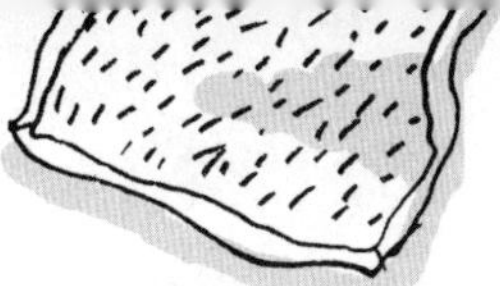

her eyes, and put her nose up in the air. And Suzanne said how when they had Barney, he hated being bathed. And he would never just stand still and let you do it, like Beatrice, and they had to hold him down.

And then we rinsed the conditioner off, and dried Beatrice with the towel. And she shook herself. And we got Suzanne's Mom's hair dryer, and plugged it in, in the garage, and put the diffuser attachment on, for curly hair, and dried her with that. And Suzanne trimmed Beatrice's bangs with her Mom's hairdressing scissors. And I did two squirts of Mom's perfume on Beatrice's bum.

And then me and Suzanne stood back, to have a proper look at Beatrice. And she looked a lot better. And she smelled a lot better too, especially at the back, because

we did a sniff test. And we couldn't smell dead vole. But she still smelled like Mrs. Constantine's green pond when the fish died at the front.

"We'd better brush Beatrice's teeth," Suzanne said.

Suzanne ran into her house and got some toothpaste, and I ran into mine and got the old toothbrush Mom keeps under the sink for cleaning between the tiles. And we put the Blu Tack back in our noses and put the dust masks on, and I put the rubber gloves on and held Beatrice's mouth open, which Beatrice didn't mind. And Suzanne brushed Beatrice's teeth. And it took quite a long time and a *lot* of toothpaste, because Beatrice had lots of teeth and they were very big and very dirty.

And Suzanne did the sniff test again.

She shook her head. "We need something stronger."

So I went into my house and I got mouthwash. And Suzanne went into her house and got her Dad's electric toothbrush. And she switched it to high and brushed Beatrice's teeth again. And then we flossed in between them. And put some of the mouthwash in Beatrice's water bowl for her to rinse. And we both did the sniff test again, together, and we could still smell Mrs. Constantine's pond a bit, so Suzanne went inside and got a pack of extra-strong mints. And she put one into Beatrice's mouth. And she put her arms around Beatrice's neck, and rested her cheek against Beatrice's, and gave her a squeeze. And Beatrice closed her eyes, and moved her

head up and down against Suzanne, like she does with Great-Aunt Deidra's gate. And I stroked Beatrice's back, and her chest, and her fur felt all warm and soft, and I rubbed behind her ears. And then we went to take Beatrice to see some family and friends, to get affection from them, because that's what it said on the list.

"What's that dog doing in here?" Mom said.

"Beatrice is depressed," I said. "You have to say something nice."

"You smell better, Beatrice. Is that my *perfume*, Anna?"

"No. And now you have to stroke her."

Mom patted Beatrice on the head and stroked her behind the ears. "Poor old Beatrice. There. Now get her out please, Anna, before she pees all over the...oh, no, *Beatrice*..."

Tom came into the kitchen. "What's that?"

"Pee," Mom said. She got some paper towels and started cleaning it up.

"Beatrice is sad," I said.

"Does she need a cookie?"

"No," Mom said, "she doesn't need a cookie. Don't stand *there*, Tom, you'll get your feet in it. What she *needs* is a diaper."

"That's it!" Suzanne ran home.

"You're only supposed to say nice things to Beatrice," I said. "Now you've upset Suzanne."

But Suzanne wasn't upset. Because she came straight back. With a packet of baby Carl's diapers. She pulled one out. "Locks in leaks for up to twelve hours of protection."

"It's a bit small," I said. "How are we going to attach it?"

"We could put it inside some big underpants, and put the underpants on Beatrice?"

"No one wears underpants big enough to fit Beatrice," Mom said.

"What about bears?" Tom said.

"Or Mrs. Rotherham?" I said. Because her underpants are enormous. Even bigger than Nana's underpants used to be. I've seen them hanging on the line.

"You are *not* to go and ask Mrs. Rotherham for underpants," Mom said.

"Come on, Beatrice." Suzanne pulled the leash. Beatrice didn't budge. I got down underneath her and levered her up.

"Anna, did you hear me?"

But we were already outside.

Suzanne explained to Mrs. Rotherham about how Beatrice was depressed. And

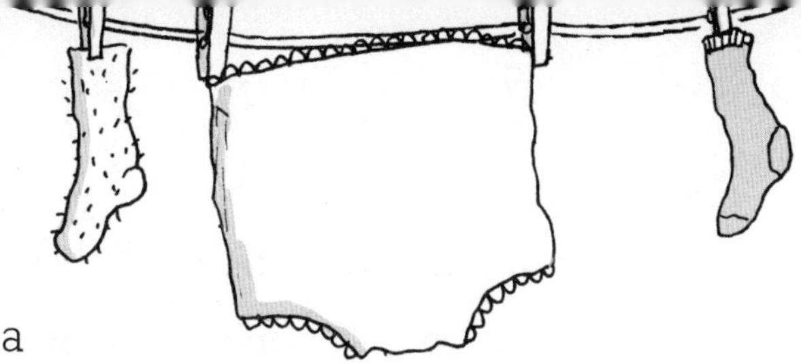

how we had made a list of things to do to help her get better. And how it was hard to get people to give her affection when she was peeing all over their kitchen floor.

And Mrs. Rotherham said, "I quite understand," and she put some newspaper down, and she asked us in.

And Suzanne showed Mrs. Rotherham Carl's diaper and said how we didn't know how to attach it.

"If only we had some really big underpants . . . ," I said.

Mrs. Rotherham looked at Beatrice. And she looked at me and Suzanne. And she winked. And she went into her cupboard, and she brought out a packet with some underpants in it, and she passed it to Suzanne.

Suzanne read the back: "High-waisted, low-legged hosiery with controlling compression zones for security and confidence. Large." Suzanne took a pair out of the pack and held them up against Beatrice. "They're too small."

Mrs. Rotherham got out some scissors, and she cut right down each leg of both of the pairs of underpants, and went over to her sewing machine, and sewed the two pairs together to make an even bigger pair, and she cut out a hole for Beatrice's tail.

Suzanne lifted up Beatrice's back paws, and put them into the legs of the pants, and we started pulling them up. Which was quite hard because of the "controlling compression zones."

Mrs. Rotherham started getting The Hysterics when she saw Beatrice in the underpants. And me and Suzanne got The Hysterics as well. But not as much as Mrs. Rotherham. Because she had to lean against the wall and get her breath back. And then Suzanne said we should stop laughing because it wasn't very nice for Beatrice.

And Mrs. Rotherham said, "Quite right."

Suzanne pulled Beatrice's tail through the hole and put the diaper in, underneath.

And then Mrs. Rotherham got us some ice cream because, like Nana used to say, ice cream is good when you need to calm down. And she got a bowl of water for Beatrice. And Beatrice lay down, and fell asleep on the black sheepskin rug in front of Mrs. Rotherham's fire. And Mrs. Rotherham sat in her chair,

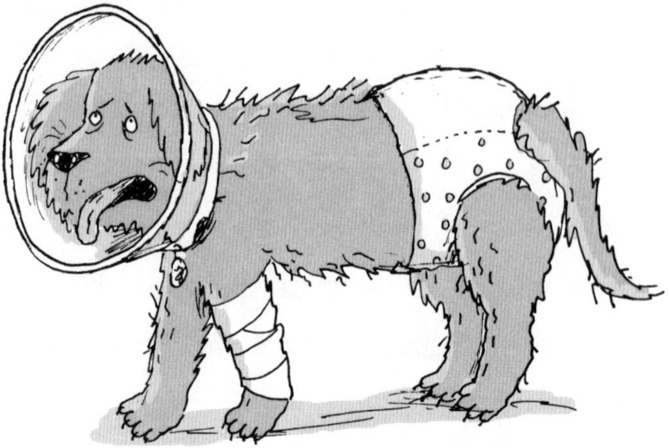

next to Beatrice, and stroked Beatrice's ears, while me and Suzanne ate our ice cream. And you could hardly tell Beatrice was there, apart from the cone and the bandage, and the underpants, because she blended right into the rug.

Me and Suzanne showed Mrs. Rotherham the list of things we were going to do to make Beatrice better. And Mrs. Rotherham said she could help us with Number 2, because we could take Beatrice round to her house in the mornings, if we liked, before school, so Beatrice wouldn't have to stay in the garage on her own all day.

And we said thank you to Mrs. Rotherham, and we took Beatrice to get affection from other friends and family, like Mr. Tucker, and Joe-down-the-street, and Joe-down-the-street's Mom, like it said on the list. And they were all pleased to see Beatrice, and her underpants. And Suzanne said she thought the underpants *had* given Beatrice security and confidence, like it said on the pack. Because her head wasn't down, looking at the ground anymore. And we went back to the shed and ticked off Number 1 on the list, and Number 2 as well, which was "Make arrangements so that your dog is not left alone."

Number 3 was to take Beatrice places to lift her spirits. And the next day was

Sunday, so Suzanne said that in the morning, after we had taken Beatrice for her walk, we should take her to church, because that's where they talk about lifting spirits and all that.

CHAPTER 13
The Ark

When she saw Beatrice, Mrs. Constantine said, "No, definitely not, no pets, I'm afraid." Mrs. Constantine is the Vicar's wife. She is in charge of Sunday School.

"If I allow one, I'll have to allow everyone. Next thing, Graham Roberts will have his ferret in the font again."

Suzanne told Mrs. Constantine about Beatrice being depressed, and how she wasn't supposed to be left on her own, and how we had brought her to church to have her Spirit Uplifted. And she showed her the list of things to help Beatrice get better.

"I see. Why is she wearing underpants?"

"To keep her diaper in place."

"Mmm."

Mrs. Constantine didn't look very pleased. "You can bring her in just this once. Keep her away from the model ark, please. The Vicar wants it on the trestle table in the north transept before Communion starts."

We had been working on the ark at Sunday School for three weeks. It was papier-mâché and painted in all bright colors with a ramp for the animals to walk up, and there was a piece of blue satin to put underneath it for the flood waters. And we had each made a pair of animals, out of colored paper, and pasta shapes, and

bits from the fabric box and all that, to put in it. Apart from Emma Hendry, because she had made Noah and his wife. And Graham Roberts, because he had made cages. Mrs. Constantine didn't want cages in the ark, because she said she didn't think cages would be very pretty.

But Graham made them anyway because, he said, "it

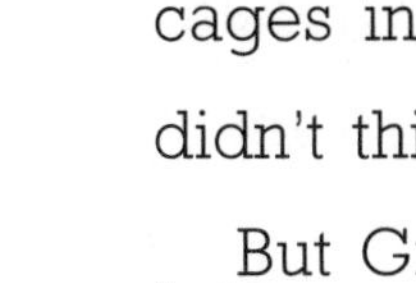

won't be pretty if we *don't* have cages. It'll be a *bloodbath*."

Anyway, Emma Hendry put Noah and his wife in, and Joe-down-the-street put his rabbits in, and Tom put in his slugs (which were meant to be cats at first, but Tom made them out of a toilet paper roll and tissue paper, and he poured the glue on, instead of using the spatula, and they collapsed). And then Shelly Wainwright put her sheep in, and Suzanne went to put her dogs down next to Shelly's sheep.

"Are those sheepdogs?" Graham Roberts asked.

"No, they're terriers."

"You can't put terriers there," Graham said. "They'll worry the sheep. They'll have to have a cage."

Suzanne stuck the dogs down. "Yes,

you can. My dog Barney's a terrier and when he stopped living with us, my Dad took him to *live* on a farm. He roams free, in the fields, and he's better off."

"If a farmer sees a dog in with his sheep, he's allowed to shoot it." Graham lives on a farm. With his Gran.

"Farmers aren't allowed to shoot dogs."

"Yes, they are. My Granddad told me." Graham's Granddad was a farmer. Before he died. "He once had to shoot a dog himself."

"That's a lie," Suzanne said. And Graham got cross and said it wasn't a lie because his Granddad didn't tell lies. It was Suzanne's Dad who was a liar. Because he probably said her dog was roaming free on a farm so he didn't have to tell her it was dead.

"Barney isn't dead!" Suzanne *pushed* Graham Roberts. And Graham Roberts fell over.

And then he got up, and he pushed Suzanne back. "Yes, he is. And your Dad probably had him put down." And Suzanne fell onto Beatrice. And Beatrice fell onto the ark.

And Emma Hendry shouted, "Bad dog!" And Beatrice started making her whale noises. And Shelly Wainwright started shouting about her sheep. Me and Suzanne levered Beatrice up. The ark was squashed flat. And so were all the animals. And it was wet as well. Because Beatrice's diaper had leaked.

"This is *exactly* why I said No Pets in the *first* place!" Mrs. Constantine told us to take Beatrice home.

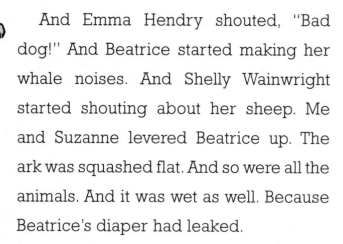

Me and Tom and Suzanne and Beatrice went outside. The sky had gone dark, like at night.

"It's the dog cloud," Tom said. "Look." He pointed at the storm cloud he and Mr. Tucker had spotted before. We passed the side door of the church, which was open, and we could hear the Vicar inside: "And God looked upon the earth, and God said unto Noah, the earth is filled with *violence*, and behold I do bring a *flood of waters*. . . ."

CHAPTER 14
Misty

When we got to our road, Mr. Tucker was in his front garden, tying up Mrs. Tucker's plants. Tom showed him his slugs, and told him all about the ark and how it got squashed. And how he was going to have to get his *own* ark now, to put his slugs in, for when the flood started, and he was going to use the dinghy from the shed.

"Good plan, Basher. Look at those cirrus clouds there. And a sudden fall on the barometer too this morning. Doesn't bode well for Mrs. Tucker's honeysuckle. Hope there's space in the ark for an Old Lag like myself." And Tom said that there was. And Tom and Mr. Tucker looked at the barometer, and the weathercock, and got the logbook out and all that.

And me and Suzanne took Beatrice to the shed. And put the lock on. And made up a password. And I asked Suzanne if she thought Graham Roberts was right about Barney being dead.

"Because," I said, "even though Graham doesn't know about lots of things, like talking in French, and doing investigations, and Lifesavers, like we do, he might know more about sheep, and dogs, and farms and all that. Because of living on one."

Suzanne didn't answer. She got out the list of things to do to help Beatrice.

"We've done Number One, and Number Two, and Number Three. The next thing is Number Four: 'Get another dog to keep your dog company.'"

So that's what we decided to do. Suzanne's Mom didn't look very pleased when Suzanne asked her if she could get another dog.

"Is this a *joke*?"

"No," Suzanne said. Because it was serious.

Suzanne's Mom pointed to the list of reasons on the fridge for why it was a good idea for the Barrys to get Suzanne's Mom's Aunt's dog. And the part where Suzanne had put that if they got the dog, she would never ask for anything else, and especially not another dog. And if she did, they could give Beatrice back to Aunt Deidra's Nephew, Mick.

So me and Suzanne went to my house, to ask Mom if *we* could get a dog instead.

Mom wasn't pleased to see Beatrice, especially not in Mrs. Rotherham's underpants. Because she said it wasn't polite to go asking old ladies for their underwear to put on your pets. And she had already told us we weren't allowed.

"We didn't ask," I said, which was true. "Mrs. Rotherham offered." Mom still didn't look very pleased. So I waited for a bit. And then I said, *"Mom?"*

"Yes?"

"Can we get a dog, please, to keep Beatrice company, and be her friend, and stop her from being depressed?"

"Ha!" Mom said. "If there is one thing that Beatrice has made clear, it is that we are never, *ever*, getting a dog."

So me and Suzanne went back to the

shed to try to think of where we could find a dog for Beatrice to be friends with.

"What about Misty?" Suzanne said.

"I don't think Misty makes friends," I said. Because she just runs backward and forward behind Miss Matheson's fence all day, baring her teeth and yapping and snapping and attacking anyone who comes close.

"Some dogs get aggressive when they're guarding their homes," Suzanne said. Which is probably true. And some *people* do too, because whenever Miss Matheson sees us trying to get over her gate, she bangs on the window and shouts, **"PRIVATE PROPERTY, PRIVATE PROPERTY!"**

"Maybe if Beatrice just bumped into Misty, in the road, she might be more friendly."

So we decided that Beatrice and Misty should meet without me and Suzanne. Because Miss Matheson might not want Misty to be Beatrice's friend if we were there with her.

So we made a plan to sit in the shed and look through the spy hole and wait for Miss Matheson and Misty to come back from their morning walk.

We took the lock off the door, and got Beatrice in position in front of it. And I stood behind Beatrice, ready to push. And Suzanne looked through the spy hole. And we waited. And waited. And it started to rain. And then Suzanne said, "They're coming. Quick, Anna!"

Miss Matheson had picked Misty up, and started to hurry. I gave Beatrice a push. And then I pushed her a bit harder. And then I got down, and wriggled my shoulder underneath Beatrice's bum, and pushed forward and up as hard as I could.

Beatrice snored.

"Now, before it's too late."

My arms shook. **"Nngnngya!"**

Beatrice's back end wobbled a bit. Then she went forward, and the shed door swung open, and she fell into the lane. Right at Miss Matheson's feet. Miss Matheson screamed, and threw her hands up in the air, and Misty went up in the air too. And Beatrice shook herself, and yawned, and then Misty came down. And Beatrice caught her, in her mouth. And then she spat Misty out. On the ground. Beatrice nudged her with her nose, but Misty didn't move.

And Miss Matheson picked Misty up and hurried into her house, calling,

"HELP, HELP, POLICE!"

And me and Suzanne got Beatrice back into the shed. And we put the lock on the door. And sat very still. And listened to the rain on the roof.

CHAPTER 15

The Farm

There was a knock on the shed door. Suzanne looked through the spy hole.

"It's your Mom, Anna. And your Dad. And *my* Mom and Dad. And a *Policeman*."

"What's the password?" I asked.

"Open the door, Anna, please. There's a Policeman to see you."

"That's not the password," I said.

"Where's his badge?" asked Suzanne. The Policeman held a police badge up to the spy hole. Suzanne looked at it. And she opened the door a crack.

The Policeman was standing in front of it. "I understand there's been an incident, involving a Newfoundland and your neighbor's Chihuahua."

He looked round the door, into the shed, at Beatrice. "I take it this is the animal in question?"

Suzanne nodded. "Yes."

And the Policeman said we needed to tell him exactly what happened.

"You'd better come in," Suzanne said. And he did. And we told him all about how Beatrice was depressed, and showed him the list of things we were doing to help her, and how we were up to Number 4, which was to find her a dog companion. And the Policeman nodded, and wrote in his notebook.

And after a bit he said, "I'm going to just step outside, if you don't mind. It's a bit tight in here." Which was true, because he was squashed in the corner, behind the door, because Beatrice took up most of the room. "And a bit ripe, too." Which was true as well. Because Beatrice's bath was wearing off, and her diaper was full, and we'd run out of extra-strong mints.

So we all went into Suzanne's house. Apart from Beatrice. Because Suzanne's Dad put her in the garage. And the Policeman asked me and Suzanne lots of questions. About Beatrice. And Misty. And Miss Matheson. And what had happened. And we answered them. And told him all about our plan for Beatrice to meet Misty. And how I pushed her out into the lane. And how she landed in front of Miss Matheson. And how Miss Matheson jumped, and threw her hands, and Misty, up in the air. And how Misty came back down and Beatrice caught Misty in her mouth.

"Is Misty going to be all right?" Suzanne asked.

"Time will tell. Punctured lung." He closed his notebook. And then he talked to Suzanne's Mom and Dad for a bit about Miss Matheson, and how she had reported Beatrice and wanted to press charges against Suzanne's Mom and Dad. "There are a range of possible charges. From failure to control your dog in a public place, to setting or urging a dog to attack. And a range of penalties to accompany them. Worst-case scenario, if it goes to court, is a fine of five thousand

pounds." And he said how Miss Matheson thought Beatrice was a dangerous dog and needed to be put down.

"You're not going to have Beatrice *put down*, are you?" Suzanne asked.

Suzanne's Mom and Dad looked at each other. "No."

Then Suzanne's Dad said, "But it might be better if Beatrice went to live on the farm where Barney is, where she can run in the fields."

And Suzanne's Mom said, "She'll be better off."

CHAPTER 16
What Happened to Barney?

Me and Mom and Dad went home to have lunch.

"Mom?"

"Yes?"

"Where's Barney?"

"Urm, I think he went to live on a farm, isn't that what Suzanne's Dad said?"

"Where is it?"

"I'm not sure."

"What's it called?"

"I can't remember."

"I want to go and see him."

"Oh, I don't think so, Anna. It's too far away."

"Me and Suzanne could go on our bikes."

"It's too far for that. You'd have to go in a car."

"We could go on the bus."

"Buses don't go out that way."

"I thought you didn't know where it was?"

"I don't. Eat your broccoli."

I ate my broccoli. And went upstairs. And knocked three times on the wall. Suzanne knocked back. I opened the window. And stuck my head out. It was still raining. *"Bonjour."*

"Bonjour."

"It's wet."

"Anna, do you think Barney is dead?"

And I was going to say *"Non"* (which is French for "no"), because I knew Suzanne didn't want Barney to be dead, and because when Graham Roberts said he was, Suzanne pushed him. I waited a bit. And picked some of the paint off the window ledge. And then I said, "Yes. I think Barney's dead." Because I did. Suzanne didn't say anything. Because she cried instead. And we stayed with our heads hanging out the windows. And the rain soaked our hair and ran down our necks.

And then after ages Suzanne said, "Meet me at ze shed."

We put the lock on the door and made up a new password, which was *mort*, because Suzanne said that's French for "dead." And Suzanne got a piece of paper, and she put "Anna's And Suzanne's Investigation Into

What Happened To Barney" on the top of it. And then she put:

Things We Need To Find Out

1. Is Barney dead?
2. How did he die?
3. What about Beatrice?

And we made a plan.

Which was that Suzanne would go to her house and get her Mom and Dad into the front room, and keep them there as long as she could, asking questions about Barney, and the farm, and where it was, and why she couldn't visit. And I would sneak in the back, through the garage, and look for evidence. In case Suzanne's Mom and Dad didn't admit that Barney was dead. And when Suzanne couldn't keep her Mom and Dad in the front room any more, she would cough, three times, to warn me to get out.

"Good plan," I said. And then I said, "What kind of evidence should I look for, exactly?"

And Suzanne said, "Every kind."

"Okay."

So Suzanne went round the front of her house. And I waited for a bit.

And then I walked down to sneak in through the Barrys' garage. And on the way, I looked along the flower beds in the lane, in case there was a big mound of earth where Suzanne's Mom and Dad had buried Barney, out the back. Where our Old Cat is buried, and the nine hamsters, and Joe's old rabbit. But there wasn't.

I went in the Barrys' garage, and through the kitchen, and I sneaked into

Suzanne's Dad's office. Because that's the room Suzanne's Dad is always telling her to get out of. And I looked on Suzanne's Dad's desk. There was a photo of Suzanne's Mom and Dad, when they were married, and one of Carl, when he was just born, and one of Suzanne and Barney in the garden. There was a calendar. I flicked through the pages in case it said, "Killed Barney today" or something like that. But it didn't. I put it in my pocket anyway.

There was a big drawer in the desk with files in it, with labels on, in order, saying "Appliances," and "Bank," and "Car," and all that. And each file was full of papers, and letters, and bills. And Suzanne's Dad had written "PAID" across some of them, in big red letters. I looked along the line of files in case there was one that said "Barney," or "Beatrice," or "Dogs."

Then I heard Suzanne. "Eh hem, eh hem, eh *hem*." It was the three warning coughs. I flicked through the files quickly. Until I came to the last one. It said "Vet."

"EH HEM, EH HEM, EH *HEM*."

I shoved the file up my sweater and sneaked back out of the office and through the kitchen and the garage, back to the shed. And waited for Suzanne.

There were three knocks on the door. *"Mort."* I opened it.

"They didn't admit *anything*," Suzanne said. "What evidence did you get?"

I passed Suzanne the calendar and the vet file. She opened it. There were two bills for Beatrice inside, one that said, "Abscess lancing, earwax removal, antibiotic

injection, worming pill. Cost: £150." Which was all the things Beatrice had had done the day me and Suzanne and Suzanne's Mom took her to the vet's. And there was another bill that said, "Tumor biopsies, tooth extraction, teeth scaling, gastric probe, MRI scan, bladder lifting surgery, vaccinations. Estimated cost: £1500." Which was for all the things she hadn't had done yet. And then there were lots of bills for Barney for having his teeth scaled, and his toenails clipped, and vaccinations, and worming, and one that said "Brain tumor biopsy." And they all had "PAID" and a date written across them. And the last bill in the file said "Euthanasia for dog: £65." Suzanne looked at the bill. It had a date on the top: Friday, June 26. And she got her Dad's calendar, and flicked back through the pages.

"Friday the twenty-sixth of June. Anna, *look*."

At the top of the page in the calendar her Dad had written: Barney to Farm.

Suzanne passed me the dictionary. This is what it says about "euthanasia":

euthanasia [yoo-thu-ney-zee-uh] ◆ *noun*
the act of killing painlessly to relieve suffering from an incurable illness; for animals, see "put down"

We looked again at Barney's euthanasia bill. It had "PAID" written across it, in big red letters. Suzanne picked up her Dad's diary and started flicking through it again. She pointed to a date. "Monday, September twenty-seventh. That's tomorrow's date. Look, Anna." It said:

9:45, Beatrice to Farm.

It was time for us to make another list.

ANNA'S AND SUZANNE'S LIST OF THINGS WE NEED FOR OUR PLAN TO HELP BEATRICE ESCAPE

- ☐ Beatrice
- ☐ Tom
- ☐ Tom's dinghy
- ☐ Mrs. Rotherham's black sheepskin rug
- ☐ The Lifesavers' practice rope
- ☐ Dog food
- ☐ Bottle of water
- ☐ Anna's and Suzanne's lunch boxes
- ☐ Backpack

Tom was sitting in the dinghy, in the hall, with Batman, and Bob the Builder, and his two slugs from Sunday School. I told him about Barney, how he wasn't on a farm, roaming free where he was better off, because Suzanne's Mom and Dad had had him euthanized.

"What's that?"

"Put down"

"What's that?"

"Dead."

"Oh," Tom said. "Who killed him?"

"The vet."

"Why?"

"Because Suzanne's Mom and Dad asked her to."

"Why?"

"It doesn't matter," I said. Because once Tom starts asking why, he won't stop. And we didn't have much time to do the plan

to help Beatrice escape. And I told him how he had to come with us to the shed because he was on our list of things for our plan to save Beatrice. And how we needed his dinghy as well.

"It's not a dinghy; it's an ark."

"Your ark, then."

But Tom said he didn't have time because he had to get his ark ready before the flood came up.

"I'll get you some cookies," Suzanne said. So Tom said he would come. And Suzanne went to her house and grabbed him some cookies.

And Tom took them, and picked up the dinghy, and said, "But when the flood comes, it's just for me, and Batman and Bob the Builder, and my slugs. Because

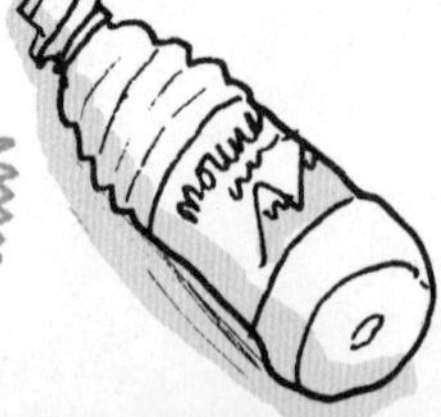

there's not much room. And I've got to leave space for the New Cat, and Mr. Tucker, and my cookies."

So we took Tom's ark to the shed. And then we went to get Mrs. Rotherham's rug. Mrs. Rotherham didn't really want to give us her rug. Because she said, "Why?" And we said how it was for Beatrice to sleep with tonight because tomorrow she was going to live on the farm, like Barney, and we wanted her to have a comfortable last night.

"I'm all for comfort," Mrs. Rotherham said. And she gave us a big trash bag to put it in, so it didn't get wet.

And then we went back to the shed and we put the rug in a backpack with the practice rescue rope from Lifesavers, and the lunch boxes

packed with dog food, and the water. And we put a new diaper in Beatrice's pants. And got our coats on, and our wellies. And Suzanne ticked each thing off on the list.

CHAPTER 17
Beatrice Escapes

Suzanne clipped the leash onto Beatrice's collar.

"Walkies."

Beatrice got up. Without me having to get underneath her to lever her up.

And me and Suzanne and Tom and Beatrice started walking down the back lane, in the rain. And we didn't push and pull, and stop and start, all the way like we normally do. Because Beatrice just walked, like other dogs do. And Suzanne said she thought that Beatrice must know that she was meant to be getting put down tomorrow. And maybe she was *psychic*. Which Suzanne said means she could see what was going to happen in the future. Because she said, "Some dogs *are*." Because she saw a program all about it on TV called *Telepathic Pets*. And I said I thought that was probably why Beatrice was so much faster. And also because the wind was blowing behind us. And it was so strong that Tom couldn't hold on to the dinghy, and we had to tie it onto Suzanne's backpack, so we didn't lose it. And the wind kept getting under it, and Tom kept getting blown forward. And the rain got heavier.

Down in the village, people were running to get indoors, and someone's umbrella had blown inside-out. And the sweet shop lady was chasing her ice-cream sign, which had blown into the road.

We came to the bridge. And turned right, down to the river, and the path down was so wet that it was hard to stay standing up, and Tom had to slide down on his bum. Down on the riverbank we walked close together, with the dinghy over our heads, to keep the rain off. Apart from Beatrice. Who walked ahead. And had her tail wagging, and her nose up.

"Beatrice likes the rain," Tom said.

We stopped at Aunt Deidra's cottage, and Suzanne climbed over the gate, and opened it, and let me and Tom and Beatrice inside. And we walked up the garden, to the top, and Suzanne unclipped Beatrice's leash, and took the cone off her neck. And we got our packed lunch boxes out. And put them down in front of the kennel. And Suzanne poured the dog food into hers. And I poured the water into mine. And I put Beatrice's cone round Tom's neck, and clipped her leash onto his coat. And we put the dinghy on his back, upside down, and Mrs. Rotherham's black sheepskin rug over, to cover it, and Tom held the handles. And in the dark, and the wind, and the rain, if you

half closed your eyes, he looked *exactly* like Beatrice. And Suzanne tied one end of the practice rope to Beatrice's collar, and the other end to a ring in the ground, next to Beatrice's kennel.

And Suzanne said we should each give Beatrice a hug, and say something nice, to keep her going through the night with affection, so she didn't get depressed again.

And I said, "Beatrice, I'm glad you aren't going to get put down."

And Suzanne said, "You are the best dog I have ever had. Apart from Barney."

And Tom said, "You are too big to get in my ark."

And we told Beatrice we would be back in the morning, before school, with some fresh water and some more food. And we said good-bye. And walked back down the garden. And turned right out of the gate, and went up over the field. And the wind kept trying to blow the dinghy off Tom's back. And me and Suzanne had to hold it on. And the rain collected in Beatrice's cone around Tom's neck. And we kept having to stop, to empty it out, and to wring Mrs. Rotherham's rug out as well.

We got onto the road that leads back to the village, and there wasn't anyone out, because they had all gone indoors. And it was as dark as if it were the middle of the night. And then there was thunder. And it sounded like when our class went on a trip to the fort, and they fired the hundred-ton gun.

And we ran until we came to the bottom of our road.

Mr. Tucker was coming down it. "Popsie, Blondie, that you?"

"Yes."

"Where's Basher?"

Suzanne nudged Tom.

"Here," Tom said, from under the dinghy.

"Can't see a thing in these specs in this weather. Thought you were the dog, Basher. Better get inside. Mom's out looking for you." He did the salute. "Into the old ark, eh?"

We went up the back lane. Suzanne's Mom banged on the kitchen window. **"WHERE HAVE YOU BEEN?"**

"Taking Beatrice for her walk," Suzanne said. And her Mom wasn't pleased, because she said Suzanne's Dad was out looking for us all in the car.

We went into the garage, and Suzanne took Beatrice's cone and leash off Tom, and put them in the backpack, and we wrung out Mrs. Rotherham's rug, over the drain, and ran out to the shed with it, and hung it over the ladders, at the back, to dry.

And me and Tom took the dinghy home. And we'd just got in when Mom came in the front door. And she was very wet and she wasn't very pleased, because she said she thought we were all in the shed. And we had no business going for a walk without telling her, and especially not in a storm. And Tom told her how it was fine because he had his ark with him and all that. And me and Tom had a bath, and our dinner.

And I knocked on the wall, and Suzanne knocked back, and we tried to put our heads out, but it was raining so hard that the rain came in sideways through the gap, and it was so loud that we couldn't hear each other speak. So we went back in, and went to bed. And then Tom came and slept in my room. Because he didn't like the noise of the storm. And he brought his ark with him. And we talked about Beatrice a bit and listened to the thunder.

And we didn't hear anything else until the morning, when Suzanne's Dad said, **"WHERE ON EARTH IS THAT DAMNED DOG?!"**

CHAPTER 18

The Rain Came Down

Mom came into my room. "Suzanne's Dad is going to drive you all to school this morning."

"I want to walk."

"Don't be ridiculous, Anna. You're not walking. Have you seen it outside?"

I looked out the window. It was raining harder than ever. I waited until Mom had gone, and I knocked three times on the wall. Suzanne knocked back, and we opened our windows. And stuck our heads out. And then we brought them back in again, because the rain was so heavy that you couldn't keep your eyes open, and it hurt your ears, and you couldn't speak.

I shouted through the window, "What are we going to do?" Because we were supposed to set off for school early, to go down to see Beatrice, and check if she was all right, and take her some food.

"We could sneak out of school at lunchtime," Suzanne said, "and go and see Beatrice and get back before the bell goes. I'll bring the dog food to school."

But at lunchtime Mrs. Peters said it was too wet to play, and everyone had to stay inside. And the rain kept on coming. And in the afternoon the people who come in to school on buses, and live out of the village, got sent home early because the rain was getting worse, and if they waited they might not get through.

When the bell rang, Suzanne's Mom was waiting for us at the gates in her car.

When we got home, I tried to sneak out to meet Suzanne in the shed. But Mom saw me. "Don't be ridiculous, Anna. The shed's half full of water. I've been in there today and put buckets under all the leaks. What on earth was that sopping wet rug doing there?"

After dinner the rain still hadn't stopped. And it kept raining all through the night. Because I could hear it, in bed, and I couldn't sleep because it was so loud, and I kept thinking about Beatrice, and Suzanne, and whether Beatrice was all right, and how she would need a new diaper, and whether her food had run out.

CHAPTER 19

The Floods Came Up

In the morning, when I woke up and went downstairs, Tom was already up and dressed and sitting in the hall in the dinghy.

"The flood has come," he said.

"No, it hasn't."

"It has. Ask Mom."

I looked out the window. The rain had stopped. Mom had the news on.

"Tom says the flood's come."

"Shh, Anna," Mom said, pointing to the TV. "Look."

There was a man on the TV standing by the bridge in the village. "That's right, Carol, I'm here on the north side of the bridge, and, as you can see behind me, over there on the south side, the river has already burst its banks. Many people on the south side were evacuated in the night, and with severe weather warnings again for this afternoon and evening, police are now advising people living close to the river on the north side to move to higher ground as well. Schools in the immediate area are closed. . . ."

I ran upstairs and knocked on the wall three times, and Suzanne knocked back, and I opened my window and stuck my head out, and Suzanne opened hers.

"We have to evacuate Beatrice and move her to higher ground."

I got dressed and ran downstairs.

"Where are you going?"

"To look at the flood."

Tom was still in the hall sitting in the dinghy. "I'm coming." And he picked up the dinghy by the string. And his packet of cookies.

Mom shouted after us, "Stay where everyone else is, Anna. And don't go down near the water!"

CHAPTER 20
The River

We couldn't get to Sorrel Cottage by going past the shops and turning right before the bridge, like we normally do. Because everyone was out in the village, looking at the river, and filming the flood. So we walked along the back road behind the church, and down over the fields instead. And the grass was so wet that we could pull Tom along behind us, in the dinghy.

As we got closer we could hear the river getting louder. And down on the riverbank it was so loud, Tom put his hands over his ears. We stopped and stared at the river.

"It's gone big," Tom said.

And it had. Because the fields on the other side of the river had all disappeared underneath it. And the island in the middle was missing. And you could just see the highest branches of the trees, sticking out the top.

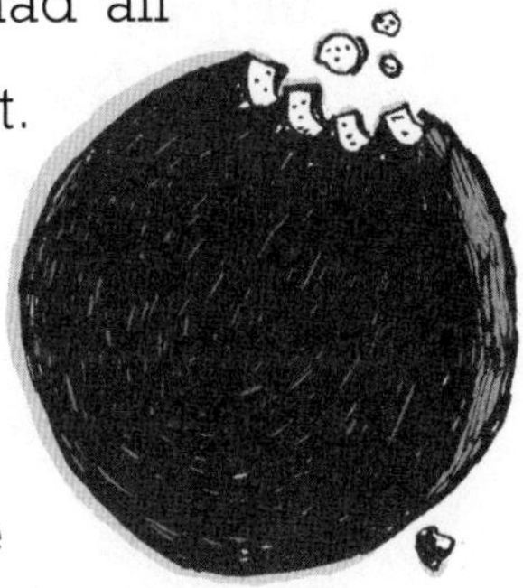

"I don't like it," Tom said. And he started eating his cookies.

I didn't like it either. Because the water was so fast, it went past white, and swirled round in rapids, and there were waves under the bridge. And looking at it made me feel a bit sick.

We carried on along the riverbank

until we came to Sorrel Cottage. Suzanne looked over the gate. "There she *is*."

Beatrice was lying in a puddle, next to the kennel, at the top of the garden.

"Beatrice!" Suzanne climbed over the gate and opened it from the inside. Beatrice stood up. And wagged her tail. And barked. Like a proper dog. Me and Suzanne walked up to meet her.

Tom stayed with the dinghy, on the riverbank and stared at the river and ate his cookies.

Beatrice was as wet as Mrs. Rotherham's black rug, the night it got soaked in the storm. Suzanne put her arms around Beatrice. And Beatrice rubbed her face against Suzanne, like she was Great-Aunt Deidra's gate. I could hear the river, at the top of the garden. And then I heard another noise. **"Quack."**

"What was that?"

"What?"

"I heard something."

"Quack."

I turned around. There were three ducks on the other side of Aunt Deidra's gate, waddling toward Tom.

"Shoo!" Tom shouted. "Go away!" He took a step backward toward the river, with the string of the dinghy in one hand and his packet of cookies in the other. Three more ducks came out from the gorse bushes.

"Quack."

"On your left, Tom."

"Quack."

"And your right."

"Shoo." Tom took another step back. And waved his cookies. And the ducks started coming toward him all together,

opening their beaks and flapping their wings.

"Throw the cookies, Tom!"

But Tom didn't. He just kept walking away. Backward. Toward the river.

I ran down the garden and through the gate. Tom was nearly at the edge of the riverbank.

"HONK!"

Tom jumped. "What was that?"

The Swan Duck pushed its way through the others to the front. It looked at Tom, and his cookies, with its good eye. And the white eye, which looks off the wrong way, looked behind it. Then it reared up, and stuck out its chest, and opened its wings, then hissed, **"TSSSSS!"**

It ran at Tom, and the ducks followed behind it, hissing and pecking and flapping like mad. Tom was right at the edge of the riverbank now. He looked behind him. "HELP!"

I could hear the river, loud, like when the trains go over at the crossing.

And suddenly the bank gave way, and Tom disappeared into the river, and shot down it, holding on to the dinghy.

"Tom! Tom!"

Tom grabbed on to the branch of a tree, which was sticking out of the water where the island used to be. He let go of the dinghy and it shot off through the rapids.

"My ark!"

On the bridge, people started pointing. "There's a boy!" "Look!" "Somebody do something!"

"The rope!" I shouted to Suzanne.

Suzanne started trying to untie the rope from Beatrice's collar.

"It's too wet!" Suzanne called. "I can't undo the knot!"

She ran down from the top of the garden, and through the gate, and over to the riverbank. "I'll dive in, Anna. Stand back!" She took her wellies off and put her arms up over her head. But before she could dive in, Beatrice did something she had never done. She ran. She ran so hard that the ring with the rope on it came out of the ground, and she dragged it behind her. She dived into the water, in front of Suzanne, and swam across the current. And stopped just in front of Tom. They both went under. And I thought they had both drowned. Because I counted to thirty. Which is the longest Tom has ever held his breath. And then they came back up, above the water, and Beatrice had the hood of Tom's jacket in her mouth. And she dragged him back to the riverbank.

CHAPTER 21

In the News

Two ambulance men came, and wrapped Tom in a silver blanket, and put an oxygen mask on him, and put him on a stretcher. And people from up on the bridge, who had seen what happened, ran down and gathered round. And one of the ambulance men tapped Tom on the cheek and asked, "Can you hear me?"

And Tom could. Because he nodded his head.

And the ambulance men asked Tom

some questions. About who he was and where he lived and all that, and shone a little flashlight in his eyes. And Tom couldn't answer because his teeth were chattering so much, and his lips had gone blue, and then he was sick. And he started crying because he'd lost his ark, and his cookies. And there was a lady from the newspaper trying to ask questions too. And I said how Tom was my brother. And the lady from the paper started asking me questions instead. And I told her how we had come to have a look at the flood. And how Tom got attacked by the ducks. And how Beatrice was Suzanne's dog, and she'd gone missing on Monday. And I started to say how Beatrice had nearly killed Misty by mistake, and Miss Matheson wanted to take her to court, and Suzanne's Dad was going to have her put down.

But Suzanne kicked me in the shin, and put her eyebrows up, and made her lips go small, like she does when she wants you to shut up.

And then I saw Mom and Dad running down the riverbank, and Suzanne's Mom and Dad as well. And they had seen everything, on the news. And Mom and Dad went with Tom in the ambulance. And

Suzanne's Dad asked the lady who she was. And the lady from the paper tried to give Suzanne's Dad her card, in case he would like to tell her his story.

And Suzanne's Dad said, "No thanks."

And the lady shook my hand, and put a card in it, and went off. And we all went home.

The next day a big picture of Beatrice was on the front page of the paper.

THE DEADLY CURRENTS OF A FLOODED RIVER PROVED NO MATCH FOR THE LOVE OF A DEVOTED FAMILY PET WHEN THE DOG CAME TO THE RESCUE OF A DROWNING CHILD.

Anna Morris (9) and her brother Tom (5) and their friend and next-door neighbor Suzanne Barry had a brush with tragedy yesterday morning as a section of riverbank collapsed, plunging the five-year-old boy into the raging river. Eyewitnesses were incredulous at the sight of Beatrice, an aged Newfoundland, diving in and dragging the helpless child out of the water. The dog, which was recently bequeathed to the Barry family, had gone missing on Monday. "Beatrice appeared from nowhere," Suzanne Barry said. "I was about to dive into the river, to rescue Tom, when Beatrice went in first."

I knocked on the wall three times. Suzanne knocked back. We opened our windows.

"Look!" And I showed Suzanne the paper. Suzanne didn't look pleased. "Don't you like it? Beatrice is a hero."

And Suzanne said how it didn't matter that Beatrice was a hero because her Mom and Dad had explained everything to her about Barney, and what was wrong with him, and how he'd had to be put down. And how they had to think about how old Beatrice was, and how much the vet's bills would cost. And how even though Misty was starting to get better, if the Barrys didn't have Beatrice put down, Miss Matheson was still going to press charges, and they couldn't afford the fine.

And if they lost the case, they might have to cover Miss Matheson's court costs.

"Want to come in the shed and make a plan?" I said. "Because we could put all our pocket money together. And . . ."

But Suzanne didn't want to come in the shed. And she closed the window and went inside.

So I went out to the shed myself. And I got the buckets of water that Mom had put under the leaks and I emptied them out in the back lane. And I got Mrs. Rotherham's rug, and I went up the road to take it back.

And I showed Mrs. Rotherham the paper, and the photo of Beatrice. And I told her all about how Beatrice wasn't well, and how she needed lots of things done at the vet's, and how she was too old, and it was too expensive. And how she had nearly killed Misty, by mistake. And how Miss Matheson wanted her to be put down. Because Miss Matheson said she was a dangerous dog. And how she was going to take the Barrys to court. And I said how we couldn't get enough money to help because even if me and Suzanne sold everything we owned and did stalls at the bottom of the road and gave all our pocket money, we still wouldn't have enough, because it would cost hundreds and maybe even thousands of pounds.

And Mrs. Rotherham listened, and looked at the pictures in the paper. And said, "Well, well, well," and "Dear, oh dear," and "Poor old Beatrice." And she started flicking through the pages, like she was looking for something. "Aha! Here it is." She pointed to a bit on the back page.

Got a story?

From celebrity exclusives to cheating politicians, to heartwarming tales of triumph over tragedy, we want your stories on all of them. Find out how much YOU could make: Call us now.

I wasn't sure if Suzanne would want me to call the newspaper. Because when I was talking to the lady on the riverbank, Suzanne didn't like it. And nor did her Dad. And then I saw something else, under the phone number to call. "You can remain anonymous. We always protect our sources."

Mrs. Rotherham passed me the phone.

The next day Beatrice was in the paper again.

HOW BEATRICE THE HERO DOG SUFFERS IN SILENCE

Beatrice, who saved a five-year-old boy from drowning this week, has suffered with depression and has a list of health problems as long as your arm, but can't afford the medical care she needs. . . .

And the day after that.

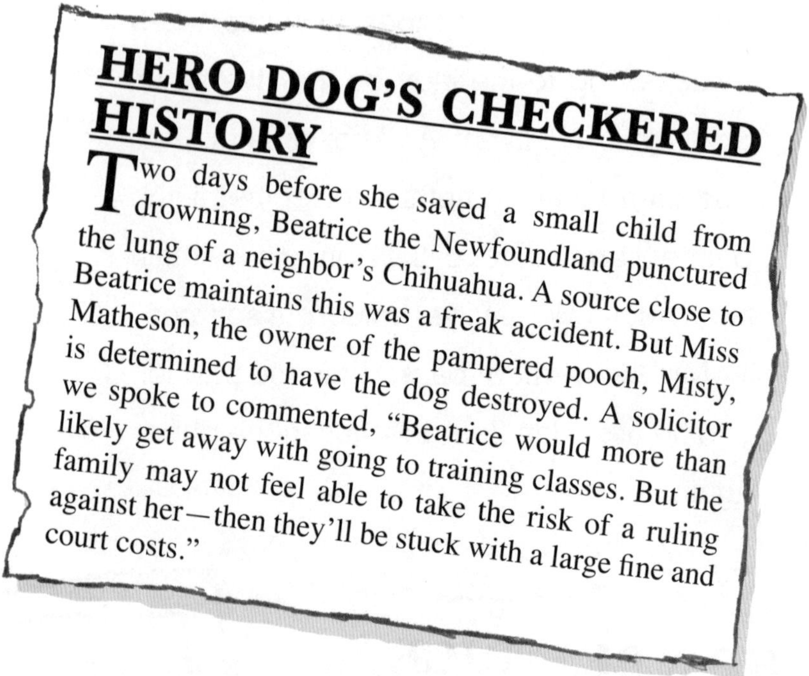

HERO DOG'S CHECKERED HISTORY

Two days before she saved a small child from drowning, Beatrice the Newfoundland punctured the lung of a neighbor's Chihuahua. A source close to Beatrice maintains this was a freak accident. But Miss Matheson, the owner of the pampered pooch, Misty, is determined to have the dog destroyed. A solicitor we spoke to commented, "Beatrice would more than likely get away with going to training classes. But the family may not feel able to take the risk of a ruling against her—then they'll be stuck with a large fine and court costs."

Beatrice was in the paper every day that week.

On Saturday Suzanne knocked three times on the wall. And I knocked back. And we said, *"Bonjour,"* and all that.

And Suzanne said, "Meet me at ze

shed." Because she had something important to tell me.

So I did. And she said how she had been sent five checks, for £200 each, from "a well-wisher" to pay for Beatrice's vet's bills. And how since Beatrice had been in the paper, people kept calling her house, like a solicitor who said that he would represent Beatrice for free. And a Policeman who said Beatrice had been nominated for a Commendation of Bravery award. And the vet, who said that she would knock some money off Beatrice's vet bills. And how Beatrice wasn't going to have to be put down.

CHAPTER 22

Life in the Old Dog Yet

That's pretty much everything that happened in the Great Dog Disaster. Me and Suzanne still take Beatrice for two walks every day. But not always down to Great-Aunt Deidra's. Because we go all over the village. And Tom comes too. And the walks are slower than ever. Because, even though Beatrice isn't depressed anymore, and she can walk a bit faster, everyone we pass stops to give her a pat, and to look at her bravery medal, and say, "Life in the old dog yet . . . ," and all that. And Tom has to tell them the story of how Beatrice saved his life, after the ducks tried to drown him.

And on Mondays, when me and Suzanne go to Lifesavers, Suzanne's Mom takes Beatrice to her *own* swimming lesson, in a special place, just for dogs, down the road from mine and Suzanne's, called Hydrotherapy Hounds. To help with her hips. And that's Beatrice's best thing of the week. And it's mine and Suzanne's as well. Because when we've finished our lesson, we watch Beatrice do hers through the window. And Beatrice doesn't look old at all in the water. And Suzanne says that, one day, Beatrice might start jumping up, and

fetching a stick, and doing the obstacle course and all that. But I don't think so. Because mainly Beatrice likes to go and see Mrs. Rotherham, and sit by her fire. And to have a bath, in the back lane on Sundays. And to fall asleep in the shed, while me and Suzanne make our plans.

The End

Katie Davies

Katie Davies was born in Newcastle upon Tyne in 1978. In 1989, after a relentless begging campaign, she was given two hamsters for Christmas. She is yet to recover from what happened to those hamsters. THE GREAT HAMSTER MASSACRE, Katie's first novel, won the Waterstone's Children's Book Prize. She has also written THE GREAT RABBIT RESCUE and THE GREAT CAT CONSPIRACY. Katie now lives in North London with her husband, the comedian Alan Davies, and their two small children. She does not have any hamsters.

Hannah Shaw

Hannah Shaw was born into a large family of sprout-munching vegetarians. She spent her formative years trying to be good at everything from roller-skating to gymnastics, but she soon realized there wasn't much chance of her becoming a gold-medal-winning gymnast, so she resigned herself to writing stories and drawing pictures instead!

Hannah currently lives in the Cotswolds with her husband, Ben the blacksmith, and her rescue dog, Ren. Hannah and Ren do dog agility together, and they have a growing collection of "special" and "good effort" ribbons. She finds her overactive imagination fuels new ideas but unfortunately keeps her awake at night!

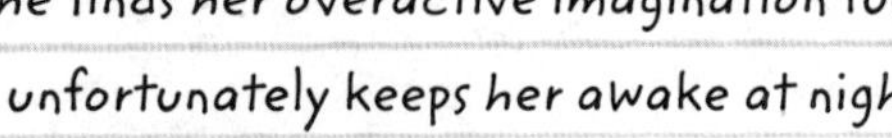

THE GREAT RABBIT RESCUE

Katie Davies

Illustrated by Hannah Shaw

Beach Lane Books
New York London Toronto Sydney New Delhi

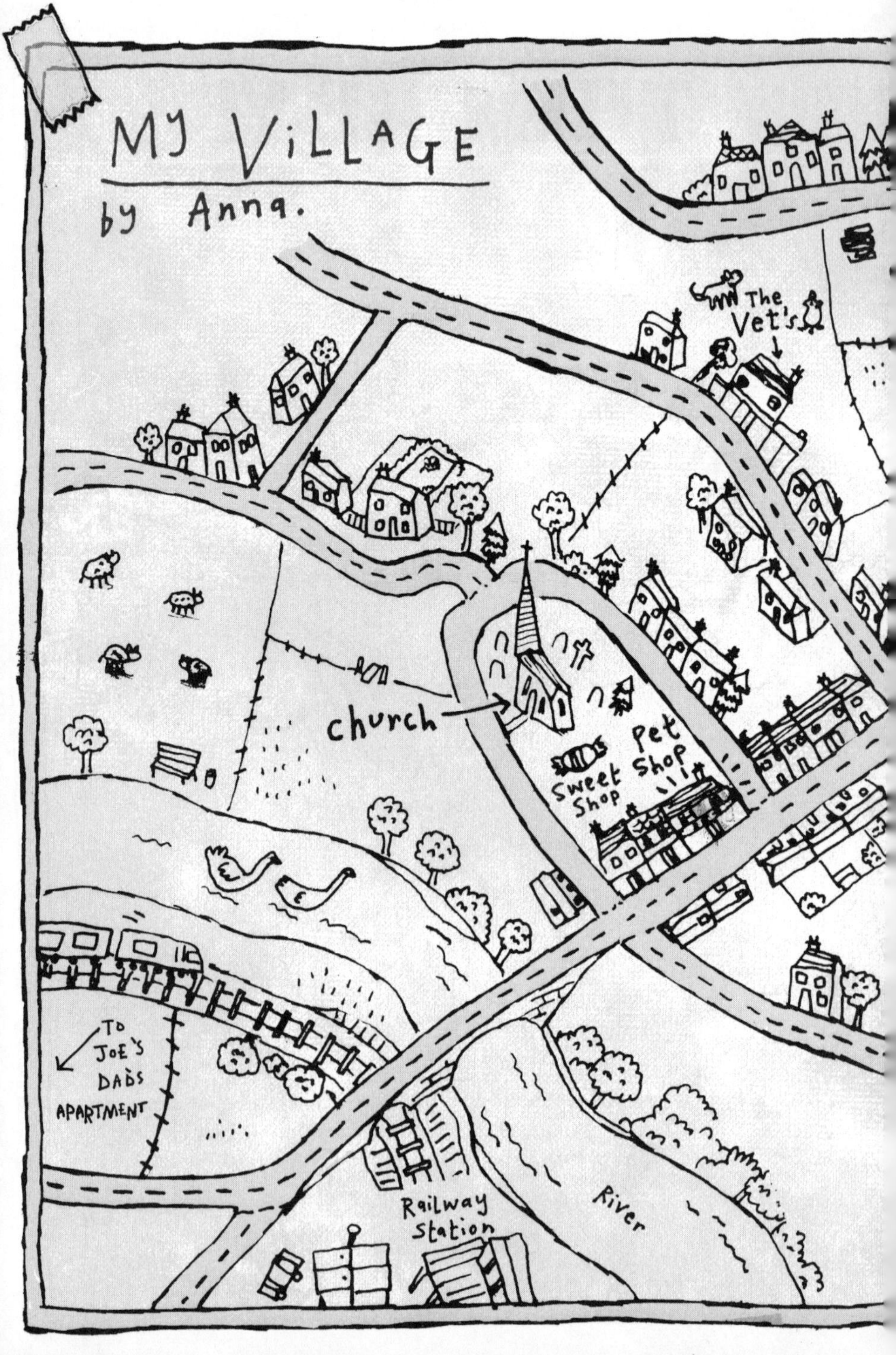

MY VILLAGE
by Anna.
The Vet's
church
Pet Shop
Sweet Shop
TO JOE'S DADS APARTMENT
Railway Station
River

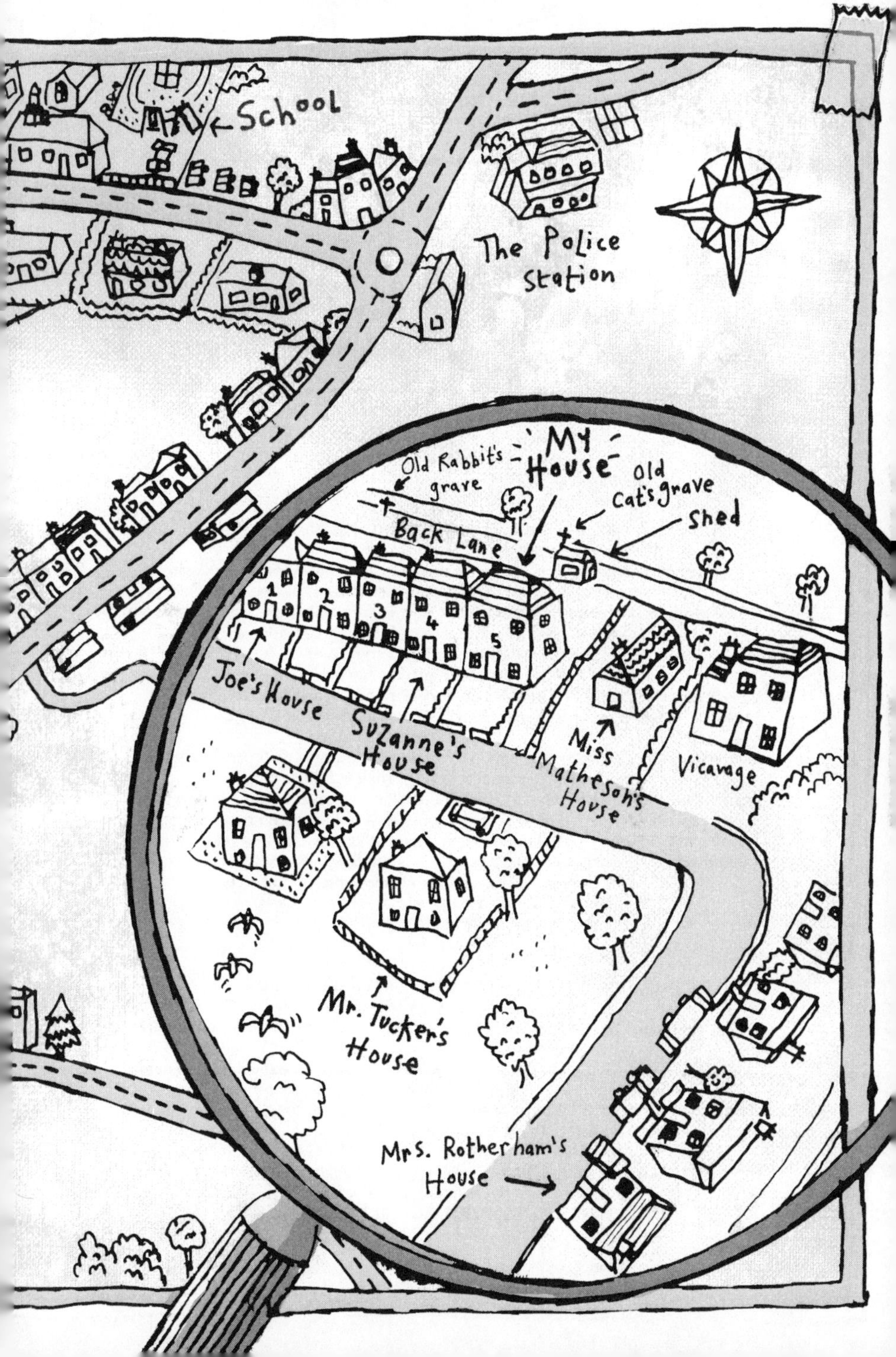
School
The Police Station
MY House
Old Rabbit's grave
Old Cat's grave
Shed
Back Lane
1
2
3
4
5
Joe's House
Suzanne's House
Miss Matheson's House
Vicarage
Mr. Tucker's House
Mrs. Rotherham's House

For Sam

Thanks to my Mum and Dad, and to my husband, Alan, for reading (and reading) it.
And thanks also to my agent, Clare Conville, and to Venetia Gosling and everyone at Simon and Schuster.

BEACH LANE BOOKS
An imprint of Simon & Schuster Children's Publishing Division
1230 Avenue of the Americas, New York, New York 10020

Originally published in Great Britain in 2010 by Simon and Schuster UK Ltd.
Published by arrangement with Simon and Schuster UK Ltd.
First U.S. edition 2011

Manufactured in the United States of America
1111 FFG
First Edition
2 4 6 8 10 9 7 5 3 1
Library of Congress Cataloging-in-Publication Data
Davies, Katie, 1978–
The great rabbit rescue / Katie Davies ; illustrated by Hannah Shaw.—1st U.S. ed.
p. cm.
Summary: When Joe goes to live with his father across town and must leave behind his beloved pet rabbit, his friends Anna and Suzanne try to take care of it for him, but when the rabbit becomes ill and then Joe follows suit, the girls are certain that both will die unless they are reunited.
ISBN 978-1-4424-2064-9 (hardcover)—ISBN 978-1-4424-3321-2 (eBook)
[1. Rabbits as pets—Fiction. 2. Sick—Fiction. 3. Friendship—Fiction.]
I. Shaw, Hannah, ill. II. Title.
PZ7.D283818Gs 2012
[Fic]—dc22
2011008326

CHAPTER 1
A Real Rescue

This is a story about Joe-down-the-street, and why he went away, and how he got rescued. Most stories I've read about people getting rescued aren't *Real-Life* Stories. They're Fairy Stories, about Sleeping Beauty, and Rapunzel, and people like that. And they probably aren't true, because in Real Life people don't prick their fingers on spindles very much and fall asleep for a hundred years. And if they did, they probably wouldn't wake up just because someone gave them a kiss on the cheek, like Sleeping Beauty did. Even if the person who kissed them was a Prince.

Because, in Real Life, when people are really *deep* asleep, you have to shake them, and shout, "WAKE UP!" in their ear, and hit them on the head with the xylophone sticks. Otherwise they don't wake up at all.

My Dad doesn't, anyway. And nor does my little brother, Tom. He falls asleep on the floor, and he doesn't wake up when Mom carries him upstairs and puts him in his pajamas and stands him up at the toilet. Not even once when he peed on his feet.

Tom is five. He's four years younger than me. I'm nine. My name is Anna.

Also, in Real Life, people don't let down their hair from towers for other people to climb up and rescue them and things, like happens in *Rapunzel*. Because you can't really climb up *hair* very well, especially not when it's still growing on someone's head. You can't climb up Emma Hendry's hair, anyway, because Graham Roberts once tried to, in PE, when Emma was up the wall bars. And Emma fell off, and Mrs. Peters wasn't pleased. And neither was Emma. She was winded. Emma's got the longest hair in school. She can sit on it if she wants to. It's never been cut. Mrs. Peters sent a note home to Emma's Mom because Emma's hair kept getting caught in doors, and drawers, and things like that, and she said, "Emma Hendry, that hair is a Death Trap!"

Which is true. Especially with Graham Roberts around. So now Emma's hair gets tied up, and on PE days it has to go under a net.

Anyway, this story isn't a Made-Up Story, or a Fairy Story like *Sleeping Beauty* or *Rapunzel* or anything like that. It's a Real Rescue Story. And that means that everything in it Actually Happened. I know it did, because I was there. And so was my little brother, Tom. And so was my friend Suzanne Barry, who lives next door.

This is what it says in my dictionary about what a rescue is . . .

rescue [res-kew] ✦ *verb*
to help someone or something out of a dangerous, harmful, or unpleasant situation

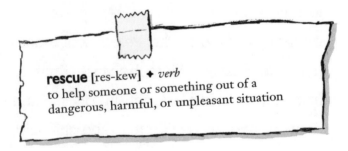

And this is what it says in my friend Suzanne's dictionary . . .

rescue [res-kew] ✦ *informal*
to free or deliver from confinement or peril

Mom said that me and Suzanne and Tom were wrong about Joe-down-the-street and that he was never even *in* any danger or peril in the first place.

She said, "Anna, Joe has gone to live with his Dad because he *wants* to. He definitely does *not* need to be rescued!"

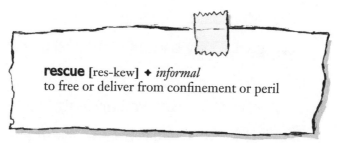

But moms don't always know everything about who might need rescuing. Because once, when I was in Big Trouble for falling through the shed roof in the back lane by mistake, I decided that I didn't like living at our house anymore, and I told Mom, "I wish I lived with Mrs. Rotherham up the road!"

And Mom said, "So do I!"

So I packed my bag, and I went off up the road.

When I got to Mrs. Rotherham's house, I decided I didn't *really* want to live there. But I had to by then, because that's what I'd said. So I went in. And I sat in the window by myself and stared out and didn't speak. And, after ages, there was a knock on the door. It was Tom, in his Batman pajamas and his Bob the Builder hard hat.

And Mrs. Rotherham said, "Hello, Tom. Are you all on your own?"

And Tom said, "I am Batman and Bob the Builder. I want Anna to come home."

So I did. And that was a rescue, really, what Tom

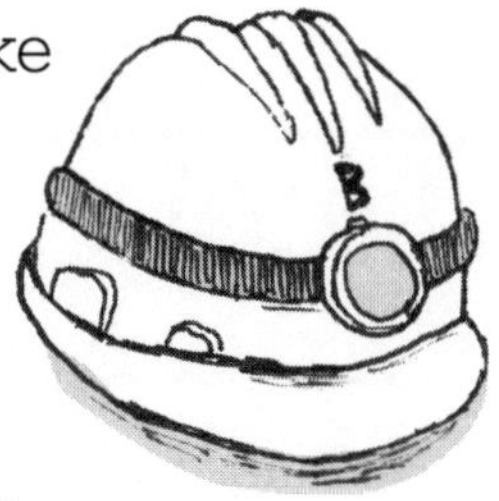

did. Because, even though I like Mrs. Rotherham a lot, I didn't *really* want to live with her. Because I'd rather live in my own house, with Tom. And Mom and Dad. And Andy and Joanne. (That's my other brother and my sister. They aren't in this story because they're older than me and Tom, and they don't really care about rabbits, or rescues.) Anyway, if Tom *hadn't* rescued me, I would probably still be living with Mrs. Rotherham now. So I'm glad he did. Because, for one thing, Mrs. Rotherham's house is at the wrong end of the road. And, for another thing, it smells a bit strange, of old things, and mothballs, like Nana's house used to. And, for an even other thing, if I lived with Mrs. Rotherham, I wouldn't live next door to Suzanne anymore.

CHAPTER 2
Anna to Suzanne

Me and Suzanne, who lives next door, have got walkie-talkies. I talk to Suzanne on my walkie-talkie in my house. And she talks to me on her walkie-talkie in her house.

I hold down the button on the side and say, "Anna to Suzanne. Anna to Suzanne. Come in, Suzanne. Over."

And then I let go of the button, and the walkie-talkie crackles, and Suzanne says, "Suzanne to Anna. Suzanne to Anna. Receiving you loud and clear. Over."

And that's the way you're supposed to say things when you're on the walkie-talkies. Because Suzanne knows all about it from her Uncle in the army. Me and Suzanne talk on our walkie-talkies all the time, wherever we are (except in the bath, because Mom says if it falls in I'll get electrocuted to death like Ken Barlow's first wife on *Coronation Street*).

Mom says she doesn't see why me and Suzanne need walkie-talkies in our houses at all, because the wall between our house and the Barrys' house is so thin we could just put a glass to the wall and talk to each other through that. Which is true. But putting a glass to the wall isn't as good as talking on walkie-talkies because me and Suzanne tried it.

For one thing, you both have to be in the exact same place on each side of the wall. And for another thing, you can't say anything secret because you have to say everything loud and clear or the other person can't hear it.

And, for an even other thing, if you've got squishy wallpaper on your walls, like Suzanne has in her house, the glass presses a circle shape in the wallpaper. And when Suzanne's Dad sees that, he says, **"GET IN HERE, SUZANNE! WHAT ON *EARTH* ARE THESE CIRCLE SHAPES ALL OVER THE PLACE?"**

You don't need a glass, or a walkie-talkie, or *anything* to hear Suzanne's *Dad* through the wall. You can hear everything he says, because Suzanne's Dad always shouts.

Before me and Suzanne got the walkie-talkies, we used to have a thing called the Knocking Code. This is how it worked:

I would knock three times on my bedroom wall, and if the coast was clear, Suzanne would knock back three times on her bedroom wall. And then we would both go to our windows, and open them, and crawl out, and sit outside on our window ledges, and talk about things. Like the road, and the roofs, and whether or not you go blind if you stare straight at the sun.

The only thing with the Knocking Code was, sometimes, if there were other noises going on, Suzanne couldn't hear my knocks. And then I had to crawl out onto my window ledge, and over to Suzanne's, to look in through her window, to see if I could see her. And one time when I did that, when Suzanne wasn't there, my window closed behind me. By itself. And I couldn't get it open again. I banged on my window. And nobody came. And I banged on Suzanne's window. And nobody came. And it started raining. And I sat on the window ledge. And I got very wet. And I shouted, "HELLO!" and "HELP!" and "I'M ON THE WINDOW LEDGE!" And after a while I wondered what would be worse, staying on the window ledge and catching my death of cold, like Nana always used to say I would, or jumping off the window ledge and breaking both my legs.

And just when I was wondering that, Mr. Tucker, who lives opposite, came out of his house to put his trash cans out.

So I shouted down, "HELP! Mr. TUCKER! UP HERE! I'M ON THE WINDOW LEDGE!"

Mr. Tucker's got a lot of medals from the War. For flying planes, and fighting, and blowing things up and all that. He doesn't fly planes anymore, though. He's too old. Most of the time what Mr. Tucker does is go up and down the road picking up litter. Nana used to say Mr. Tucker was "waging a one-man war against rubbish."

Mr. Tucker put his trash cans down, and he said, "HALLO, LOOK KEEN, WHAT'S THIS?"

I said, **"IT'S ME!"**

"AHA, POPSIE. ON A PROTEST UP THERE, ARE YOU?"

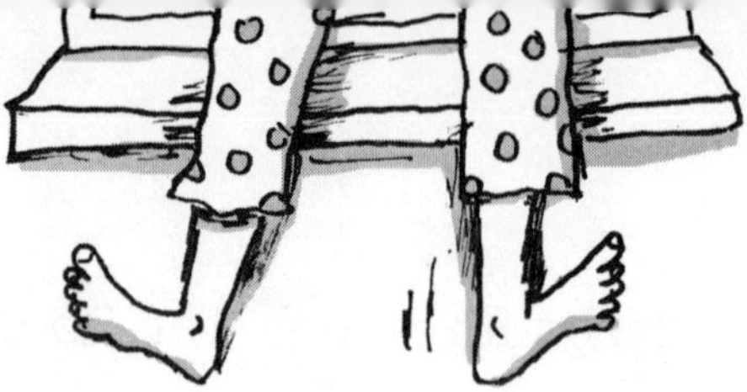

I don't like being called Popsie. Sometimes when Mr. Tucker calls me it, I pretend I can't hear him. But I didn't do that this time because of being stuck out on the window ledge in the dark and the rain and everything, and needing to get rescued.

So I said, "NO, I'M NOT ON A PROTEST." Because I wasn't. "I'M STUCK."

"STUCK, IS IT?"

"YES," I said. "I CAME OUT, AND NOW I CAN'T GET BACK IN."

Mr. Tucker said, "NOT BINDING ON?"

And I said, "WHAT?"

Because sometimes it's hard to know what Mr. Tucker means, with him having been in the War and everything.

"COMPLAINING ABOUT THE CONDITIONS?"

"NO," I said. "I CAME OUT TO SEE SUZANNE, AND THE WINDOW CLOSED BEHIND ME."

"AHA, BOTCHED OP, EH? SIT TIGHT. I'LL GET ME KIT."

And he went and got his long ladder, and he put it up to the window and held it steady at the bottom, and said, "THAT'S IT. YOU'VE GOT THE GREEN. CHOCKS AWAY."

And I climbed down.

I stood behind Mr. Tucker, and Mr. Tucker rang our doorbell.

Mom opened the door. And Tom was with her, in his Batman pajamas, and he was pleased to see Mr. Tucker, because talking to Mr. Tucker is one of Tom's favorite things.

Tom gave Mr. Tucker the salute. And Mr. Tucker gave Tom the salute back. Because that's what Tom and Mr. Tucker always do when they see each other.

And Mr. Tucker said, "You're in your best blues there, Old Chum. Bang on target, those jimjams. Batman, eh? Smashing, Basher."

And Tom stuck his chest out.

And Mr. Tucker said to Mom, "Missing one of your mob, Mrs. Morris? Found this one trying to bail out."

And he pointed behind him. I poked my head round.

Mom said, "Anna, what are you doing? Why are you wet?"

We went inside, and I told Mom about what had happened with the Knocking Code, and how I went out the window, and climbed over to Suzanne's, and how my window closed behind me, and how I couldn't get back in, and how the rain came down, and how I banged on the windows, and shouted for help, and how I climbed all the way down the long ladder by myself.

Mom didn't look very happy. And I thought I was going to be in Big Trouble again, because she said "*Anna* . . ." the way she always does.

But Mr. Tucker butted in. "What a line!" he said. "No, no, no. *Here's* how it went. I *smell* something's up, you see—instinct. Go out on me own, no Second Dickey. Clock Popsie, dead ahead, ten angels up and about to bail. Say to myself, 'Look lively, Wing Commander. Your twelve o'clock, young blond job doing the dutch!' I get weaving right away. Caught some bad flack off Mrs. Tucker, *'RAYMOND!'* and all that. Corkscrew out of it. Ladder up. Popsie down. Safe and sound. Spot on. (Be surprised if I don't get a gong as it goes.) No need to debrief Blondie, though, Chiefy. Caught a packet on her way down, lot of offensive fire. Tore a strip off her myself, of course. Badly botched op, and the clot hadn't packed her chute correctly. All in order now, though. No harm done. Prob'ly do with a brew up."

Mom looked at me. I was cold. And I was dripping quite a lot on the carpet. And she started smiling. And Mr. Tucker started smiling too. And then Mom and Mr. Tucker started laughing. And they got The Hysterics, which is what you get when you start laughing and then you can't stop.

But I didn't get The Hysterics. Because

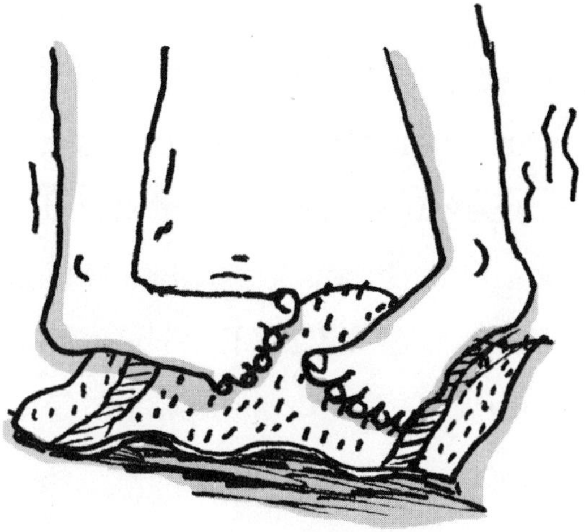

my feet were going blue, and anyway, like Tom said, "It's not that funny."

Mom got me a towel and made some tea.

And Mr. Tucker drank his and said, "Better get on, or I'll catch another packet off Mrs. Tucker. If you fancy pulling your finger out tomorrow, I shall be out plugging away at this litter situation again. Four Coke cans, three grocery bags, and a half-eaten carton of chicken chow mein today. Doesn't do, Popsie, doesn't do. O-eight-hundred hours, eh?"

Normally, I tell Mr. Tucker I'm too busy

to pick up litter. Especially on a Saturday morning. Because I'd rather watch cartoons, or work on the Super-Speed-Bike-Machine with Suzanne, or sit on the shed roof or something. But seeing as how Mr. Tucker had rescued me, I said, "Okay."

And Tom said that he was coming too, because he loves doing things with Mr. Tucker. Especially picking up litter. He follows him up and down and holds the trash bag open for Mr. Tucker to put the rubbish in.

Mr. Tucker said, "Spot on, Tom." And he messed up

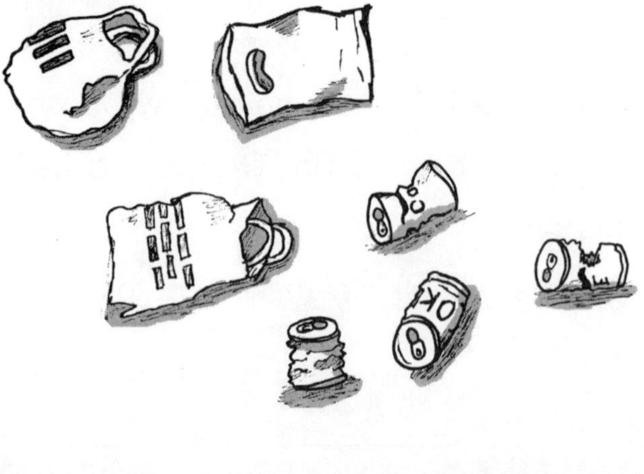

Tom's hair. And Tom and Mr. Tucker gave each other the salute again. And then Mr. Tucker went home.

Mr. Tucker isn't like the people who do rescues in Made-Up Stories or Fairy Tales or anything like that. Because no one ever makes Sleeping Beauty or Rapunzel go on a litter pick.

Anyway, after that I didn't go out on the window ledge again.

The next day, me and Suzanne told Mrs. Rotherham all about what happened with Mr. Tucker, and the Knocking Code, and how we couldn't go out of our windows to talk anymore. Mrs. Rotherham got us some ice cream, and she said, "Mmm, let me think. . . ." And then she winked. "I've got just the things for you two if I can lay my hands on them."

And she went into one of her cupboards. And she found two walkie-talkies. Not toy walkie-talkies like some people have. Real walkie-talkies that Mrs. Rotherham used to use when she was in the police about a million years ago.

Mrs. Rotherham cleaned the walkie-talkies up, and got them working, and she gave them to us to keep.

If anything ever happens to my Mom and Dad, I'll probably go and live with Mrs. Rotherham, as long as she doesn't mind

Tom coming too, even though she's old, and her house smells a bit strange. Because she's got lots of good stuff in her cupboards, and she always gives you ice cream, and she never tells you not to do things.

CHAPTER 3

The Old Rabbit and the New Cat

Before everything happened with Joe-down-the-street, before he went away and had to get rescued, I didn't really mind all that much whether he was down the road or not. Because most of the time, when he *was* down the road, Joe just did things on his own. And partly that was because Joe didn't want to do the things me and Suzanne were doing. And partly that was because me and Suzanne didn't want to do the things Joe was doing. But mainly it was because Joe wouldn't come out of his garden because he had to guard his New Rabbit.

Most people who've got rabbits don't really guard them all that much. Because they probably think that when a rabbit's in its hutch, nothing bad can happen to it. But Joe-down-the-street knows that even in their hutches, rabbits aren't always safe. Because Joe used to have another rabbit, called the *Old* Rabbit, that he got from his Dad, when his Dad still lived at Joe's house, before he went away.

And once, when Joe was playing out the back with me and Suzanne, a cat went in Joe's garden, and looked in at Joe's Old Rabbit, sitting in its hutch. And the Old Rabbit was so scared when it saw the cat that it panicked and died. And that's why, when Joe's Mom got him a New Rabbit, Joe started guarding it straightaway.

Joe's Mom's Boyfriend said, "The Old Rabbit was daft to die just because a cat *looked* at it." Because "It's not like the cat could open the hutch."

But the Old Rabbit *wasn't* daft really, because, like Suzanne said, "You don't have time to think about things like that when you're about to die of fright."

And it isn't just rabbits that can die of fright either. Anyone can. Suzanne knows all about it, after she saw a show on TV called *Scared to Death*.

And she said, "A man died of fright when his wife jumped out on him from inside the wardrobe."

Which the wife said was meant to be a joke. But like Tom said, "It wasn't a very funny one."

Suzanne always gets to watch all the good stuff on TV. Not like me and Tom. My Mom changes the channel and puts *Coronation Street* on instead. When Suzanne told Joe all about the *Scared to Death* show, and the man who died of fright, Joe said he was going to jump out on his Mom's Boyfriend from their wardrobe and see if it worked.

But he never got the chance because Joe's Mom's Boyfriend stopped being her Boyfriend soon after that. And he started being Joe's Babysitter's Boyfriend instead. And Joe never saw him again.

Joe's got a different babysitter now, called Brian.

Anyway, the thing with Joe's Old Rabbit was, it wasn't just *any* old cat that scared it to death. In fact it wasn't an *old* cat at all. It was a *new* cat. *Our* New Cat, which is a wild cat that we got off a farm. And everyone is scared of it: me, and Mom, and even the Milkman. Because the New Cat is a *mad* cat. And it attacks anything it can. The only one who isn't afraid of the New Cat is Tom.

This is a list me and Suzanne made of all the things that the New Cat has killed . . .

ANNA'S AND SUZANNE'S LIST OF THINGS THAT THE NEW CAT HAS KILLED

6 mice

2 frogs (One might have been a toad. After the New Cat got it, it was hard to tell.)

4 blackbirds

2 jackdaws

1 rat

12 spiders

4 moths

1 shrew

3 bees (the New Cat doesn't even mind when it gets stung)

Whenever the New Cat kills something, me and Suzanne do a funeral for it. We put the body in a box, and we bury it in the back lane. We've buried so many things in our bit of the back lane that we've run out of room. So now we have to bury things in Miss Matheson's bit too. Miss Matheson lives next door, on the other side. Our house is between hers and Suzanne's.

Miss Matheson doesn't like it when she sees me and Suzanne burying things in her bit of the back lane.

She shouts, **"YOU GIRLS GET OUT OF IT! THAT'S MY GARDEN, NOT A GRAVEYARD. GET AWAY FROM MY GLADIOLI!"**

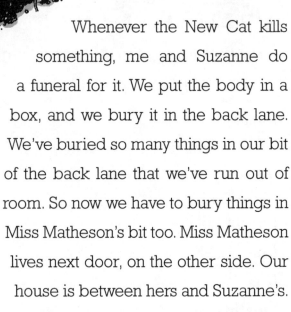

And she phones Mom to complain.

I think we should be allowed to bury whatever we want in Miss Matheson's bit of the back lane. Because Miss Matheson ran over our Old Cat, which never used to kill anything, and if she hadn't done that, we would never have got the New Cat in the first place. And then it wouldn't be here to keep killing things all the time.

CHAPTER 4
You Be the Dog

Joe guards the New Rabbit with a Super Soaker water pistol. Sometimes he marches up and down in front of the hutch with his Super Soaker. And sometimes he stands still by the hutch with his Super Soaker. And sometimes he sits on the hutch with his Super Soaker. And if anything comes anywhere near Joe's garden, like a cat, or

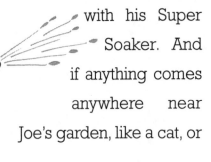

a pigeon, or an ant, Joe blasts it and shouts, "TAKE THAT! AND DON'T EVER COME BACK!"

Before Joe started guarding his rabbit all the time, me and Suzanne and Joe used to do lots of things together, like going on the rope swing at the top of the road, and sliding down the stairs in sleeping bags, and seeing who could hold their breath the longest before they die. And sometimes we played games that everyone knows, like Shops, and Schools, and Prisons, and things. And sometimes we played our own made-up games, like Dingo the Dog, and Mountain Rescue, and breaking the world record on the Super-Speed-Bike-Machine.

Here's what happens in Dingo the Dog. There's a school, for dogs, and Suzanne is the teacher. (Suzanne knows all about dog schools because she used to take her dog

Barney to one, before her Dad said he was allergic and sent Barney to live on a farm.) Anyway, Suzanne tells all the dogs what to do, like "Stay," and "Roll over," and "Heel," and all that. (There aren't real dogs in the class. We just pretend. There's only one real dog on our road, and it belongs to Miss Matheson. It's the same size as a guinea pig, and we aren't allowed to play with it.)

Anyway, there are lots of pretend dogs in the class, and they're all doing what they are told. And I come to the class with my dog, which is a bad dog called Dingo. (It's really Joe-down-the-street, on his hands and knees, with Barney's old collar on and a leash.) And Dingo goes around sniffing all the other dogs, and Suzanne tells him off. And then Dingo spots a dog he really hates, and he barks, and goes crazy, and slips his collar off, and chases the dog around the room, and right out of the class. And I run up and down the road shouting, **"Dingo, Dingo, here, boy!"** and try to get him back. But Dingo hides in the bushes, and howls, and tears up the flower beds, and pees on trees and everything. And all the other dogs in the class go mad and start chasing each other too. And their owners complain, and ask Suzanne for their money back.

It's a pretty good game.

But it's no good without Joe, because no one else can do Dingo. Because Suzanne is only good at telling the dogs what to do. And I'm only good at doing the chasing. And once Tom tried to be Dingo, but he didn't like the leash, and he wasn't any good at being bad. Because he just sat when Suzanne told him to sit, and stayed when she told him to stay. And then, when Suzanne told him he was supposed to be

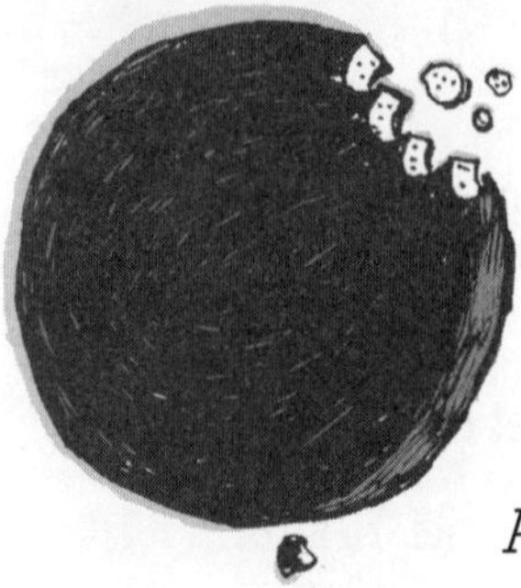

a *bad* dog, he bit her. On the arm. Really hard. And Suzanne screamed. And went home. And Tom had to go in the house and sit with Mom and have a cookie.

And Mom took Tom off the leash, and said, "Best not to play Dingo the Dog anymore, Anna."

Another game we used to play with Joe-down-the-street is the Mountain Rescue Game. We play it inside when it's really raining and we aren't allowed out. We don't play it in Suzanne's house, though, not since her Dad tripped over the rescue rope and went flying down the stairs, and said, **"THIS IS A STAIRCASE, SUZANNE, NOT SNOWDONIA! YOU CHILDREN COULD'VE KILLED ME!"**

Anyway, what happens in Mountain Rescue is, Suzanne goes to the top of the stairs, which is the top of the mountain, because she's best at screaming for help and dangling from the banisters and everything. And me and Joe have to rescue her, and we're tied together with ropes. (It used to be real ropes, but Mom took them away, so now we get tied together with Mom's tights instead.) And Joe has his stopwatch, and he keeps looking at it and saying, "She's only got two minutes of air left at the top before she dies." And things like that.

And then we start climbing up, which takes ages because it's all windy and icy and high. And Joe says, "We're approaching the summit."

And then he says, "AVALANCHE!"

And that's when we fall all the way down. And land at the bottom. And then we have to climb all the way back up again. In the end we bring Suzanne down on a stretcher, which is a sleeping bag. And sometimes she's alive, and other times she's dead. We don't do the Mountain Rescue Game anymore, though, because Joe's the only one with a stopwatch, and last time, when me and Suzanne played Mountain Rescue on our own, when I got to the top, we argued about whether Suzanne was dead or not. Because Suzanne said she was, even though she wasn't. And she wouldn't help me get her down the mountain. And that's why the stretcher slipped and Suzanne went all the way down on her own, and landed on her head. And then she went home.

And Mom said, "Best not to play Mountain Rescue anymore, Anna."

And we aren't allowed on the Super-Speed-Bike-Machine anymore either. The Super-Speed-Bike-Machine is my bike, with Joe's stunt pegs on the back wheel for standing on, and Tom's old training wheels on the sides, and Suzanne's trailer tied on behind. Before Joe's Dad stopped living at Joe's house, me and Suzanne and Joe-down-the-street used to work on the Super-Speed-Bike-Machine all the time, cleaning it, and putting spokies on the wheels, and streamers on the handlebars, and stickers on the crossbar, and painting the trailer, and pumping up the tires, and repairing the punctures, and all that. And after we worked on it, we would take it right up to the top of the back lane, by Miss Matheson's garden, which used to drive her dog mad, and

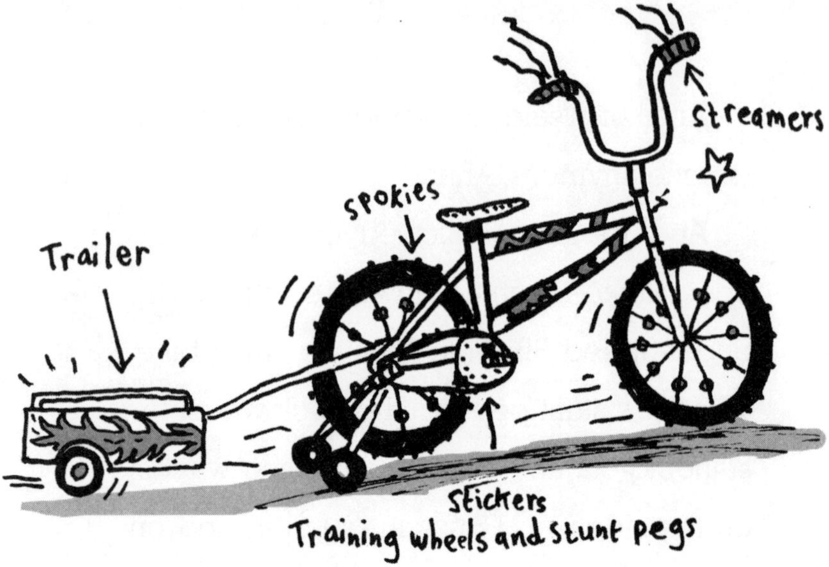

Miss Matheson would run out and shout, "YOU KIDS GET THAT CONTRAPTION AWAY FROM MY GATE!"

And then I would get on the seat, and Suzanne would sit on the handlebars, and Joe would stand on the stunt pegs, and Tom would kneel in the trailer, and Joe's Dad would stand at the bottom of the back lane. And we'd all say, "THREE, TWO, ONE, BLAST OFF!"

And then Joe pushed off from the stunt

pegs, and Suzanne leaned back, and Tom held tight to the trailer, and I pedaled my fastest, and we all went flying down the back lane, over the hump, right to the bottom, where Joe put his foot out to slow the Super-Speed-Bike-Machine down, and Joe's Dad grabbed hold to stop us from going into the road. And then we checked the seconds on the stopwatch, and if it was a world record, we put it in the record book. And if it wasn't, we went all the way back up to the top and did it again. And sometimes we did it all day.

Once, after Joe's Dad stopped living at Joe's house, and Joe's Old Rabbit died, and Joe started guarding his New Rabbit all the time, me and Suzanne and Tom went on the Super-Speed-Bike-Machine on our own. But Joe wasn't there to put his foot out at the end to slow us down, and his Dad wasn't there to grab the Super-Speed-Bike-Machine and stop it from going in the road, and it did go in the road, and it only stopped when it hit the curb on the other side, and then Tom flew out of the trailer, and the Super-Speed-Bike-Machine went over on its side, and a van had to screech to a stop. And Tom had to go to the hospital and get six sticky stitches in his head.

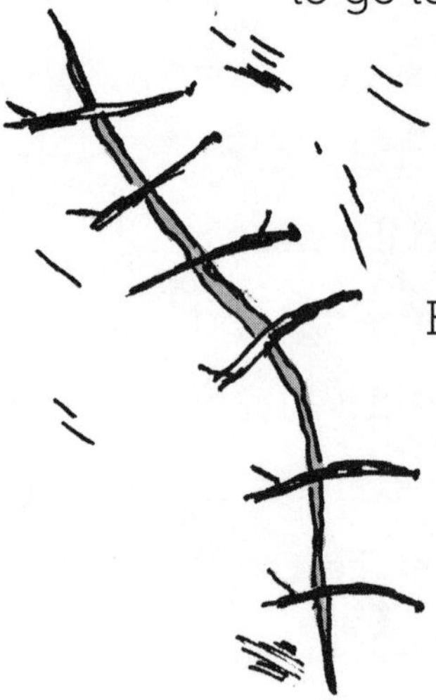

And Mom said, "Best not to go on the Super-Speed-Bike-Machine again, Anna."

And she put it at the back of the shed, under an old sheet, behind the stepladders, and the plant stakes, and the broken old floorboards.

Anyway, when Joe first started guarding the New Rabbit, me and Suzanne sometimes used to go and guard it with him. Joe told us all the rules, and we took our Super Soakers and we marched up and down and blasted anything that moved. But after a while, especially when nothing much came except squirrels and starlings and daddy longlegs and things, me and Suzanne got sick of guarding the New Rabbit.

And we said, "Let's go and do something else, like make plans, or do Dizzy Ducklings, or sit on the shed roof instead."

But Joe always said, "No."

And one day, when Tom came to guard the New Rabbit with us, Joe said that Tom wasn't allowed in his garden because of him liking the New Cat. And he blasted Tom with the Super Soaker and said, **"Take that! And don't ever come back!"**

And Tom fell over. And he ran up the

road. And me and Joe argued after that. And Joe's Mom sent me home. And I got in Big Trouble. Even though it was Joe's fault in the first place, because, like I said, "It's not Tom's fault that the New Cat is his friend!"

But Mom said she didn't care, because, "Whatever happens, Anna, you don't beat people about the head with Super Soakers."

And after that I didn't go and see Joe-down-the-street and guard the New Rabbit much anymore. Apart from when Mom made me. Because I'd rather do other things. Like going on the walkie-talkies, or doing funerals, or finding wood lice. And, anyway, me and Suzanne had our clubs to do, which no one else was allowed in.

TOP
SECRET
CLUB
IN PROGRESS

ANNA'S AND SUZANNE'S CLUBS THAT NO ONE ELSE (EXCEPT SOMETIMES TOM) IS ALLOWED IN

1. Shed Club

Make up a password

Don't let anyone in who doesn't know the password (except Tom when he forgets it)

Make plans

Don't tell anyone the plans

2. Worm Club

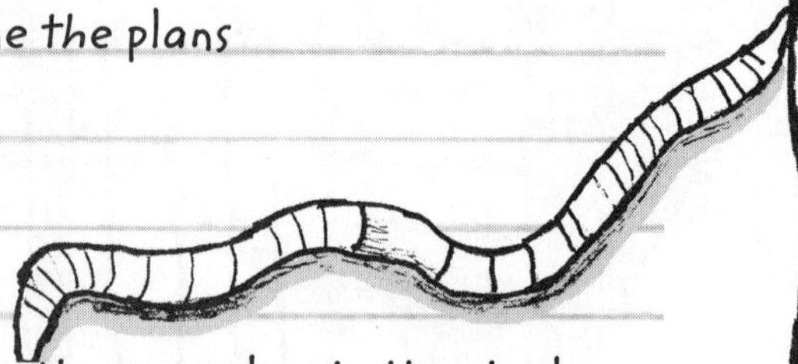

Collect worms

Put the worms in the worm box in the shed

Write down how many worms there are in the record book (most number of worms in a day so far = 43)

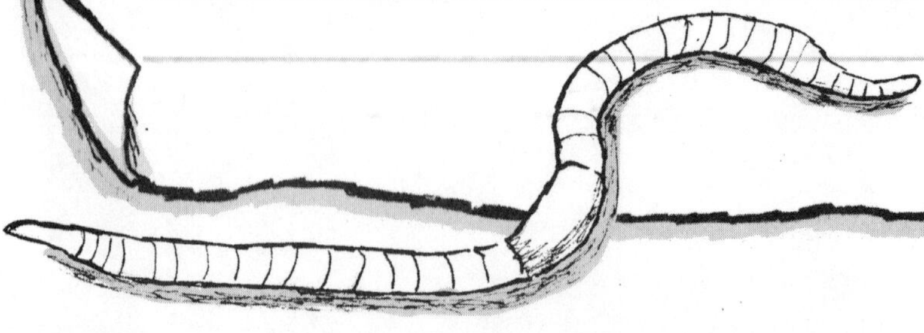

3. Bug Club

Same as Worm Club but with bugs instead of worms

Cover the bugs with a lid or they get away

Put holes in the lid or they die

4. Spy Club

Spy on people with the binoculars Mrs. Rotherham gave us

Write what people are up to in the notepad

People we have got pages on in the notepad are . . .

1. Miss Matheson
2. The Lollipop Lady
3. Mr. Tucker
4. Suzanne's Dad
5. Joe's Mom
6. Joe's Mom's Old Boyfriend
7. Joe's Old Babysitter

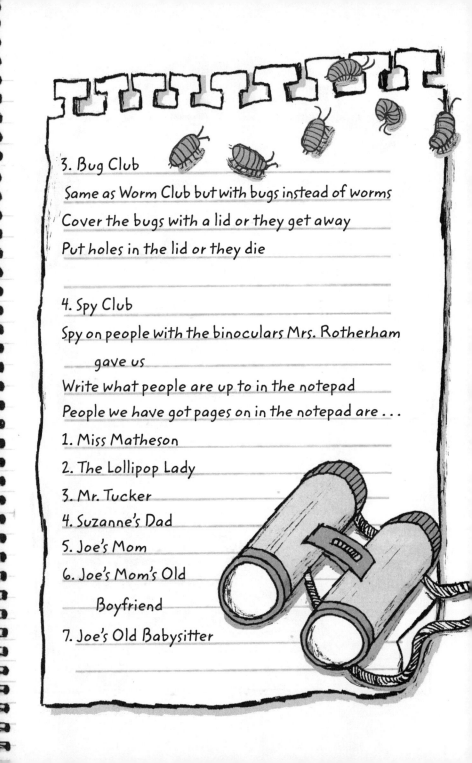

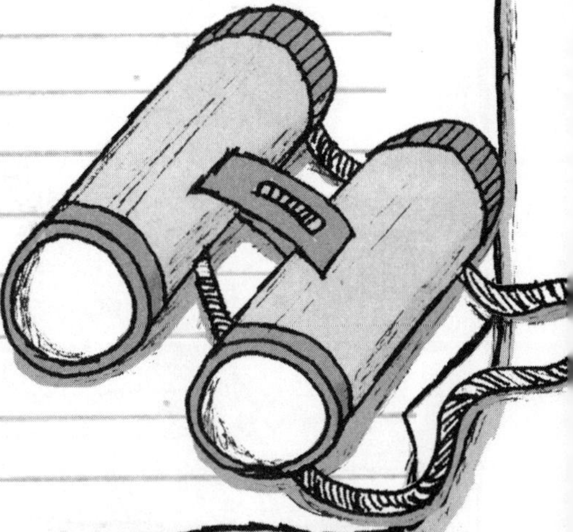

Me and Suzanne aren't supposed to do Spy Club anymore because last time Miss Matheson saw us looking in at her through her window, and she phoned Mom to complain.

And Mom said, "It's rude to spy on people and write down what they're doing, Anna. Especially when they're in the bathroom."

And she said if she found out that we were doing Spy Club again, we would be in Big Trouble.

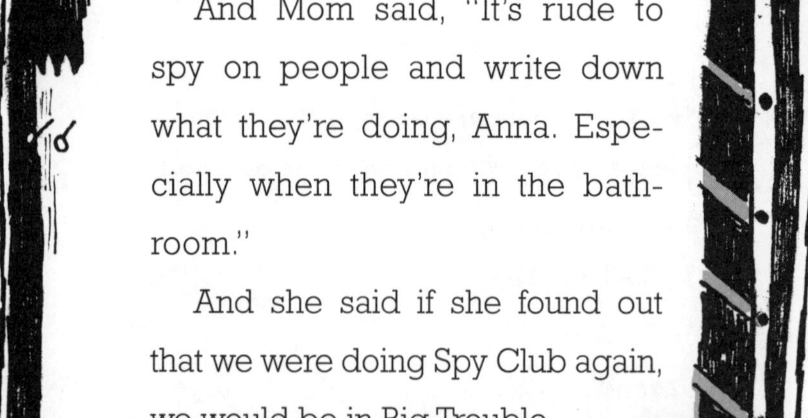

So we put the binoculars and the notepad away, at the back of the shed, on the shelf above the broken floorboards and the stepladders and the Super-Speed-Bike-Machine.

Sometimes Tom does clubs with me and Suzanne, except Worm Club, because he says worms wriggle his skin, but most of the time he forgets he's meant to be looking for weevils and wood lice and things, and goes to see Mom and get a cookie, or to talk to Mr. Tucker about his old sports car instead. Doing clubs is pretty good, and so is sitting on the shed roof, and going on the walkie-talkies and things, but not as good as before, when Joe didn't have to guard his rabbit, and Joe's Dad was still on the road, and we did Dingo the Dog, and Mountain Rescue, and going on the Super-Speed-Bike-Machine.

CHAPTER 5
A Rabbit Pie Chart

Joe couldn't guard his New Rabbit *all* the time though, because, like his Mom said, "Sometimes you have to do other things, Joe, like sleep, and eat, and go to school."

But whenever he *wasn't* doing those sorts of things, Joe stayed in his garden, because he said, "The less time the New Rabbit gets guarded, the more chance there is of the New Rabbit getting got."

Which is probably true.

But some people didn't think Joe needed

to guard his New Rabbit at all. Mrs. Peters told Joe that she didn't think so, the day we made pie chart mobiles at school.

That morning Mrs. Peters said, "Right, everyone. Here is a math problem. There are twenty-four hours in a day. If Janet spends ten hours in bed, and six hours at school, how many hours has Janet got left for doing other things?"

And she wrote it on the whiteboard. Some people put their hands up, like Emma Hendry, but not Joe, because even though Joe is good at math, he isn't very good at putting his hand up. Which is different from Emma Hendry. Because Emma Hendry is good at putting her hand up, but she isn't very good at math.

Anyway, even though Joe didn't put his hand up, Mrs. Peters said, "Joe, why don't you have a go?"

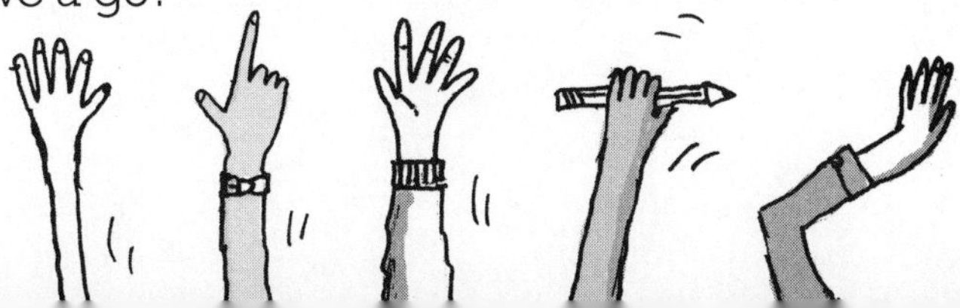

And Joe said, "Twenty-four hours minus ten hours sleeping equals fourteen hours; and fourteen hours minus six hours at school equals eight hours, so Janet's got eight hours left to do what she wants."

And he said it really fast. Just like that. And he was right, because Mrs. Peters said, "Very good. Well done, Joe."

And she wrote it on the board like this:

$$24-10=14$$
$$14-6=8$$

I didn't get that answer. I didn't get any answer, because for one thing, I'm even worse at math than Emma Hendry is, especially if I have to do it in my head. And for another thing, Mrs. Peters had said here is *a* math problem and that was actually *two* problems. And for an even other thing, Graham Roberts, who sits next to me, drew a picture in his book of a girl called Janet.

And he drew some fumes coming off Janet's bum, and he wrote, **Janet has eight hours a day to drop bum bombs.** And I got The Hysterics. And

Mrs. Peters said I had to go and stand outside the classroom and do deep breathing until I calmed down.

When I came back, Mrs. Peters drew a big circle on the whiteboard, and she said that the circle was "a day." And she drew twenty-four slices in the circle, which was "one for each hour." And she colored some of the slices in to show the different things Janet did in a day. And she said it was called a "pie chart."

This is what Mrs. Peters's pie chart of Janet's day looked like:

In the afternoon Mrs. Peters helped us all do our own pie charts. And we could put anything we liked in them. Mine was like this:

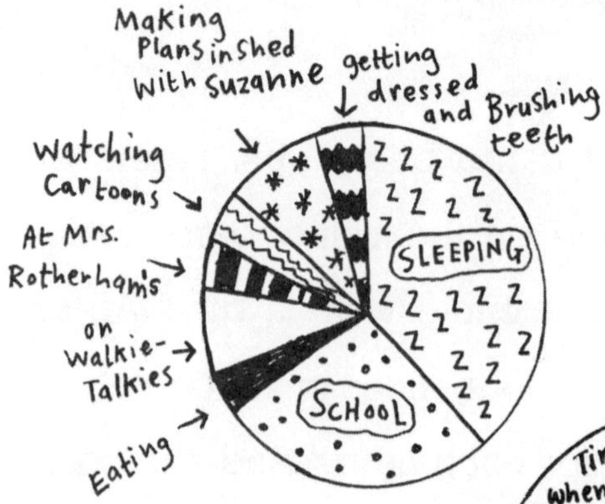

And Joe's was like this:

Later on we colored our pie charts in. Mrs. Peters said our pie charts were so good, she was going to cut them out and put a string through each one and hang them from the ceiling to make mobiles. Emma Hendry asked Mrs. Peters why pie charts are called pie charts. And Mrs. Peters said it's because they look like pies. Which is true. They don't taste like pies, though, because Graham Roberts licked his. And he got blue felt-tip all over his tongue. And I got The Hysterics again. And Mrs. Peters sent me back out of the classroom. And Graham Roberts had to put his tongue under the tap.

When the bell rang, Mrs. Peters said she wanted to talk to Joe about his pie chart and some other work he'd done, like his poem about the rabbit that dies when it gets dark, and his story about the rabbit that can't get to sleep, and his painting of the rabbit being guarded with guns. Me and Suzanne stayed behind to wait for Joe, to walk home. Mrs. Peters told Joe he wasn't in trouble. She said she just wondered whether he might be worried about something. Like his rabbit, maybe.

Joe told Mrs. Peters that he wasn't worried. And Mrs. Peters asked if he was sure.

And Joe said, "Yes."

And Mrs. Peters said that that was good. Because she didn't think that Joe needed to worry about his rabbit. Because she thought his rabbit was very safe.

"Because," she said, "rabbits are pretty tough, you know, Joe."

And Joe said, "I know."

Even though he didn't really think so.

Mrs. Peters asked me and Suzanne what we thought.

And I said, "*Some* rabbits are tough."

And Suzanne said, "Joe's Old Rabbit wasn't. It got scared to death by Anna's Cat."

"Did it?" said Mrs. Peters.

And Suzanne said, "Yes."

And Mrs. Peters asked, "How?"

And Suzanne told her, "In its hutch."

"Oh. I see. That's not very nice, is it?"

And Suzanne said, "No."

Because it wasn't. Especially not for Joe. Or the Old Rabbit.

Mrs. Peters asked, "Do you want to tell me about your Old Rabbit, Joe?"

And Joe said, "No."

And Mrs. Peters said, "Okay."

And then she said that she thought that what had happened to Joe's Old Rabbit was "very sad and very bad luck." But she didn't think that it meant that something bad was going to happen to Joe's *New* Rabbit. Because she thought that it was "a one-off." Which is when something only happens once. And then she said, "Lightning doesn't strike twice, as they say."

Joe didn't say anything.

Mrs. Peters said, "What do you think, Joe?"

And Joe said, "Okay."

And Mrs. Peters smiled at Joe and said, "Okay, then." And she gave him a stroke on the head, which Mrs. Peters doesn't normally do. And then she said, "Have a good weekend." Because it was Friday. And me and Suzanne and Joe walked home.

On the way, I asked Joe if he was going to stop guarding his New Rabbit now.

And Joe said, "No. Mrs. Peters is wrong about lightning not striking twice, because there was a man in America called Roy Sullivan who got struck by lightning seven times."

And that's true, because I looked on the computer when I got home, and before he died, Roy Sullivan was always getting struck by lightning. And his wife got struck by lightning too. So if anyone ever says that lightning doesn't strike twice, they're wrong. Because sometimes it does. And sometimes it strikes seven times, like it did with Roy Sullivan. And that's why they called him "The Human Lightbulb."

I told Suzanne what it said on the computer about people getting struck by lightning millions of times and everything. And about Roy Sullivan. And how he was the human lightbulb and all that. And I said, "Want to see?"

And Suzanne said, "No."

And I said, "Oh."

And Suzanne said, "I already know."

Suzanne always says she already knows when you try to tell her things.

I said, "Well, Roy Sullivan and his wife aren't the only ones, because there are lots of people who've got struck by lightning twice, like his wife, and lots of trees too."

And Suzanne said, "I know" again.

And I said, "No, you don't."

Because she didn't.

And Suzanne said she did know actually, and even if she *didn't* know, she didn't care. Because what she *really* didn't know was why everyone kept going on about lightning all the time. Like me, and Joe, and Mrs. Peters.

Because, she said, "Lightning hasn't even got anything to do with it, because it isn't lightning that Joe is guarding the New Rabbit from. It's other things, like cats!"

I said I wouldn't show Suzanne anything on the computer ever again. Or tell her any more things about anything. Especially not Roy Sullivan. Not even if she asked.

CHAPTER 6
Joe-Down-the-Street's Dad's Van

Sometimes me and Suzanne go down to the bottom of the back lane, and we take the walkie-talkies, and we stand back-to-back. And Suzanne walks *down* the road, and I walk *up* the road, because we want to know how far apart we can go before the walkie-talkies stop working. When we've gone twenty

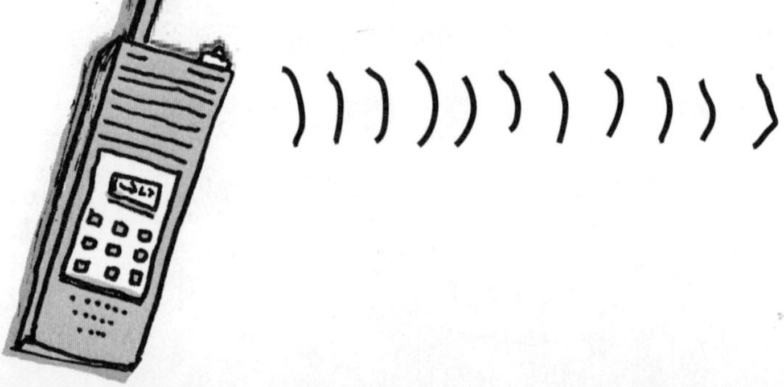

steps apart, we stop, and Suzanne says, "Suzanne to Anna. Suzanne to Anna. Come in, Anna. What's your position? Over."

And I say, "Anna to Suzanne. Anna to Suzanne. I'm at the chestnut tree. Over."

And then Suzanne says, "Copy that. Chestnut tree. Are you receiving me? Over."

And I say, "Yes. Over."

And then Suzanne says, "You're supposed to say, 'Receiving you loud and clear. Over.'"

And I say, "Oh. Receiving you loud and clear. Over."

And Suzanne says, "Copy that. Over and out."

And then we walk twenty more steps apart, and say the same stuff

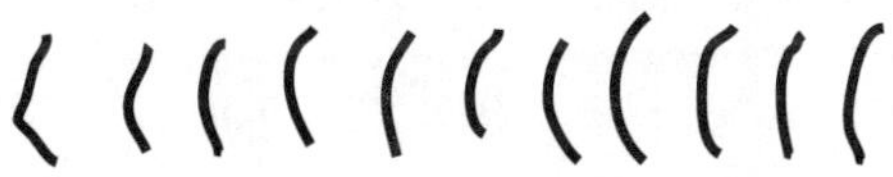

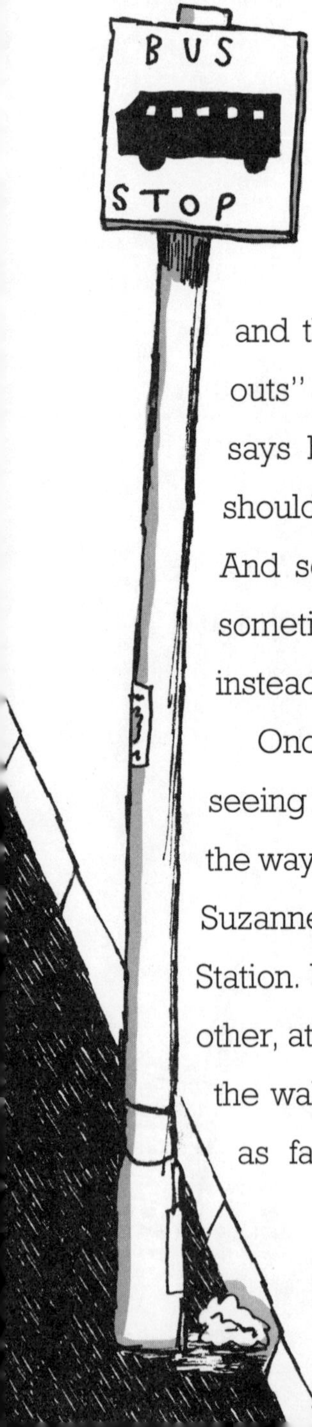

again, about where we are, and whether we can hear each other and everything. Only I don't always do all the "Come ins," and the "Copies," and the "Over and outs" and all that, even though Suzanne says her Uncle in the army said you should. Because sometimes I forget. And sometimes it takes too long. And sometimes I'd rather say something else instead.

Once, when me and Suzanne were seeing how far apart we could go, I got all the way down to the Bottom Bus Stop, and Suzanne got all the way up to the Police Station. Which are *ages* apart from each other, at opposite ends of the village, and the walkie-talkies still worked. But that's as far apart as we've got, because

Suzanne's not allowed past the Police Station, or the Bottom Bus Stop, because her Dad says it's **"OUT OF BOUNDS!"**

I don't know if I'm allowed past the Police Station or the Bottom Bus Stop or not. My Dad has never said anything about bounds to me before. I probably am, though. I'm normally allowed to do more things than Suzanne.

Because even though Suzanne's Mom doesn't mind Suzanne doing most things, like going out of the back lane, or not taking a coat, or doing relay races up the road in bare feet, Suzanne's Dad minds Suzanne doing a *lot* of things. And if it was only up to him, Suzanne probably wouldn't be allowed to do anything at all. Except eat her dinner, and brush her teeth, and go to bed, and things like that. Suzanne's Dad is different from my Dad. If you ask my Dad if you can do something, he says, "You can play on the highway as far as I'm concerned, Anna. But you'd better ask your Mom."

But Suzanne's Dad just says, **"NO!"**

And he's not the sort of Dad you can say, "*Ahhhh, but whyyYYYyy, though, Dad? PleeEEase?*" to. Because he won't change his mind. He'll only say, **"RIGHT, THAT'S IT. ROOM!"**

Anyway, this time we didn't get anywhere near the Bottom Bus Stop and the Police Station because we were just standing back-to-back at the bottom of our road, ready to go, when we saw Joe's Dad's van coming.

We knew it was Joe's Dad's van because it said BARRY WALKER: SMALL BUILDING WORKS, RENOVATION, AND REFURBISHMENT on the side.

The van stopped right outside Joe's

house, where it always used to stop when Joe's Dad still lived there. So me and Suzanne stopped doing the walkie-talkie testing and decided to do some spying instead. Because, even though we aren't supposed to do Spy Club anymore because Mom says we're banned, sometimes we *have* to do it if it's really important.

Suzanne ran up the road and got the binoculars, and the notepad, and we turned the walkie-talkies off and crouched down low behind a car at the bottom of the road. Suzanne looked round from behind the car through the binoculars.

"What can you see?" I said.

"Joe's Dad's hair."

Suzanne passed the binoculars to me.

She was right. You *could* see Joe's Dad's hair. And you couldn't see much else. Because for one thing we were too close to Joe's Dad to really need the binoculars. Because the whole point of binoculars is that they are for looking at things that are far away. And for another thing, Joe's Dad has got a lot of hair. It's long and brown and curly.

"He's got split ends," Suzanne said. "And he's going gray." She wrote in the notepad: Saturday, 9:45 a.m. Joe's Dad outside Joe's house in his van.

And then she put: Split ends. Going gray.

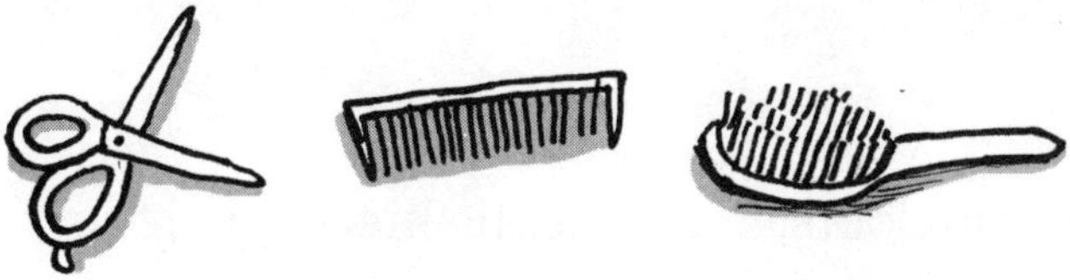

Suzanne knows all about hair because her Mom is a hairdresser.

Suzanne's Mom cut Joe's Dad's hair when he still lived on our road. When Joe's Dad stopped living on our road, Suzanne's Mom said to my Mom, "What a shame."

And my Mom said, "I know. Such a lovely man."

And Suzanne's Mom said, "And such lovely hair."

And my Mom said, "Yeah."

And they both shook their heads for ages.

Suzanne's Mom cuts my Dad's hair too, and Suzanne's Dad's. She doesn't say *they've* got lovely hair, though. My Dad and Suzanne's Dad are mostly bald.

Anyway, Joe's Dad got out of his van, and he went round to the back of it and opened the van doors, and took out three big brown boxes, and he carried the boxes up the path to Joe's house, and he rang on Joe's doorbell and went inside.

Suzanne wrote down: 9:48 a.m. Joe's Dad takes three big brown boxes into Joe's house.

"Maybe Joe's Dad has come back to live at Joe's house," said Suzanne.

And I said I hoped he had. Because then he would fix the rope swing at the top of the road, where the rope was caught up and the tire had come off.

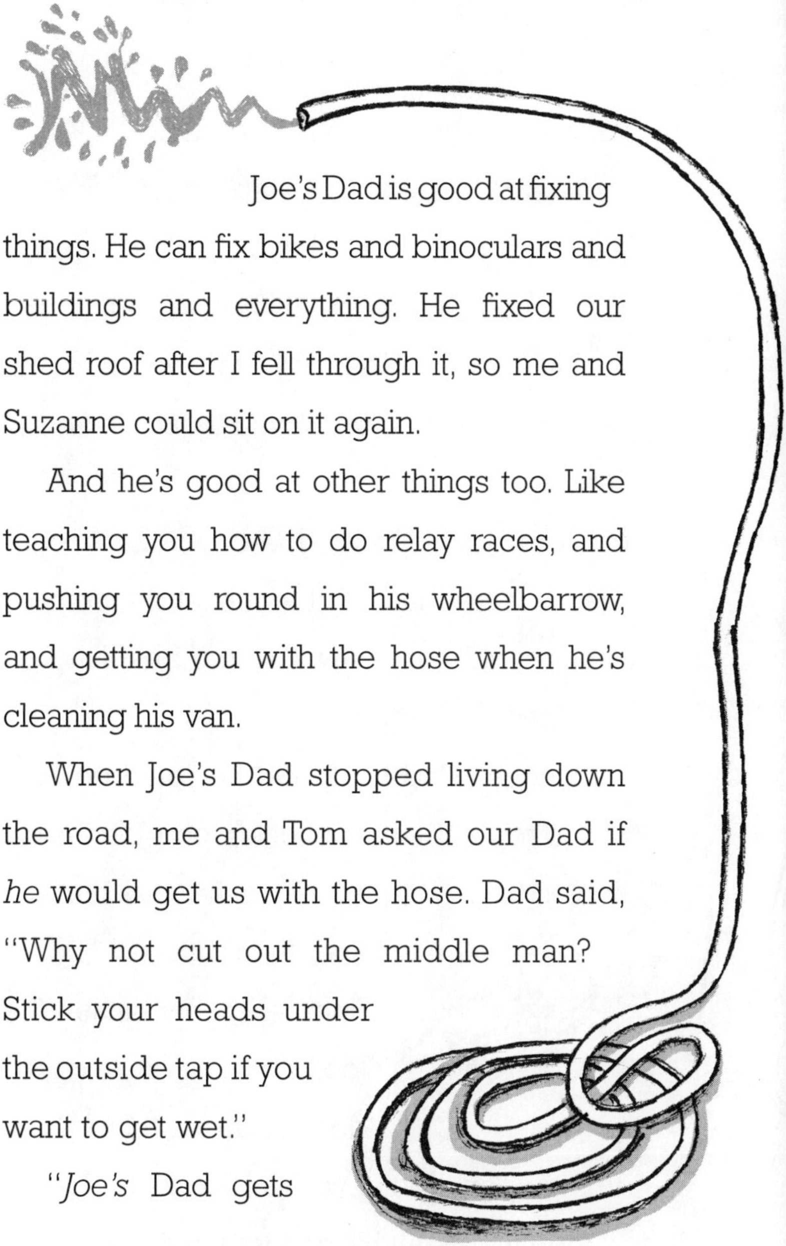

Joe's Dad is good at fixing things. He can fix bikes and binoculars and buildings and everything. He fixed our shed roof after I fell through it, so me and Suzanne could sit on it again.

And he's good at other things too. Like teaching you how to do relay races, and pushing you round in his wheelbarrow, and getting you with the hose when he's cleaning his van.

When Joe's Dad stopped living down the road, me and Tom asked our Dad if *he* would get us with the hose. Dad said, "Why not cut out the middle man? Stick your heads under the outside tap if you want to get wet."

"*Joe's* Dad gets

us with the hose," I said. "It's fun."

"Yeah, yeah, yeah," Dad said. "I used to be fun. And I used to have hair."

I asked Dad when his hair fell out.

Dad said, "The day you were born." And then he laughed. Even though it wasn't funny.

Tom told Dad, "Joe-down-the-street's Dad has got hair, and a van, and a cement mixer, and that's why he's the best Dad on the road."

"Right!" Dad said. And he grabbed Tom and tickled him. But not for long, because if you tickle Tom too much, he wets himself. And then he gets upset. And also because the football came on. And Dad doesn't do anything when that happens. Except drink his beer and shout at the TV, and put his hands over his eyes.

Anyway, me and Suzanne were crouching quietly behind the car at the bottom of the road, waiting to see what happened.

And then Tom came running down the road, and he saw us and he shouted, **"WHAT ARE YOU DOING?"**

"Shh," I said, "we're spying. Get down."

And Tom got down behind the car as well.

Joe's Dad came out of Joe's house, holding one of the big brown boxes. He went round to the back of the van, and he opened the doors and put the box in the van.

And Tom stood up, and he said, "Hello."

Joe's Dad looked around to see where the voice had come from.

"Tom!" I whispered. "Get down!"

But he didn't. Tom doesn't really care about spying. He cares more about other things, like Joe's Dad's van.

"Hello, lad," said Joe's Dad.

"Can I go in your van?" Tom said.

"Ah, not today, Tommy."

"Why?" Tom said.

Because that's Tom's favorite question. And because Joe's Dad always used to let him get in his van and look at all the tools, and once he let Tom put sand in the cement mixer. And that was about the best thing Tom had ever done. Except for when Mr. Tucker let Tom sit on his knee in the driver's seat of his old sports car and put his driving gloves and goggles on. And drive up and down the road, and honk the horn.

Anyway, Joe's Dad said, "Bit busy today. Next time, eh, Tom? Promise."

And Tom said, "Okay."

And they shook on it. And Joe's Dad went back into Joe's house. And Tom went to talk to Mr. Tucker. Mr. Tucker is never too busy. Especially not for Tom.

Me and Suzanne stayed waiting. After a while Joe's Dad came out of Joe's house again with another brown box. And he went round the back of the van, and opened the doors, and put it in. And then he went back into the house, and got the last brown box and put that in the van too. He shut the van doors. And got in the van himself.

And then Joe and his Mom came out of the house. And Joe went over to his rabbit hutch, and he checked the latch, and arranged his plastic soldiers on the roof, and then he got his Super Soaker, and he pumped it up, and blasted some ants. And

then he gave his Mom a cuddle. And he got in the van, in the front, next to his Dad. And he put his seat belt on. And then he took his seat belt off again, and he got out of the van. And he went over to the rabbit hutch. And checked the latch again. And rearranged his plastic soldiers.

And then Joe's Dad got out of the van too. And he talked to Joe's Mom for a bit, and he gave Joe a cuddle. And then Joe's Dad got back in the van by himself. And he drove away.

And Joe ran out of his garden, down the road after the van. And the van stopped. And Joe got in it. And the van drove off. And Joe looked out the window. Me and Suzanne waved at Joe, but Joe didn't wave back.

When Joe and Joe's Dad and the van were gone, Joe's Mom sat down on the doorstep by herself. Suzanne looked through the binoculars. And she wrote in the book: 10:45 a.m. Joe-down-the-street 's Mom sits down on the step and cries.

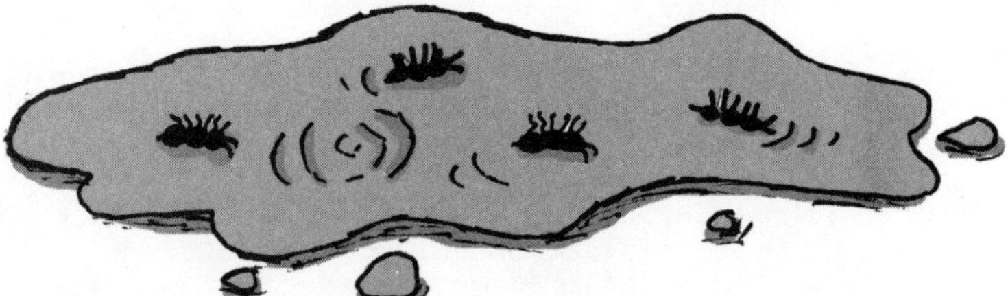

CHAPTER 7
The Tale of Peter Rabbit

Me and Suzanne told my Mom all about Joe's Dad, and his van, and Joe, and the boxes.

Mom said, "Oh, poor Pam." (Which is Joe's Mom's name.)

I asked, "Why?"

"Never mind," Mom said. "I'm popping down the road."

"What for?"

"Nothing."

"Are you going to spy?" asked Suzanne.

"No, Suzanne," Mom said, "I am not going to spy. I'm just going to see Joe's Mom."

And I said, "We'll come."

"No," Mom said, "you won't."

Suzanne asked Mom, "Why?"

"Because I want to talk to Pam on my own," Mom said. And off she went.

When Mom came back, after ages, me and Suzanne were waiting for her on the garden wall.

"Where has Joe gone?" I asked.

Mom said, "To stay with his Dad."

Me and Suzanne followed Mom into the house.

Suzanne asked, "Where's that?"

"Not far," Mom said. "At his apartment."

"In the village?" I asked.

And Mom said, "Not quite. Over the bridge."

Which *is* far. It's ages. Because you have to go on the bus, or at least on a bike.

"Why has he gone?" Suzanne asked.

And Mom said, "I don't know."

I asked, "How long has he gone for?"

And Mom said, "I don't know."

And Suzanne said, "What about his rabbit?"

And Mom said, "For goodness' sake, girls, I don't *know*!"

And I told Mom she should have let me and Suzanne go with her to Joe's house, because she had hardly found out anything about Joe, or his rabbit. Because she hadn't asked the right questions. And she probably only asked Joe's Mom about work, and the weather, and washing, and things like that.

So I said, "Come on, Suzanne."

And Mom said, "Where are you going?"

And I said, "To see Joe-down-the-street's Mom to ask her when Joe will be coming back, and what is going to happen with his rabbit while he's gone, of course."

And Mom said, "No, Anna, you are not. Here, have an ice pop. Go out the back. And don't bother anyone, *especially* not Joe's Mom."

So me and Suzanne went outside with our ice pops. And we climbed up on the shed roof and ate them up there. And when they were finished, we lay flat on our backs to see how long we could stare at the sun. Graham Roberts says if you stare straight at the sun, you go blind. But me and Suzanne tried it one day, at exactly the same time, so

that if we did go blind, it would be together. And afterward we could still see fine. When we told Graham Roberts, he said we mustn't have stared for long enough.

Anyway, we didn't stare very long this time because there were too many clouds so it didn't count. So we sat up and dangled our legs over the edge of the shed instead. And we tried to think of things to do. Which was hard, because the rope swing was broken and we weren't allowed to do Spy Club or Mountain Rescue, or Dingo the Dog, or go on the Super-Speed-Bike-Machine. And we were sick of doing Worm Club and Bug Club and Shed Club and all that.

Suzanne said she wondered what Joe was doing now. And I said I wondered too. Because even though we hadn't done anything with Joe for ages, I didn't really mind not doing things with Joe when I knew that he was down the road, guarding his rabbit. But now that I didn't know *what* Joe was doing, or when he was coming back, I couldn't stop wondering. Like when Mom gave my old teddy to Mrs. Constantine for the Sunday School Jumble Sale. Because before she gave it away, I forgot I even had it. But afterward I kept thinking about the teddy all the time, and how it was mine, and how it was meant to be in my toy box, and how I wanted it back.

Suzanne said we should never have told my Mom about Joe's Dad and his van and the boxes and all that. Because before we told her, we could have gone and asked Joe's Mom whatever questions we wanted. But now we couldn't because Mom had said we were banned.

We got down off the shed because it was starting to rain. And we went inside the shed, and sat on the boxes, and listened to the rain on the roof, and wondered about Joe, and what he was up to, and whether anything bad had happened to his rabbit since he had gone. And I said I thought it probably hadn't, because Joe only went about an hour ago, and Suzanne said I was probably right, but it would be nice to know for certain. Which was true. Then there was a knock on the shed door.

Suzanne looked through the spy hole (which is a knot in the wood that you can pop in and out).

"It's Tom," she said.

Tom put his eye to the spy hole and said, "Hello."

Suzanne said, "What's the password?"

"I don't know," said Tom. "What is it?"

And then me and Suzanne remembered we had forgotten to make one up. Which we never normally do because making up the password is the first rule of Shed Club.

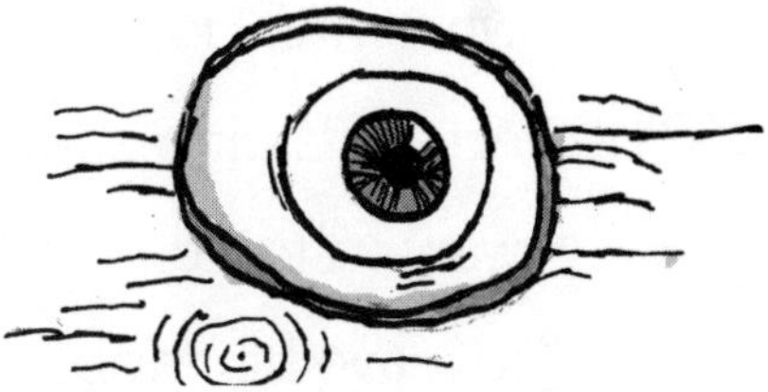

So Suzanne told Tom to guess.

And Tom guessed, "Open sesame."

Which is what he always says, and Suzanne said, "Yes."

And Tom was very pleased, because "Open sesame" had never been right before.

We let Tom in, and we told him all about Joe, and how he had got in the van with his Dad, and the boxes, and how he got out again. And how his Dad had driven away. And how Joe chased his Dad down the road. And how they drove away together. And how he didn't take his rabbit with him. And how Mom said Joe had gone to stay with his Dad, in an apartment, over the bridge. And how we didn't know why, or for how long, or what was going to happen to Joe's rabbit. And Suzanne said that she didn't think Joe wanted to go. And I said that he didn't want to leave his rabbit.

And Tom said, "Joe didn't want to go, and he didn't want to leave his rabbit, but he really, really, really didn't want to be left behind."

And Tom was probably right, because being left behind is one of Tom's worst things, so he knows all about it.

Because, when Tom was little, if Mom wanted to go somewhere without him, Dad had to take Tom out of the house first so that Tom was the one doing the leaving, not the one being left. Otherwise, if Tom was in the house and he found out that Mom had gone somewhere and left him behind, he would stand at the door and look through the letter box and cry until she came home.

But the thing about taking Tom out, even just to the shops, is that you have to do a lot of other things on the way, like talking to Mr. Tucker, and walking on the wall, and wetting your wellies in the horse trough. So that's why, if Mom only wants to buy an onion or something, she tries to sneak out before Tom notices.

And then she runs down the road as fast as she can. Most of the time Mom doesn't get that far, though, because, like she says, "Tom has got supersonic ears."

And he nearly always hears the door handle turn, even from upstairs.

And then he runs down, quick, and puts his wellies on, and says, "Are you going out?"

And Mom says, "Oh, for goodness' sake, Tom, I'm only going to get an onion."

And Tom says, "I'll come."

And she has to take him with her. Because if she doesn't, Tom gets what Nana used to call "The Screaming Habdabs," where he screams, and cries, and bangs his fists on the door, and dribbles all over the doormat.

Anyway, me and Suzanne told Tom how we wanted to know why Joe had gone to his Dad's, and when he was coming back, and what was going to happen to his rabbit while he was gone. And how we couldn't ask Joe's Mom about it because Mom had said we were banned.

And Tom said, "*I'm* not banned."

Which was true. So we decided that Tom should go instead. And Suzanne said we better make sure Tom knew exactly what to ask Joe's Mom first, before he went. And she wrote it all down on the notepad.

SUZANNE'S AND ANNA'S LIST OF THINGS FOR TOM TO ASK JOE'S MOM

1. Why has Joe gone to his Dad's?
2. When is Joe coming back?
3. What is going to happen to Joe's rabbit?

Tom looked at the list for a while, and then he said, "What does it say?"

Because even though Tom goes to school, and he knows all his letters, he's only in kindergarten, and he doesn't really know what the letters say when you put them all together. So I said that Suzanne should just tell Tom what to say, and Tom would remember. And Tom said that was a good idea, because even though he isn't a very good *reader* yet, he is a *very* good rememberer. So that is what we did.

"Right," Suzanne said. "The shed is Joe's house, and Anna is Joe's Mom."

And Tom had to go out of the shed and knock on the door. And I answered it as Joe's Mom. And Suzanne told Tom exactly what he should say. And this is how it went:

Tom: "Hello."

Me being Joe's Mom: "Hello."

Tom: "How are you?"

Me being Joe's Mom: "Fine."

Tom: "Why has Joe gone to his Dad's?"

Me being Joe's Mom: "For a vacation."

Tom: "When will he be coming back?"

Me being Joe's Mom: "On Thursday."

Tom: "What about his rabbit?"

Me being Joe's Mom: "He will be back in a minute to take it with him."

Tom: "Thank you, Joe's Mom. Bye."

We practiced it again and again. And Suzanne told me to say different answers every time because she said, "Who knows what answers Joe's Mom might say."

Which was true. And she said it was best for Tom to get used to Joe's Mom saying all sorts of answers so he wouldn't get flustered and forget everything if she said something he didn't expect. We practiced it over and over again until Tom said all the questions exactly right, every time.

And, after about a million times, Suzanne said, "Tom is ready."

And Tom was pleased, because he said, "I'm a *very* good rememberer."

And we went off down the road.

Tom knocked on Joe's door. And me and Suzanne crouched behind the hedge.

And Joe's Mom answered the door and said, "Hello, Tom." Just like we thought.

And Tom said, "Hello, Joe's Mom. How are you?" Just like he was supposed to.

And Joe's Mom said, "Oh, I don't know, Tom, not very good."

And Tom said, "Oh."

And then he said, "Can I have a cookie?"

Which he was not supposed to say.

And Joe's Mom said, "Umm . . . Have you had your lunch?"

And Tom said, "No."

And Joe's Mom said, "You shouldn't really."

And Tom said, "Just a plain one."

And Joe's Mom said, "Okay."

And she went in the house and she brought the cookies out and she said, "Shall I have one with you?"

And Tom said, "Have you had your lunch?"

And Joe's Mom said, "No."

And Tom said, "Okay."

And they sat down on the doorstep. And they got a cookie each. And Tom had a bite of his cookie. And Joe's Mom had a bite of her cookie. And

Tom had a bite of his cookie. And Joe's Mom had a bite of her cookie. And they took turns having bites like that until their cookies were finished.

And then Tom said, "Shall we have a story?"

And Joe's Mom said, "Okay."

And she went and got some books, and Tom picked *Peter Rabbit* because, he said, "*Peter Rabbit* is one of my favorites."

And Joe's Mom said it was one of Joe's favorites too, when he was Tom's age. And they sat on the step. And Joe's Mom read *Peter Rabbit*. And when it was finished, they had another cookie, and they took it in turn to have bites.

And then Tom said, "Shall we have *Peter Rabbit* again?"

And Joe's Mom said, "All right."

And she read *Peter Rabbit* again. And she cuddled Tom in, and rubbed her cheek on his head. When the story was finished, Tom said, "That was nice."

And Joe's Mom said, "Yes."

And Tom said, "I'm going home now."

And Joe's Mom said, "Okay."

And she brushed the cookie crumbs off Tom, and off herself. And she smiled and said, "Don't tell about the cookies." And she put her finger over her mouth. And Tom put his finger over his mouth too. And he walked down the path, and back up the road.

And me and Suzanne followed, and I said, "Tom! You didn't ask why Joe has gone to his Dad's, and when he's coming back, and what's going to happen with his rabbit!"

And Tom said, "I forgot to remember. I had a story instead."

And I said, *"Tom!"*

And Tom said, "I didn't have cookies."

And then he said, "Joe's Mom cried on my head."

And she had as well, because Tom's hair was all wet.

Me and Suzanne went back to the shed and decided to wait until Monday at school, when we could ask *Joe* why he had gone to his Dad's, and when he was coming back, and what was going to happen with his rabbit.

CHAPTER 8
The Spare Seat

Most of the time I'm not very good at getting ready in the mornings. And that's why Mom always shouts things up the stairs like, "Anna, if you don't hurry up, I'm going to come up there and dress you myself."

But the Monday after Joe-down-the-street went away with his Dad in the van, I got ready really fast. And I packed my bag and got my uniform ready the night before. Because, like Suzanne said, "We have to get there early to talk to Joe before the bell rings."

I was eating my breakfast when the walkie-talkie crackled, "Suzanne to Anna. Suzanne to Anna. Are you ready? Over."

"Anna to Suzanne. Anna to Suzanne. Just finishing my cornflakes. Over."

"Copy that," Suzanne said. "Cornflakes. I'm putting my coat on. I'll be out the back. Waiting on the wall. Over and out."

And I ran and brushed my teeth, and got my bag, and my coat, and Tom.

It's good talking on the walkie-talkies in the mornings. Better than ringing on the doorbell like most people have to. It would be even better if we could take the walkie-talkies to school, but Mom says she doesn't think Mrs. Peters would like it, so we have to leave them at home.

When we got to the crossing, me and Suzanne and Tom were the first ones to arrive.

The Lollipop Lady said, "The early bird catches the worm, eh?" We call her that because her sign looks like a lollipop.

Tom said, "I don't like worms."

"No?" said the Lollipop Lady.

"They wriggle my skin," Tom said.

"Fair enough," said the Lollipop Lady. "Some like carrots and others like cabbage."

"Come on," I said, "we've got to go."

And the Lollipop Lady said, "Time is money," and took us over the road.

Tom loves talking to the Lollipop Lady. Sometimes he talks to her for ages. But we didn't have time to talk to the Lollipop Lady for long that day, because we needed to get into the playground, to wait for Joe, to find out why he had gone to his Dad's and when he was coming home, and what was going to happen to his rabbit and all that.

Me and Suzanne and Tom were the first ones in the playground. After a while other people started coming in: the ones who walk, and the ones on bikes, and the ones from the bus, and Graham Roberts on his Grandad's tractor. Graham Roberts comes to school in all sorts of ways. On his brother's motorbike, and his cousin's combine harvester, and once with his Nan on her electric shopping scooter. But

Joe-down-the-street didn't arrive at all. And then the bell rang, and everyone went inside.

Mrs. Peters said, "Right, Class Five. Coats on pegs, bags down, bottoms on seats."

There was a space next to Emma Hendry, where Joe always sits.

When everyone was quiet, Mrs. Peters said that she had "an announcement to make," which means she had something to say. And she said that Joe wasn't coming to school this week, because he was going to go to another school, which was a very nice one, just like ours, in another village, on the other side of the bridge, and he was going to see if he liked it there. And if he *didn't* like it, he was going to come back to our school after Easter, and if he did like it, he was going to stay.

Emma Hendry put her hand up, and

Mrs. Peters said, "Yes, Emma?"

And Emma said, "Can I take the attendance sheet to the office when it's Joe's turn?"

And Mrs. Peters said, "No, because if he's not here, Joe won't have a turn, will he?"

And Suzanne said, "Won't you say Joe's name?"

And Mrs. Peters said, "No."

And I said, "What about when Joe comes back?"

And Mrs. Peters said, "If Joe comes back, I will say his name again."

And then she said, "Hands up who knows whose will be the last name on the attendance sheet now."

And Emma Hendry put her hand up.

"Jake Upton?"

And Jake Upton said, "Shelly Wainwright is after me."

And Mrs. Peters said, "That's right. Shelly Wainwright, you will be last on the attendance sheet."

And Shelly Wainwright said, "I don't want to be last. I like being second to last."

And Mrs. Peters said, "Well, that's the way the alphabet works."

Emma Hendry asked, "Who is going to sit in Joe's seat next to me if he's not coming back?"

And Suzanne said, "He probably is coming back, because he's left the New Rabbit behind."

And I said, "Yes, because Joe lives down the same road as me and Suzanne."

Graham Roberts said, "That's probably why he went away."

And I said, "No, it isn't."

And Graham Roberts said, "Yes, it is."

And I said, "No, it isn't."

And Graham Roberts said, "Yes, it is."

And I said, **"NO, IT ISN'T!"** And I kicked Graham Roberts under the table. And Graham Roberts kicked me back.

And Mrs. Peters said, "Excuse me! Anna Morris! I am not impressed! Graham Roberts, come and sit next to Emma Hendry, please."

Emma Hendry did not look very happy that Graham Roberts was going to sit next to her, because Graham Roberts swings on his chair, and copies other people's work, and puts their pencils up his nose. And Emma Hendry doesn't like those kinds of things. And also, Graham Roberts always tries to touch Emma Hendry's hair. And then Emma puts her hand up and

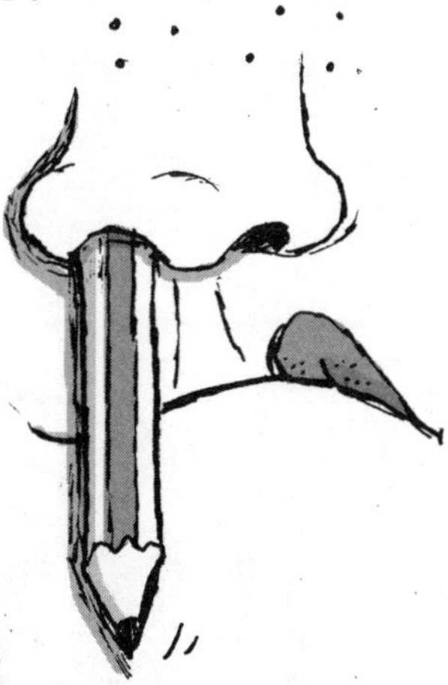

says, "Mrs. Peters, Graham Roberts is touching my hair again."

I wouldn't tell Mrs. Peters if Graham Roberts touched my hair.

Graham Roberts picked up his things and went to sit with Emma Hendry. And I wished I hadn't kicked him.

"Who's going to sit next to me?" I said.

"For the time being, Anna, you can sit by yourself. If you're good this week, I will have another think."

I undid my laces, and then I did them back up again. And I didn't say anything. Because everyone was looking. And because I didn't want to sit on my own. And

because no one can be good for a *week*. And because Joe-down-the-street was moving *schools* as *well* as houses, and no one had told us *that*. And if he still lived at his Mom's house, instead of ages away with his Dad, I wouldn't have to sit on my own, because there wouldn't be a spare seat next to Emma Hendry for Graham Roberts to go and sit in in the first place.

I wrote a note to Suzanne: "What are we going to do about Joe-down-the-street?"

Mrs. Peters said, "Anna, writing notes is *not* being good."

And she took the note from me. And she put it in the trash. And then she took roll. And she stopped at Shelly Wainwright.

After school Mrs. Peters said she had some pictures and work and things that she wanted me and Suzanne to take home to give to Joe next time he came to his Mom's.

Me and Suzanne put all Joe's work up on the walls in the shed. There were paintings and drawings and poems and stories and collages and cutouts and math problems and everything. And they were *all* about his rabbit.

I said, "How are we going to get Joe-down-the-street back?"

And Suzanne looked at all Joe's work on the walls. "I don't know," she said, "but it's got to be something to do with the New Rabbit."

CHAPTER 9
Keeping the Rabbit Alive

We didn't know how yet, but me and Suzanne were sure that the New Rabbit was the thing that could make Joe come back and live down the road. And that's why, even though Mom said we had to stay out of it, and stop sticking our noses in, me and Suzanne decided that we'd better start looking after the New Rabbit ourselves. Because if anything bad happened to the New Rabbit, like it died, then Joe would never come back. But while the New Rabbit was here, there was a chance that he might.

Because me and Suzanne heard Joe's Mom talking to my Mom on the phone when we listened in upstairs. And Joe's Mom said Joe didn't really know *where* he wanted to live, or *what* he wanted to do. And the only reason he hadn't taken the New Rabbit with him to his Dad's was because the landlord at Joe's Dad's apartment had said, "No Pets Allowed."

Suzanne said she bet Joe was worrying about the New Rabbit all the time, now that no one was guarding it. Because even though Joe's Mom said Joe would be coming back for Easter, and weekends, and that sort of thing, it still meant the rabbit was hardly ever getting guarded. And, like Joe always said, and like it shows on his pie chart, which we hung up in the shed, "The more time the rabbit gets guarded, the less chance there is of the rabbit getting got."

Joe's Mom told my Mom that she was going to look after the rabbit herself.

When Mom got off the phone, me and Suzanne put the other phone down and went downstairs.

"Who was on the phone?" I asked.

"Joe's Mom."

"Oh."

I said, "Why are no pets allowed at Joe's Dad's apartment?"

And Mom said, "Were you listening in again, Anna?"

I said, "No."

And Mom said, "Mmm."

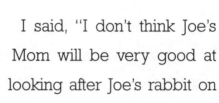

I said, "I don't think Joe's Mom will be very good at looking after Joe's rabbit on her own."

"I'm sure Pam is quite capable of looking after a rabbit, Anna."

But me and Suzanne didn't think she was.

Because we had got the binoculars and the notepad out again and done some more spying. And for one thing, Joe's Mom was at work most of the time. And for another thing, she never went in the garden and marched up and down with the Super Soaker. And for an even other thing, she didn't give the rabbit anything to eat. Except millions of dry brown pellets. And you can't just eat those on their own.

Because, like Suzanne said, "Remember what happened when you tried to eat that whole pack of crackers?"

Which I had bet Suzanne I could. But in the end I could only eat two because I couldn't even swallow them down. And then a bit went down the wrong way, and I nearly choked to death. And Suzanne had to hit me on the head and throw cold water in my face. And the brown pellets that Joe's Mom gave the New Rabbit were even drier than crackers. Because I tried one.

I said I thought Suzanne was right, and anyway, even if it didn't choke to death, the New Rabbit shouldn't just eat pellets every day because, like Mom says, "You have to eat fruit and vegetables, Anna, or you will get scurvy and die, like a seventeenth-century sailor."

This is what it says in my dictionary about what scurvy is:

> **scurvy** [skur-vee] ✦ *noun*
> a disease marked by swollen and bleeding gums, livid spots on the skin, and suppurating wounds, due to a diet lacking in vitamin C

And this is what it says in Suzanne's dictionary:

scurvy [skur-vee] ✦ *noun*
a disease caused by a deficiency of ascorbic acid characterized by spongy gums, the opening of previously healed wounds, and bleeding from the mucous membranes

And we definitely didn't want Joe's rabbit to get that.

Me and Suzanne decided that as well as making sure it didn't choke to death, or die of scurvy, we'd better start guarding the New Rabbit, in case something else killed it, like the New Cat.

"It isn't just the New Cat that could get the New Rabbit either," I said, "because I looked on the computer, and *everything* wants to get rabbits, especially at night.

Dogs, and cats, and hawks, and owls, and weasels, and foxes, and farmers, and old ladies who want rabbits' fur for hats."

And Suzanne said, "I already knew that."

And then she said we should make a list of all the things we had to do to make sure the New Rabbit didn't die.

ANNA'S AND SUZANNE'S LIST OF THINGS TO DO TO MAKE SURE THE NEW RABBIT DOESN'T DIE

1. Put a bell on the New Cat's collar so it can't sneak up and scare the New Rabbit to death like it did with the Old Rabbit
2. Put Suzanne's little brother Carl's old baby monitor under the New Rabbit's hutch so we can hear if anything is happening
3. Guard the New Rabbit with Super Soakers
4. Feed the New Rabbit fruit and vegetables so it doesn't get scurvy and die
5. Throw the rabbit's pellets away so it doesn't choke to death

It took quite a long time trying to put a bell on the New Cat's collar. First of all we had to find one. So we went to see Mrs. Rotherham, and we told her all about how we needed to put a bell on the New Cat's collar to stop it from sneaking up on the New Rabbit and scaring it to death.

Mrs. Rotherham said, "I see. A Cat Attack Alarm . . . I wonder if I can lay my hands on a bell." And she went in her cupboard for ages until she did. And then we all had a bowl of ice cream.

And then we had to find the New Cat, and catch it, and then the New Cat attacked us, and then we had to find Tom, to ask him to put the Cat Attack Alarm on the New Cat for us, because he is friends with the New Cat, so it might not mind so much.

And at first Tom said, "No."

Because, he said, "I don't think the

New Cat would like to have a Cat Attack Alarm on."

And Suzanne said, "We'll give you some cookies."

So Tom said, "Okay."

And Suzanne pinched some cookies from her house, and I pinched some from ours, and we gave them to Tom. And Tom put the Cat Attack Alarm on the New Cat's collar. And the New Cat *didn't* want the Cat Attack Alarm on at all. She had a fight with it. But she didn't win, because the Cat Attack Alarm stayed on. Tom said he felt sorry for the New Cat. And he sat down and stroked the New Cat on the head so its ears went flat. And Tom ate all his cookies.

CHAPTER 10
The Tale of the Fierce Bad Rabbit

The next day after school, while Joe-down-the-street's Mom was still at work, me and Suzanne went to see if Mrs. Rotherham

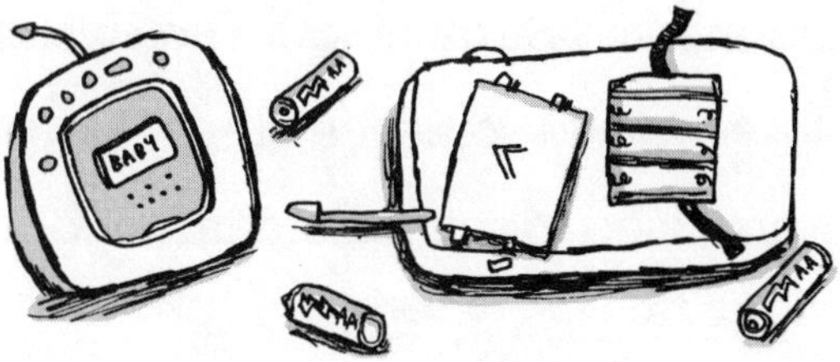

had any batteries to put in Carl's old baby monitor. And we told her all about how we needed it to listen out for Joe's New Rabbit now that Joe wasn't down the road anymore.

Mrs. Rotherham said, "Of course. A Rabbit Monitor. No rabbit should be without one."

And she checked inside it and said, "Mmm . . . Four double A batteries. . . . I'll see if I can lay my hands on some."

And after ages in her cupboard, she did. And she put the batteries in the monitor, and she checked that it worked by leaving one end of the monitor with us and taking the other end upstairs and saying, "Help! Help! It's me, Mrs. Rotherham. I'm trapped in the baby monitor. Can anybody hear me?"

And me and Suzanne got The Hysterics. And then we had some ice cream. Because, like Nana used to say, ice cream is good for calming down.

And then we went down the road and put the listening part of the Rabbit Monitor on the shelf in the shed. And we put the hearing part under the New Rabbit's hutch. And we peered in to have a look at the New Rabbit. There was a lot of hay in the way, all piled up against the wire mesh at the front. Suzanne reached her hand in through the hay and felt around.

"Oh," she said, "I can feel it. It's all soft, and fluffy, and warm."

And then she screamed, "AGH!" and she pulled her hand back. Her finger was bleeding. She put it in her mouth.

"It bit me!" she said.

I said, "Maybe it was asleep, and it got frightened when you put your hand in." Because when me and Tom had hamsters, our Hamster Manual said that hamsters only bite when they are frightened. And it's probably the same with rabbits.

So I said, "Things only bite when they're frightened."

And Suzanne said, "No, they don't. Some things bite because they like to."

And I said, "Like what?"

And Suzanne said, "Like the New Cat!"

"The New Cat is different," I said. "You don't get rabbits like that. Rabbits just hop around, and eat lettuce, and wear yellow ribbons on Easter cards and things."

Suzanne took her finger out of her mouth. It was still bleeding.

"You put *your* hand in its hutch, then."

"I will," I said.

I undid the latch, and opened the door a crack, and slowly put my hand in the hutch, lying it flat on the bottom, like the Hamster Manual said you should.

I heard something rustle, and then I felt the rabbit's fur

against my hand, and its whiskers, and its wet nose.

I kept very still.

"It's sniffing me," I said. "It tickles."

And then I said, "*Nice* New Rabbit."

And then I said, **"AGH!"**

And pulled my hand away. And put my finger in my mouth. **"It bit *me*!"**

"See," Suzanne said.

And she put the latch back on.

The New Rabbit rustled in the hay. It pushed its way through to the front of the hutch. It was white. And it had pink eyes. And it was Absolutely Enormous. The New Rabbit stared out at us through the wire mesh.

Suzanne said, "Look at its eyes!"

And I said, "Look at its ears!"

And Suzanne said, "Look at its teeth!"

And I said, "Look at its claws!"

And Suzanne said, "When did it get so *big*?"

Because the last time me and Suzanne had seen the New Rabbit, it was tiny. And its eyes were closed. And it fitted inside Joe's hand.

The New Rabbit gnawed on the wire on the front of the hutch. It had long yellow teeth.

Suzanne said, "It's not like Joe's *Old* Rabbit, is it?"

And it wasn't, because if you put your hand in the Old Rabbit's hutch, the Old Rabbit would rub its head against you, and hop onto your hand to be taken out. And then, if you let it, it would go up your sweater and nuzzle your neck.

You couldn't fit the New Rabbit up your sweater. Not even if you wanted to. And you wouldn't want to anyway.

We stared at the New Rabbit. And the New Rabbit stared back at us.

Suzanne said, "It's too big for the hutch."

Which was true. It was almost as big as the hutch itself.

"Maybe that's why it looks angry," I said.

Because the Old Rabbit had lots of room to hop around. But if the New Rabbit stretched out, its feet would touch both ends of the hutch.

I said, "We could let it out for a bit."

And Suzanne said, "How will we get it back in?"

"We won't let it *out* out," I said. "We'll just let it out in the run. For a few minutes. And then we'll shoo it back in."

And Suzanne said, "Good idea."

Which Suzanne hardly ever says, so that meant it was.

We picked up the run from the corner of the garden and put it on the front of the hutch. And it fitted just right. Because that's how Joe's Dad had made it, ages ago, for the Old Rabbit, when he still lived with Joe and Joe's Mom.

There was a small hole in the wire mesh, in one corner of the run. We looked at the hole, and we looked at the rabbit. The hole was about the size of a jam jar. And the rabbit was about the size of a dog. In fact, it was bigger than a dog. It was bigger than

Miss Matheson's dog, anyway, because that's only the same size as a guinea pig.

"The rabbit can't fit through the hole," I said.

"No, definitely not," said Suzanne.

So we opened the door of the hutch. And the rabbit hopped out into the run. And it stood very still in the middle of the run, and it sniffed the air, and it put its ears right up. And then it hopped over to the corner with the hole. And it looked at the hole. And then, in a second, it squeezed through it.

Suzanne said, "It's out!"

And I said, "The gate!"

I ran to the gate and slammed it shut. The

rabbit looked angrier than ever. It thumped its back leg on the ground. I tried to grab the rabbit. And Suzanne tried to grab the rabbit. But whenever we got near it, the New Rabbit ran at us and scrabbled and scratched and tried to bite.

I said, "We need gardening gloves." Like Mom uses to put the New Cat in its carrying case to take it to the vet.

And I ran up the road to the shed to get them.

When I got back, Suzanne was running round Joe's garden in circles, and the New Rabbit was running after her.

"Suzanne," I said. "Turn around and run *at* the rabbit, to shoo it toward me. I'll get it with the gardening gloves."

And she did.

I grabbed hold of the rabbit. It scrabbled

and scratched and clawed and kicked. But I held on to it, tight.

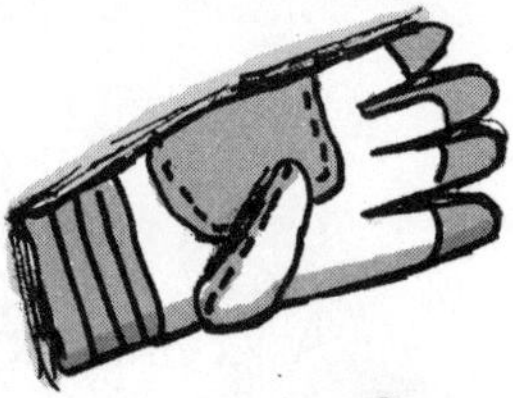

And then I felt it bite. My blood came right through the gardening gloves. I dropped the rabbit. And ran up the road with my finger in my mouth.

I got a Band-Aid from the house for my hand. And I went into the shed and got my big brother Andy's football pads and his bike helmet. I put them on. And I put his mouth guard in my mouth. I took his shin guards, some old oven mitts, and a balaclava for Suzanne. And I got two fishing nets.

When I got back, Suzanne was in the corner of Joe's garden, pressed against the fence, and the New Rabbit was in front of her, and it was making a growling sound. There were scratches all over Suzanne's legs.

I said, "I didn't know rabbits growled."

And Suzanne said, "HELP!"

"You need to get to the gate!"

"I can't! I'm stuck."

"Jump!" I said.

Suzanne jumped right over the rabbit and ran for the gate. And when she got through it, she slammed it shut. I gave Suzanne the shin guards, and the oven mitts, and the mouth guard and the balaclava.

And she put them on.

Then we got The Hysterics because we looked quite funny, and we had to lie down on the pavement for a bit.

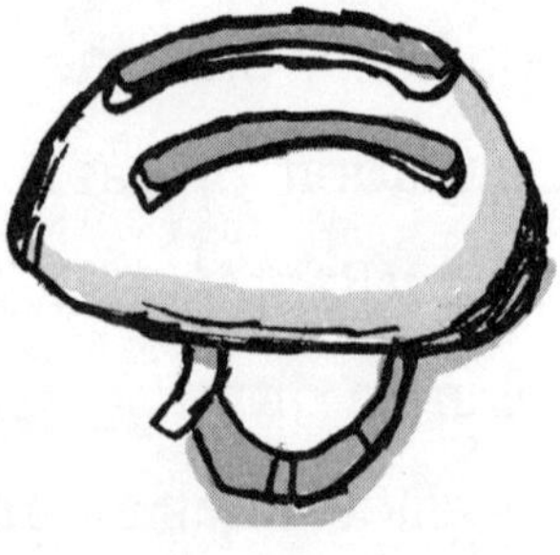

And then we stopped having The Hysterics, because it wasn't funny really, because, like Suzanne said, "This is *serious*."

So we went back in.

The rabbit stood still in the middle of the grass, sniffing the air, with its enormous ears up. We took a step toward it, and it thumped its back leg on the ground, and growled again.

"Ready?" I said.

And Suzanne said, "Yes."

We ran at the New Rabbit, and we tried to catch it under the fishing nets, but the New Rabbit was too quick. And the fishing nets were too small. And it hopped and jumped and ran all around the garden, and the more we chased it, the farther away it got.

And then, suddenly, the New Rabbit stopped, and it got up on its hind legs, and it put its ears right up, and it sniffed the air.

And it stared at the gate. And it froze.

The gate started to open. And I thought me and Suzanne were in Big Trouble then, because it was probably Joe's Mom.

But it wasn't. It was Tom. And he wasn't on his own. He was with the New Cat.

When it saw the New Rabbit, the New Cat's eyes went very wide, and it got down very low. And it stared at the New Rabbit. And the New Rabbit got down low too and stared back at the New Cat. And they stayed very still.

And the rabbit went, **"Ggrrrrrrrr."**

And the cat went, "Ttssssss."

And then the New Rabbit turned and shot back through the hole in the run and up into its hutch. And Suzanne closed the door, and I fastened the latch.

When I got home, Mom said, "Anna, where did you get all those scratches?"

And I said, "From Suzanne."

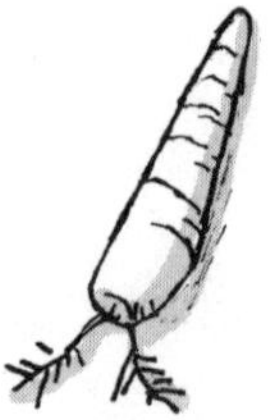

CHAPTER 11
Rabbit Food

After that, even though me and Suzanne decided we didn't really like the New Rabbit, we started looking after it all the time. We sat on the pavement outside Joe's house with Super Soakers, and we took turns to take the Rabbit Monitor to bed at night. We fed the New Rabbit every morning on the way to school, and every

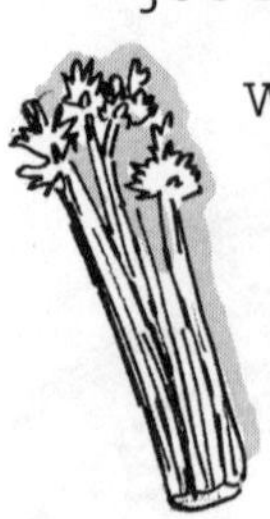

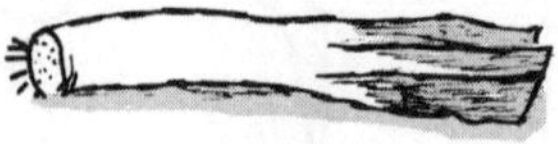

afternoon on the way back. And at first we put in things we found at home, but then Mom said, "I could have sworn I had some spinach."

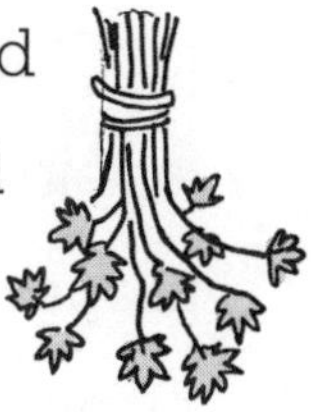

And, "Has anyone seen the celery?"

And, "How can you *lose* a *leek*?"

And when Suzanne's Dad said, **"WHAT ON EARTH HAS HAPPENED TO ALL MY HERBS?"** we started getting things from other places instead.

We got apples from Mr. Tucker's tree, and cress from the window ledge in the classroom at school, and privet leaves from Miss Matheson's hedge.

And we wanted to get the

parsley from Miss Matheson's back garden too. But Miss Matheson kept spotting us and tapping on her window, saying, **"Private property! Private property! I won't have my plants purloined!"**

And then she phoned Mom to complain.

This is what it says in my dictionary about purloining . . .

purloin [pur-loyn] ✦ *verb*
to take dishonestly; filch; pilfer

This is what it said in Suzanne's dictionary . . .

purloin [pur-loyn] ✦ *verb*
steal

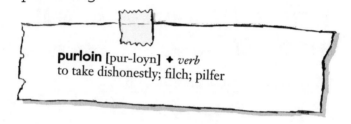

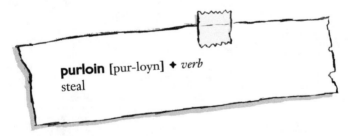

Suzanne didn't used to have her own dictionary. She used to borrow her Dad's. But the last time Suzanne took it, it went in the toilet by mistake, and Suzanne's Dad said, **"FOR CRYING OUT LOUD, IT'S COMPLETELY RUINED, SUZANNE!"** And he threw it in the trash.

He bought a new dictionary, and he said, **"IF YOU GO ANYWHERE NEAR IT, SUZANNE, YOUR LIFE WILL NOT BE WORTH LIVING!"**

But Suzanne didn't need to go anywhere near it anyway, because we got the old dictionary out of the bin and dried it out in our airing cupboard, and stuck the pages that had torn back together, and now it's as good as before, except the pages are a bit wobbly and it smells a bit strange.

Anyway, when me and Suzanne first started feeding the New Rabbit, we had to be quick getting our hands in and out of the hutch, because as soon as we opened the latch, the New Rabbit attacked us.

But on the second day it didn't bite, and on the third day it let us stroke it. And at first we thought it was because the New Rabbit was starting to like us. But on the fourth day, when the New Rabbit didn't even get up, and hardly opened its eyes, Suzanne said, "I don't think the New Rabbit is very well."

And I said that I didn't think it was either. Because its fur looked funny, and it had red patches all over its chest.

When we told Tom all about how the New Rabbit was sick, Tom said, "When Peter Rabbit is poorly, Mrs. Rabbit gives him chamomile tea."

Me and Suzanne looked in the cupboards in Suzanne's kitchen, and then we looked in the cupboards in my kitchen, but we couldn't find any chamomile tea. We did find some other tea, though, which it said on the box was "made only with the finest tips." Which we thought would be just as good.

I'm not supposed to make hot drinks because, once, I tried to make coffee, and I forgot to put water in the kettle, and I put half a jar of coffee granules in instead, and when I turned it on, the kettle made a fizzing noise and went **BANG!** And that's why there's a big black patch on the kitchen counter.

So we made the tea very quickly, and went outside and waited for it to cool, and then we took it down the road and we tipped the New Rabbit's water out of its bowl and we poured the tea in instead. Then we went back to the shed.

And after a while Mom came and she knocked on the door and she said, "Have you been using the kettle again and trying to make tea in the kitchen?"

And I said, "No."

And Mom said, "Mmm."

And then she said, "What are you two *up* to?"

And Suzanne said, "Nothing."

And Mom said, "Mmm."

And then she said that Joe-down-the-street was coming home tomorrow for Easter, and that me and Suzanne should call on him and try to be kind, and that we should do the things Joe wanted, even if it was boring, like guarding his rabbit.

CHAPTER 12
Joe's Down the Street Again

In the morning, when Joe's Dad's van pulled into the road, me and Suzanne were standing at Joe's gate with our Super Soakers.

Joe and his Dad got out. Joe's Dad said, "Armed guard, eh, girls?"

And we said, "Yes."

"Can't be too careful," he said, and he held up his hands, and we let him pass, and he went inside. And me and Suzanne told Joe all about how we had been guarding the New Rabbit, in secret, and how we had put the Cat Attack Alarm on the New Cat's collar so it couldn't sneak up and scare the New Rabbit to death, and we showed him the Rabbit Monitor, under the hutch, and told him how the other end was in the shed, and how at night we took turns taking it to bed so we would hear if anything happened.

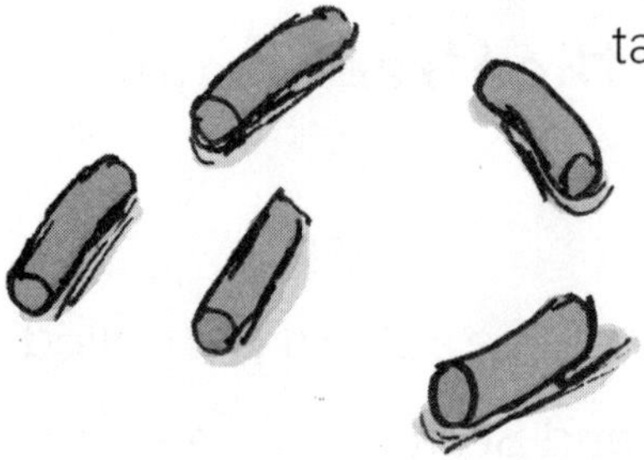

But we didn't tell him about how we had let the New Rabbit out by mistake, or how the New Cat had seen it, or how Joe's Mom was only giving it bowls of brown pellets, and how we had to feed it ourselves, because like Mom said to us before we left the house, "Don't go worrying Joe about his rabbit."

Joe looked in at the New Rabbit, and he

opened the hutch, and he put his hand in and pushed back some of the straw.

"I don't think the New Rabbit is very well," he said. "Normally, the New Rabbit bites."

"Oh," I said.

"Does it?" said Suzanne.

And we pulled our sleeves over our hands to cover our scratches and Band-Aids.

Joe looked in the hutch again. He said that the New Rabbit's poos were all wrong, because they're supposed to be small and hard, not wet and stuck to its bum. Then he looked at the New Rabbit's chest. And he said its fur had gone strange, and it didn't normally have red patches like that.

And then Joe's Dad came out of the

house. And he mended the hole in the wire in the rabbit run. And he went to the van, and he got a paper bag out, and he gave it to Joe.

And he said, "I've told your Mom about the medicine. Don't forget to take it, champ."

And Joe said, "No."

Joe's Dad gave him a cuddle. And he scrubbed him on the head. And he got in the van and drove away.

Joe watched the van go.

"What medicine?" said Suzanne.

Joe showed her. There was a tube of cream, and a bottle of liquid. The tube

said FLORASONE and the bottle said IMODIUM.

Suzanne looked at the bottle, and at the tube. And then she looked at the rabbit. And then she looked at Joe.

And then she said, "You and the rabbit are *both* poorly."

And Joe said, "Yes."

And then Joe's Mom came out. And she kissed Joe all over his face until Joe went red. And then she said, "Sorry, Joe." And then she kissed him again.

Joe told his Mom that he thought the New Rabbit was poorly.

And Joe's Mom said that she knew, and that she was keeping a close eye on the rabbit, and she checked the New Rabbit's chest, and she looked in its mouth and she said, "He hasn't been himself. I've spoken to the vet, and if he's not any better tomorrow, we'll take him to see her."

And then she lifted up Joe's T-shirt, and she looked at *his* chest too, and it had a red rash all over it, and she looked in his mouth. And she said, "And if *you* aren't any better tomorrow, we'll take you to the vet as well."

And she kissed Joe again. And then she said that her and Joe were going to have some lunch.

And me and Suzanne said that if Joe wanted, he could come up to the shed after, and we would let him be in our clubs.

On the way up the road, Suzanne said, "Let's go on the computer and look something up." Which Suzanne never normally wants to do.

We sat down at the screen, and Suzanne put in "Florasone," and it said, "`Florasone: a cream for eczema.`"

And then she put in "Imodium," and it said, "**Imodium: for upset stomachs and diarrhea.**"

And then she put in "diarrhea and eczema" and she said, "Let's print these pages off."

I went and asked Mom. I'm not allowed to print things without asking anymore, after I printed off two hundred and forty-three pages for Tom about Batman and Bob the Builder.

Mom came with the printer cable, and she looked at the screen and she said, "Why do you want to print off descriptions of eczema and diarrhea?"

"It's for Suzanne," I said.

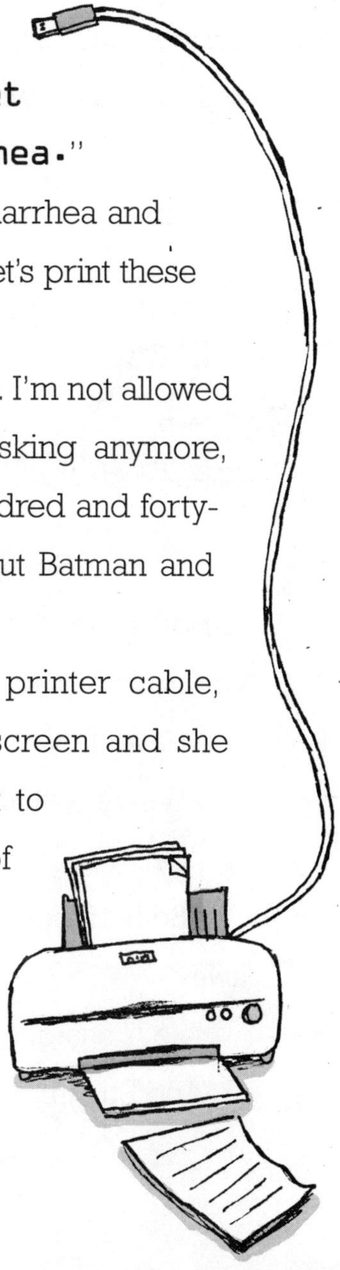

Suzanne scratched her chest and rubbed her stomach. "I'm not well," she said.

Mom said, "Mmm," and pressed print.

Suzanne put the pages in her pocket.

And Mom made us some cheese sandwiches and some squash, and we took them out to the shed, and we ate our sandwiches and read what it said about eczema and diarrhea.

Suzanne said, "Joe and the New Rabbit have got exactly the same things wrong with them."

"Have they?"

"Yes. At exactly the same time."

"Oh."

"Both of them were fine before Joe went away."

"So?" I said.

And Suzanne said, *"So . . . "*

I asked Suzanne if she wanted the rest of her sandwich.

And Suzanne said, "No."

So I had it instead. And I said, "It's probably a coincidence."

"It *could* be a coincidence," Suzanne said. "But it could be *connected*."

"Why?"

"Because," Suzanne said, "Joe and the New Rabbit were both fine. And then Joe and the New Rabbit got separated. And that's when Joe and the New Rabbit got poorly. So now that Joe and the New Rabbit are back together again, what's going to happen?"

"I don't know," I said. Because I hate riddles and things like that because I never know the answer.

"They might both get better again. And if they do, it can't just be a coincidence, can it? It has to be connected."

And I said, "I don't know." Because I didn't.

This is what it says a "coincidence" is in my dictionary:

coincidence [co-in-si-dense] ✦ *noun*
a striking occurrence of two or more events at one time, apparently by mere chance or accident

This it what it says "connected" is in my dictionary:

connected [con-ec-ted] ✦ *adjective*
joined together or linked

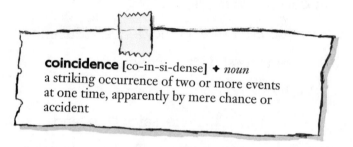

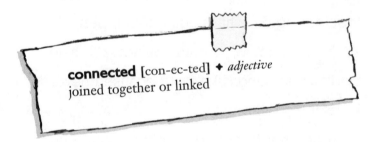

I didn't know if Joe and the New Rabbit being poorly with the same thing at the same time was a coincidence, or if it was connected, but I was glad we didn't have to look after the New Rabbit for two weeks while Joe was back down the road for Easter.

Because it's quite hard work, looking after a rabbit. Especially when you aren't supposed to be looking after it, and you have to do it in secret, and hide behind the hedge to guard it, and steal all its food for it, and listen to it on the Rabbit Monitor in bed every other night.

Now that Joe was back to look after his rabbit himself, me and Suzanne could do all the other things that we used to do before we had to look after the New Rabbit all the time.

So I said, "Let's do something."

And Suzanne said, "What?"

"I don't know."

We sat on the roof and tried to think.

And Suzanne said she wondered what Joe was doing now. And whether he had finished his lunch.

And I said so did I.

And Suzanne said she wondered if Joe would come up to the shed.

And I said that he probably wouldn't, because he would probably just go back to guarding his rabbit all the time.

And then we saw Joe coming up the back lane.

And we got down from the roof, and we told Joe the password, and we let him in the shed, and we showed him how we had put all his work up on the walls, and how we had the Rabbit Monitor on the shelf to listen out for the New Rabbit. And Joe looked pretty pleased.

"Shall we play Dingo the Dog?" I said.

At first Joe didn't want to, but Suzanne gave him the Rabbit Monitor to put in his pocket so he could hear if anything happened. And then he said, "Okay."

And Suzanne went and got Barney's old collar and leash, and we went out the back and played Dingo the Dog.

And afterward we went to Joe's house, and we played Mountain Rescue. And Joe's Mom got us fish and chips. And she said me and Suzanne could stay the night, if we liked. And we did.

So we went home to

get our pajamas and toothbrushes and all that.

And Suzanne told Joe about how it isn't as good in Mrs. Peters's class without him. And how Shelly Wainwright is last on the attendance sheet, and how she doesn't like being last because she liked being second to last, like she was when Joe was there.

And I told Joe about how Mrs. Peters made Graham Roberts move and sit in Joe's seat, and how I had to sit on my own, and I didn't like it. And I said that it was probably much better at Joe's new school.

But Joe said it wasn't, because he liked Mrs. Peters because she didn't mind him not putting his hand up, and doing all his work about rabbits and everything, but his new teacher did mind. And everyone called him Joseph instead of Joe.

And Suzanne said, "Mrs. Peters said you could come back to our school after Easter if you didn't like it at your new one."

And Joe said, "I can't, because after Mom shouted at me about always guarding the New Rabbit, I shouted back and said, **"I WANT TO LIVE WITH DAD!"** And Mom said that I could if I really wanted to. And I said I did. And I phoned Dad and he said that he would come and get me in the morning. And when the morning came, I didn't want to go, but I had to then because that's what I'd said. And I didn't want Dad to think I didn't want to live with him." Which is like when I went to live with Mrs. Rotherham. When I didn't really want to. Before Tom came to rescue me.

And then Joe showed us a list that he had done, and it said:

GOOD THINGS ABOUT LIVING WITH MY DAD:

I see my Dad every day

BAD THINGS ABOUT LIVING WITH MY DAD:

The New Rabbit isn't there

The food

My bed

There's no one to play with

Dad's New Girlfriend

I don't like the school

Mom isn't there

And then Joe drew us a picture of his Dad's apartment, and where his bedroom is at the back, and how you get there.

You go down our road and past the horse trough, and the shops, and the Bottom Bus Stop, and over the bridge and round the roundabout, and down the track, and through the old tunnel, and through the gate, and across the field, and then you're there.

And Joe said that maybe me and Suzanne could come and see him soon, after school.

And Suzanne said that we probably couldn't, because it was way past the Bottom Bus Stop and everything, which is Out-of-Bounds.

And Joe said, "You could come on the Super-Speed-Bike-Machine, and bring me back on the stunt pegs."

And I said how we weren't allowed to get the Super-Speed-Bike-Machine out anymore after we went into the road and Tom hit his head and had to have six sticky stitches.

And Joe said, "Oh."

And then he wrote, "Map to Joe's Dad's apartment" on the top of the paper. And he said we could have it anyway, just in case.

And I said we would pin it on the wall in the shed. And we would go when we were old enough.

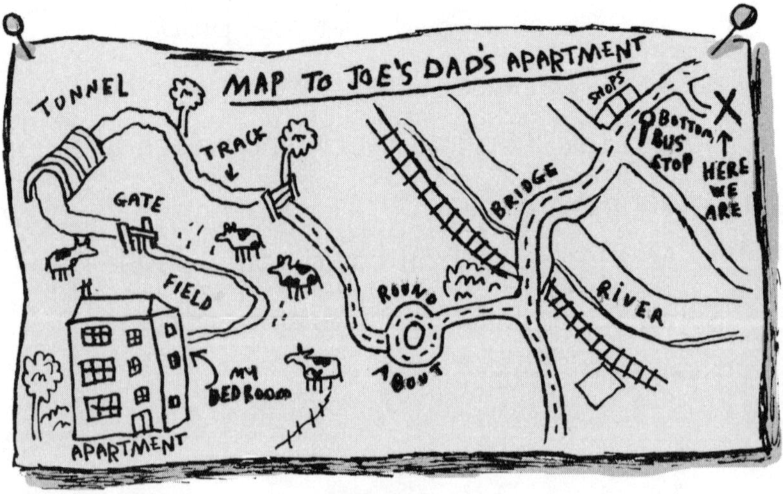

And Joe said I should put the list of things he didn't like about living with his Dad in the shed as well, because he didn't want his Dad to see it.

So I folded the list and the map up, and I put them in my bag.

And then Suzanne started making funny noises and opening and closing her mouth. And snoring. And I held her nose, and me and Joe got The Hysterics.

And Suzanne woke up and said it wasn't funny, actually, because she couldn't help it and she might have to have her adenoids out.

This is what it says about adenoids in my dictionary:

adenoid [ad-en-oyd] ✦ *noun*
one of two soft masses of flesh between the back of the nose and the throat, which sometimes make breathing difficult

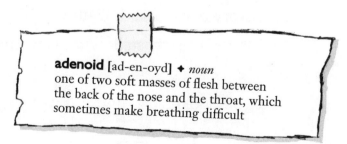

In the morning me and Suzanne and Joe-down-the-street played Mountain Rescue again, and Dingo the Dog, and Tom played too. And we sat on the shed roof and did other things, like seeing how long we could stare at the sun before we went blind, and how long we could hold our breath before we died, and talking about the Super-Speed-Bike-Machine.

And after that, as soon as he had finished his breakfast and looked after his rabbit, Joe came up the road to meet me and Suzanne every day.

And every day Suzanne said, "How's the New Rabbit?"

And every day Joe said, "Better."

And then Suzanne said, "And how are *you*?"

And Joe looked at her a bit funny,

because it's not like Suzanne is always asking people how they are or anything.

And he said, "I'm better too."

And Suzanne kept looking at Joe's chest and asking him about his poo. And looking in on the New Rabbit and checking its poos and its chest too. And when Joe wasn't looking, she wrote it all down in the Spy Club notebook: 10:00 a.m., Tuesday. Joe much better. Rabbit much better too.

And she said to me, "Joe and the rabbit are getting better every day."

And I said, "So?"

And Suzanne said, "They were both fine, and then when Joe went away, they both got poorly. And now that Joe is back, they are both fine again."

And then she said, "It *can't* just be a coincidence."

CHAPTER 13
Purloining Miss Matheson's Parsley

The day Joe gave us the Rabbit Monitor back and left to go to his Dad's, me and Suzanne promised him we would keep looking after the New Rabbit.

So that afternoon we collected privet leaves and daffodils. And then we got the binoculars and the Spy Club notebook out of the shed and we started to spy on Miss Matheson because

even though we were banned, we had to get some of her parsley for the New Rabbit in case it got poorly again, because, like Tom said, "Before the chamomile tea, Peter Rabbit eats some parsley to make him feel better."

We looked over Miss Matheson's fence with the binoculars.

And Suzanne wrote down in the notebook:

2:45 p.m.–Miss Matheson digging her parsley up
3:15 p.m.–Miss Matheson putting parsley on her compost heap
3:30 p.m.–Miss Matheson going into her house

We sneaked in over the gate, and we ran to the compost heap and took as much of the parsley as we could carry, and we put it in the shed. The parsley that grows in Miss Matheson's garden is just like normal parsley, except much taller, and fatter, and it smells strange. And then we shut the shed, and locked the padlock, and we went down the road with the privet leaves and the daffodils and a little piece of parsley.

The New Rabbit was back to how it used to be, before Joe left, and it tried to bite us when we put our hands in.

We sat and watched it eat the privet and the daffodils. And we gave it the little bit of parsley, just to make sure.

And I said, "Maybe the New Rabbit is going to be fine."

And Suzanne said, "Maybe."

CHAPTER 14

Till Death Do Us Part

In the morning it was the first day back at school, and me and Suzanne and Tom looked in on the New Rabbit on the way, and gave it some more of the parsley to eat, but the rabbit didn't try to bite. It was just lying still again.

Suzanne said, "The rabbit was fine, and then Joe went away and the rabbit was poorly. And then Joe came back, and the rabbit got better. And now Joe has gone away again and the rabbit is poorly again. It

can't be a coincidence."

And I said, "It *has* to be connected."

We must have fed the rabbit for too long because Suzanne looked at her watch and jumped up and said, "It's five to nine!"

I haven't got a watch because I lost mine, and anyway, like Suzanne says, even when I did have one, it didn't help because I'm not very good at telling the time.

We closed the hutch and fastened the latch and ran as fast as we could, and at first we thought the Lollipop Lady had gone home because she wasn't standing at the crossing. But when we got closer, we saw she was sitting on the bench, under the chestnut tree, reading a paper.

The Lollipop Lady stood up, and a gust of wind whipped her newspaper out of her hands, and the pages went everywhere and

she ran around trying to grab them.

"Well, if it's not one thing, it's another," she said.

And me and Suzanne and Tom ran around as well, picking up the pages, and we gave them all back, except I saw Suzanne take one page and fold it up and put it in her pocket.

And Suzanne said, "We're late."

And the Lollipop Lady said, "Shake a leg, then."

And she took us over the road.

And we shouted, "THANKS" and went over the wall and into the playground.

And the Lollipop Lady shouted after us, "BETTER LATE THAN NEVER. BLAME IT ON THE RAIN!" even though it wasn't raining.

Tom ran to his classroom, and me and Suzanne ran to ours.

And Miss Peters looked at the clock and said, "What time do you call this?"

And I didn't know what time to call it because I can only do the o'clocks and the half pasts, and it wasn't one of those.

And Suzanne said she called it, "Quarter past nine."

And then she said, "The Lollipop Lady's newspaper blew away, and we had to help her catch it."

And Mrs. Peters said, "Mmm."

And then she said, "Sit down."

At recess, me and Suzanne went up into the top corner of the field, and Suzanne showed me the piece of newspaper that she had folded up and put in her pocket. It said:

WOMAN'S SHED NEARLY BURNS DOWN.

"Not that bit," said Suzanne. "Look!" And she pointed to the part underneath. It said:

CAN'T LIVE APART

Local couple Sidney and Edith Armstrong both died last week within hours of each other, having been separated into different care homes. A friend said, "Sidney and Edith were fine before. Doctors can say what they like, but I know that they died of broken hearts."

I read it twice. And I said, "It's just like Joe and the New Rabbit."

On the way home from school, me and Suzanne and Tom went to get some of Miss Matheson's tall parsley from the shed. The smell wafted out when we opened the door.

We took a piece down to the New Rabbit. It looked even worse than ever.

Suzanne said, "What if the New Rabbit dies?" We went back to the shed.

Suzanne got the newspaper page out of her pocket and pinned it on the wall next to the map to Joe's Dad's apartment and the list of things Joe didn't like about living at his Dad's.

"What are we going to do?" I asked.

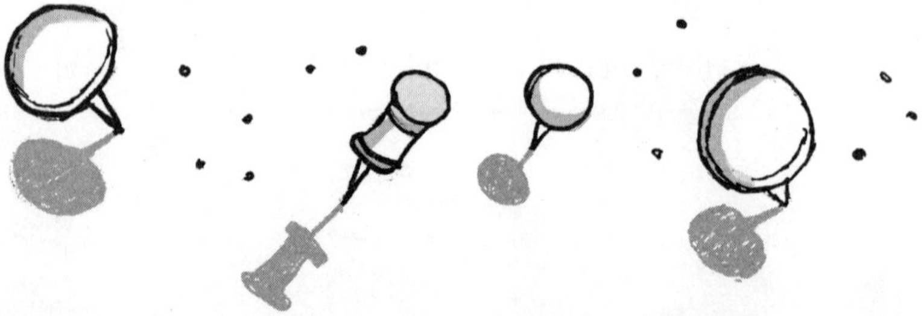

Suzanne said, "We have to get Joe and his rabbit back together."

We started making a plan.

ANNA'S AND TOM'S AND SUZANNE'S PLANS TO GET JOE-DOWN-THE-STREET AND THE NEW RABBIT BACK TOGETHER AND RESCUE THEM BEFORE THEY BOTH DIE

PLAN NUMBER 1

Tell Mom that Joe and his rabbit are going to die and ask her to go and rescue Joe

PLAN NUMBER 2

Get Joe's Dad's phone number and phone Joe and tell him that his rabbit and him are going to die if he doesn't come home

PLAN NUMBER 3

Write Joe's Dad a letter pretending to be the landlord and tell him that the rules have changed from "NO PETS" to "NO PETS EXCEPT RABBITS"

PLAN NUMBER 4

Go and rescue Joe ourselves

There was a knock on the shed door.

"What's the password?" I said.

Mom said, "Trouble. Your dinner is ready. And Suzanne's Dad's been on the phone."

So we pinned the plan on the wall, and Suzanne took the Rabbit Monitor because it was her turn, and we came out of the shed, and I locked the padlock.

And Mom said, "What is that awful smell?"

And Suzanne said, "Tom," even though it was really Miss Matheson's parsley.

And Mom said, "Tom, that's a big smell for a small person. Maybe you should go to the toilet."

And me and Tom went inside. And Suzanne went home. And we heard Suzanne's Dad shouting through the wall about what time it was, and where she'd been, and coming straight home from school and all that.

After dinner, when Mom was watching *Coronation Street*, I said, "Mom . . ."

And Mom said, "Yes . . ."

"Can you drive to Joe-down-the-street's

Dad's apartment and rescue Joe, please?"

And Mom said, "Mmm?"

And then she said, "No."

And Tom said, "Why?"

"Because it's a school night."

And I said, "Please."

And Mom said, "No."

And Tom said, "Why?"

"Because."

And Tom said, "If you don't, Joe's New Rabbit and Joe will die."

And Mom said, "Joe's Rabbit is fine. And so is Joe. No one needs to be rescued!"

And I said, "What's Joe's Dad's phone number?"

And Mom said, "Why?"

And I said, "Because."

And Mom said, "Are you going to tell Joe this rubbish about his rabbit dying?"

"No."

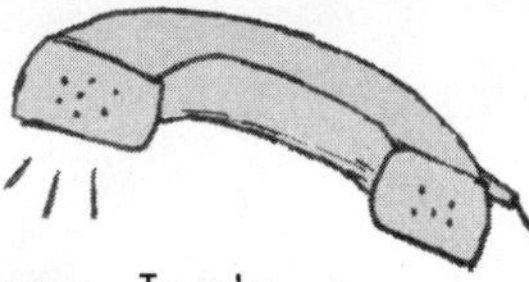

Mom gave me Joe's number. I dialed it. Mom was still standing in the room, so I said, "Did you want something?" Because that's what Mom always says to me when I hang around when *she's* on the phone.

Mom said, "*Watch* it, Anna," and went away.

Joe's Dad answered.

"Is Joe there?"

And he put Joe on.

"Hello, Joe."

I heard Mom pick up the other phone upstairs. Mom doesn't know that you have to hold the quiet button down if you don't want the other person to know you're listening in.

So I couldn't say anything about the New

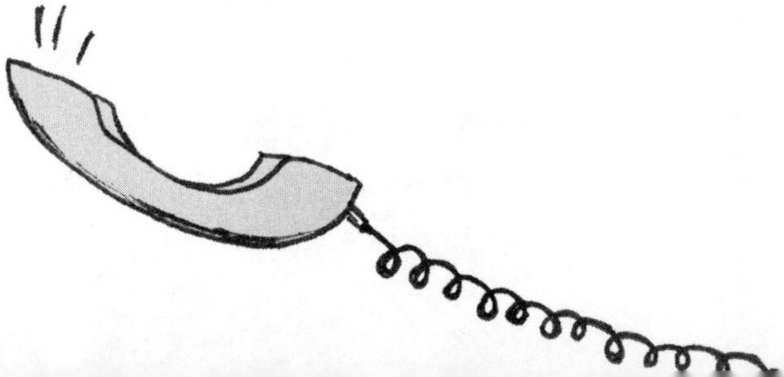

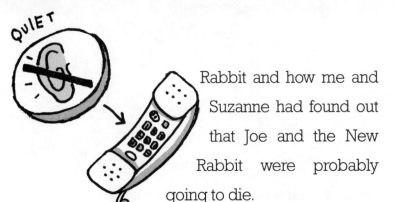

Rabbit and how me and Suzanne had found out that Joe and the New Rabbit were probably going to die.

So I just said, "Can you tell me your address, please, because me and Suzanne want to send you a birthday card."

And Joe said, "It isn't my birthday until August."

And I said, "So?"

"That's in four months."

I said, "We have to make it first."

"Oh."

Joe told me the address, and I wrote it down.

And then he said, "Is the New Rabbit okay?"

And I was going to say, "No," but I heard Mom say, "Ahem" on the other phone, so I said, "Yes. It's fine."

And then I said, "How are *you*?"

And Joe said, "Itchy. My eczema's back."

And I said, "Okay, then. Bye." And I put the phone down.

Mom came down and said, "Why do you want Joe's address?"

And I said, "Were you listening in?" Because that's what Mom always says to me.

And Mom said, "*Anna* . . ."

And I said, "I'm going to see Suzanne."

And Mom said, "No. You're not. You're going to do your homework, and read your book, and then it's time for bed."

I went into my bedroom and I got the walkie-talkie. "Anna to Suzanne. Anna to Suzanne. Come in, Suzanne. Over."

"Suzanne to Anna. Suzanne to Anna. Receiving you loud and clear. Over."

"I have tried Plan One." (Which was the one about getting Mom to drive to Joe's house to rescue him.) "But Mom says she won't rescue Joe. And I have tried to do Plan Two." (Which is the one where we phone Joe to tell him to come home.) "But I couldn't talk to Joe about it because Mom was listening in and she said I wasn't allowed to say anything to Joe about his rabbit. Over."

"Copy that. We will have to try Plan Three. Over."

Which was the one where we write a letter to Joe's Dad from the landlord.

I was going to tell Suzanne about how Joe had said that his eczema had come back again, but I didn't get a chance to say anything else because Mom came in and she took the walkie-talkie off me and she said, "Homework!"

And I heard Suzanne saying, "Anna? Anna? Are you receiving me? Over."

CHAPTER 15
"Rabbits Don't Scream"

In the morning we went and looked in on the New Rabbit again and took it some more of the tall smelly parsley from the shed. The rabbit looked even worse than before. On the way to school, Suzanne said that she had had a dream in the night, and in her dream the rabbit was screaming.

I said, "I don't think rabbits scream."

And Suzanne said, "In my dream it did."

After school Suzanne brought all her pens

to the shed. We decided that Suzanne should write the letter because she has got the best handwriting. And I said what she should write down. We had to do a lot of practice letters, because for one thing Suzanne isn't very good at spelling and she kept putting the words all wrong. And for another thing, I kept changing my mind about what the words should be, like whether it should say "from" or "love from" or "yours sincerely."

Anyway, in the end we put . . .

Dear Mr. Walker (Joe 's Dad),
I have changed the rules about pets from NO PETS to NO PETS EXCEPT RABBITS. If you see me, do not ask me about rabbits, though, please, because I don 't want to talk about it.
Yours sincerely,
The Landlord

P.S. Please do not let the rabbit go on the stairs or in the elevator, because I do not want poos and rabbit fluff getting trod into the carpet.

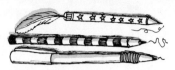

We put the letter in an envelope, and Suzanne wrote the address on it, and I put a stamp on and licked the envelope shut, and we took it to the post box at the bottom of the road, and we lifted Tom up to post it, because posting letters is one of Tom's favorite things.

And Suzanne said she couldn't stop thinking about her dream with the rabbit screaming.

So we went home, and we put "rabbit screaming" in the computer, and this is what it said . . .

"A rabbit scream is a
shrill sound, not unlike
the scream of a small child.
It generally signifies the
rabbit is dying."

CHAPTER 16
A Real-Life Rescue

I was in bed when I heard it. It woke me up.

Mom came into my room. "Anna, what's the matter?" She felt me on the forehead. "You screamed," she said. "Did you have a bad dream?"

I said that I had.

Mom stroked me on the head. And I lay back down and pretended to fall asleep until she went back to bed.

Because it wasn't *me* who had screamed.

It had come from under my bed. Where the Rabbit Monitor was.

I got my walkie-talkie and I whispered, "Suzanne, are you asleep?"

Suzanne didn't speak.

"Suzanne, are you there?" I went under the covers. "SUZANNE, THE RABBIT SCREAMED!"

The walkie-talkie crackled. "Copy that," Suzanne said. "Meet me at the shed. Over and out."

I got out of bed and felt my way, in the dark, through my bedroom door and along the wall in the corridor, until I came to the top of the stairs. I'm not scared of the dark, because I'm nine, but some things in our house aren't nice at night, when the lights aren't on. Like the photo of Dad's Great-Grandma with the black lace veil on her face, and the spider plant with the tentacles that touch you when you go past, and the post with the coats on it at the bottom of the stairs that sometimes looks like a person.

And this time the stair post looked *a lot* like a person. And as I got near it, I saw one of the arms was reaching out. And when I got to the bottom, I thought it tried to touch me.

I ran past it, into the kitchen, to the back door, and turned the handle fast. And then I felt something behind me, tapping me on the back. I froze.

"Are you going out?"

"Tom?"

"Yes?"

"Oh." I turned around. He was in his Batman pajamas and his Bob the Builder hard hat.

"I thought you were something else."

"No," Tom said. "Where are you going?"

"To the shed."

"I'll come."

And I said that he could, because, for one thing, he was already putting his wellies on, and for another thing, I didn't want him getting the Screaming Habdabs and waking up Mom, and for an even other thing, I was glad it was him who had tapped me on the back, and not a coat that had got down off the stair post on its own, or anything like that.

It was cold outside, and the moon was out, and the stars. The sky was big. And when I looked up, it made me feel a bit sick. It was quiet. I held my nose and popped my ears, to hear clearer.

Tom turned on the light on his Bob the Builder hard hat. The light shone on Suzanne. She was waiting by the shed.

"Follow me," she said.

The back lane looked different in the dark.

"Come on, Tom," I said, and I told him it was best to look straight ahead, not out to the sides, where the bushes are, because in the dark you can sometimes see things that aren't really there. And I said that if he wanted, he could hold on to my hand. But Tom said he was Batman, and Bob the Builder, so he wasn't scared.

When we got to the bottom of the lane, I looked up at Joe's house. It was so dark, you couldn't see the windows, or the door, only the shape of the outside. Like the houses Mrs. Peters cut out of black card, to put at the back of the stage when we did the school play.

Suzanne opened the gate.

We crouched down by the hutch. I opened the latch and pushed back some of the hay. The New Rabbit was on its side. There was dribble round its mouth. And its eyes were all strange.

"Is it dead?" Tom said.

The New Rabbit groaned, and twitched its feet.

"Not yet," said Suzanne.

"What are we going to do?" I asked.

Suzanne said we should go back to the shed and make a plan.

I was glad to get away from the New Rabbit, and to be inside the shed with the worms and the wood lice and the wasp trap and all that. I closed the door. We looked at the plans pinned up on the wall.

"We've tried Plan Number One, and Number Two, and Number Three," Suzanne said.

There was only one plan left. It was Plan Number Four: Rescue Joe Ourselves. I looked at the map to his Dad's apartment that Joe had drawn. It was a long way away. Past the Bottom Bus Stop, and over the bridge, and round the roundabout, and down the track, and through the old tunnel, and through the gate, and across the field. All in the dark.

"Joe's Dad might come and collect the New Rabbit in the morning when he reads our letter from the landlord," I said. "And if he doesn't, we could rescue Joe tomorrow, straight after school."

"Tomorrow might be too late," Suzanne

said. "We need to go tonight."

"How are we going to get there?" I asked.

"We'll walk," said Suzanne.

I said I didn't think walking was a good idea.

"How else?" Suzanne said.

"Erm . . . bus?"

Suzanne made her eyebrows go up, and said, "*Anna*," the way I hate. "You don't get buses in the middle of the *night*."

And I said how you did, actually, and that's why it's called a night bus.

Suzanne said she had never heard of a night bus, and there was, "no such thing."

And I said that just because she didn't know about it didn't mean it didn't exist. Because there were millions of things in the world that Suzanne had never heard of. And I tried to think of one, which was hard because Suzanne has actually heard of most things, and because Tom kept pulling at my pajamas and saying, "Anna . . . Anna . . . ANNA . . ."

So I stopped trying to think, and said, "WHAT?!"

"Look." Tom was pointing to something shiny at the back of the shed, near the floor, underneath an old sheet. The light from his Bob the Builder hard hat was making it glint.

I went closer. It was a reflector, on the spoke of a bicycle wheel. I pulled away the old sheet. *"The Super-Speed-Bike-Machine!"*

Me and Suzanne checked the training wheels, and the tires, and the lights. And Tom rang the bell and made the wheels spin round, and all the reflectors shone, and the spokies went up and down.

And Suzanne said we should write a list of things we needed.

So we did. This is what it said . . .

ANNA'S AND SUZANNE'S AND TOM'S LIST OF THINGS WE NEED TO RESCUE JOE-DOWN-THE-STREET

The Super-Speed-Bike-Machine

Tom's Bob the Builder hard hat with the light turned on

Walkie-talkies

2 flashlights (one for Anna, one for Suzanne)

A whistle

A compass

Cookies

Life jacket

Snorkel

Camouflage

When the list was finished, Suzanne said we had too many things, and they would take too long to find. So we crossed the compass off because, like she said, we didn't know whether Joe's house was north or south or anything anyway. And we crossed off the life jacket, and the snorkel, and the whistle as well. And Suzanne wanted to cross off the cookies, too, but Tom said if we weren't taking cookies he was staying at home, so I sneaked back into the house to get some. And I got two flashlights as well, one for me and one for Suzanne. And then we went into the garden and smeared camouflage mud on our faces from Miss Matheson's flower bed.

We got the Super-Speed-Bike-Machine out of the shed. And we walked it down the back lane. And Suzanne said we should have one last look at the New Rabbit, just in case. Because, like she said, there wasn't much point in going to rescue Joe, to bring him back to his rabbit, if it was already dead.

Suzanne shone her light into the hutch. The New Rabbit opened its eyes and groaned. I said maybe we should take the New Rabbit with us, in case it died while we were gone. And Suzanne said that was a good idea.

So I picked the New Rabbit up, and I wrapped Suzanne's coat around it. And I passed it to Tom, in the trailer, to hold. The New Rabbit closed its eyes. Tom

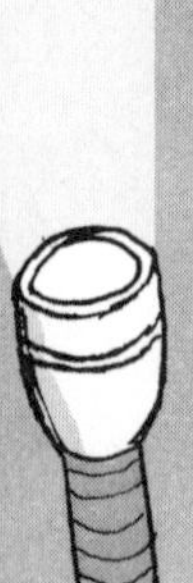

held it close, and stroked it behind the ears, and spoke to it nice and low.

And then Suzanne said, "Shh . . ." because she had heard something.

I listened. There was a jingling sound. I saw two yellow eyes, in the dark, up the road. "It's the Cat Attack Alarm!" I said.

"Quick," said Suzanne. "Let's go."

I got on the saddle of the Super-Speed-Bike-Machine, and Suzanne got on the stunt pegs. And the New Cat came nearer. And when it saw the New Rabbit, it stared, and got down low, and its eyes went very wide.

Suzanne looked at the map. "Turn left!" she said.

I turned on the light. Tom held on tight, and Suzanne pushed off, and I started to pedal as fast as I could, and we all said,

"THREE, TWO, ONE, BLAST OFF!"

And we went off, flying, down the hill, right in the middle of the road, because we were the only ones out. And we whizzed past the horse trough where Tom wets his wellies, and the shops, and the Bottom Bus Stop.

And Suzanne said, "NOW WE'RE OUT-OF-BOUNDS!"

And I rang the bell, and the wind made my eyes water, and Tom did the Batman song in the trailer in the back. And me and Suzanne got The Hysterics.

And when we came to the bridge, Suzanne said, "Stop!" and she put her foot out, and I slammed on the brakes, because the traffic lights were on red.

We waited until the light went green. And we rode over the bridge. It was so quiet, we could hear the river underneath. When we got to the roundabout, Suzanne said, "Go left."

And I did. Well, I *thought* I did, but I'm not very good with my left and my right. And roundabouts are hard.

"That's *right*," Suzanne said. "Not right, *left*!"

"Left?"

"Right, yes!"

"Make up your mind!"

In the end we went round it about a million times. And Tom said he felt sick, and Suzanne told him to stop eating all the cookies. And then she said, "Anna, *here*!" And she grabbed the handlebars, and the Super-Speed-Bike-Machine turned, and we came off the roundabout, and hit a bit of gravel, and skidded, and the trailer hit a bump, and Tom and the New Rabbit and the trailer went flying, up in the air, and the trailer and Tom came down again with a thump.

And Tom said, "Ouch."

But he wasn't hurt because he said he was, "saved by my Bob the Builder hard hat!"

"Where's the New Rabbit?" I said.

Tom looked down at his hands. It was gone.

Me and Suzanne got the walkie-talkies out. We stood back-to-back. And Suzanne walked one way, and I walked the other, and we shone our flashlights from side to side.

"Suzanne to Anna. Suzanne to Anna. Come in, Anna. I'm at the gorse bush. What's your position? Over."

"Anna to Suzanne. Anna to Suzanne. I'm at the traffic cone. Over."

"Copy that. Traffic cone. Are you receiving me? Over."

"Yes."

Suzanne said, "You're supposed to say, 'Receiving you loud and clear.'"

And I said, "We haven't got time to do all the 'Come ins,' and the 'Copies,' and the 'Over and outs' and all that. Let's just look for the New Rabbit!"

And then Suzanne started going on about her Uncle again, and how he's in the army. And about how I shouldn't have wrapped the New Rabbit in her coat because she was cold, and if it was lost, she would be in Big Trouble with her Dad.

And I said how losing someone's coat wasn't as bad as losing someone's rabbit, and what were we going to say to Joe-down-the-street? And then I saw something.

"Look. In the river!" I shone my light on the water.

Me and Suzanne and Tom stood on the bank. Suzanne's coat floated past.

"Can rabbits swim?" Tom asked.

And me and Suzanne didn't answer, because we both knew that they can't. And that the New Rabbit must have drowned. And Tom started to cry.

And I told him he was Batman and Bob the Builder, to try to make him stop. But he didn't. And he took his hard hat off, and put it on the ground.

And then Suzanne said, "Shh, listen." There was a jingling sound. It was coming from the bridge. There were two yellow eyes, in the dark, on the wall. "It's the Cat Attack Alarm again."

The New Cat came close, and it got down very low, and its eyes went very wide, and it stared at something near the edge of the river. And then it disappeared down the bank. And when it came back up, it was dragging something in its mouth. It dropped something white next to Tom's feet. I shone my flashlight on it. The white thing opened its eyes. They were pink.

"The New Rabbit!" Tom said. And he stopped crying and stroked the New Cat on its head until its ears went flat. And he gave it a cookie. Which the New Cat didn't really like. And then the New Cat went back off over the bridge.

Tom got back in the trailer with the New Rabbit, and I sat on the saddle, and Suzanne stood on the stunt pegs. And Suzanne pushed off and I started to pedal. And we carried on down the track, on the Super-Speed-Bike-Machine, until we came to the old tunnel.

We went inside.

It was so dark in the tunnel, even with the flashlights, that we couldn't see the sides.

Suzanne shouted, "Hello . . ."

It echoed back, "Hello . . . *low* . . . *low* . . . "

"Is there anybody there?" Suzanne said.

And the echo said, "There . . . *ere* . . . *ere* . . ."

And we called out our names, and they echoed back, until we came out on the other side.

Suzanne looked at the map. "We have to go through the gate and across the field."

We got off the Super-Speed-Bike-Machine and hid it in the bushes.

Tom wasn't sure about going into the field because when we got near, we could see there were cows. And Tom doesn't like cows because he says they're too big. But I told Tom how cows never hurt anyone. And in the end Tom said okay.

We opened the big gate. And Suzanne held the rabbit. And then we closed it again. Like the sign on it said.

And the cows turned to look at us, and one of them said, "**Mooo . . . ,**" but they didn't move.

The field was full of cowpats, and it was so muddy, it was hard to get across. And Tom's wellies kept getting stuck.

When we got to the other side, there were some buildings straight ahead. We looked at the picture that Joe had done. It matched. We counted the windows along to where Joe's bedroom was. And we threw stones up at it.

A light came on, and the curtains went back, and we saw Joe's face. The window opened.

I said, "Hello, Joe."

And Joe said, "Who's that?"

Because it probably didn't look very like me because of the dark, and the cowpats, and the camouflage on my face and all that.

And I said, "It's Anna."

And Suzanne said, "And Suzanne."

And Tom said, "And Tom."

"We've come to rescue you," said Suzanne.

Joe closed his window. And his curtains. And at first we thought he had gone back to bed. But then a door opened, downstairs.

Joe came out. And we told him all about how the New Rabbit had got poorly again, after he'd gone. And about the old couple in the paper, who got separated and died of broken hearts. And about Suzanne's dream. And how the New Rabbit had screamed.

And Joe held the New Rabbit very close, and he put it inside his pajama top, and he kissed it all over its face. And he said, "Let's go home."

And me and Tom and Suzanne and Joe started back across the field. Which Tom said he didn't mind this time because the cows had gone.

Until we got to the middle, when one appeared, right in front of us, in the dark.

"Mooo . . . ," it said.

We stopped. The cow stared. And then another cow came, and another, and another.

I told Tom to ignore them.

Because of how cows had never hurt anyone.

And I said, "Isn't that right, Joe?" Because Joe always knows about things.

And Joe said how that wasn't *exactly* right, because cows had hurt some people, and once it was someone who was walking his dog, and it was definitely true because it was on the news, and he was called Chris Poole.

And I said how they probably didn't hurt him very badly, and it was probably only by mistake.

And Joe said how they had kicked him, and broken his ribs, and he was only saved because he was in the police and his friend

rescued him in his helicopter. And if he hadn't, the cows would have trampled him to death.

"Oh," I said.

The cows came around us in a circle. And they rolled their eyes and licked their lips. And I heard something roar, and at first I thought it was the noise cows make just before they trample you. So I closed my eyes.

But then I heard it again, and this time it sounded more like a car. So I opened my eyes. And I saw two headlights. And I heard a car horn. And I heard, "Spot on, Skipper. Four sprogs. And they're surrounded. Got 'em in the old illuminators. Fall out."

It was Mr. Tucker. In his old sports car, wearing his driving goggles and his gloves. And Mrs. Rotherham was with him.

Mrs. Rotherham got out of the car, and she opened the gate, and then she got back in, and Mr. Tucker drove the car right into the field, and he flashed the lights and honked the horn. And Mrs. Rotherham waved her walking stick. And the cows all scattered.

And Mr. Tucker stopped the car and he said, "Hallo, Basher." And he gave Tom the salute.

And Tom gave Mr. Tucker the salute back.

And Mr. Tucker said, "Hop in!"

And Tom got on Mr. Tucker's knee, and Mr. Tucker said, "Bit of cowpat in the cockpit there, Basher."

And the rest of us piled in the back.

And Mr. Tucker said, "Good God. Overload."

And he put his goggles over his eyes and tightened his driving gloves and he said,

"Honk, honk!" Like Toad of Toad Hall does in my *Wind in the Willows* book at home.

And Mr. Tucker drove us home even faster than the Super-Speed-Bike-Machine.

CHAPTER 17
The Poisoned Parsley

That was just about everything that happened in the Great Rabbit Rescue.

When we got home, there were two police cars outside. Mom and Dad, and Suzanne's Mom and Dad, and Joe's Mom, and two policemen were in our kitchen.

I thought we were in Big Trouble then, but nobody shouted, not even Suzanne's Dad.

And Mom cuddled me and Tom in.

And Suzanne and her Mom and Dad went to their house.

And Joe and his Mom and the New Rabbit went to their house.

And the policemen filled in their forms. And they went home as well.

And Mom made some tea for Mrs. Rotherham. And Mr. Tucker said he'd prefer something stronger. And Dad brought him some brandy. And Mr. Tucker said, "That's the ticket. Just a snifter." And he drank it down in one.

And Mom made some hot milk for me and Tom. And Tom fell asleep on Mr. Tucker's knee before his milk even came. And Mr. Tucker fell asleep too.

And he started snoring. And Mom and Mrs. Rotherham got The Hysterics.

And then Mrs. Rotherham told Mom the story of how her and Mr. Tucker found us. And how she had seen the police cars, and come down the road, and how Mr. Tucker was out, asking the police what was going on. And how the policemen said we were missing. And how Mrs. Rotherham had seen the tire tracks from the Super-Speed-Bike-Machine at the bottom of the road, and that the hutch was open, and that the New Rabbit was gone, and how she went up to the shed and saw all Joe's pictures about his rabbit, and the list about what he didn't like about living at his Dad's, and our plans on the wall, and how they had all been ticked off, except number four, which was, "Rescue Joe Ourselves."

And how she found the piece of paper

with Joe's Dad's address. And how her and Mr. Tucker tried to tell the police, but they said they had to take statements from everyone first. And how Mr. Tucker said, "Humph, Old Gendarmerie, load of old bull and bumph." And got his old sports car out of the garage.

And that's all I remember, because then I fell asleep as well.

The next day me and Suzanne and Tom and Joe stayed home from school. And Joe came round in the morning to tell us that his Mom had taken the New Rabbit to the vet, and how the vet had given the New Rabbit some pills and said that the New Rabbit wasn't dying of a broken heart at all. It was dying because it had been poisoned.

And Suzanne said we had better do an investigation to find out who had poisoned it.

So we went to see Mrs. Rotherham to ask her to help us, because of how she used to be in the police and everything.

And Suzanne said, "Who could have done it?"

And Mrs. Rotherham said, "Who *indeed*?"

And she gave me and Suzanne a file with a label on it that said, "The Case of the Poisoned Rabbit." And inside it was our Spy Club notebook, which Mrs. Rotherham had taken from the shed. And she had highlighted the bits about Joe going away, and about us feeding the New Rabbit, and the New Rabbit being unwell. And there were some privet leaves, and daffodils, and apple seeds, and some of the strange-smelling parsley from

Miss Matheson's garden in the file as well. All in see-through plastic bags, sealed up. And they had tags on them that said, "*Evidence.*" And there was an old book with pictures of poisonous flowers and plants, and one of the corners of the pages was folded down. And on the page it said, "Common house and garden plants toxic to leporid creatures." And all of the things in the little bags inside the file were on the list. And at the bottom of the list it said, "*Aethusa cynapium,* or fool's or

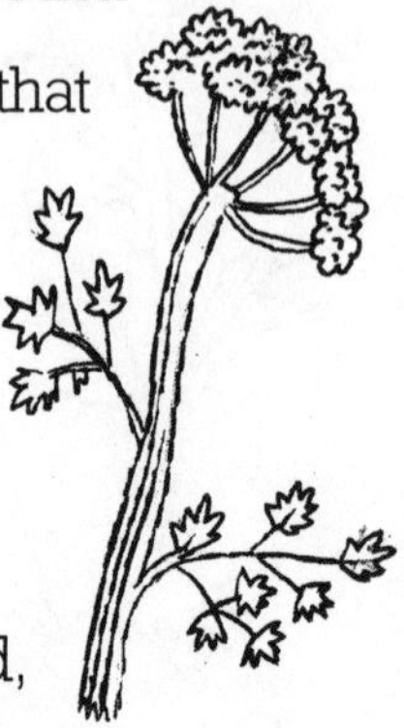

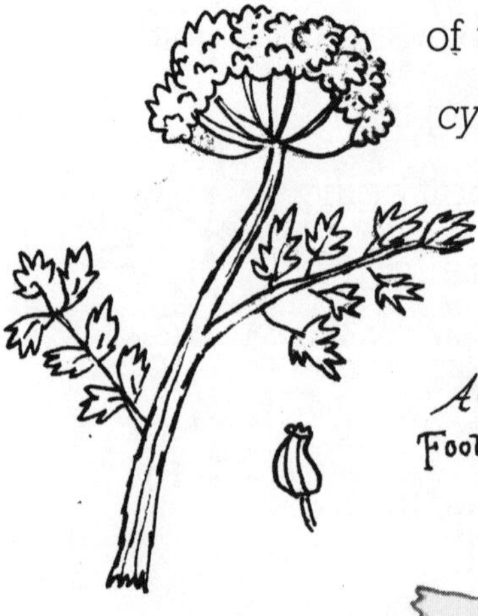

Aethusa Cynapium
FOOL'S PARSLEY

poison parsley, easily distinguished from parsley proper by its height, girth, and foul-smelling odor."

Me and Suzanne looked up "leporid" in my dictionary. It said . . .

leporid [lep-uh-rid] ✦ *noun*
an animal of the family Leporidae, comprising the rabbits and hares

And we looked in Suzanne's as well. It said . . .

leporid [lep-uh-rid] ✦ *noun*

rabbit

The next day, at school, Joe sat back in his old seat. And Mrs. Peters called Joe's name out last, taking roll. And Joe said, "Here."

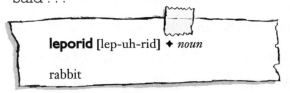

Mrs. Rotherham didn't tell anyone what had really happened with Joe-down-the-street and his rabbit and why it nearly died. And neither did me and Suzanne.

But we took the rest of the parsley out of the shed. And we put it on Miss Matheson's compost heap. And we hid the file of the Case of the Poisoned Rabbit next to the Spy Club notebook, behind the worms and the wasp trap, on the shelf in the shed.

Me and Suzanne don't go on the walkie-talkies as much anymore. Not now that Joe is back down the road. Because mostly we play Dingo the Dog, and Mountain Rescue, and see how long we can stare at the sun before we go blind and all that.

We aren't allowed back on the Super-Speed-Bike-Machine, though. Dad took me and Tom to find it, in the bushes, by the field by Joe's house. And when we got it home, and Mom saw how the training wheels were hanging off, and the back wheel was bent, and one of the tires had burst, she said, "That contraption is condemned."

And she tried to put it out with the trash cans.

But me and Tom begged, and in the end she let us put it back in the shed. Under the dust sheet, behind the stepladders, and the plant stakes and the broken old floorboards.

Suzanne says that when we're older, and we haven't got any bounds to be in, we can take the walkie-talkies as far away as we want. And one of us can go on the Super-Speed-Bike-Machine, and the other one can go on buses and boats and things like that.

And then Suzanne says she will say, "Suzanne to Anna. Suzanne to Anna. I'm in America. Are you receiving me? Over."

And I will say, "Anna to Suzanne. Anna to

Suzanne. I'm in Afghanistan. Receiving you loud and clear. Over."

Because those places are about the same far apartness from here. We've measured it on a map.

And when we do it, I'm going to get Tom to come with me, and Suzanne is going to take Joe-down-the-street.

Because Tom and Joe love the Super-Speed-Bike-Machine, and buses, and boats and things like that. And they don't like being left behind.

The End

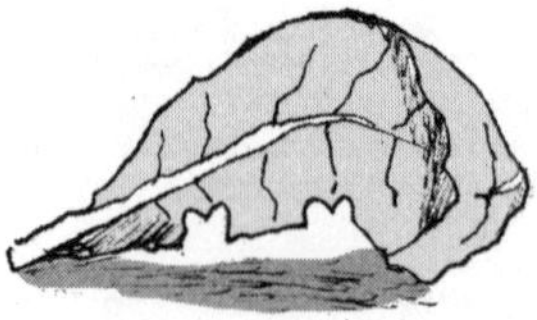

THE GREAT CAT CONSPIRACY

Katie Davies

Illustrated by Hannah Shaw

Beach Lane Books
New York London Toronto Sydney New Delhi

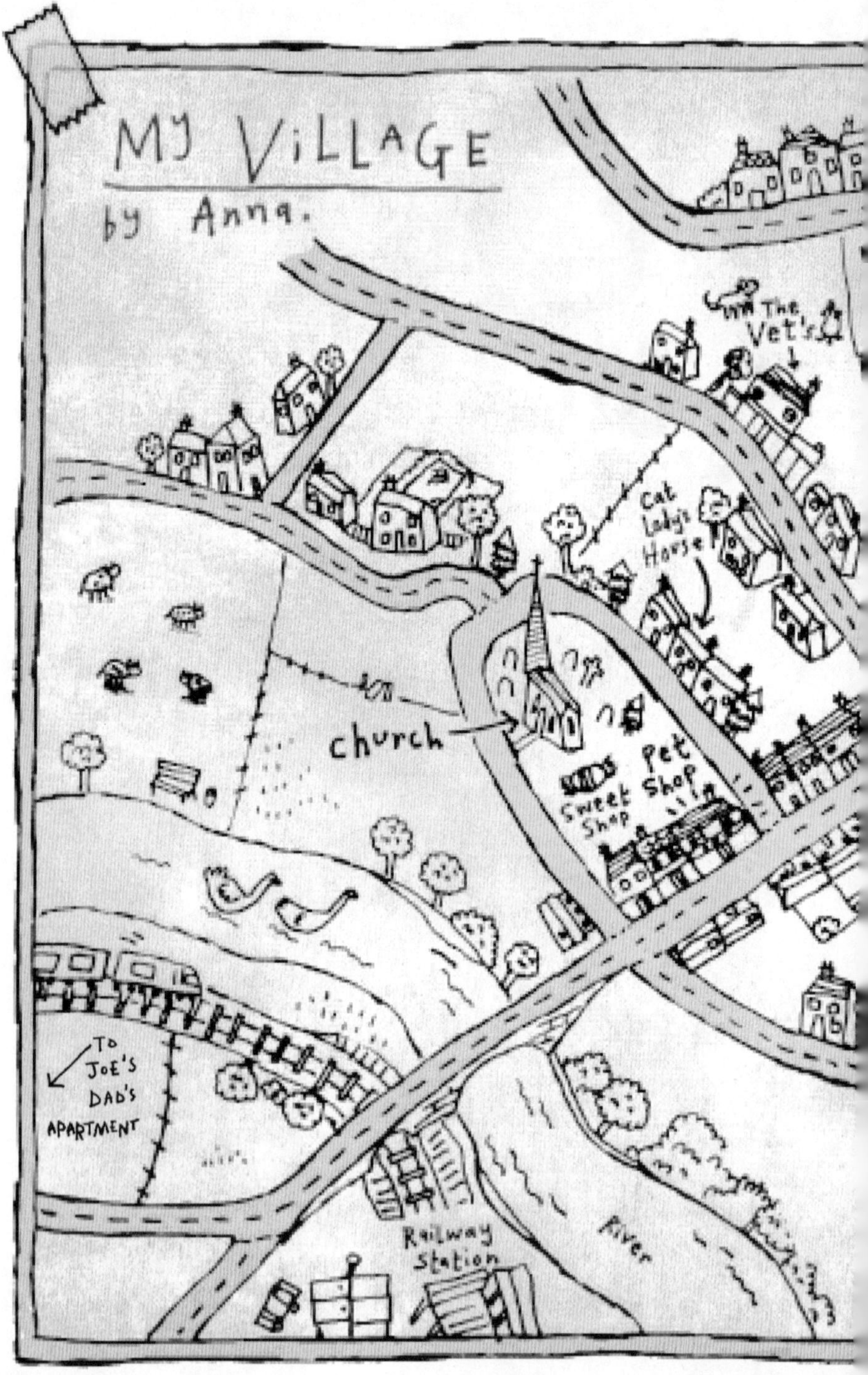

MY VILLAGE
by Anna.
The Vet's
Cat Lady's House
church
Pet Shop
Sweet Shop
TO JOE'S DAD'S APARTMENT
Railway Station
River

School
The Police Station
MY House
Shed
Back Lane
1
2
3
4
5
Joe's House
Suzanne's House
Miss Matheson's
Vicarage
Mr. Tucker's House
Mrs. Rotherham's House

For Harry, of course

Thanks to Alan, and Mum and Dad,
and Venetia at Simon and Schuster.

BEACH LANE BOOKS
An imprint of Simon & Schuster Children's Publishing Division
1230 Avenue of the Americas, New York, New York 10020

The story "The Cat That Walked by Himself" is taken from
Rudyard Kipling's *Just So Stories*, published 1902.
Originally published in Great Britain in 2011 by Simon & Schuster UK Ltd.
Published by arrangement with Simon & Schuster UK Ltd
First U.S. edition 2012

Manufactured in the United States of America
0312 FFG
2 4 6 8 10 9 7 5 3 1
Library of Congress Cataloging-in-Publication Data
Davies, Katie, 1978–
The great cat conspiracy / Katie Davies ; illustrated by Hannah Shaw.—1st U.S. ed.
p. cm.—(The great critter capers)
Summary: When their naughty cat disappears while being disciplined for bringing home the head of the vicar's most expensive koi carp, three siblings suspect a kidnapping and start an investigation.
ISBN 978-1-4424-4513-0 (paper over board)
ISBN 978-1-4424-4515-4 (eBook)
[1. Mystery and detective stories. 2. Cats—Fiction. 3. Brothers and sisters—Fiction. 4. Family life—England—Fiction. 5. England—Fiction. 6. Humorous stories.] I. Shaw, Hannah, ill. II. Title.
PZ7.D283818Gp 2012
[Fic]—dc23
2011045508

CHAPTER 1
Cat Conspiracy

This is a story about Tom, and the Cat Lady, and everything that happened when the New Cat vanished. After it went missing, Mom said that me and Tom had to stop talking about the New Cat, and telling everyone how it had been kidnapped by the Cat Lady, and all that. She said, "*Anna*," (that's my name) "you can't go around accusing old ladies, and bandying words like 'conspiracy' about, which you don't even understand." But, like I told Tom, I *did* understand what a conspiracy was. Because me and my friend Suzanne looked it up in my dictionary, when we first heard there was one from Graham Roberts at Sunday School. This is what it said:

conspiracy [kun-spir-uh-see] ✦ *noun*
an evil, unlawful, treacherous, or surreptitious plan formulated in secret; plot

And what the dictionary said was probably right. Because ours wasn't the only cat that had vanished. Emma Hendry, in Mrs. Peters's class, couldn't find her cat either. And nor could Joe-down-the-street's babysitter, Brian. And Graham Roberts said he had *seen* the Cat Lady kidnapping cats, and taking them into her house, himself.

And he said, "With my *very own eyes,*" and swore it was true on Mrs. Constantine's *life*. Mrs. Constantine is in charge at Sunday School. She is the Vicar's wife.

Suzanne said that Graham swearing on Mrs. Constantine might not count, because Graham sometimes lies. And you're only supposed to swear on the life of someone you *like*. And Graham didn't even have Mrs. Constantine going to heaven when he did his big collage called "IT'S *JUDGEMENT* DAY!" Because he made her out of an egg carton and she was too big to fit on it.

Anyway, like I told Mom, me and Tom did know *some* things about the Cat Lady, and where the New Cat was, and what had happened to it, and so did Suzanne. Because we were the ones who had sent out the Search Party. *And* we were the ones who were actually *in* it. And the whole *point* of a Search Party is to find things out.

It was Tom who first noticed that the New Cat had vanished. Tom is my brother. He's five. He's four years younger than I am. I'm nine. I've got another brother and a sister too, called Andy and Joanne, but they're not in this story because they're older than me and Tom and they don't really care about cats or conspiracies or anything like that.

If it wasn't for Tom, no one might even have minded that the New Cat had gone anywhere. Because, before we couldn't find it, Tom was the only one in our house who cared about the New Cat, and what it got up to.

Mom said that *she* cared about what the New Cat got up to as well because, she said, "*I'm* the one who has to clean up after it all the time."

But that isn't really the same kind of caring.

Most cats don't need to be cleaned up after. That's why Mom said we could get a new one, after our *Old* Cat died, and why we weren't allowed a dog, like me and Tom wanted. The New Cat isn't like most cats, though. The New Cat makes more mess than anyone's dog does. It makes more mess even than Tom. And it's not easy-to-clean-up mess, either. Not like jigsaws, and sticklebricks, and Spider-Man pants, and all that. The mess that the New Cat makes is normally *dead.* Because, whenever it leaves the house, the New Cat *hunts.* And, after it's been hunting, it brings the things it has hunted inside, and puts them in places for people to find. Sometimes the things it brings in are still a bit alive.

Like the hedgehog curled up in a ball, which it rolled in through the front door. And the greenfinch with one wing, which was flapping behind the fridge. And the frog in the log basket, which me and Suzanne were going to bury, until we got it in the garden and it hopped out of its box.

Most of the time, though, the things that the New Cat brings in are *definitely* dead. And sometimes they're so

dead it's hard to tell what they *would* have been when they were *alive*. And that's when you only find a few feathers, or a bunch of bones, or a pile of slimy insides.

CHAPTER 2
The Petition

Suzanne lives next door. Her bedroom is right next to mine. If there wasn't a wall between our houses, our family and Suzanne's would live in one big house together, instead of two small houses apart, which would be a lot better. Because then me and Suzanne wouldn't have to ring on each other's doorbells, or bang on the wall, or shout through the letter box every time we needed to talk. We could talk all the time, whenever we wanted, while we're supposed to be doing other things, like brushing our teeth, or remembering our spelling, or staying in our rooms until we've thought about what we've done.

I asked Mom if we could knock down the wall between our house and Suzanne's house.

Mom laughed, even though it wasn't funny, and said, "You and Suzanne practically live together already." Which isn't true because we only have our dinner together on Tuesdays and Thursdays. And we aren't allowed to stay round each other's houses on school nights. And we don't go swimming together because Suzanne's got grommets.

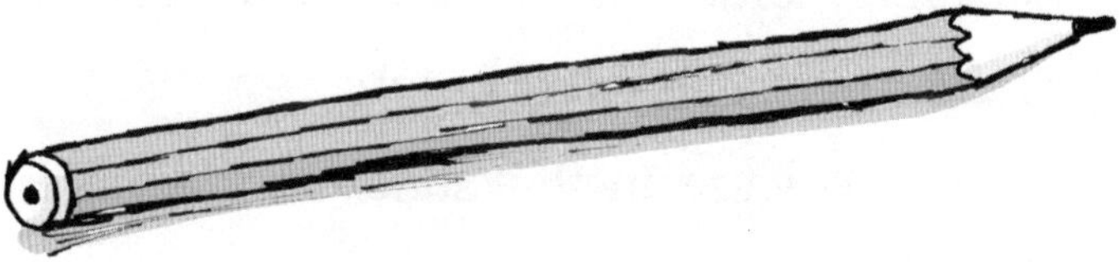

This is what it says about "grommets" in my dictionary:

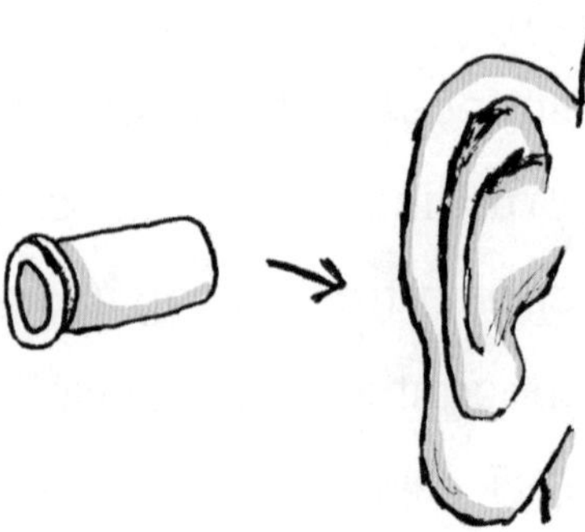

grommet [grom-it] ✦ *noun*
a tube-shaped device used for the treatment of persistent middle-ear infections where thick gluelike fluid builds up behind the eardrum

So me and Suzanne decided to do a Petition to see if we could get the wall knocked down that way, because, like Suzanne said, "When you do a Petition, people can see you're serious."

So we went in the shed, in the back

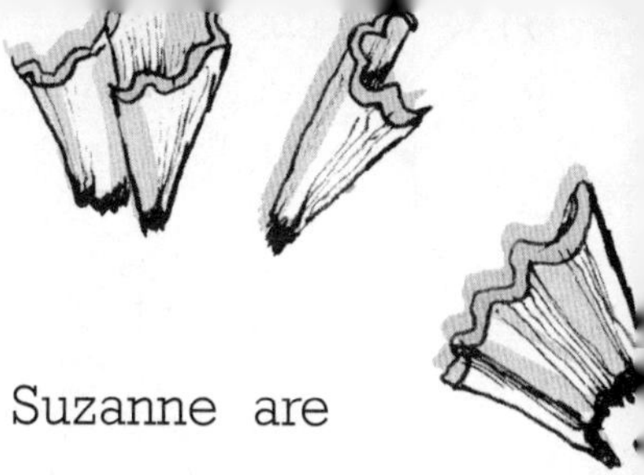

lane, which only me and Suzanne are allowed into (except for Tom if he wants, when he remembers the password), and Suzanne wrote "Purtishun" at the top of a piece of paper. And then she stopped because she said before she *wrote* the Purtishun, she just wanted to check exactly what one *was*. So we looked it up in the dictionary (which took a long time because Suzanne wasn't exactly sure how to spell it, either). This is what it said in my dictionary:

petition [puh-tish-un] ✦ *noun*
a formal request addressed to a person or persons in power, soliciting some favor, right, mercy, or other benefit

And this is what it said in Suzanne's:

petition [puh-tish-un] ✦ *noun*
a document signed by a large number of people demanding some action from the authorities

And, after that, we knew *exactly* what a petition was. And Suzanne said we could probably write one by ourselves, but just in case we might miss something out, we should go and see Mrs. Rotherham up the road. Mrs. Rotherham is really old. Her house smells a bit strange, of old things and mothballs, like Nana's house used to. But she's good at playing cards, and getting everyone ice cream, and showing you how to do things when you aren't exactly sure.

Mrs. Rotherham said, "A Petition? Sounds

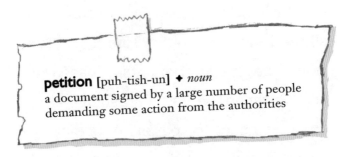

serious. You'd better come in."

So we did. And we told her all about the wall, and how we thought it would be better if it wasn't there, because we couldn't talk to each other through it anymore, not since Suzanne's Dad took Suzanne's walkie-talkie off her, in the middle of the night, and rang on our doorbell in his dressing gown, and made Mom get me out of bed, and said, **"*HAND* THE DAMN THING *OVER!* IF I HEAR, *'ANNA TO SUZANNE . . . ANNA TO SUZANNE,'* ONE MORE TIME, I'LL GO OUT OF MY *MIND!*"**

Mrs. Rotherham listened and said, *"Well,"* and, "I *see*," and, "Oh *dear*, oh dear, oh dear." And she said she thought a Petition was *just* what was called for. And that she would start us off, and me and Suzanne could finish.

This is what our Petition said:

We the undersigned (which Mrs. Rotherham said means "we the people who have signed this underneath") *are in agreement that the wall between the Morris house* (which is mine) *and the Barry house* (which is Suzanne's) *should be torn down in the name of peace and unity* and because it gets in the way and stops you being able to talk when you really need to, like in the middle of the night, when you aren't allowed out, and you haven't got walkie-talkies anymore, and you've thought of something important, which can't wait until the morning in case you forget it.

The people we got to sign it were . . .

A Morris (me)
S Barry (Suzanne)
K Rotherham (Mrs. Rotherham)
CB (Carl Barry, Suzanne's brother)

Suzanne's Mom said Carl's signature didn't count because he's only a baby, and he can't write, and Suzanne must have held his hand. Which Suzanne admitted afterward that she did, but only a bit.

We didn't exactly get a *large* number of people to sign the Petition, like Suzanne's dictionary said we should. Because getting people to put their names on was harder than we thought. Dad wouldn't sign it, and nor would Andy, or Joanne.

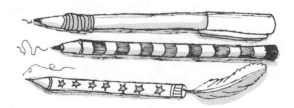

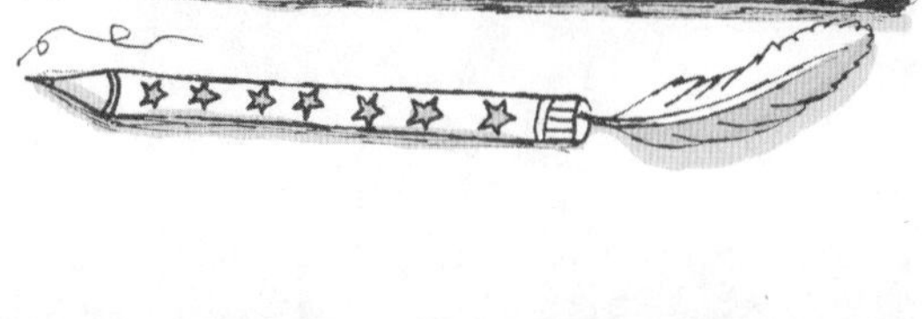

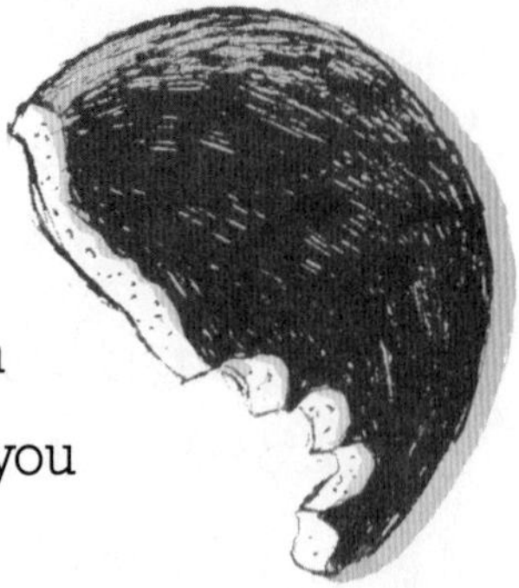

Even Tom wouldn't put his name on. And you can normally get Tom to do anything, as long as you give him a cookie.

I showed Tom the Petition, and the cookie, and he looked at it for ages. And then he said, "What does it say?" Because he's only five and he can't really read yet, except for "the," and "cat," and his name. So I read the Petition out loud, and Tom asked, "What does it mean?" So I told him how it was a serious thing, which people were putting their names on, to say they wanted the wall knocked down.

"What wall?"

"*This* one."

"Why?"

"Because," I said, "if the wall isn't there, our family and Suzanne's will all live in one *big* house, which would be a lot better."

Tom said, "Where will Suzanne's Dad live?"

Suzanne told Tom her Dad would live in the house as well.

But Tom said he didn't want to live with Suzanne's Dad because "he shouts too much." Which is true. We hear him all the time through the wall, when he's **"COUNTING TO *THREE*"** and when he's **"NOT GOING TO SAY IT *AGAIN*"** and when he's **"LOSING THE WILL TO *LIVE*!"**

Suzanne said she didn't think her Dad would shout at anyone on *our* side of the house, because he will only be in charge of the people on *her* side.

But Tom wasn't sure. And he said he would rather keep the wall where it was. Because some of it was in his bedroom, and it had his bookshelf on it, and his Batman stickers, and the bit he had colored in black with a crayon. And he went and asked Dad for a cookie instead.

I didn't say anything to Suzanne, but Tom was probably right about living with her Dad. And how he would be in charge.

Like he was the time our family and Suzanne's family went on a walk, which no one wanted to go on. He was definitely in charge of everyone then. Because he had a map, and a compass, and a stick that turned into a seat, which we weren't allowed to touch. And he told us what everything was, and how long it had been there. Like the bridge, and the battlements, and the boulders.

And there wasn't enough time to stop and play Pooh Sticks. And he walked in front and said, **"ONLY NINE MORE MILES,"** and **"WE WON'T BE BEATEN BY A BIT OF RAIN,"**

and ***"RUN FOR COVER, FOR CRYING OUT LOUD!"***

And he made Tom leave all his best things behind, which he had been collecting on the way, like a brick, and a sheet of blue plastic, and a bag of gravel. Because he said Tom was slowing us down.

And after that Tom refused to walk at all, and he lay facedown on the wet ground,

and had what Nana used to call the Screaming Habdabs. And Dad had to carry him the whole way home.

Anyway, it probably wouldn't have made any difference *how* many people me and Suzanne had got to sign the Petition. Because when I showed it to Mom, she said,

"Don't be ridiculous, Anna. The wall is not coming down. This is a dictatorship, not a democracy. Get that eggplant eaten."

This is what it says a dictatorship is in my dictionary:

dictatorship [dik-tey-ter-ship] ✦ *noun*
a form of government in which absolute power is exercised by a dictator with imperious, overbearing control

And this is what it says a "democracy" is:

democracy [de-mok-ruh-see] ✦ *noun*
a form of government in which the supreme power is vested in the people and exercised by them or by their elected agents

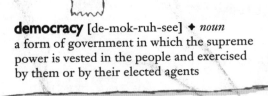

I hate eggplant. Especially the ones from Suzanne's Dad's garden. Anyway, I stopped wanting to get the wall down so much after that because for one thing, I thought Tom might be right about living with Suzanne's Dad, and for another thing, I found out that the wall had a *hole* in it.

CHAPTER 3
Three Blind Mice

The day I found out about the hole in the wall there was a strange smell in the house, like there is sometimes, when Mom stops what she's doing, and sniffs, and says, "*Ooh,* what on *earth* is *that*?"

And Dad says, "What?"

And Mom says, "I can *smell* something. Can't you?"

And Dad says, "Nope." And stares at the TV and tries not to talk about it.

And Mom goes sniffing round the house, on her hands and knees, until she finds out what it is. Sometimes it might be a moldy potato in the bottom of the vegetable rack. Or dog poo that came in on someone's shoe, and got trod into the carpet. But most of the time it's something that's dead somewhere, which the New Cat has dragged in from outside.

Mom followed the smell into the hall, until she came to the closet under the stairs, where the laundry basket is, and the ironing pile, and all Dad's things, at the back, that aren't really allowed to be there, like the bag of worn-out footballs, and the broken tennis rackets, and the pile of newspapers he hasn't got round to reading yet. The closet under the stairs has got so much stuff in it that when you open the door, all the ironing falls out. And then you have to pick it all up, and shove it back in, and close the door quick, and put the catch down to keep it in. The closet under the stairs didn't *used* to have as much ironing in it as it does now. Because, before Nana died, whenever she came round, she always said, "My program's on in a bit. Get me set up, Duck, and I'll attack your ironing pile."

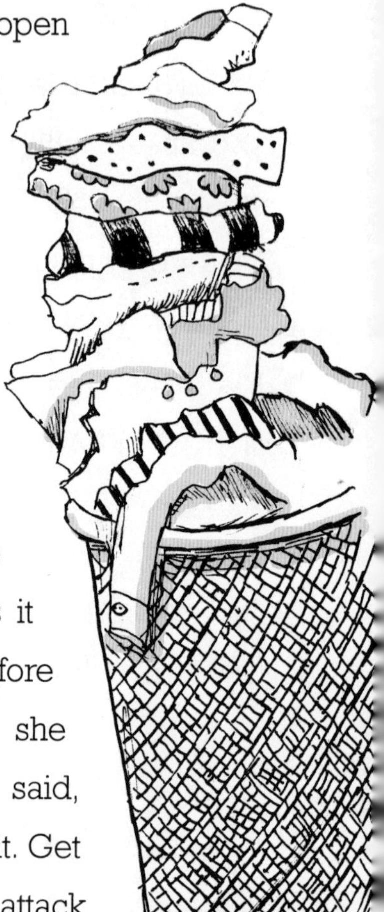

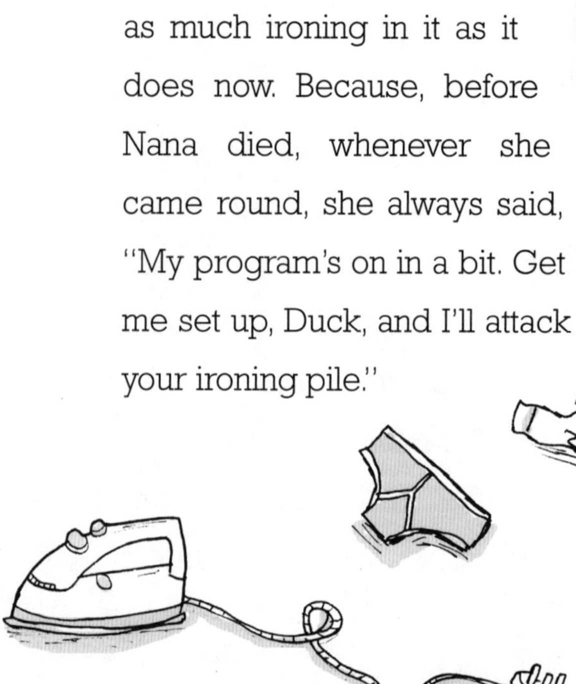

And then Mom got the ironing board out. And put it up in front of the TV. And Nana ironed everything, even things that Mom said were daft, like dishcloths, and hankies, and Tom's underwear. Because no one can iron as fast as Nana could, or as neatly. And at the end of *Coronation Street*, Nana stopped ironing and sat down. And Mom brought her half a cup of tea, in a china cup (because Nana didn't like mugs and she said if she had more than half a cup, she would be up and down to the toilet all night).

Anyway, this time, Mom was sniffing around. And when she came to the closet under the stairs, she stopped. And she opened the door. And all the ironing fell out. And she sniffed again, and said, "Oh no, it's coming from in *here*."

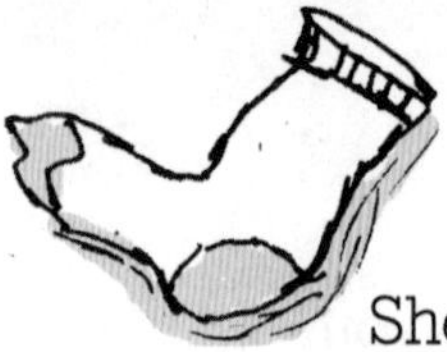

She sniffed through the ironing. And then she got the dirty laundry basket out, and sniffed through that. (I wouldn't sniff the things in the laundry basket because it's full of old football socks, and gymnastics leotards, and Dad's dirty pants, but Mom doesn't mind because she's a mom and that's what they do.)

And, after that, Mom started pulling Dad's things out of the closet as well, so she could get right inside. And she piled them all up in the hall. There was the alarm clock that doesn't go off, and the toaster that doesn't pop, and the kettle that me and Tom blew up by mistake.

Mom said, "No wonder there's not enough room for the ironing. It's like the electrical afterlife in here." And she pulled out some more stuff. A stool with one leg, and a bucket with a hole in the bottom, and half a broom handle without a head.

Me and Tom sat on the stairs and watched. And Mom said, "I thought I threw those out *years* ago." And, "Why on *earth* are we keeping *these*?" And, "*That's* as much use as a chocolate teapot."

After a while, there was so much stuff in the hall that you could hardly see the carpet. When Mom got to the very bottom of the closet, she found a black trash bag. And she sniffed inside. And then she put her

hand over her mouth, and made a sound like she was about to be sick, which went, "Eur-*ugh*-eka!"

And she put a pair of rubber gloves on, and laid some newspaper on the floor. And she reached inside the trash bag, and started pulling things out, one at a time.

The bag was full of Dad's clothes from the olden days, like we've seen in photos, from before he was even bald. There was a flowery shirt with a flappy collar, and some purple velvet flares, like Willy Wonka wears, and some massive underpants, with brown-and-orange stripes and a flap at the front, called Y-fronts.

Tom wanted to pull something out of the bag himself, because, he said, "It's a *lucky dip*."

But Mom said, "No! There's nothing

lucky about it. Stand *back*, Tom. It stinks!"

And she reached in again, and felt around, and she pulled something out, and held it up in the air, by its tail, and she said, *"Aha,* a *mouse*!" And she laid it on the newspaper. And then she tipped the trash bag upside down. And two more things fell out. And they were mice as well. Mom laid them on the newspaper, next to the first one.

Tom asked, "Are they dead?"

"*Dead?*" Mom said. "They're practically decomposed!" And then she shouted, *"PETE!"* (which is our Dad's name). Dad put the TV on pause and came into the hall. Mom pointed to the

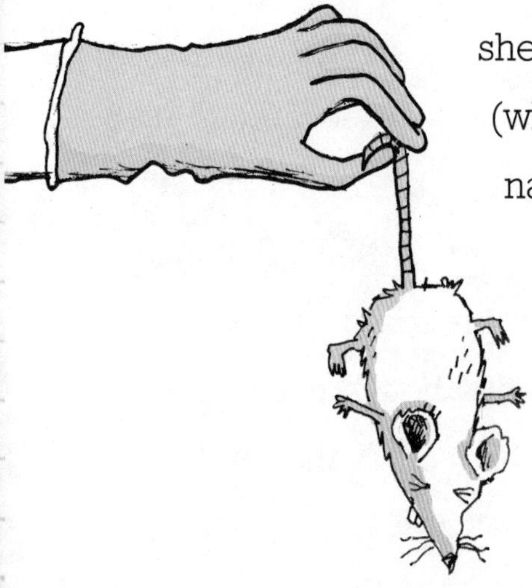

newspaper with the mice on it, in a line. And she said, *"What* do you call *this*?"

Dad said, "Urm . . . Three Blind Mice?" And he got The Hysterics (which is what you get when you start laughing and then you can't stop). And I got The Hysterics a bit as well. But Tom didn't, because he said he didn't think three blind mice were very funny, especially not when they were dead as well.

And neither did Mom, because she said, "It's a mass grave, Pete, for goodness' sake! The New Cat is disposing of its bodies in your trash bag."

And she told Dad to start sorting all his stuff out, under the stairs, like she had been asking him to "for *ten years*!" Because, she said, it was a breeding ground for bacteria, and a serious health hazard, and she had seen something on TV that said you shouldn't have anything in your house that isn't beautiful or useful.

And Dad said, "Well, we'd better get rid of Anna in that case." And he got The Hysterics again. But only a bit. Because nobody else did.

Mom said, "I mean it. Two piles: one for the dump and the other for the charity shop. I'm going to see Pam. I want it gone when I get back."

Pam is Joe-down-the-street's Mom. She lives with Joe and Joe's New Rabbit at number 1.

And Tom went as well. Tom loves it at Pam's house, even on the weekends when Joe's at his Dad's and it's just Mom and Pam, drinking tea and talking about boring things. Like work, and laundry, and Joe's Mom's New Boyfriend. Tom sits on Pam's knee and stays quiet, and eats all the cookies.

I didn't want to go to Pam's. And sorting things into piles and throwing them out isn't the kind of thing Dad is very good at, so I said I would stay and help. Because putting things in the trash is one of Dad's worst things. That's why he eats all the leftovers off my and Tom's plates, which is good when it's eggplant, and Mom hasn't noticed, or the black bit in our bananas, or the skin off our fish. Dad eats the bits that no one wants, even when he's already full up himself. And then he says, "Ugh, I've *eaten* too much," and has to go and lie down, in the dark, on the sofa, because he's too sick to help with the dishes.

CHAPTER 4
The Hole in the Wall

Dad looked at all the things in the hall. And he started putting them into two piles. And, after a while, he said that instead of *two* piles, he would do *three*: one for the charity shop, one for the dump, and one for things that might come in useful. And he said we wouldn't need to tell Mom about the *third* pile because we could put it all up in the loft. In secret.

So I held each thing up, and said what it was. Like, "a clock with no hands," and "an umbrella with a hole in it," and "a shoe with no sole." And Dad said which pile it should go in.

"Dump. No, charity shop. No, keep. Just *in case.*"

When we had finished, there was a small pile for the charity shop. And a small pile for the dump. And a BIG pile of "useful" things to keep. And Dad said we had to hurry up and get the "useful" pile up into the loft before Mom came back.

So he got the stepladder from the shed, and took it up to my room, where the hatch for the loft is. And he climbed up and opened it. And some dust, and dirt, and dead flies fell out on his head.

And I went downstairs and got as many things as I could carry from the "useful" pile in the hall, and brought them back up, and passed them to Dad on the ladder. And I ran up and down doing that, as fast as I could. Because Dad said if we got it all done before Mom came back, he would let me go up the ladder, into the loft, myself.

Without getting off the ladder, Dad balanced all the things on top of one another, close to the loft hatch. And when he was finished, he let me go up.

Dad handed me his flashlight. I had never been in the loft before. It was dark, and dusty, and Dad said there were bats. And he said you have to be careful to walk on the beams. Otherwise you can come straight through the ceiling.

"Quick, Anna, before Mom comes. And don't knock anything. If that stuff falls through, my life won't be worth living."

Careful not to knock Dad's pile of things, and holding on to the beams above me, I stepped from beam to beam toward a wall I could see across the other side. On my left the roof got lower and lower, and on my right higher and higher. I reached the far wall, and ran my hand along. My hand went through a hole where some bricks were missing, and I grazed my arm.

"Hurry up!" Dad called out. "Don't go too far back."

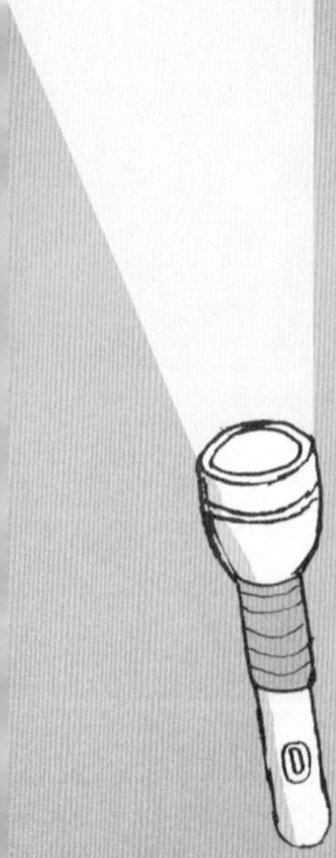

I shone my flashlight through the hole. I could see beams and boxes, just like in our loft. Only these boxes were all in rows, and they were on top of boards that had been put down.

"All right, come back now, Anna."

I stuck my head right through

the hole, and squinted to see. Some of the boxes had writing on them. There were "Christmas Decorations," and "Camping Equipment," and one of the boxes said "Suzanne's old toys," in Suzanne's handwriting. The hole went straight into *Suzanne's* loft.

"Anna!" said Dad. "If you don't come back now, I'm closing the hatch."

I went back the way I had come, and careful not to touch Dad's pile of useful things, I followed him back down the ladder.

"What were you doing?" Dad said.

"Urm, I saw a bat," I said. And I slid down the ladder, and ran downstairs.

"Oi, I thought we were going to the dump? Wash your hands before Mom gets back. *Anna?*"

But I didn't answer. And I didn't have time to wash my hands. And I hadn't seen a bat. I needed to see Suzanne to tell her about the hatch, and the loft, and the wall, and the hole.

I ran round to her house. And I rang on the Barrys' doorbell three times. Me and Suzanne always do three rings if it's something important.

And then I ran away again because it was a Saturday, which meant Suzanne's Dad would be home, and he doesn't like people ringing the doorbell more than once. He sticks his head out the window and says, **"YES? IS THERE A FIRE? I HEARD IT THE *FIRST* TIME, FOR *CRYING OUT LOUD*!"**

I waited in the shed until Suzanne came round. And I told her all about the hatch, and the loft, and the wall, and the hole.

"We need to do a plan," Suzanne said. So we did. This is what the plan looked like when it was finished:

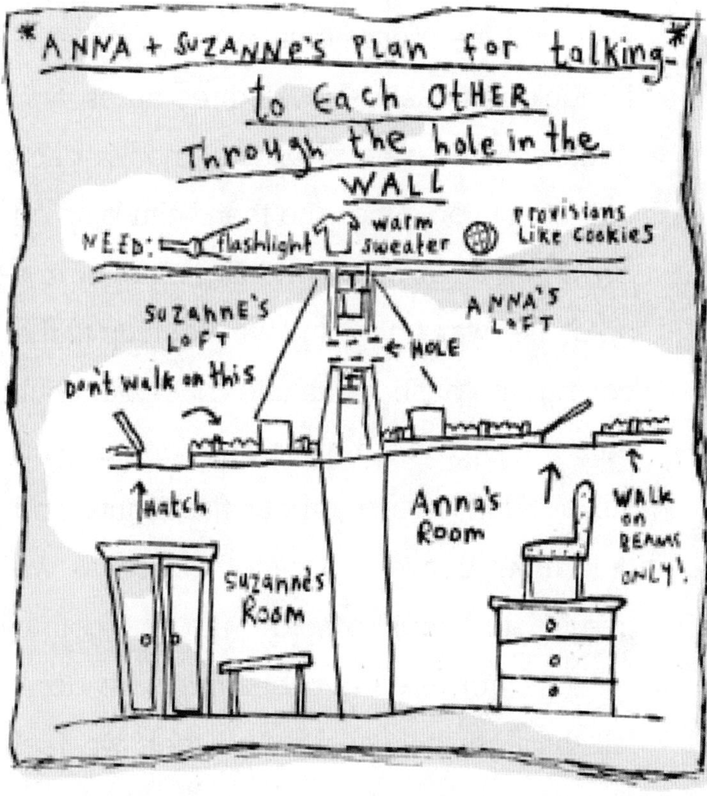

Since then, whenever me and Suzanne really need to talk, like in the middle of the night, when we aren't allowed out, and we've thought of something important, which can't wait until the morning, in case we forget it, I knock on Suzanne's wall three times, and if the coast is clear, Suzanne knocks back three times on mine. And then I climb up on my chest of drawers, and Suzanne climbs up on her wardrobe, and we reach up to the ceiling, and push the hatches back. And pull ourselves up on our arms, and scramble up inside. And we turn on our flashlights, and hold them between our teeth, because we need both hands to hold on to the roof, to balance from beam to beam, so we don't fall through the ceiling. And then we feel along the wall, and we meet at the hole. And we stay up there and talk about things, like the beams, and the bats, and whether there are holes in all the walls, in all the lofts, the whole way down the road. And how, if there are, you could climb through each one, and come out at the house at the bottom, which is Joe-down-the-street's.

CHAPTER 5
Miss Matheson's Dog

Before the New Cat vanished, when it wasn't busy hunting, and killing things, and hiding their bodies round the house, it used to follow Tom around and watch what he was doing. Most of the things Tom does aren't that good for watching, like walking in a straight line with his eyes closed, or collecting gravel, or helping Mr. Tucker pick up litter. But the New Cat didn't mind. It just waited nearby, with one eye open, watching Tom, and washing its whiskers.

Mr. Tucker lives on the other side of the road, in the house opposite. When he was young, Mr. Tucker was important in the Second World War, flying planes, and fighting enemies, and getting shot at, and all that. He's got lots of medals, and a pair of flying goggles with the glass smashed, and an old parachute to prove it. Mr. Tucker doesn't fight enemies anymore. He's too old. (Unless they've been throwing their beer cans into Mrs. Tucker's chrysanthemums.)

Mr. Tucker was there when the New Cat *saved* Tom, the time he got attacked by Miss Matheson's dog. Mr. Tucker was going up and down the road, picking up litter, like he always does, and Tom was with him, holding the trash bag for Mr. Tucker to drop the litter into. And Mr. Tucker was half-way inside a rosebush,

trying to reach a packet of pickled onion Monster Munch. And Miss Matheson's dog got out. And it went running at Tom, barking, and baring its teeth. And Tom panicked, and dropped the trash bag, and all the litter spilled out, and he ran off down the road. And Mr. Tucker tried to untangle himself from the bush.

And Miss Matheson's dog chased Tom right down to the bottom of the road, and got him up against Joe-down-the-street's hedge. And, even though Miss Matheson's dog is only the same size as a guinea pig, Tom couldn't get away. Because, for one thing, Tom is only five, and he was born in August, and he's the smallest in his class, and that made Miss Matheson's dog seem much bigger. And, for another thing, Miss Matheson's dog isn't the kind of dog that people say, "Oh, its bark is worse than its bite" about. It's the opposite kind of dog to that. Because its bark is only a yap. But, like the Milkman said, "Its bite takes you by surprise." And that's why he leaves Miss Matheson's milk on her wall, instead of taking it up to her doorstep.

Anyway, Miss Matheson's dog was jumping up, and baring its teeth, and snapping between Tom's legs. And Mr. Tucker was running down the road, to rescue Tom, when the New Cat came flying over the top of the hedge, hissing, with its ears flat, and its eyes wide, and its fur big. And it swiped

Miss Matheson's dog right between the eyes. And Miss Matheson's dog yelped, and put its head between its paws. And the New Cat held it down on the ground with its claws. And then Miss Matheson came running down the road, in her slippers, with her coal shovel in her hand, and she whacked the New Cat on the head until it let her dog go. And she picked her dog up, and put it under her arm, and kissed it, and said, "What are you doing to my *poor* little Misty?" and took it home.

If Miss Matheson hadn't come out, the New Cat would probably have dragged her dog in dead through the cat flap, like it does with everything else.

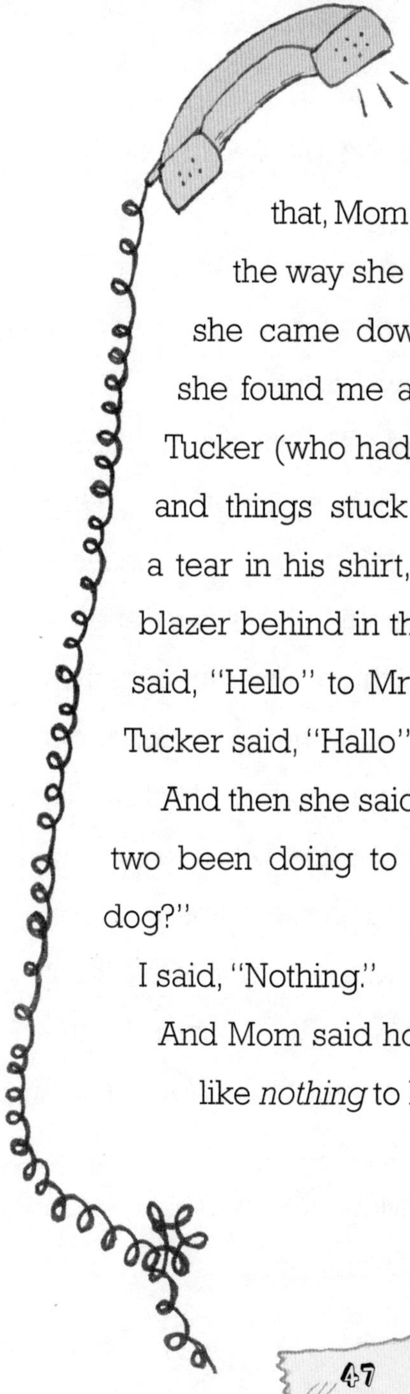

Anyway, after that, Mom called, *"Anna . . . ,"* the way she always does. And she came down the road. And she found me and Tom, and Mr. Tucker (who had leaves and twigs and things stuck in his hair, and a tear in his shirt, and he'd left his blazer behind in the bush), and she said, "Hello" to Mr. Tucker, and Mr. Tucker said, "Hallo" back to Mom.

And then she said, "What have you two been doing to Miss Matheson's dog?"

I said, "Nothing."

And Mom said how it didn't sound like *nothing* to her. Because, she said, "Miss Matheson phoned. And she's *very* upset."

And Miss Matheson had told Mom that me and Tom had been tormenting her dog, and setting the New Cat on it.

Mr. Tucker said, "Unreliable intel, Mrs. Morris. Duff gen. Here's how it went. Dog comes flying out, full pelt, no provocation. Drives Basher downhill till his port engine packs up. Damned thing's got him frozen on the stick, up against the hedge here, going for his goolies, pardon my French. New Cat comes at it, low over the old hedge, and downs bandit with a single burst, bang on target. Then Miss M.'s out. Ten of the best to the New Cat's head. Tears a strip off the sprogs. Your mob not at fault. Wonder old Tommy here hasn't got the twitch."

And then I told Mom what had happened as well. Because sometimes it's hard to understand what Mr. Tucker means, with him being from the War. And Tom said how Miss Matheson's dog had tried to *kill* him, and that the New Cat had *saved his life.*

Mom said, "I think Miss Matheson's dog might be a bit small to kill you, Tom."

Tom said, "It's small, but it's nasty."

And Mr. Tucker said, "I should say it is. Smallness inversely proportionate to its viciousness, Mrs. Morris." And he said the New Cat made a great Rear Gunner.

And Tom said, "It's a *Guard* Cat."

And Mr. Tucker said, "A Guard Cat, Basher, exactly that."

And Tom stuck his chest out. And he gave Mr. Tucker the salute. And Mr. Tucker gave him the salute back.

I wasn't sure if the New Cat was *that* good a Guard Cat. Because, like I told Tom, it attacks things inside the house as well. Like *us*. And our *feet*. And a Guard Cat shouldn't do that, because we are the ones it's meant to guard. The New Cat even attacks Tom, if he hasn't got socks on.

Tom says the New Cat doesn't know that feet belong to *people*. Because whenever it's wet outside, the New Cat stops hunting animals, and comes inside and hunts *us* instead. Sometimes it stands still, *just* inside a door, flat against the wall, and when the door opens, the New Cat flies out from behind it, and throws itself on your feet, and locks on with its claws, and sinks in its teeth. Other times the New Cat goes partway up the stairs, and lies flat, pressing itself against a step, so you can't see it from the top, and when you step down onto the stair it's on, it shoots its paws out and gets you with its claws, and clings on to your ankle.

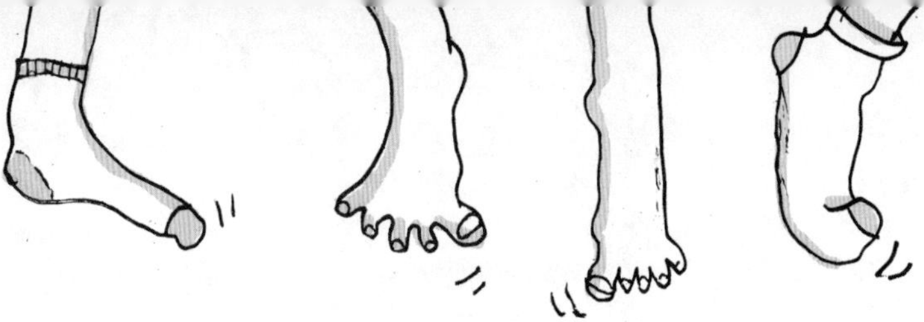

And sometimes the New Cat gets inside the beds, under the covers, right down at the bottom, and waits until you get in to go to sleep. And when you slide your feet down, it pounces, and gets its teeth in, and digs its claws into your toes, trapped under the covers.

And that's why everyone in our house has got scratches, and scabs, and scars on their feet.

And they're always running round in circles screaming, "*Help,* the *New Cat*!" and kicking their legs, to try to shake it off.

And that's why, when the New Cat first went missing, no one, apart from Tom, really cared very much.

CHAPTER 6

The Vicar's Koi Carp

The night before it went missing, the New Cat caught a fish in the Vicarage pond. Not a small fish like Joe-down-the-street once won at the school summer fete. Or a middle-size fish like Mom gets on Friday from the fish-and-chip shop. This was a Really Big Fish. It was the biggest thing the New Cat had ever brought in. And it must have taken ages to catch it, and kill it, and drag it down the road, and get it in through the cat flap.

In the morning there were bits of fish

all over the house. There was a tail on the kitchen table, and scales all up the stairs, and a backbone on the bath mat, and on Tom's pillow, when he woke up, was a big fish head with its eyes wide open.

I wouldn't like it if the New Cat put a fish head in *my* bed, but Tom didn't mind. He shouted out, "Hey, Anna, come and see *this*!"

So I went into Tom's room. And he sat up in bed. And he pointed at his pillow.

"It's a fish head," I said.

Tom said, "Do you think it's a present from the New Cat?"

And I said I thought it probably was. Because I didn't think anyone else would give a present like that.

"The New Cat likes me *best*," Tom said. And he got out of bed, and he picked up the fish head, and he took it into Mom's room, where she was still asleep, and said, *"Look!"*

And he held it near Mom's face.

Mom opened her eyes, and said, "*What the . . . ? Tom*, it's a *fish head*!"

And Tom said, "Yes."

"Where did you *get* it?"

"In my bed."

"Give me *strength,*" Mom said. And she looked at her clock, and then she shot out of bed, because she had overslept. And she grabbed the fish head off Tom, and ran downstairs, and she got the tail off the kitchen table, and put them both in the trash. And then she ran back up, and brushed her teeth, and picked the bones up off the bath mat, and vacuumed the trail of scales all up the stairs.

And she said, "I'm going to Church. . . ."

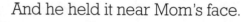

Because it was Sunday. "If anyone's interested? *Stinking* of *fish*."

Mom didn't used to go to Church much because she only went sometimes to keep Nana company. But after Nana died, when it was her funeral, Mrs. Constantine asked Mom if she could put her name down on the handing-out-the-hymnbook roster. And Mom meant to say "no," but she said "yes" by mistake. And after that she had to go to Church all the time. Because the other people who hand out the hymnbooks were always going away on holiday, and getting mono, and things like that.

When Mom goes to Church, me and Tom go to Sunday School, next door, and do painting and putting on plays instead, and Tom eats all the cookies.

Dad doesn't go to Church. He doesn't even believe in God. He says he believes in staying in bed.

After Church was over, and the Vicar had finished standing by the door, and shaking everyone's hands, and saying, "Go in peace and serve the Lord," he came back inside where Mom was putting the hymnbooks away, and I was waiting, and Tom was collecting up all the cushions for kneeling, and putting them in a big pile by the pulpit (which is the thing the Vicar stands on to speak). And the Vicar said, "Hello," and, "Lovely day," and, "Put the cushions back now, please." And then he asked Tom what we had done in Sunday School.

Tom said how we had eaten cookies.

And the Vicar said, "Anything *else*?"

And Tom shook his head.

And the Vicar said, "I'm sure you *did*. I

know Mrs. Constantine was going to do the story of the loaves and the fishes with you, and make a start on the frieze for the far wall." Which she probably was, but Graham Roberts locked the door when he went to the bathroom, which we're not supposed to do, because he forgot about it again, and he didn't see the big sign that says, DO NOT USE THIS LOCK. IT GETS STUCK!

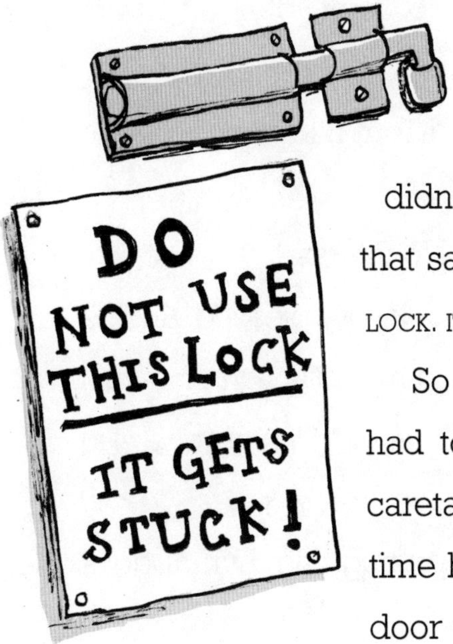

So Mrs. Constantine had to go and get the caretaker, and this time he had to take the door off. And everyone watched. And after that there was only time to do the prayer, and have juice and cookies.

Anyway, the Vicar asked Tom if he knew the story about Jesus and the five loaves, and the two fishes, and how he had fed the five thousand.

And Tom said he didn't.

And the Vicar said how it was from the Gospel according to Saint John, and from

Matthew, chapter 14, verses 13 to 21. And he asked Tom if he would like to hear it.

And Tom said, "No thanks."

The Vicar didn't look very pleased. And he breathed in deep, and he did a sigh. And then he did a sniff. And he said, "Can anyone else *smell fish*?"

Mom stopped putting the hymnbooks away.

And the Vicar said, "I've got fish on the brain. Several of mine have gone missing from my pond. There was another one gone this morning when I got up—my best Koi Carp."

Mom didn't say anything. But Tom did. He said, "Mom smells of fish."

The Vicar said, "I'm sure she doesn't."

Tom said, "She does, because the New Cat brought a big fish in through the cat flap and it killed it and put its bits all over the house. And Mom had to clean it up. Its head was on my pillow."

And the Vicar said, "Oh? What did this fish *look* like?"

And Tom said, "Like *this*."

And he held his eyes wide apart and rolled them around and stuck his tongue out.

And the Vicar said, "What color was it?"

And Tom told the Vicar how it was hard to tell what color it was because it was in lots of different bits because its scales were

all up the stairs, and its tail was on the table, and its bones were on the bath mat. And some of it was missing, but its head, which was in his bed, was white and orange with black spots.

And the Vicar said, "That's my best *Koi Carp*! I bought him for breeding. . . ."

And Tom said, "He's in the trash." And then he said, "Are there any more cookies?"

And the Vicar said, "*No.* There *aren't.*" And his neck went all red.

And Mom said, "I am so sorry about your Koi Carp. Can we buy you a replacement?"

The Vicar said, "If you insist."

Which Mom hadn't. Because she only said it once. And if you insist about something, you say it lots of times. Over and over again. Until the other person gives in. But Mom got her purse out of her handbag and said, "How much is it?"

The Vicar said, "Two hundred and twenty pounds."

Mom looked surprised. And then she looked in her purse.

The Vicar said, "I can take a check."

And Mom said, "Oh . . . right . . . yes."

And she got her checkbook out, and wrote "two hundred and twenty pounds" on one. And she gave it to the Vicar. And he put it in his pocket.

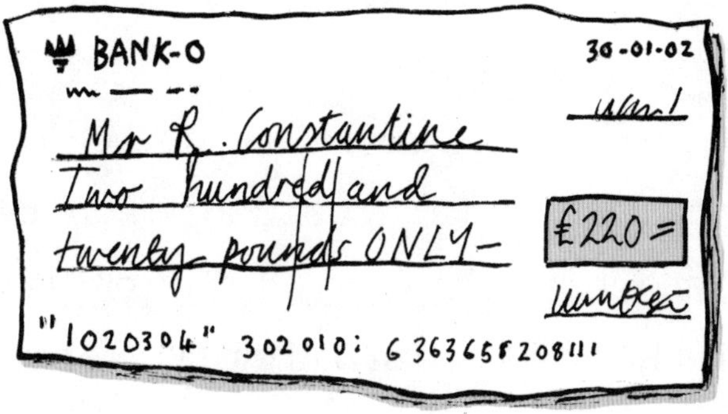

When we got home, Dad was still in bed. And me and Tom went in to bounce on it, and wake him up, and Mom came as well, and she told him about the Vicar's Koi Carp, the New Cat, and the check for two hundred and twenty pounds.

Dad said the Vicar would be lucky if there was two hundred and twenty pounds in their bank account. And then he said, "That's *enough bouncing*." And he got out of bed, and started going downstairs to make breakfast, saying things to himself, about the Vicar, and how he should spend less on his pond and more on the poor, like he's always going on about.

The New Cat was halfway up the stairs, lying flat against a step, so Dad couldn't see it, and it probably hadn't had its breakfast either, because when Dad put his foot down onto the stair it was on, the New Cat shot out its paws, and clung on with its claws, and sank in its teeth. And Dad screamed, "Agh, the **NEW CAT!**" And he fell down the rest of the stairs, with the New Cat attached.

When he got to the bottom, he kicked the air until the New Cat came flying off, and hit the wall, and then, while it was still stunned, Dad grabbed the New Cat by the scruff of its neck, and put it out the back door.

And slammed the door shut. And said, **"AND STAY OUT!"** And after that Dad put the lock down on the cat flap.

Tom asked Dad to take the lock off. Because, he said, it wasn't the New Cat's fault, really, about the Vicar's fish. Because cats are *supposed* to catch things. And they don't know how much they cost. And he told

Dad how the New Cat didn't know that feet belonged to people. And how it didn't like it outside. Because it was raining. And that was why it kept running at the cat flap, and banging its head.

But Dad just said, "Tough." And put the bacon under the grill, and cracked the eggs into the frying pan, and turned the radio right up.

And the New Cat put its tail in the air, and walked away down the road.

And Tom watched it through the window.

CHAPTER 7
The Search Party

The New Cat hadn't come back by the time we went to bed.

In the morning, which was Monday, when Tom woke up, he asked, "Has the New Cat come back?"

And Mom said, "No."

And when Tom got home from school, he asked again, "Is the New Cat back?"

And Mom said, "Not yet."

And on Tuesday, and Wednesday, and Thursday, and Friday, Tom asked again about the New Cat, and where it was, and whether it was coming back. And when Saturday came, Tom wouldn't sit with me and have his cereal, in his pajamas, and watch cartoons, or go and meet Suzanne to make plans in the shed. He put his wellies on instead, and went down the road, on his own, and stood at the bottom, and looked up and down.

Mr. Tucker was out picking up litter, and he saw Tom standing at the bottom of the road, and he gave him the salute and called down, "Out early today, Old Chum. Getting a head start on collecting the gravel up, eh?"

Tom shook his head.

"Walking-in-a-straight-line-with-the-old-eyes-closed today, is it?"

Tom shook his head.

"How about plugging away with me at this litter situation, then?"

Tom shook his head again.

So Mr. Tucker went down the road, and he sat on the wall at the bottom, and Tom sat down too. And he said, "Not *woman trouble*, is it, Old Chap?"

And Tom said it wasn't, and he told Mr. Tucker all about what had happened with the New Cat, and the Vicar's fish, and how it had hunted Dad's feet. And how Dad had thrown it out. And locked the cat flap. And how he didn't think it was coming back.

Mr. Tucker said, "Old Rear Gunner missing in action, eh? Black do all round, Basher. Can't have that. What about a recon, eh? Send out a search party, Tom, what do you say?" Tom wiped his nose on his sleeve. And Mr. Tucker got his hankie out, and he held it to Tom's nose, and said, "Give it a good blow." And Tom did. And then he said, "That's the ticket. Now, look tidy. Fling one up."

And Tom stood up straight. And he gave Mr. Tucker the salute. And Mr. Tucker gave him the salute back. And he took Tom down into the village. And they asked everyone they passed if they had seen the New Cat. And no one had. And Mr. Tucker told Tom he thought that the New Cat had probably gone on holiday, or something like that. And it was sure to come back. Because cats were always doing things like that. And he had heard of one cat that went to Spain on a ferry. On its own. By mistake. And it came back in the end. Because, he said, "Thing with cats is, *top-notch navigators*."

After they had been round the village, and asked in all the shops, and bought a bag of sweets, and stopped halfway up the hill for a rest on the

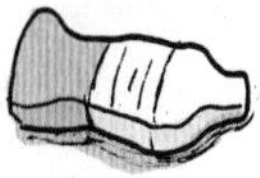

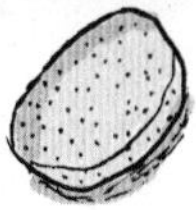

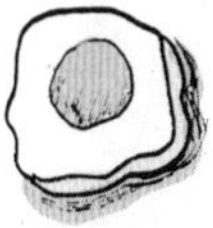
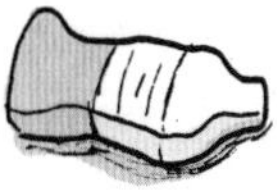

bench—while Mr. Tucker had his puffer, and Tom wet his wellies in the horse trough—they walked back up into our road. Mrs. Tucker came out, and Mr. Tucker said, "Hallo, Tom, look sharp, Squadron Leader."

Mrs. Tucker said, "Hello, Poppet," to Tom, and she said, "*Raymond!* Where have you been?"

And Mr. Tucker said, "Reconnaissance, Dickey. Tom's cat's gone AWOL."

Mrs. Tucker said, "Oh dear, poor old Tom, I'm sorry to hear *that*."

And then she said, "Raymond, your breakfast is cold, and you're late to take your pills, and in case you've forgotten, your cousins are *still* here."

Mr. Tucker said, "Roger that. T minus two minutes, Dickey."

And he asked Tom, "Where's the rest of your wing? Popsie and so on?" Popsie is what Mr. Tucker calls me. Even though it's not my name. And I've told him I don't like it.

Tom told Mr. Tucker I was in the shed, making plans with Suzanne.

"Old chairborne division, eh?" And he told Mrs. Tucker to take Tom inside and give him a cookie. "Back in a jiffy."

And he went round the side of our house, into the back lane. And he knocked on the shed door.

Me and Suzanne looked through the spy hole, which is a knot of wood at the front of the shed that you can pop in and out.

Suzanne said, "What's the password?"

"Press On Regardless."

Which it wasn't. But we opened the door anyway because Mr. Tucker had never knocked on the shed before so it was probably important. He came inside, and he looked at the wasp trap, and the worm box, and he tried to look at the plan that me and Suzanne were working on. Which we hadn't got very far with because we had only done the title, which was too long, and took up most of the piece of paper. It said:

Anna's And Suzanne's Plan To Find Out If There Are Holes In All The Walls In All The Lofts In All The Houses In The Road And, If There Are, Whether We Can Climb Through Them And Come Out In The House At The Bottom, Which Is Joe-Down-The-Street's.

I rolled the plan up so Mr. Tucker couldn't see it.

Mr. Tucker said, "Look here, I can see you bods are hard up against it with your bumph and all that, but this briefing comes down from Brass Hats, so look lively; simple enough op for your division, Popsie. As of eleven hundred hours, we want all personnel assisting Basher with this damned Cat Situation. Went AWOL on Sunday, of course, and so far it's still Missing In Action. Don't like to mention moral fiber, or the lack of, but it doesn't do to leave a chap's cat unaccounted for, so fingers out for you and Blondie on this one, eh, Popsie, what do you say?"

I said, "Okay."

And Mr. Tucker said, "That's the ticket. Best of British. Your group's got the green, Popsie, chocks away."

And he gave the salute. And Suzanne gave him the salute back. But I didn't, because the last time I gave Mr. Tucker the salute, which was ages ago, when I was about eight, Mr. Tucker said I didn't do it right, and he made me do it again, about a million times, and he kept saying, "More power on the up." And also because I didn't really *want* to try to find the New Cat, because I wanted to do the plan for the loft and the holes, and climbing through all the houses in the road, and coming out at the bottom in Joe-down-the-street's.

Tom came to the shed with the cookies from Mrs. Tucker.

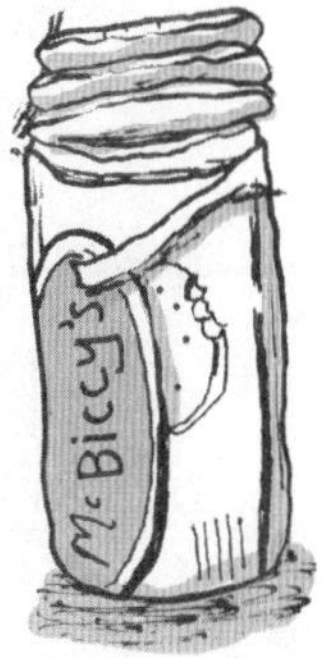

And Mr. Tucker said, "Right-o. Relatives now, Basher. Black do all round."

And he messed Tom's hair up. And then he went home.

When he was gone, Suzanne said how she didn't know why Mr. Tucker called her "Blondie" when her hair was brown. And she said, "I don't know why he says that it's *your* division, and *your* group, either, because it's not like you're in charge." Which is true. Because normally Suzanne is. Especially when it comes to investigations. Because Suzanne knows everything about stuff like that, because her Mom lets her watch all the police dramas on TV, and one of her uncles is a Special Constable, and she's got a book from the Brownie Jumble sale called, *Private Detective: A Practical Handbook.* Which she keeps under her bed. And she's read it a billion times.

Suzanne said, "You didn't tell me the New Cat was missing."

Which was true, because I forgot. And because I didn't really care about the New Cat. Not until Tom came into the shed, after Mr. Tucker left, and his eyes were all red, and his T-shirt was wet, and he was chewing his coat sleeve like he sometimes does when he's upset.

And he said, "Are you making a plan for finding the New Cat?"

And then I said, "Yes." And so did Suzanne.

And Tom stopped chewing his sleeve, and he sat down and started eating his cookies.

And Suzanne put the plan for the loft and the holes behind the stepladders, under the shelf with the wasp trap on it and the worm collection. And I got my dictionary, and I looked up "AWOL." Because that's what Mr. Tucker said the New Cat was.

And this is what it said:

AWOL [A.W.O.L.] ✦ *noun*
Absent With Out Leave (A.W.O.L.) normally used about a soldier or other military person who is absent from duty without permission, but without the intention of deserting

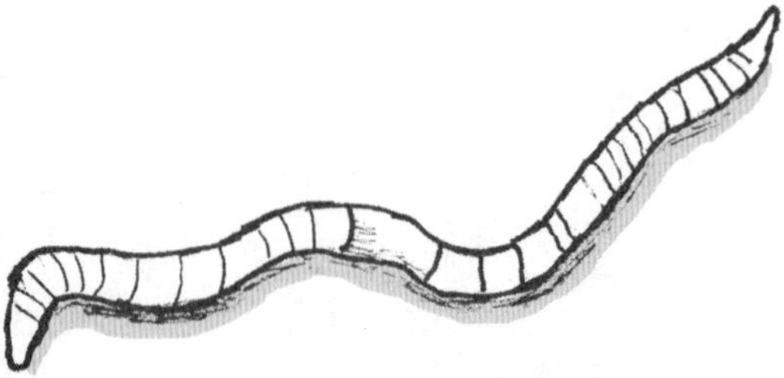

CHAPTER 8

What Might Have Happened to the New Cat

Anna's And Suzanne's And Tom's List Of All The Things That Might Have Happened To The New Cat

1. Killed
   (By A Dog Or Wolves Or Bears Or A Car)
2. Gone Off In A Huff
3. Gone Hunting
4. Gone On Holiday

The first thing on the list was "Killed." I didn't think a dog would be able to kill the New Cat because we had never met one that it was even scared of. And Tom agreed, because, he said, "In a fight with a dog, the New Cat would win. But," he said, "it might not win against wolves or bears. Especially if they were hungry, or in a big pack."

You don't really get packs of wolves or bears round here, but I put it on the list anyway because Tom's eyes were still pink and he had finished all his cookies.

I said maybe the New Cat had been hit by a car. Like happened to our *Old* Cat, in the back lane, when Miss Matheson ran it over.

But Suzanne said she

didn't think Miss Matheson *had* run over the *New* Cat, because when she ran the Old Cat over, Suzanne found cat blood on Miss Matheson's car tires. And there wasn't any blood on them this time, because Suzanne went out and checked. And anyway, like Tom said, we didn't *just* find cat blood when the Old Cat got run over. Because we also found the Old Cat, squashed flat, out the back, by Miss Matheson's gate. And no one had found the New Cat squashed flat anywhere.

So we crossed number 1, "Killed (By A Dog Or Wolves Or Bears Or A Car)," off.

Number 2 on the list was "Gone Off In A Huff." Which was Suzanne's idea. Suzanne goes off in huffs, if you do something she doesn't like, and then you have to wait for ages, and

try and find her, and say sorry, and all that. But the New Cat doesn't go in for huffs much, because it's not the sort of cat that wants people coming after it. You can't even touch it without gardening gloves on. And, anyway, the New Cat had been gone for nearly a week. And even Suzanne has never stayed in a huff *that* long. But Suzanne said that she would, if she had been thrown out, and it was raining, and she kept banging her head on the cat flap.

So we went up and down the road, looking for the New Cat, and we put bits of ham out, and banged on a saucer of milk with a spoon, and shouted, "Puss, puss, puss, puss, puss." Like Nana sometimes did, before she died, to get the Old Cat to come in at night. But the New Cat didn't come. So we crossed "**Huff**" off the list as well.

The next thing was "**Gone Hunting.**"

Because, like Suzanne said, "The New Cat is always off killing things. And maybe it has had to go farther to find some, because it has already killed all the things in the garden, and there probably wasn't anything left alive, nearby."

But Tom told Suzanne how the New Cat always brings the things it has hunted back, to hide them in the house. And how it doesn't go hunting when it's wet outside. Because that's when it stays in, and sleeps, and hunts feet in the house. And it had been raining all week. So we crossed "Gone Hunting" off too.

Tom said the New Cat might have "Gone On Holiday," like Mr. Tucker said. And he told us about the cat that went to Spain on the ferry by itself, by mistake, and found its way back. Suzanne said she didn't think cats went on holiday on their own,

even if it wasn't on purpose, because she thought that was only the kind of thing that grown-ups say to shut you up and stop you getting upset. So we went into the house and put "cat, Spain, holiday, mistake" into the computer. And what Mr. Tucker said was true. Because there was a picture of the cat, and it had got in the news. And it said:

Missing Cat Found on Ferry

Stowaway Sandi was discovered by stunned ferry staff under a truck on the P&O Pride of Bilbao, which had traveled all the way from Portsmouth. The ferry crew took the tom to a vet, who was able to tell from an embedded microchip where he was from. Sandi had a luxurious return trip, fed on a special menu of fresh salmon, grilled chicken, and milk in an en-suite cabin with a sea view.

But the New Cat didn't have an embedded microchip. It didn't even have a collar, so no one would know where to bring it back to. And, like Suzanne said, it could have got off the boat in Spain, or something like that. And we couldn't go there to look for it, because Suzanne isn't even allowed past the bottom bus stop because her Dad says it's **"OUT OF BOUNDS."** And that meant all we could do was wait, to see if the New Cat came home. Which wasn't much of a plan. And that was all the things on our list.

So I said, "Let's go and see Mrs. Rotherham." And Suzanne said that was a good idea, because of how Mrs. Rotherham used to be in the police so she knows about these kinds of things. And Tom said it was a good idea too. Because Mrs. Rotherham always has cookies.

CHAPTER 9

The Suspect List

We told Mrs. Rotherham all about what had happened with the New Cat and the Vicar's Koi Carp and how Dad had thrown it out and locked the cat flap, and how it still hadn't come back. And Mrs. Rotherham went and made some tea, and Tom asked if she had any cookies, and she brought out the tin, and she said, "When I was in the police," which was probably about a million years ago, "the first thing we did when a person went missing was to fill

out a *Missing Person Alert* form." And she went inside her cupboard. And she found a form. And she brought it out. And she crossed "Person" out, and put "Pet" instead. And me and Tom and Suzanne sat by the fire and drank the tea and ate the cookies and filled it in. And when it was finished, the Missing Pet Alert Form looked like this:

PET

Missing ~~Person~~ Alert

SURNAME: Cat

FORENAME: The New

DOB (Mrs. Rotherham said this means Date of Birth): Unknown

PHYSICAL DESCRIPTION: small, angry animal with four legs and a tail

HEIGHT: About up to Tom's new bruise

BUILD: scrawny

HAIR, COLOR AND STYLE: Gray, matted

EYE COLOR: Green

CLOTHING: *None*
(it used to have a flea collar, but it chewed it off)
ANY DISTINGUISHING FEATURES:
A tooth that hangs down over its mouth
KNOWN RISKS: *Hunts most things, especially birds, mice, moles, voles, rats, rabbits, spiders, wasps, flies, and feet*
ADDITIONAL INFORMATION: *Do not approach without gardening gloves*
CONTACT DETAILS: *Anna and Tom Morris, Number 5, Spoutwell Lane*

Mrs. Rotherham looked at the form and said she thought it was very good.

Suzanne asked, "What did you do after that?"

"I'd ask myself, has this person gone somewhere of their own accord, or are we dealing with something altogether more untoward? Then I'd do some poking about the place. More often than not, if there's a suspect, it'll be someone very close to the person who's missing. A neighbor, maybe. A family member, more often than not. And then it's motive, of course, and whether or not the suspect had an opportunity, and are there any prior convictions?"

Suzanne wrote down everything that Mrs. Rotherham said in the notepad.

"After that, it's a rather less interesting business. Putting up 'Missing' posters, talking to passersby, handing out fliers. Offer a reward."

We finished our tea. And Tom ate the last cookie. And Suzanne finished writing, and put the notepad in her pocket. And we said "thank you" to Mrs. Rotherham. And went back down the road.

When we got back to the shed, Suzanne wrote on the top of a piece of paper, People Who Might Have Taken The New Cat, and she underlined it.

I said I couldn't think of anyone who would take the New Cat. Because it wasn't the sort of cat that people would want. Because before it went missing, *we* didn't even want it ourselves.

Tom said, "Someone might take it to make a fur coat, like Cruella de Vil does in *101 Dalmatians*."

But I didn't think *anyone* would wear the *New Cat's* coat. Even if it was washed, and had conditioner put on it, and was given a blow-dry. Because the New Cat's coat isn't very nice, and it's got lots of bits missing from all the times it's been in fights.

Suzanne said, "There might be another reason why someone would take it."

And I said, "Like what?"

And Suzanne said, "*Revenge.*" And then she wrote on the paper:

1. The Vicar, for killing his Koi Carp
2. Miss Matheson, for attacking her dog
3. Anna's Dad, for costing £220 to buy the Vicar a new fish

I thought Suzanne might be right about the Vicar and Miss Matheson, but I didn't think Dad really wanted revenge much, because all he ever wants is to watch football, and drink beer, and he probably couldn't be bothered to kidnap the New Cat.

But Suzanne looked in the notepad, at all the things Mrs. Rotherham had said, and she read, *"More often than not it's a family member."* And she wrote, Motive? Yes. Opportunity? Yes. And then she said, "Has your Dad got any prior convictions?"

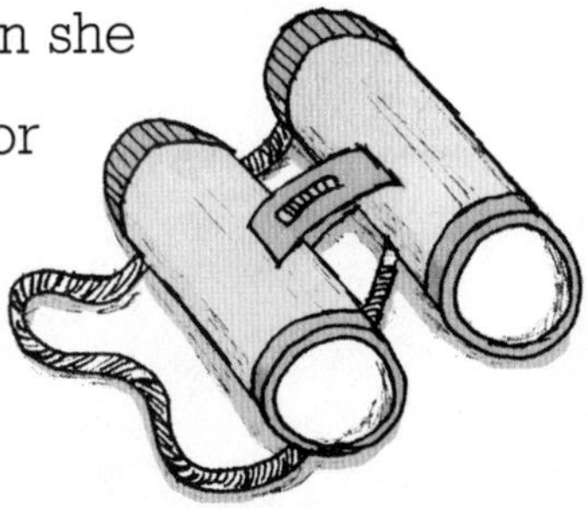

And I said, "I don't know."

And Suzanne wrote, Possible prior convictions. And she underlined Anna's Dad. And she put the notepad in her pocket, and she got the binoculars, and she said, "Let's go to the Vicarage."

And Tom asked us to wait while he went inside, and got his swimming goggles, even though, like Suzanne said, "You won't really need them."

And we went up the road.

CHAPTER 10
Poking About the Place

Suzanne looked through the Vicarage gate with the binoculars. And then I looked as well. And then Tom. But none of us could see the New Cat, especially not Tom because he had his goggles on, and the binoculars backward. And then we opened the gate and went in because, like I told Suzanne, it was a Saturday, so the Vicar would be doing weddings.

We held the binoculars up to the letter box, and up to all the windows at the front of the house. And then me and Suzanne went round the back. And Tom stayed at the front, behind the hedge, to keep watch.

Me and Suzanne looked through the binoculars into all the windows at the back. And we couldn't see the New Cat there, either.

Suzanne said, "The New Cat isn't the sort of animal that someone could take easily." Which was true. "Which means there was probably a fight. So if the Vicar took it, we should see signs of a struggle."

So we went all round the Vicarage looking for some. But we didn't find any. And, after a while, Suzanne said, "The New Cat isn't here." So we went back round to the front.

When we got there, Tom wasn't standing behind the hedge, looking out. He was lying on the ground, with his face in the fishpond.

"Tom?!" I said. "What are you doing?"

Tom lifted his head up. "I'm looking for the New Cat, in case the Vicar has drowned it." And he put his face back in the water, and blew out, so bubbles came up, like he learned at swimming club. And then his head came up again, and he said, "It's not here." And he wiped his goggles with his sleeve, and his tongue as well, because, he said, "I forgot to close my mouth," and it had quite a lot of green slime on it.

And then we went down the road, and round the back, to Miss Matheson's.

We got down on the ground in the back lane beside Miss Matheson's fence, and looked through the binoculars.

I said if she *had* taken the New Cat, I didn't think Miss Matheson would keep it in the garden. Because, for one thing, it would be too easy for it to escape. And, for another thing, someone might spot it. And, for an even other thing, it might attack Miss Matheson's dog.

And Tom said he didn't think Miss Matheson would keep the New Cat in her house, either, because it would hunt her feet, and tear up her furniture, and it might attack her dog there as well.

And Suzanne said that she thought we were right, and if Miss Matheson was going to keep the New Cat anywhere, it would have to be in her garage, and it would probably be tied up.

So me and Suzanne and Tom climbed over the gate, and we crept over the gravel, and ran over to the garage, and I gave Suzanne a boost up, and she looked in through the garage window. And then we swapped around.

Miss Matheson's garage was very neat. There were rakes and brooms and hoes all

in a line. And plant pots in order of size. And one shelf for jars, and another for paint, and one for string and twine. But there wasn't any sign of the New Cat anywhere.

"It's not here," I said.

I got down from the garage window. And we started walking back toward the gate. And when we were halfway across we stopped, because we heard someone say, "Ahem."

Miss Matheson was standing on the other side of the gate. In the back lane. With her arms crossed. Watching us. And Mom was standing beside her.

Miss Matheson said, "This is the kind of thing I'm talking about, Mrs. Morris." And she said how she wasn't the only one on the street

who was upset with our family, and our pets. Because she had spoken to the Vicar, and he had told her about our cat, and what it had done to his Koi Carp. And she had seen us all in his garden, just now, meddling in his pond.

And Mom said, "*Anna*, is that true?"

And I said, "No."

And Mom said, "Why has Tom got goggles on? And what's that green slime?" And Mom took me and Tom and Suzanne inside.

And Miss Matheson called, "If it happens once more, I shall call the *police*."

Suzanne said that we could call the police on Miss Matheson, actually, because of her dog, and how it attacked Tom. Because, she said, "Miss Matheson's dog should wear a muzzle." Which Suzanne knows all about from when her cousin went to court.

Mom said she was pretty sure Miss Matheson's dog wasn't covered by the Dangerous Dogs Act, because it was a Chihuahua, and they didn't have to have muzzles on. And then she said, "And in any case, Suzanne, that's not the point."

And Tom said, "What does 'the point' mean?"

And Mom said, "It means you had no business going in her garden, and looking into her garage. Or the Vicar's. What were you doing?"

I didn't say anything and nor did Suzanne. Tom said, "The Vicar and Miss Matheson have taken the New Cat, and drowned it and tied it up and things like that."

And Mom said, "No one has taken the New Cat, Tom."

And she said me and Suzanne had to stop filling Tom's head with rubbish. Because it wasn't fair, and it wasn't funny.

And I said how it wasn't meant to be funny because, I said, "It's very serious. And that's why me and Suzanne and Tom are trying to find it."

Mom said, "If someone's got the New Cat, it's more likely to have been *adopted* than *abducted.*"

I got my dictionary and looked "adopted" up. This is what it said:

adopt [a-dopt] ✦ *verb*
to choose or make one's own by selection;
to rear as one's own

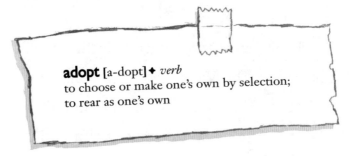

And this is what it said about "abducted":

abduct [ab-duckt] ✦ *verb*
to carry off or lead away in secret or by force, often using threats or violence; to kidnap

But whether the New Cat had been abducted or adopted didn't make much difference, I didn't think. Because you can't just go round adopting pets that already belong to other people.

Because, I said, "Imagine if someone just came and adopted me or Tom?"

Mom said, "Ha. *Imagine!*"

And she told us we had to play inside for a while.

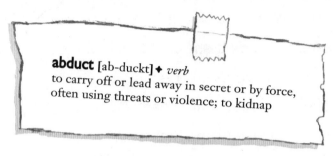

And Suzanne got the notepad out and crossed the Vicar and Miss Matheson off the list because, like she said, we had done a search, and we hadn't seen the New Cat, and there weren't any signs of a struggle. And Miss Matheson would have had scratches on her hands if she had touched the New Cat. And she didn't, because Suzanne had checked. And that meant there was only one person left. And that was *Dad.*

"Let's interrogate him," Suzanne said.

This is what my dictionary says "interrogate" means:

interrogate [in-ter-o-gate] ✦ *verb*
to ask someone a lot of questions for a long time in order to get information, sometimes using threats or violence

Suzanne said, "We need to do a lie detector test."

Because, she said, her book tells you all about how when people tell lies, their eyes look up, and off to the left, and they touch their mouth with their hand.

So she said, "We'll ask him all about the New Cat, and what has happened to it. And the lie detector test will say if he's telling the truth."

Dad was watching football with his hands over his eyes.

I told him how we were trying to find out what had happened to the New Cat.

Dad said, "Uh-huh." Like he does when he isn't listening.

So I said how it was very important and we needed to ask him some questions.

And Dad said, "Yup."

And I said, "Now."

And Dad said, "Yeah, yeah." And then he said, "At halftime."

And Suzanne said, "Or we could go and tell your Mom about the loft, Anna, and how all the broken things from under the stairs are up there."

And then Dad jumped up, out of his chair, and said, "No, no, don't do that! I'll answer your questions."

And Suzanne said, "I thought so." And she turned the TV off. And she told Dad to turn his chair around. And she closed the curtains. And she turned on the lamp, and she pointed it at Dad. And she walked around the room.

And she whispered to me to ask Dad a question I knew he would lie to, so I said, "Do you like going on long walks with Suzanne's Dad?"

And Dad said, "Urm, yes, I do." And he touched his mouth and his eyes went up to the left. And Suzanne said, "That's a *lie*! Ask him again."

So I said, "I'm going to ask you again. Do you like going on walks with Suzanne's Dad?"

And Dad said, "Urm, well, no, not that much." And he didn't put his hand on his mouth, or move his eyes. So we knew that the lie detector test was working.

And after that Suzanne asked Dad lots of questions really fast, close to his face, like, "Do you like the New Cat?" and, "Are you glad it's gone?" and, "Do you hope it never comes back?"

And Dad said, "Urm, no, yes, I do, I'm sorry, Tom."

And Suzanne said, "And that's why you took it and tied it up, or killed it, isn't it?"

And Dad said, "What? Oh, yes, of course, that's *exactly* it." But his hand touched his mouth, and his eyes went up, and to the left, which meant he was lying.

And then Tom went very close up to Dad, with the lamp, and he pointed it right in his face, and Dad said, "*Ah*, I'm *blind*."

And Tom said, "Have you kidnapped the New Cat, Dad?" And he looked right in his eyes.

And Dad said, "No, Tom, of course not." And it wasn't a lie because he looked straight back at Tom and his hand didn't touch his mouth.

So Suzanne said, "No further questions."

And she opened the curtains, and turned the lamp off, and put the TV back on, and Dad turned his chair around and started watching the football again.

And me and Tom and Suzanne went back to the shed and looked in the notepad for what Mrs. Rotherham said to do next.

CHAPTER 11
Missing

The next thing after "poking about to see if it's a neighbor or a family member" was to put up "Missing" posters and hand out fliers and offer a reward.

So Suzanne drew two pictures of the New Cat, one big one for the poster and a smaller one for the flier. And Tom started coloring them in.

And then Suzanne had to draw the big one again, because Tom put green stripes on the New Cat's body, and gave it red feet, which, like Suzanne said, was nice, but wasn't exactly what the New Cat looked like.

And she told Tom to color the New Cat in gray, so people would know what cat it was. And when the pictures were finished, I put the words on.

This is what the poster looked like:

And the flier was like this:

MISSING
If you have any information about this cat, please bring it to the shed out the back of Spoutwell Lane, behind number 5, and knock three times and ask for Anna, or Tom, or Suzanne

And then we all went to see how much money we had for the reward.

Suzanne asked her Dad for her pocket money, which is meant to be three pounds fifty, but after Suzanne's fines for not eating her onions, and for losing her shoes, and not coming home straight from school, it was only eighty-five pence.

I had already had my pocket money, and

next week's. I asked Mom if I could have the week after next's as well, but she said, "No, you can't. You do this every week. When it's spent it's spent." I checked in my pocket to see if I had any left. There was only £1.49.

Tom said he had lots of money. Which he always does. Because he doesn't have anything to spend it on so it just adds up. He brought his piggy bank out to the shed, and we opened it up. And tipped the money out on the table. And I counted it. And Suzanne said she didn't think I had counted it right. So I said, "You count it then." And she did. Out loud, and when she was finished, she did it again, to check. And she took ages. And said every sum out loud. And I undid my shoes and did them back up again, because I was sick of hearing sums. Because I don't like them in school, and I especially don't like doing them on a Saturday, in the shed, when it isn't time for math because it's supposed to be time for finding out who took the New Cat.

Suzanne put the amount for the reward on the bottom of the poster, and the flier, which was £26.79. And then we started to make more. Suzanne drew another outline of the New Cat, a big one for the poster and small for the flier, and Tom started coloring them in, and I had to keep an eye on him so he didn't do it green stripes with red feet again. And I wrote the words. And put the reward amount on the bottom of each one. It was already starting to get dark, and we had only finished two posters. "If we had a photocopier, we could make as many as we liked," I said. There's a photocopier in Suzanne's house.

Suzanne said, "No, we're not using it." Because last time, when we tried to photocopy her Dad's dictionary, because he wouldn't let us borrow it, Suzanne's Dad went mad about us using all the paper. And the ink. And because the photocopier overheated. And he said, **"THE DICTIONARY IS TWENTY-ONE THOUSAND THREE HUNDRED AND FORTY-THREE PAGES LONG, FOR CRYING OUT LOUD, SUZANNE!"** And he had to get a man to come out and fix it.

"There's a photocopier in the cottage at the Church," Tom said. Which was true. And it was Sunday the next day.

So Suzanne said that in the morning we should all get up early, and go to Sunday School, to use it. And afterward we could put loads of posters up, and hand fliers out, all around the village.

And then we heard Suzanne's Dad in the back lane, saying,

"SUZANNE, YOU'RE LATE. I WANT FIFTY PENCE OF THAT POCKET MONEY BACK!" And Suzanne took it out of the reward money on the table. And changed the amount on the poster and the flier. And then she went home.

CHAPTER 12
Cats

I set my alarm, and in the morning, when it went off, I went into Tom's room and woke him up. Tom got out of bed and put his Spider-Man suit on, with the built-in muscles. I wasn't sure if you're allowed to wear a Spider-Man suit in Church. But Tom said he would put his coat on top, and wear his smart shoes, and leave the mask behind. So I said it was all right. Because once Tom has decided what

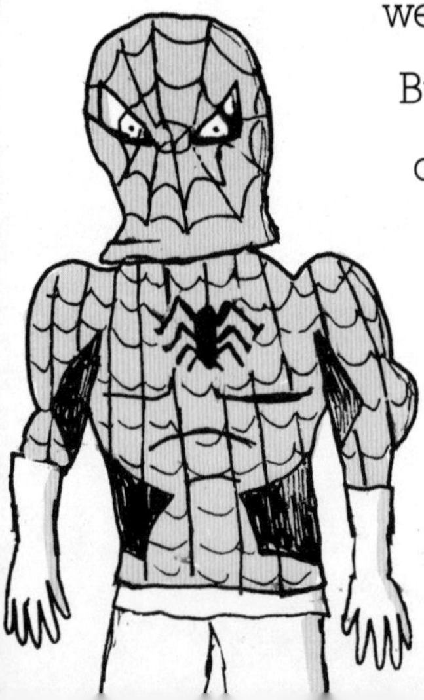

he's wearing, it's hard to make him change his mind. Unless you pin him down. Like Dad had to, for a wedding, when Tom was meant to be a page boy and he refused to take his frog wellies off.

Me and Tom had our cereal, and brushed our teeth. And when we were ready, we went in to see Mom, who was still in bed.

Mom said, "Why are you up?"

"For Sunday School," I said.

Mom said she wasn't going to Church because it wasn't her turn for handing out the hymnbooks and she'd gone off it since everything with the Vicar and his Koi Carp.

I asked if me and Tom could go on our own, since we were ready. Mom looked at the clock and said, "You're going to be very early."

So I said we would probably just sit and read the Bible, with Mrs. Constantine, until everyone arrived.

Mom looked at me a bit strange, with her eyebrows up, like she does sometimes. And she shook her head, and said, "Fine." And she asked Tom, "Are you going dressed as Spider-Man?"

Tom said how he wasn't because he was going to put his coat on top, and his smart shoes, and he was leaving his mask behind.

And me and Tom said good-bye, and went out to the shed, and got the poster and the flier. And then we went next door to call on Suzanne.

We rang three times, and Suzanne's Dad opened the window really fast, and leaned out in his dressing gown, and shouted, **"YES? IS THERE A FIRE? IT'S SUNDAY MORNING, FOR CRYING OUT LOUD!"**

Mrs. Constantine said it was nice to see Suzanne at Sunday School, because she doesn't normally come. And she asked what Suzanne would like to do.

And Suzanne said that she would like to use the photocopier.

And Mrs. Constantine said, "Oh."

And Suzanne showed Mrs. Constantine the "Missing" poster and the flier about the New Cat.

Mrs. Constantine said that the photocopier was only supposed to be used for things that were to do with the Church, like the parish magazine, and hymn sheets, and community things.

Suzanne said, "The New Cat was in the community. Before it went missing."

And then Graham Roberts came in, and he said that he had seen the Vicar use the photocopier to copy a magazine, called *Pond Construction and Koi Carp Keeping*. And that wasn't to do with the Church. And then he said that he could show us how to use the photocopier, if we liked, because he

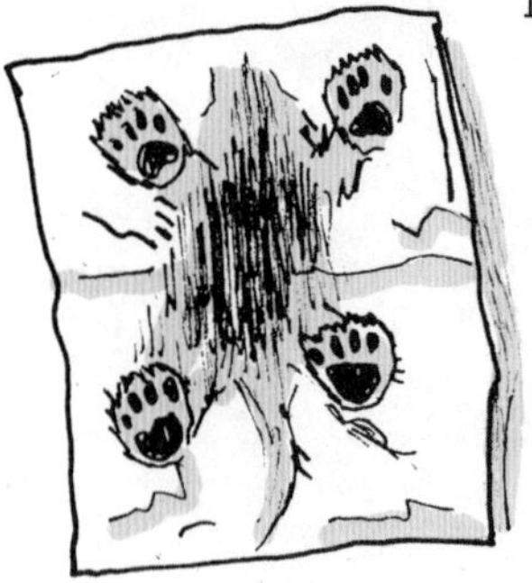

had used it before, to photocopy his dog, before it died. And he brought a piece of paper out of his pocket, which was all crumpled, that had the photocopied dog on it. And he showed it to Mrs. Constantine.

You couldn't see much, apart from the pads on the dog's paws. And a bit of fur. Mrs. Constantine said, "All right, fine, but don't use all the paper. And if anyone needs the toilet today, you'll just have to whistle so we know you're in there, because we're still without a door until the caretaker can put it back on."

So me and Tom and Suzanne and Graham Roberts went upstairs to the room where the photocopier is, where all the old hymnbooks are, and the cloths for the altar, and the gold crosses. And Graham switched the photocopier on. And Suzanne gave him the poster, and the flier.

And Graham looked at them, and then he said, "Emma Hendry has lost her cat as well. That's why she was upset at school on Friday. And that's why Mrs. Peters said I should say sorry, even though I hadn't done anything, except paint her hair by mistake."

Suzanne said, "Joe-down-the-street's babysitter Brian has lost his cat too." And she said, "So that's three cats that have vanished."

And Graham said, "There could be more."

And Suzanne said, "Yes." Because, she

said, "Those are only the ones we know about."

And Graham said, "It's probably a *conspiracy*." And he started the machine. And then he said, "Have you ever heard of the Cat Lady?"

And Tom said he had, because he said, "She's in *Batman*, and Batman is one of my favorites, after Spider-Man, and Bob the Builder."

Graham Roberts said, "That's *Catwoman*. She has cat ears, and a tail, and black boots. This is the *Cat Lady*. She doesn't look like that. She wears a blanket, and when it's raining she puts a carrier bag on her head, and she never has any shoes on."

Tom said how he hadn't heard of the Cat Lady in that case. And neither had me or Suzanne.

Graham said, "It's probably her who is kidnapping the cats." And he said he would show us where her house was, if we liked, after Church.

Suzanne said she wasn't sure, because we would be busy handing out fliers, and putting posters up, and all that. And because, like she told Tom afterward, Graham sometimes tells lies, like the time it was Emma Hendry's turn to talk about "Something I Like," on the carpet, in Mrs. Peters's class, and she did it all about unicorns. Afterward Graham told Emma that his Gran had a unicorn, on her farm, and Emma could come for dinner, and see it, if she liked. And, after she went, Emma said that Graham's Gran's unicorn was only an old Shetland pony that had an ice-cream cone tied on its head, on a piece of elastic.

Graham said, "The Cat Lady's house is

only in the marketplace. You can see it from the Church gate."

So we said we would go. And the photocopier was finished, so we took the posters and fliers, and went back downstairs.

Mrs. Constantine said it was time for the prayer.

Tom asked if she would put the New Cat in it. And Mrs. Constantine said she would.

And then she said, "Right, eyes closed, hands together."

And she did the prayer, which went,

Dear God most high, hear and bless
Thy beasts and singing birds:
And guard with tenderness
Small things that have no words.

And then she said, "And please take care of the New Cat, which is missing."

And Graham Roberts said, "It's been kidnapped by the Cat Lady."

And Mrs. Constantine said, "Right . . ."

And Graham Roberts said, "You can ask my Gran, because she knows all about her and she doesn't tell lies."

And Mrs. Constantine said, "Amen." Which means, "So be it," and, "That's the end," and also, like Tom says, "It's time for cookies." And Tom ate about ten. Until Mrs. Constantine took the tin from him. And then we all went into Church for the last bit at the end. And the Vicar was saying, "Ye have heard that it hath been said, an eye for an eye, and a tooth for a tooth: But I say unto you, that ye resist not evil: but whosoever shall smite thee on thy right cheek, turn to him the other also."

And Suzanne whispered, "See, Anna, *revenge*."

When Church was finished, the Vicar went and stood outside, by the door. And when all the people came out, he shook their hands, and asked if he would be seeing them at Evensong, and told them to "Go in peace and serve the Lord."

And then me and Tom and Suzanne gave each person a flier, and said, "And look out for the New Cat."

When everyone was gone, Graham Roberts said, "Follow me," and we went over to the Church gate. And we looked through it. And Graham pointed to a big house, on the other side of the marketplace, and he said, "*That* is where the Cat Lady lives."

And then he went home.

Me and Tom and Suzanne stood and looked at the house. Suzanne said, "It doesn't look like anyone lives in it." Which it

didn't. Because all the paint on the front was cracking, and peeling off. And two of the windows were broken, and one had cardboard in it, instead of glass. And there were lots of tiles missing from the roof. And there was a bird's nest at the top of the drainpipe. And the chimney looked like it might fall off. And there were dead plants in the window boxes.

We crossed the marketplace to look at it close up. Next to the door was a big window, like you get in a shop. The window was so dirty you could hardly see through it.

I wiped it with my sleeve, but it didn't make much difference because most of the dirt was on the inside. Behind the window, a little way back, was an old net curtain, which had gone all greasy and gray. And, in front of the curtain, on the window ledge, there were three fruit boxes, like you get from the greengrocers. And inside each box was a dirty old blanket. And on top of each blanket was a cat. Beside the cats there was a sign. I breathed on the window and wiped it again, and tried to read what the sign said. "These . . . cats . . . are not . . . forced to sit . . . here. They do so of their own . . . free . . . will. . . ."

Me and Tom and Suzanne looked at one another. And then we looked back at the sign.

Suzanne said, "If nobody lives here, who wrote the sign?"

And Tom said, "And who looks after the cats?"

And I said, "Maybe Graham Roberts is right about the Cat Lady. And the Kidnapping. And the Conspiracy."

We pressed our faces against the window.

"Let's put the posters up and go home," I said.

But we stayed, looking. Then the curtain twitched, and I saw two hands, pulling it apart, and in the gap, above them, there was a face, with a blanket round it, and it looked out, and its eyes were wide, and its mouth was open.

I screamed. And the face in the window screamed back.

And I dropped all the posters and fliers.

And Suzanne said, "RUN!" And we did.

And we didn't stop until we got to the shed.

CHAPTER 13

The Stakeout

We locked the shed door. And stood against it. And we stayed very quiet.

After ages, Suzanne popped out the little knot of wood in the spy hole. And looked through.

Tom was jumping from foot to foot, like he does when he gets excited. And then, if he doesn't get to the toilet quick, he wets himself and gets upset.

"Do you need to pee?" I said. Tom

nodded his head. He reached for the door. "Don't open it," I said. "Can't you go in the shed?" I looked around for something.

"No!" said Suzanne. "He can't." And she got the binoculars down from the shelf and opened the door a crack, and looked up and down the road. "Quick. Just go there, on Miss Matheson's side."

Tom's not really allowed to pee outside because last time he did it, when Mom saw him, from in the kitchen, she tapped on the window, and said, "*Oi*, do you *mind*? Those are my herbs. We don't want your pee in our shepherd's pie." But he didn't look like he would make it into the house. So I held the shed door open, and kept watch, just in case the person whose face we saw in the window had followed us.

Once Tom was back inside, and I'd locked the door again, Suzanne started writing on a piece of paper:

Whose was the face in the window?
Was it the Cat Lady?
Has she got the New Cat?

And she said, "These are the things that we need to find out."

"How?" I asked.

And Suzanne said, "We'll have to go back to the house. Who's going to come?"

I said, "Urm . . ."

Tom said, "I am."

So I said I would too. "But only to look, from far away, like in the Churchyard, through the gate, or from behind the stone cross in the marketplace, through the binoculars."

Suzanne said, "It will be a Stakeout." And she wrote, Anna's and Suzanne's And Tom's

Plan to steak out the Cat Lady's House on the top of a piece of paper. And she said how detectives do "steak outs" all the time.

I looked "steak out" up in my dictionary, which wasn't easy. And, when I found it, this is what it said:

> **stakeout** [steyk-owt] ✦ *noun*
> the surveillance of a location by the police, as in anticipation of a crime or the arrival of a wanted person

And then we looked in Suzanne's dictionary as well. And it said:

> **stakeout** [steyk-owt] ✦ *noun informal*
> a period of secret surveillance of a building or an area by police in order to observe someone's activities

And Suzanne said that after we had done the stakeout, we would probably have to do a

raid, which is where you shout, "GO GO GO," and bash down the door, and stomp up the stairs, and shout, "HANDS IN THE AIR," and, "YOU'RE SURROUNDED," and all that.

And then we made a list of things to take with us.

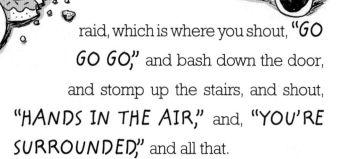

Anna's And Suzanne's And Tom's
Plan To ~~Steak out~~ Stakeout
The Cat Lady's House

Things We Will Need:

1. Coffee and doughnuts (because that's what Suzanne said the police always have in stakeouts)
2. Binoculars
3. Sunglasses (for a disguise)
4. Watch (so we know how long we've been looking for)
5. Notepad and pen

6. Gardening gloves and Cat Carrier in case we find the New Cat

What We Will Do:

1. Watch the house

I said, "What about a newspaper with eyeholes cut out, for looking through?"

But Suzanne said, "You don't have those in a *real* stakeout, Anna. That's just in cartoons, actually."

I hate it when Suzanne says "actually," so I said, "Well, some things that happen in cartoons happen in real life as well, actually."

And Suzanne said, "Like what?"

And I couldn't think of anything so I said, "Lots." And then I said, "It's not like you know everything about stakeouts."

And Suzanne said she did, actually.

And I said I didn't think so, because

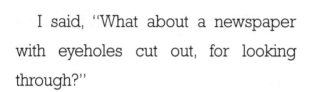

she didn't even know how to spell it. And that's why she had put an "e" in the middle, which is a piece of meat, like you eat for your dinner.

Suzanne said how you didn't have to be able to spell things to know how to do them. And I said that you did. And Suzanne said, "Then how come I can do a triple side somersault?"

And I said, "You can't. Because I've seen you try and it's just like three wrong-way-round forward rolls."

And Suzanne said it wasn't three wrong-way-round forward rolls, and she wasn't going to do the plan for finding out about the New Cat or anything until I admitted that she could do a triple somersault, and that she knew all about stakeouts. And I didn't say anything. And after ages, I said, "Sorry." But only very quiet, and fast, and with my fingers crossed behind my back.

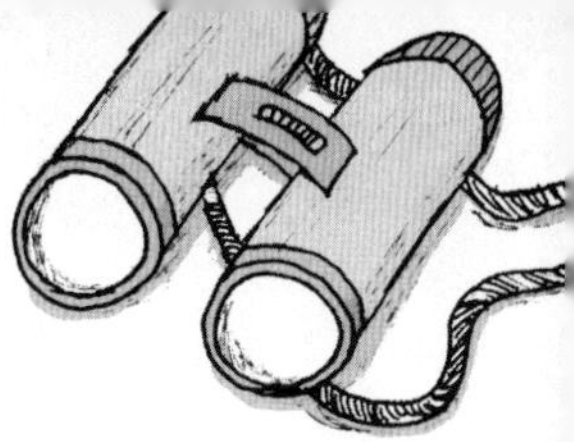

CHAPTER 14
The Cat Lady's House

Me and Tom and Suzanne stood behind the stone cross in the middle of the marketplace, and peered round, and watched the house through the binoculars.

"Oh, *look*!" Suzanne said. And she passed them to me.

Part of the window had been cleaned, and one of the Missing Pet posters I had dropped, with the picture of the New Cat, had been put in the place where the dirt was wiped away. The sign

about the cats not being forced to sit there was still on the window ledge. And the cats were there as well.

And not just three of them, one in each box; this time there were six. And one got up and stretched, and looked out the window, and scratched itself. And then it jumped down behind the curtain, so we couldn't see it anymore. And then another cat came up, from under the curtain, and pushed its way into one of the boxes, and fell asleep.

"How many cats are there?" Tom said.

And Suzanne said, "We'd better keep track." And she got the notepad out and wrote a number for each cat down the side of the page, and wrote what each one looked like beside it, like this:

cat number	looks like
1	ginger, fat
2	black with bits of white
3	Siamese, skinny
4	tortoiseshell, bits out of its ears, one funny eye

We kept count of the cats like that as they came and went from behind the curtain. Tom was the best at spotting them.

And it was me who said if they had any marks that made them stand out, so we would know it again, like, "black paws," or "a piece missing out of its left ear," or "three legs." And Suzanne added them onto the list.

And, after a bit, we took turns eating our sandwiches, and drinking our juice (which we had instead of the doughnuts and the coffee because Mom said she didn't have any doughnuts, only Kit Kats, and she

wouldn't make us a flask of coffee, and she was starting to get suspicious). And I ate Tom's sandwich as well as mine, because he said he didn't want his, because he only wanted the cookies.

And, after ages, it started to rain, and we had to keep wiping our sunglasses, and we still hadn't seen the New Cat, even though we had twenty-three others in the notepad.

And then Suzanne said, "Let's stop the stakeout for today," because it was getting too dark to see the cats, and if she wasn't back for her dinner, she would get in trouble off her Dad. So we started to pack up. And just when we were about to go, something gray shot up into the window, from behind the curtain, and pounced on the tail of the cat with three legs,

which had been hanging down over the window ledge. And the three-legged cat fought back. And then all the cats went mad, and started attacking one another. And you couldn't tell what cat was which; you could just see fur and eyes and teeth and claws.

Tom said, "That was *it*, Anna. That was the *New Cat*."

Tom wanted to go and knock on the door and ask if he could take the New Cat home.

But Suzanne said that wasn't what you did in stakeouts, because then the person being staked would know what was going on, and then Tom would have Blown Our Cover.

Tom said, "Oh." And then, "I think I'll go anyway." Because you can't really stop Tom

once he has decided to do something.

And he came out from behind the cross, and ran across the road, and knocked on the door. Just like that. No one answered. So he rang the bell. But no one came.

Suzanne looked through the binoculars. And then Tom walked round the side of the house. And started opening the gate. So me and Suzanne came out from the stakeout spot, and ran after him.

When we got there, Tom was already in the back garden.

"It's a bit messy," he said. Which it was. There was an old mattress, and a sofa, and a frying pan. And lots of things that don't normally go in the garden. And there were more cats as well.

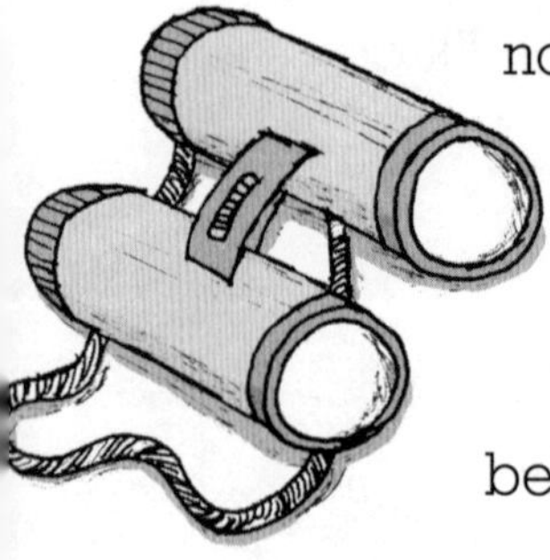

Tom knocked on the back door. We heard a noise, from behind it.

"Someone's coming," Suzanne said.

"Quick," I said. *"Run!"* And I started to go.

But Suzanne and Tom didn't follow, and when I looked back, there was just a big ginger cat, coming out of the cat flap.

Tom said, "I'm about the same size as that cat. Maybe I could get through the cat flap," and he put his head through it. And then he tried to get his shoulders in. But they wouldn't fit. So he took off his coat and tried again. And then he took off his Spider-Man suit with the built-in muscles.

And me and Suzanne got The Hysterics, watching Tom trying to get in, because he looked pretty funny just in his shoes and his underwear.

And then we stopped having The Hysterics because Tom was gone. And we hadn't really thought he could actually get

inside. Because Tom has tried to get in the cat flap at home, lots of times, and he always gets stuck. We looked in through the back windows, but they were too dirty to see through, and there were all sorts of things piled up behind them.

We banged on the back door, and ran round the front, and rang on the bell, and I shouted, "TOM!"

And then Suzanne started saying how it was her dinnertime, again, and how she would get in trouble off her Dad if she was late and all that.

And I said, "We can't leave." Because what if Tom was tied up, or trapped, or dead? And because I was supposed to be looking after him, and we were only supposed to be in the shed.

And then I saw Tom's head coming out through the cat flap. And he wriggled his shoulders through. And he said, "She's too busy looking for something now. And then she has to go shopping. We have to come back for the New Cat another time."

And Suzanne said, "Who?"

And Tom said, "The Cat Lady."

Suzanne looked at her watch. "Let's go," she said.

And there wasn't time for Tom to put his Spider-Man suit on, so he just did the first snap up, on his coat, and he didn't put his arms in, so it looked like a cape. And we ran home. Our fastest.

When me and Tom got in, we could hear Suzanne's Dad through the wall. Shouting about the time, and

Suzanne's dinner, and how it was cold.

Mom wanted to know where me and Tom had been, and why Tom only had his coat on.

"In the shed," I said.

But Mom said she had checked. And then she asked Tom. And Tom said how we had been to the Cat Lady's house, and done a stakeout and Blown Our Cover and all that. And how we had seen the New Cat. And how he got in through the cat flap. And Mom wasn't pleased. Because she said how she had told us already about poking about in other people's property, and we were not to do it. And under no circumstances should we go in through other people's cat flaps.

Tom said, "But what about the New Cat?"

Mom said that after dinner she would go and knock on the door herself, and ask if the lady had the New Cat, and if she did, she would bring it back.

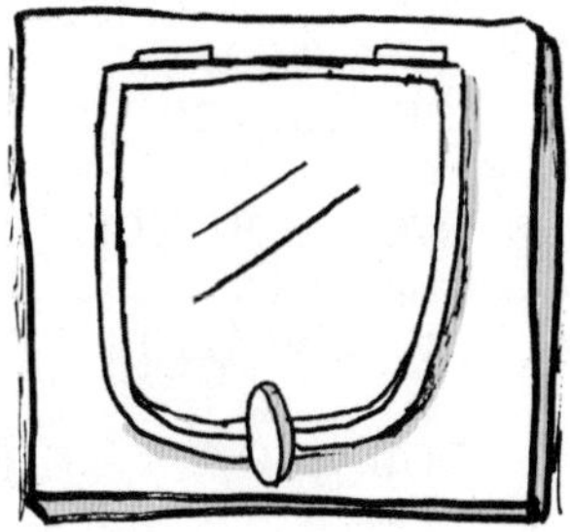

Me and Tom were waiting on the stairs when Mom got back.

"Did you get the New Cat?" Tom said.

"No," said Mom. "Nobody answered." And then she said, "I don't want you going down to that house again. It doesn't look safe." And then she said how we had to come home straight from school every day, and we weren't to go out of the road on our own again unless she said. Mom said she would call at the house again, later in the week, and maybe someone would be home then, and she would ask about the New Cat then.

When everyone was in bed, Suzanne knocked three times on the wall. And I knocked three times back, and we climbed up into the loft, and across the beams, to the hole in the wall, and we talked about everything up there, like the New Cat and the Cat Lady. And how Mom said she was going to try to get the New Cat back. And how, if she didn't, we could say we were going to Sunday School again next week, and go back ourselves.

CHAPTER 15

The New Cat's New Home

Mom went down to the Cat Lady's house three times, but she never came back with the New Cat.

And the Cat Lady had told Tom we had to come back another time. So when Sunday came round, we told Mom we were going to Sunday School. Which was nearly true because Sunday School was very nearby. And if we got the New Cat back, like Suzanne said, we could go to Sunday School afterward.

We went round the back of the Cat Lady's house, and Tom squeezed in through the cat flap again. And he opened the back door. And me and Suzanne went inside.

It was dark in the Cat Lady's house. And it didn't smell very nice, a bit like the Real Smelling Cesspit, at the Viking Center, where we went on the school trip.

It was even messier inside the house than it was in the garden. There were boxes, and books, and hats, and papers, and picture frames in piles against all the walls. And there was a bald mannequin, and a broken coat stand, and a stuffed deer's head, and some dead flowers in the sink.

Suzanne said, "Is this the kitchen, do you think?"

I said I wasn't sure because it was hard to tell, because if there was an oven, or a dishwasher, or a fridge, they must have been hidden under piles of things. It was like the Brownie jumble sale, before Brown Owl has sorted everything into stalls for clothes, and bric-a-brac, and white elephant, and all that, when all the trash bags have been emptied into the middle of the floor. Only it was more like a hundred Brownie jumble sales. Because some of the piles went right up to the ceiling.

We heard some rustling, and a crashing sound coming from the next-door room.

"That's her," Tom said. And he opened the door, and looked through. "Hello?"

"Send them away, Polly," a voice said. "I'm not inclined to receive this Sunday."

And then there was more rustling and banging and crashing. And a saucepan with no handle came whizzing past, and then a shoe, and then a stuffed owl, which hit Suzanne on the head.

"Ow," Suzanne said.

The Cat Lady came out from a pile of things, backward, and she was coughing from the dust, and she turned round and saw us standing in the door. She looked frightened. "What do you want?"

"Our cat," said Tom.

"How did you get in here? Did Polly let you in?"

"No," said Tom. "I came in through the cat flap."

"Ah, in that case, I apologize. If it's small enough to get in by itself, it's small enough to stay, that's what I say. I had thought you were someone else." And then she whispered, *"Someone official."* And she looked around her in case anyone was listening. "I should have known by your height, I suppose, but they start them so young these days, and they're often undernourished. A policeman knocked lately, and if it wasn't for his hat, I'd have sworn he was the paperboy."

And then the Cat Lady put her hand to her forehead. "I was looking for something, just now, and I can't remember what it is. . . . Do excuse me a moment. . . ."

And she went into another pile of things, and she rummaged around, and started throwing things out behind her from inside it. And one of them was a pile of our "Missing" posters, about the New Cat.

Suzanne picked up one of the posters and said, "This is the cat we're looking for."

The Cat Lady stopped looking for a moment. "You've lost something, have you? How frustrating. I was looking for something myself just now, only I've quite forgotten what it is."

Suzanne held out the poster. The Cat Lady looked at the picture. "Ah, it's not an affectionate animal, but a marvelous mouser."

The fat ginger cat, which we had seen last time coming out the cat flap, started rubbing itself against the Cat Lady's legs. "I don't encourage them—the cats—you understand. They just come. But, once they're here, it would be awfully rude not to offer them something. Some of them have traveled."

And then she tipped a big bag of dried cat food onto the floor, and all the cats came round, and started eating it. And the ginger cat ate the most. And he guarded his patch, and if the other cats came near, he went for them. And in about a minute, the food was all gone. And the cats went back to their places.

"They're all in good health, though, as you can see."

They didn't look in good health to *me*. They were the skinniest, scraggiest cats I'd ever seen. Apart from the fat ginger one.

The Cat Lady said, "He's been with me from the beginning. He was a mouser too, in his youth, but now, as you see, he's gone to fat. I've had to enlarge the cat flap. But I'm forgetting myself—do forgive me—it's been so long since we've had company. Will you take some tea?"

Suzanne said, "Yes, please."

The Cat Lady pulled a little bell out of her pocket, and she rang it, and she looked up, like she was waiting for someone to come, and she shook her head and said, "She sleeps so late these days. And who can blame her, of course, a whole life spent in service. Well, if we're to make it ourselves, we shall almost certainly require a kettle. You can never find one when you need one, and when you don't, of course, there's ten all at once. . . ." And she started looking through the piles again.

She didn't find a kettle, but she spotted the saucepan without the handle that had gone whizzing past Suzanne's head, and she said, "Aha. Here we are."

And she went outside and filled it from the outside tap by the back door. And she came back in, and lit a camping stove. And she boiled the water on that. And she said, "If I'd known you were coming, I'd have had Polly bring out the best china." And she rang her little bell again. And she listened. And then she banged with a broom handle on the ceiling, but no one answered.

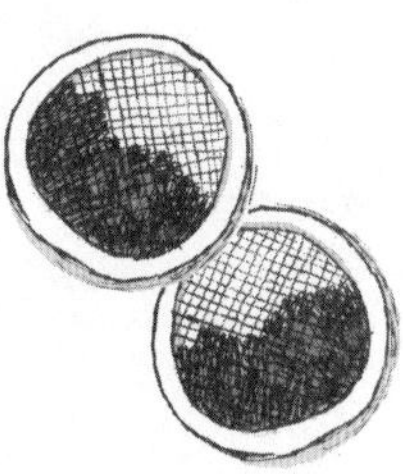

"Deaf as a post. I should replace her, I suppose, but she's *not quite right,* and who else would take her?"

She rooted around inside her pocket,

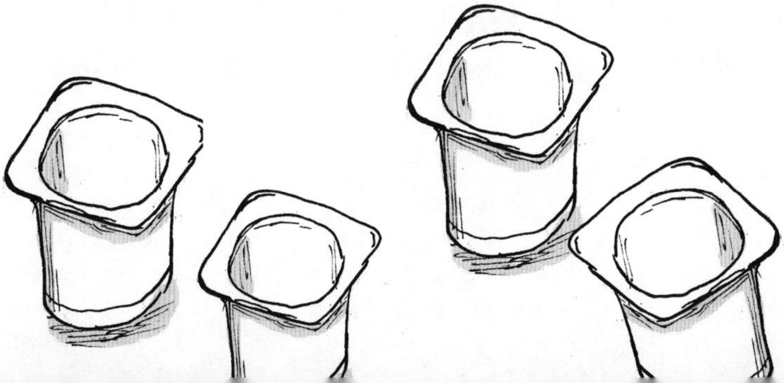

and brought out two tea bags, and she dropped them into the saucepan. Then she picked up four empty yogurt pots, and she tipped them upside down, and a few dead flies fell out, and she blew the dust off, and wiped them on her skirt.

"This set is quite serviceable. Came down to me on Mother's side, if I remember rightly." And then she brought two stools over, and two boxes, from a heap behind the front door, and a crate, which she turned upside down for a table. And she poured the tea into the yogurt pots. And we all sat down. And she said, "After you," to Suzanne, and Suzanne said, "After you," to me.

I didn't really want it to be "after me" because the tea didn't look very nice, and there wasn't any milk, and because mine still had half a dead fly in it. But I drank some anyway. Which burned a bit because the tea was very hot, and the yogurt pot was starting to melt.

Tom said, "Have you got any cookies?"

"Cookies, cookies, now where would she keep such a thing?"

She rang the little bell again, and shouted, "Polly," up the stairs. And she started throwing things out behind her, from in the piles again. Until she spotted something on the floor, in the corner, and said, "Aha. The very thing." Which it wasn't really, because it was a beer coaster, but she gave it to Tom, and he bit it, and then he put it down.

And he said, "Can we look for the New Cat now?"

And the Cat Lady said, "Of

course, of course, it is so frustrating when one loses something." And she took three candles out of her pocket, and lit them, and gave us one each to hold. "Mother never held with electricity, and as time passes, I find myself more and more in agreement. It's terribly unforgiving. I shan't come upstairs with you, if you don't mind. I never do, these days. I do hope you find your cat. I was looking for something myself, just now, and I've quite forgotten what it is. . . ." And she went rooting through a pile again.

We started going upstairs.

And the Cat Lady called after us, "Do excuse the papers and so on, which aren't quite organized. My filing system is not what it was, and Polly has grown quite hopeless. Still, no one was ever hurt by a little untidiness."

And it *was* untidy upstairs, too. Even more untidy than downstairs. And more untidy than my and Tom's bedrooms were, the week that Mom went away when Dad was in charge. And more untidy than the shed, and the closet under the stairs. And the pile of Dad's broken things up in the loft.

Because you couldn't see the carpet, except for in little paths, through the piles, and it was so dirty that your feet stuck to it, and you couldn't tell what color it was. And you had to be careful not to knock into anything because, once, when Tom did, a whole pile of things collapsed, and clouds of dust came up, and cats scattered, and boxes, and a long lamp, and a set of brass fire irons, came crashing down, and nearly hit Suzanne on the head. Some of the rooms were so full we couldn't even open the door to look inside.

We searched in all the rooms we could get into, but we didn't see the New Cat. It was quite hard to see *anything* with the candles, and the mess, and all the curtains being closed. After a while we started back downstairs. Suzanne went first. And me and Tom followed, and as we got near the bottom, when Suzanne put her foot forward, to tread onto the last step, something pounced on it, in the dark, with all its claws out, and it dug them right in, and sank its teeth into her ankle.

And Suzanne screamed, "Agh!" and kicked her leg in the air. And the thing flew off, and hit the wall.

"It's the New Cat!" Tom said.

Tom tried to pick the New Cat up, and its ears went flat, and its fur went big,

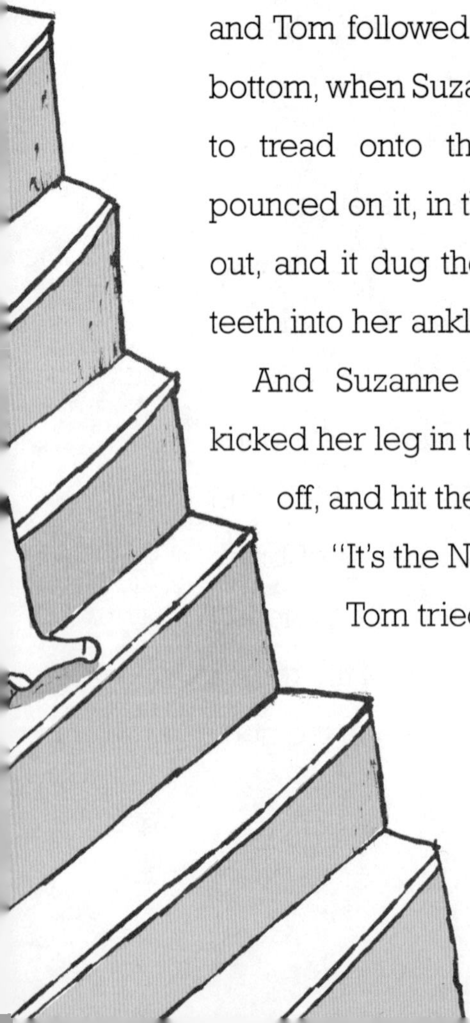

and it scratched, like it always does.

So we went and got the gardening gloves, and the cat carrier. And we got the New Cat into a corner, and we shooed it into the cat carrier. And we took it to show the Cat Lady.

"A cause for celebration," she said. "I suppose champagne would be too much, at this hour, and a Sunday after all. And heaven only knows where Polly might have put it. But will you take some more tea?"

I didn't want any more tea, and nor did Tom and Suzanne. "No thanks," we said.

The Cat Lady looked disappointed. "Have you got any stories instead?" Tom said. "Because we could celebrate with one of those."

"I suppose you know the story of the Cat That Walked By Himself?"

Tom said, "No."

And the Cat Lady said, "Shall we have that one, then?"

And Tom said, "Yes." And we sat down.

And the Cat Lady lit some more candles, and even the cats went quiet, and she said, "HEAR and attend and listen; for this befell and behappened and became and was, O my Best Beloved, when the Tame animals were wild. The Dog was wild, and the Horse was wild, and the Cow was wild, and the Sheep was wild, and the Pig was wild—as wild as wild could be—and they walked in the Wet Wild Woods by their wild lones."

And after a while the Cat Lady stopped, and put her hand up to her forehead, and said, "Oh, I've just remembered, I was looking for something, wasn't I, just now, and I've quite forgotten what it is. . . . Do excuse me. . . ."

And she went into one of the piles, and started looking through it.

And me and Tom and Suzanne went out the back door and went home, with the New Cat, with its ears flat, in the carry case.

CHAPTER 16
Shopping

We opened the front door, and let the New Cat out of the cat carrier, and shooed it inside, and Suzanne took the carry case and the gardening gloves and put them back in the shed.

When Mom saw the New Cat, she said, "Where on earth did you find it?"

"At Church," I said, before Tom said anything. Because even though I told Tom about a million times that he shouldn't say

anything to Mom about being in the Cat Lady's house, and all that, because we're banned, Tom isn't always very good at lying, because sometimes he forgets, and tells the truth by mistake.

The New Cat sat still in the corridor, and looked around. And then it ran into the kitchen, and straight out the cat flap.

"Oh," said Tom.

I said, "Maybe it's gone hunting and it'll be back in a bit."

But it wasn't. And it didn't come back all week.

So when Sunday came around, me and Tom told Mom we were going to Sunday School again, and we called on Suzanne, and we went back to the Cat Lady's house instead.

Tom went in through the cat flap, and let

me and Suzanne in, just like last time, and we told the Cat Lady how the New Cat had gone missing.

And the Cat Lady pointed to the corner where the New Cat was after a mouse.

Suzanne tried to get the New Cat away from the mouse, because it was still a bit alive, and the New Cat went mad, and shot up the curtains, and upset one of the piles, and sent all the cats scattering. And the other cats started attacking one another, and you could just see fur and eyes and teeth and claws. And the mouse got away, through a hole in the floor.

The Cat Lady tipped a bag of cat food into the middle of the floor, and the cats all came round, and started eating. Except the New Cat, which was staring at the hole where the mouse had gone.

Me and Tom and Suzanne closed in on

the New Cat, and got it into the cat carrier, and closed the door. And the New Cat watched the mouse hole through the mesh.

And we sat down on the crates, and Tom asked the Cat Lady to tell us the next bit in the story.

And the Cat Lady lit some candles and told us some more about the Cat That Walked By Himself.

And after that we took the New Cat home again. And this time we pushed it in through the cat flap, like it had come back on its own. And then we went in ourselves and put the lock on. And we put some pieces of ham in the New Cat's dish and the cream off the top

of the milk. And it had a nap, in its basket, with one eye open. And when it woke up, it tried to get out the cat flap, but it couldn't because of the lock, so it just banged its head. And after that it went and waited by the front door, and as soon as someone opened it, which was Mom to let Pam in, the New Cat ran through it.

After that, Suzanne said that she didn't think there was much point in getting the New Cat into the cat carrier every week, and getting all bitten and scratched, and bringing it back. Not if it was only going to run away again. Which was probably true.

And Tom said that, next time, he didn't mind if we just visited the New Cat at the Cat Lady's house, and took the gardening gloves so he could stroke it, and listened to the rest of the Cat Lady's story.

The next Sunday, after Tom had stroked

the New Cat, the Cat Lady asked, "Does anyone fancy a spot of shopping?"

Tom said, "Yes." Because he loves going to the shops, even when it's just the butcher's and the greengrocer's and all that. Because he carries a bag, and sits up on the counter, and dips his wellies in the horse trough on the way past.

I don't like shopping, not like Tom, because normally it's pretty boring, unless it's for sweets. So I said, "What will we be shopping for?"

"We can hardly know until we find it," said the Cat Lady.

Which is different from going shopping with Mom, because she always knows exactly what she's shopping for, because she has it on a list, on the side of the fridge, that says "milk" and "bread" and "braising steak."

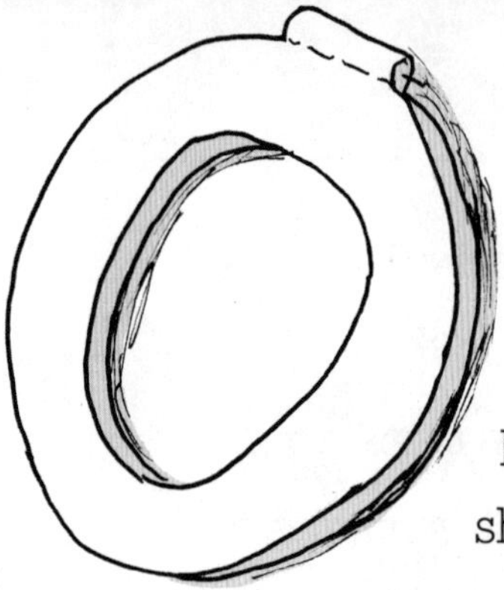

But the Cat Lady went past all the food shops, and she went in the charity shop instead. She looked around, and picked things up, and asked the man, "How much is this?" about things. Even though they all had the price on the bottom.

And the man told her, and then the Cat Lady said, "Dear, oh dear, that's daylight robbery." Even about a whole set of cutlery for fifty pence. And then she said, "We shall go elsewhere."

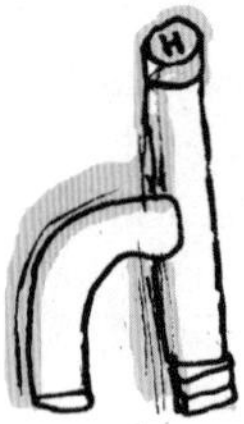

And after that we went into the park, and along by the river, and the Cat Lady said, "Keep your eyes peeled." And she poked in the bins, and then we saw a Dumpster, and the Cat Lady got quite excited. And there were all

sorts of things in there that somebody didn't want, like a broken toilet seat, and a tap with no knobs, and a big rusty hinge.

And me and Suzanne found a few things we thought the Cat Lady would like. Like a can to put her trash in, and some net curtains that looked brand new, and four china cups, which were hardly chipped at all. But the Cat Lady said, "You take them. That's not the kind of thing I need."

And then Tom found a bag of jam-jar lids, all different sizes, and a leg off a chair, and a pair of glasses with the glass missing, which only had one arm. And he showed them to the Cat Lady.

And the Cat Lady said, "Marvelous. Well, what a wonderful eye you have." And she put them straight into her cart. And when the cart was full, she said, "That's enough for today."

And we went back to the house.

Tom and the Cat Lady looked through the things that they had collected. And they found places to put them. And they were both pretty pleased. And the Cat Lady made us some tea, and Suzanne got the china cups out, which we had found. And I gave Tom the cookie I brought from home. And we lit the candles, and sat down. Tom stroked the New Cat with the gardening gloves. And the Cat Lady carried on the story about the Cat That Walked By Himself.

"And the Cat walked by himself, and all places were alike to him. Of course the Man was wild too. He was dreadfully wild. He didn't even begin to be tame till he met the Woman, and she told him that she did not like living in his wild ways. She picked out a nice dry Cave, instead of a heap of wet leaves, to lie down in; and she strewed clean sand on the floor; and she lit a nice fire of wood at the back of the Cave; and she hung a dried wild-horse skin, tail down, across the opening of the Cave; and she said, 'Wipe your feet, dear, when you come in, and now we'll keep house.'"

CHAPTER 17

The Letters

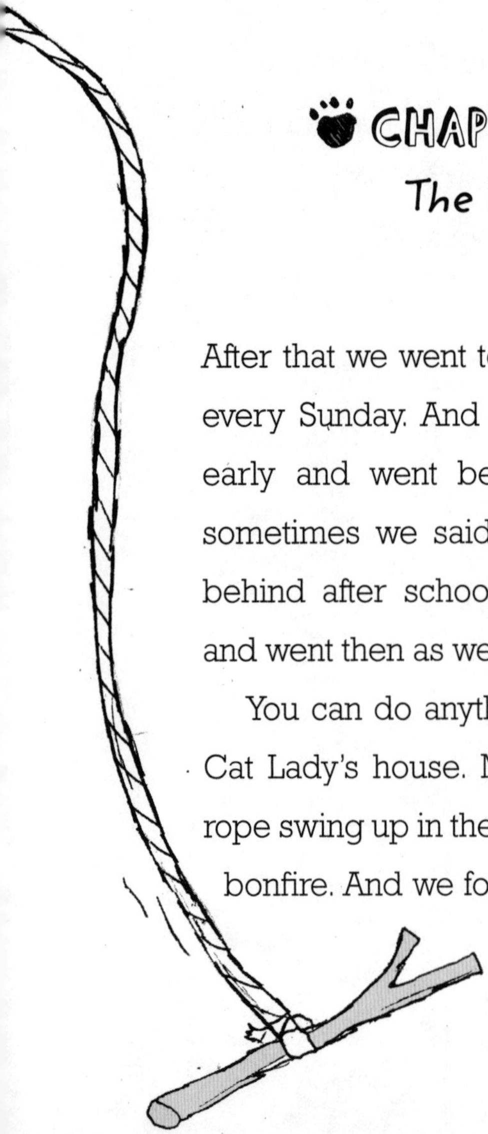

After that we went to the Cat Lady's house every Sunday. And some days we got up early and went before school, too. And sometimes we said that we were staying behind after school for Homework Club, and went then as well.

You can do anything you want to at the Cat Lady's house. Me and Suzanne put a rope swing up in the garden. And we built a bonfire. And we found a bag full of tins of sardines and cooked them outside on the camping stove.

Once, when we were there, the doorbell rang. The Cat Lady froze. "Shh," she said, "it's them."

Me and Suzanne got down on our knees, and looked over the window ledge, through the net curtains. There was a man and a woman, in suits. They rang the bell again. And they waited. And then the man put a letter through the letter box. And they went away.

Suzanne went to the door and pulled the letter from the pile of things in front of it and gave it to the Cat Lady.

"I can't imagine where poor Polly will find the time to deal with all this correspondence," the Cat Lady said. "She's not educated, of course, but Mother took care to see she knew her letters, and even in ill health, her handwriting is immaculate."

She put the letter in a bag with

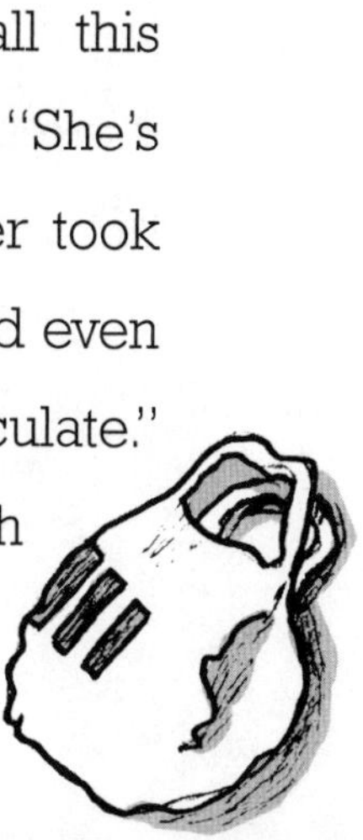

lots of others. And then she said, "Are we shopping?"

And Tom said, "Yes."

But Suzanne said, "I think me and Anna will wait here and help Polly."

And the Cat Lady looked pleased. And me and Suzanne were pleased too, because we didn't really like going down the river-bank, and looking for bits of rubbish, and getting things out of Dumpsters and trash cans, not like Tom. Shopping with the Cat Lady was Tom's favorite thing.

When they had gone, Suzanne went and got the bag full of letters. And she tipped them out, onto the floor, and she counted them all. There were forty-four. And none of them had ever been opened.

Suzanne said, "Let's put them all in order."

So we did, by the dates on the envelopes,

which said when they had been mailed.

And we laid them all out in a long line on the floor. And some of the letters were from three years ago.

"I wonder what they're about?" Suzanne said. And so did I.

"Maybe we should open one."

"Just one," said Suzanne.

So we did. This is what the first letter said:

Dear Mrs. Neville,

We have received numerous complaints relating to the buildup of refuse in the garden to the rear of your property, including several dozen black trash bags, a double mattress, two Chesterfield sofas, and a fridge/freezer. This is a formal request that these items be removed, and the garden cleared to a reasonable standard. Should you require help with the clearance, please contact us at the above number.

Yours sincerely,

Mr. A. Grabham
Senior Environmental Health Officer

And then we opened another one, from the same person, also about the garden, saying it had got worse, and how more people had complained, and asking if the Cat Lady would like someone from the council to come to her house and help her.

And then, after a year, there was one that said:

Dear Mrs. Neville,

An examination of the exterior of your property, and a partial examination of the interior (through the rear windows), has found that its condition threatens both your own health and that of other property occupiers in the immediate vicinity. In particular, we are concerned to find evidence of rats and mice in and around the property (despite the presence of at least twelve cats). We also observed rotting food items and large quantities of animal waste, both inside and outside your property, as well as generally unsanitary and unsafe conditions.

As stated in previous correspondence, failure to keep your property clean, and clear of accumulations of refuse, presents a risk to public health, and, as such, if the current situation does not improve, the council will intervene. Please contact us to arrange for assistance in this matter.

And there were letters giving times and days when people from the council would be coming to talk to the Cat Lady. And others asking to make an appointment. And there were leaflets about "Health and Well-Being in Your Home," and "Caring and Support Services in Your Community," with questionnaires for the Cat Lady to say whether they were "very useful" or "quite useful," or "not very useful," "not at all useful," or whether she was "unsure."

And me and Suzanne filled in the questionnaires, to post back. And we ticked the "unsure" box. And then we were down to the last letter, which was the one that had just arrived. It said:

Dear Mrs. Neville,

We have attempted to work with you to improve the repair and condition of your property. However, this approach has not resulted in improvements. We therefore see no alternative but to carry out works ourselves. We shall require access to the property over several consecutive days, with as many return visits as deemed necessary, in order to clear it of refuse and restore it to a reasonable standard for habitation. If we do not hear from you with alternative dates, we shall arrive to commence the clearance on Monday, October 24.

And that was in a week.

CHAPTER 18
A Reply

After the Cat Lady and Tom got back from shopping, and showed us their things, and we had all had some tea, and Tom stroked the New Cat with the gardening gloves on, and the Cat Lady had told us the next bit of the Cat That Walked By Himself, me and Tom and Suzanne went home.

And Suzanne took the bag full of letters from the council, because we didn't think the Cat Lady would notice. And, like she said, "Somebody better reply." Because a few of them said **"DELIVERED BY HAND"** in red letters on the front, and they looked pretty important. And because we knew that the Cat Lady wouldn't like it if people from the council came to clear her house out, because she doesn't let anyone in, except for the cats, and me and Tom and Suzanne. And because she hates throwing things away, even more than Dad.

So me and Suzanne started writing back, and we put at the bottom "From Polly," even though we had never met her, and like Suzanne once whispered when the Cat Lady was trying to get Polly's attention by banging on the ceiling with the broom handle, "I don't think Polly actually exists." We wrote back whenever we could, in break and lunchtime at school, and in the back of our notebooks when we were meant to be doing math problems,

and at night when we were supposed to be in bed, through the hole in the wall in the loft. And this is what some of the letters said:

Dear Mr. Grabham,

Thank you for your letter about Mrs. Neville's garden. She does not require help with it though thank you very much because it isn't actually rubbish because I think you'll find most of it is ~~air~~ heir looms that came down to her on her Mother's side (who was a hard lady but fair and taught me my immaculate handwriting despite my time of life).

Yours sincerely,
Polly

Dear Mr. Grabham,

I think it is quite rude to go round looking in people's windows, actually. Especially their rear ones. And that is probably why I keep Mrs. Neville's windows so dirty. Her health is good and so is her cats'. If her neighbors are not well that is not really Mrs. Neville's fault. I hope they get better soon. Have they tried putting their heads over a bowl of boiling water and having some Heinz chicken soup? I have not been quite right myself lately, so I have got a little bit behind with the cleaning. I am better now though and will start picking up the cat poop.

From Polly

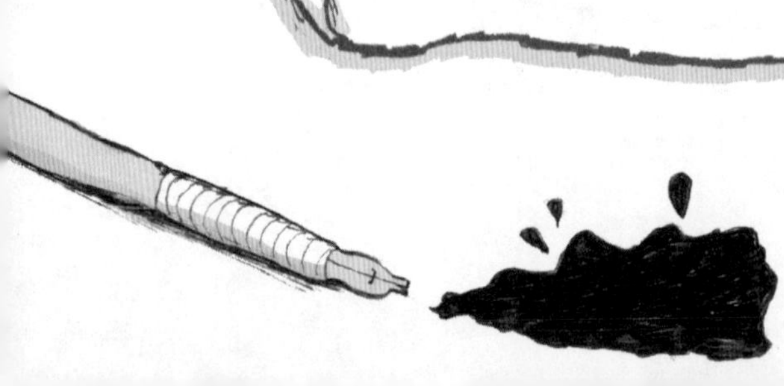

Dear Mr. Grabham,

By the time you get this I will have put new curtains up, moved the cat poop, put the dead rats in the trash, and put some flowers that aren't as dead in the window boxes. I hope that this means you do not need to come on October 24. If you do come, Mrs. Neville will be out shopping, and I am sleeping late these days (who can blame me after my life in service?) so I'm afraid you won't be able to get in.

From Polly

And, after that, a new letter came. It said:

Dear Mrs. Neville,

In light of recent correspondence from your employee, Polly, we are arranging for a new inspection of your property. We hope to find the conditions of your property improved significantly. If we do not find these to be sufficient, the clearance of your property will be rescheduled for the following week.

Yours sincerely,

Mr. Grabham

After that, every time Tom and the Cat Lady went out shopping, me and Suzanne did jobs at the Cat Lady's house. We raked the rubbish in the garden and put it into bags, and lit a bonfire, and burned it, and collected all the broken glass. We cleaned the front window, and scrubbed the front step.

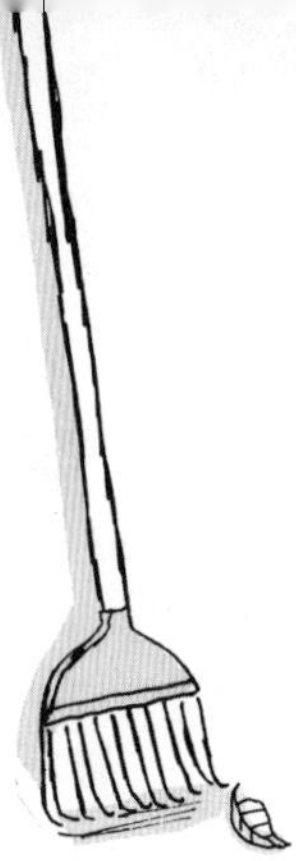

It was hard to make things look tidy because there were so many piles of things, and as soon as we put some in the trash or on the bonfire, Tom and the Cat Lady came back with a cart full of new ones.

One time, when Tom and the Cat Lady were out, and I was looking around the house for dead mice and rats, for burying outside, and Suzanne was picking all the cat poop up, and putting them in a trash bag, for burning on the bonfire, the doorbell rang.

Suzanne said, "It might be Mr. Grabham, the council man, come to do the inspection."

We looked out over the

window ledge, through the new net curtain. It wasn't the council man, though. It was Mom.

"*Anna,* I know you're in there."

Me and Suzanne stayed still and didn't say anything. And after a while we heard something out the back, and we went to look out through the cat flap.

Mom was coming up the back garden, past the broken television, and the mattress, and the rolls of chicken wire. And she saw the bonfire, with the rubbish, and the cat poop burning on it, and she saw me and Suzanne looking out through the cat flap.

And she said, "*Home*, now."

I said, "We have to wait for Tom. He's gone shopping."

"Shopping?" Mom said. "Is that what you call it? Tom is home already, Anna."

And she didn't say anything else, all the way home.

Suzanne went into her house. And me and Mom went into ours.

Mom said, "Sit down." And she told me all about how Mrs. Constantine had called round, and how Tom was with her, and how she had found him looking through the trash cans behind the Church with Mrs. Neville.

And how she had asked Mrs. Constantine where I was. And Mrs. Constantine didn't know.

And how Mom asked, "Wasn't she at Sunday School?"

And Mrs. Constantine told her how me and Tom hadn't been to Sunday School for weeks.

And then Mom started shouting, like she never normally does, almost as loud as Suzanne's Dad, and she said, "YOU LIED, ANNA, AND YOU LET TOM GO

OFF WITHOUT YOU, WITH A STRANGER, LOOKING IN TRASH CANS, AND YOU AND SUZANNE HAVE BEEN PICKING UP RATS AND CAT POOP, AND BURNING THEM ON BONFIRES. IT'S A MIRACLE YOU DIDN'T GET TOXOPLASMOSIS, OR WEIL'S DISEASE, OR BURN YOURSELVES ALIVE."

I tried to tell Mom how Tom wasn't with a stranger because he was with the Cat Lady and they had only gone shopping. And me and Suzanne were just trying to tidy up, and how we wouldn't have burned ourselves alive because we know all about fires from Brownies, and Suzanne has got her Fire Safety Badge, and she knows how to escape from a smoke-filled room and everything actually, and Mom said, *"ANNA . . . ,"* like she always does. But louder. *"ENOUGH!"*

And she said that I shouldn't say anything

else. And I should go upstairs. And think about what I'd done.

This is what my dictionary says about toxoplasmosis and Weil's disease:

toxoplasmosis [tok-soh-plaz-moh-sis]
✦ *noun (pathology)*
infection with the parasite *Toxoplasma gondii,* transmitted to humans by consumption of insufficiently cooked meat containing the parasite or by contact with contaminated cats or their feces

Weil's [vahylz] ✦ *noun (medical)*
a type of leptospirosis in humans, an infectious disease characterized by fever and jaundice, that damages the liver and kidneys, often caused by bacteria in the urine of rats

CHAPTER 19
The Cat Lady

Me and Suzanne missed going to the Cat Lady's house. But not as much as Tom did, going shopping with the Cat Lady, and stroking the New Cat with the gardening gloves, and hearing about the Cat That Walked By Himself, and all that.

After ages, when Mom stopped being cross, she said if me and Tom wanted, the Cat Lady could come to our house. And she would call round and invite her.

"The Cat Lady won't answer the door," I said.

"I'll pop a note through," said Mom.

"The Cat Lady doesn't open her post," I said, "because she thinks someone called Polly does it, who probably doesn't exist."

But Mom went anyway, and she knocked on the door. And when no one answered, she put a note through, with our address on it, and all that, asking the Cat Lady to come. And she said, "I'm sure she will if she wants to."

But the Cat Lady never came.

After a while, me and Suzanne went back to doing things in the shed, and collecting worms, and making wasp traps, and all that. And Tom went up and down the road collecting gravel, and walking in a straight line with his eyes closed, and picking up litter with Mr. Tucker.

And we didn't do much else because we weren't allowed past the bottom of the road by ourselves. Because Mom said we couldn't be trusted anymore.

Then, one day, which was Tuesday because Suzanne was there, when we were all having our dinner, the cat flap flipped open, and the New Cat came in.

The New Cat looked wilder than ever. And its fur was even more matted, and one of its ears had a bit missing, and it was so skinny you could see the bones in its back.

Mom went and got some cat food and put it in the New Cat's dish, and the New Cat ate it all, really fast, and it kept looking behind it, like one of us might take its food.

And after that it sat on the rug by the radiator. And Tom went and got the gardening gloves, and stroked it. And the

New Cat didn't scratch, or try to get away. It just stayed still, and closed its eyes, and fell asleep.

Tom said, "The New Cat has probably come to see me, because I haven't been to visit, and soon it will go back."

But the New Cat stayed all night. And in the morning, it was still there.

On the way to school, we told Joe-down-the-street all about the New Cat and what had happened, and how it had come back. And Joe said that his babysitter Brian's cat had come back as well.

And at playtime Suzanne asked Emma Hendry if she had found her cat. And she said, "It came back yesterday. All on its own."

When we got home, me and Tom and Suzanne told Mom about how Emma's and Brian's cats had come back.

And Mom said, "How strange, I wonder why."

"We could go down to the Cat Lady's house and see," I said.

And Tom said, "If she doesn't answer the door, I can go in through the cat flap."

And Mom started going on about how you shouldn't go poking round other people's houses, and going in through their cat flaps, and how the Cat Lady's house isn't safe, and all that.

And she said, "I'll go and see if she's all right myself."

When Mom came back, she said, "Nobody's home. There aren't any lights on. Maybe she's visiting relatives. I'll try again tomorrow."

But the Cat Lady never has lights on. Because she doesn't like electricity. And, like Suzanne said, "I don't think she's got any relatives." And Mom going again tomorrow wouldn't make any difference because, like we already told her, the Cat Lady won't answer the door. Me and Tom and Suzanne went out to the shed and started trying to think of reasons why the cats had come back.

Tom said, "I think the New Cat came back to see me."

"I think it came back because it was hungry," Suzanne said. Which was probably true. Because it was thin, and it had only been back for a night, and it had eaten four tins of cat food, three slices of ham, and two of Tom's cookies, which it doesn't normally like.

Suzanne said, "The Cat Lady must have stopped feeding the cats."

"Why would she do that?" I asked.

"What if she ran out of cat food?" Tom said.

And Suzanne said, "What if she just forgot?"

And I said, "What if she's not very well?"

And Suzanne said, "What if she's dead?"

Tom started chewing his sleeve.

"We need to go down and find out," Suzanne said. But, like I told Suzanne, we couldn't do that because of being banned. And because of not being allowed past the bottom of the road on our own. And because ever since everything happened with the Cat Lady, Mom was always coming out and checking where we were, and what we were up to.

"There's no way we can go without Mom noticing," I said.

But Suzanne said, "There might be *one* way." And she reached behind the stepladders, under the shelf with the wasp trap, and the worm box, and she pulled out the plan for going through all the lofts, which we did ages ago, before we started trying to find the New Cat.

The plan wasn't finished, because we had only written the title, which was "Anna's And Suzanne's Plan To Find Out If There Are Holes In All The Walls In All The Lofts In All The Houses In The Road And, If There Are, Whether We Can Climb Through Them And Come Out In The House At The Bottom, Which is Joe-Down-the-Street's." But Suzanne said we should try it anyway. Because she said we could just go up into my bedroom, and Mom wouldn't check on us if we were playing up there. And we could get up inside the loft, and go through all the holes, and come out at the bottom of the road, in Joe's. And then we could run down to the village and check on the Cat Lady, and go back the same way, without Mom knowing we had even left my bedroom.

"It's easy," said Suzanne.

It didn't sound that easy, I didn't think, because for one thing we didn't even know if the lofts *did* all have holes in them, or if they were all joined together. And for another thing when we got to the bottom, the hatch in Joe's house might be closed, and how would we get out?

Suzanne got a flashlight down from the shelf in the shed, and she turned it on, and she said, "Who wants to come?"

And Tom said, "Me." And he put on his Bob the Builder hard hat with the light on the front.

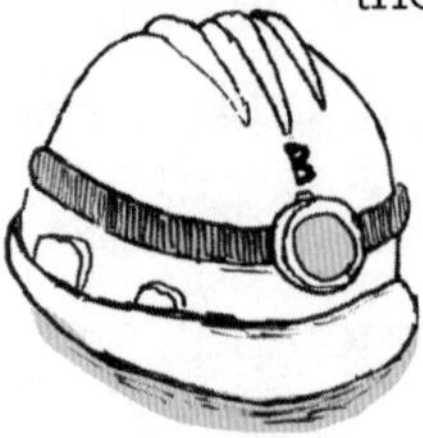

And we went up into my bedroom. And we got up on the chest of drawers, and opened the hatch, and pulled ourselves up into the loft. And we got up onto the beam and balanced on it, and I told Tom how we had to step from one beam to the next. Which was a bit hard. Because Tom's legs are only little. And when we went across, he nearly missed the beam, and slipped, and he grabbed on to Dad's pile of "useful" things, from the closet under the stairs, to stop himself from falling off.

Dad's pile of things wobbled, and the toaster fell off the top, and hit Suzanne on the head.

"Ow," Suzanne said.

And then the whole pile collapsed. And all of Dad's things came down: the bag of worn-out footballs, and the broken tennis rackets, and the pile of newspapers he hasn't got round to reading yet. And the alarm clock that doesn't go off, and the kettle that me and Tom blew up by mistake. And the stool with

one leg,
and a bucket
with a hole in the
bottom, and half
a broom handle
without a head. And
the boxes. And the
bag of clothes
from the olden
days. And it
went right
through the
ceiling.

"Oh,"
Suzanne said.

Me and
Tom and
Suzanne got down on

our hands and knees. And we looked through the hole in the ceiling, down to my bedroom underneath, where all Dad's things were on the floor.

And then Mom came running in, and she looked down at the pile of things on the floor, and she looked up at me and Tom and Suzanne through the hole, and she said, "Are you three all right?"

And I said, "Yes."

And she said *"Anna . . . ,"* like she always does, only a bit angrier, "*come down.*"

And we did. And Mom said how me and Tom and Suzanne had "NO BUSINESS BEING IN THE LOFT." And we were "NEVER TO GO UP THERE AGAIN." And she said, *"DO YOU HEAR ME?!"* And we did. Because she said it quite loud.

And Mom looked at the pile of things

on the floor, and back up at the hole in the ceiling, and she said, *"PETE . . ."*

And Dad came in. And he saw the hole, and all his things, and how they had come through the ceiling. And he said, "Ah, well, the thing *is*, you *see* . . ."

And Mom told me and Tom and Suzanne to go and play outside. So we did. And we could hear Mom talking to Dad from in the front garden. All about his "rubbish," and how she had been asking him to get rid of it for "*ten years,*" and how he was "supposed to have taken it to *the dump,*" and how "SOMEONE COULD HAVE BEEN *KILLED.*" And how now she would have to have a *"WHOLE NEW CEILING!"*

Mr. Tucker was in the road, picking up litter. "Hallo, Bods," he said, "sounds like the Blitz in there."

We told him about how all Dad's things

had fallen through the ceiling. And how Mom was cross. And what had happened with the Cat Lady, and the New Cat, and how it had come back. And how we wanted to go to her house, to check if the Cat Lady was all right, in case she was sick, or dead, or she had run out of cat food or something like that. But we weren't allowed to go past the end of the road on our own.

"Not without a grown-up," Tom said.

Mr. Tucker said, "A grown-up, is it, Basher? And, say you found one? What's the plan on landing, Popsie?"

I said there wasn't really a plan.

"Mmmmm," said Mr. Tucker. "Take a dim view of that, very dim."

"There *is*," said Suzanne, "but we haven't *written* it yet."

"We just want to look," Tom said.

"Quick shufti, is it? Recon, you say? Well,

look here, bit hush-hush, keep it under your hats, but technically speaking, I'm a grown-up myself." Which was true. And Mr. Tucker said he would come with us.

On the way we told him all about the council, and the letters, and how the Cat Lady doesn't answer the door, and how Tom goes in through the cat flap.

And Mr. Tucker said, "Cat flap? Not sure I like the sound of that."

But me and Suzanne told Mr. Tucker how Tom had done it millions of times. And how as soon as he gets in, he opens the back door, and lets us in as well.

And Mr. Tucker said, "All right, aircrew, belt up: briefing. Basher, you're skipper; Old Lag's second Dicky. Popsie and Blondie, Arse-End Charlies." He looked at his watch. "T.O.T. eighteen hundred hours. So, when I give the green, Skipper's off, in through the cat flap, back door open, bang on target, no silly beggars. Any offensive fire, straight out, Old Chap. All clear?"

And me and Tom and Suzanne said it was.

And Mr. Tucker gave us the salute. And we gave him the salute back.

Suzanne opened the gate into the Cat Lady's back garden.

"Good God. Looks like it's been hit for a six. Right-o, Old Chum, got your clobber?"

Tom took his coat off, and switched on the light on his Bob the Builder hard hat.

"Chocks away."

Tom squeezed in through the cat flap.

Me and Suzanne and Mr. Tucker waited.

After a while, Mr. Tucker pushed open the cat flap. "All right in there, Basher?"

"I can't open the door," Tom said. "There's things in the way."

And there were, because Mr. Tucker shone his flashlight in.

There was more stuff than ever. And most of the piles had collapsed. And there wasn't enough room for Tom to turn round.

Mr. Tucker said, "Reverse gear, Basher. Backward. Easy does it."

But Tom didn't come back. He wriggled a bit farther forward.

And Mr. Tucker said, "That's far enough, Old Chum. Come back."

And then we heard a crash.

And Mr. Tucker said, "Basher? Can you hear me, Old Chap?"

But Tom didn't answer.

And Mr. Tucker shook the door handle, and then he leaned against the door, and pushed his shoulder against it. Then he walked down the garden. And when he got to the bottom, he shouted, "Clear the runway. . . ." And he ran at the door, and went straight into it with his shoulder. And the door burst open.

Tom was stuck under some boxes.

Mr. Tucker pulled them off him.

"Look," Tom said. And he pointed to the big ginger cat, which was sitting at the edge of a heap of boxes and papers and things that had collapsed.

Mr. Tucker shone his flashlight over. And he said, "Good God." Because next to the cat, sticking out from under one of the piles of things that had collapsed, was a pair of feet, like happens when the house falls in the *Wizard of Oz*, only without the ruby slippers.

Mr. Tucker picked Tom up, and the big ginger cat. And he carried them both out, and then he took us all to the phone box, and he dialed 999. And said, "Ambulance."

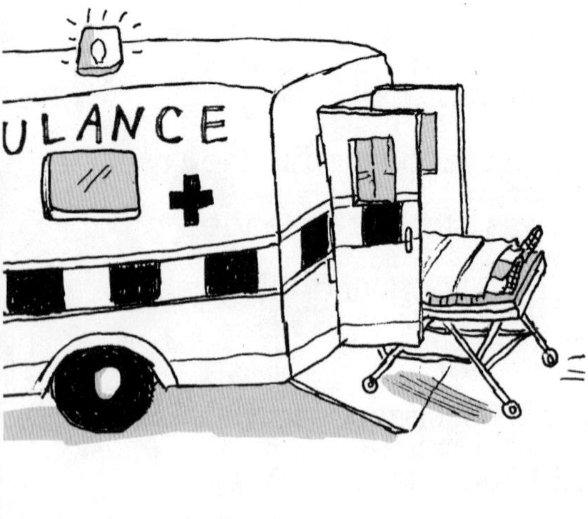

CHAPTER 20
The Hospital

The next day, at school, everyone was talking about the Cat Lady. And how the ambulance had come. And how they had had to smash the front window to get inside. And move mountains of things before they could find her. And how they brought her out on a stretcher, with an oxygen mask on. And put her in the ambulance, with the lights on and the siren. And how it was Tom who had found her. And how Mr. Tucker broke his arm, going in to get Tom. Which was all true. And that's why, after Mr. Tucker took us home, Dad took him to the hospital.

After school, Mom took me and Tom and Suzanne to visit Mr. Tucker. Mr. Tucker was sitting up in bed, with his arm in a sling. And Mom said, "Thank you," again to Mr. Tucker, for saving Tom.

And Mr. Tucker said how it was Tom who was the hero, and how he "ought to get a medal" and all that.

And Mom patted Tom on the head. And gave Mr. Tucker some grapes and said, "I'll be back for you all in an hour."

Mr. Tucker said, "Right Wing: Debriefing."

And we told him all about how the police put cones outside the Cat Lady's house, and tape that said "Keep Out." And how there

were three Dumpsters, and a fire engine, and two vans that said, "Environmental Health," and people in white space suits bringing things out of the Cat Lady's house, in bags that said "Toxic."

And Tom said, "Do you think that the Cat Lady is all right?"

And Mr. Tucker said, "Ask her yourself, Basher." And he pointed to the bed opposite. "Not sure I hold with it. All this mixed ward business." And he gave me the grapes and said, "Take her these. There's only so many a man can eat."

Both the Cat Lady's legs were in plaster, and they were up in the air. And she had lots of bruises from where all the things in the piles had fallen on top of her. And the nurse

told us we should be quiet because the Cat Lady wasn't well, and she was a bit confused, and how they thought she had been trapped on the floor for three days.

The Cat Lady didn't recognize me and Suzanne. But she smiled at Tom. And she patted the bed, beside her, and Tom sat on it. And she stroked him on the head. And Tom gave her the grapes, and asked her to tell us the rest of the story, about the Cat That Walked By Himself, because we never got to the end.

And the Cat Lady said, "Then the Man threw his two boots and his little stone ax at the Cat, and the Cat ran out of the Cave, and the Dog chased him up a tree; and from that day to this, Best Beloved, three proper Men out of five will always throw things at a Cat whenever they meet him, and all proper Dogs will chase him up a tree. But the Cat keeps his side of the bargain too. He will kill mice and he will be kind to Babies when he is in the house, just as long as they do not pull his tail too hard. But when he has done that, and between times, and when the moon gets up and night comes, he is the Cat that walks by himself, and all places are alike to him. Then he goes out to the Wet Wild Woods or up the Wet Wild Trees or on the Wet Wild Roofs, waving his wild tail and walking by his wild lone."

And Mr. Tucker started snoring in the bed opposite.

And then the Cat Lady fell asleep as well.

And me and Suzanne ate the rest of the grapes, and Tom ate Mr. Tucker's cookies, until Mom came to collect us.

CHAPTER 21
Cleaning the Cat Lady's House

That's pretty much everything that happened with Tom, and the Cat Lady, and the Great Cat Conspiracy.

All week people went in and out of her house while the Cat Lady was in the hospital. And they cleared everything out, even the carpets, and the wallpaper, and after they cleaned it, and made it so you could tell what each room was, people came in to paint the walls, inside the house and out, and the window frames, and the front step, and the door. And they put new glass in the windows, and new tiles on the roof. And made the chimney so it didn't look like it was going to fall off. And people said it took twenty-six Dumpsters to take all the things away and make the Cat Lady's house tidy.

On the day the Cat Lady came back from the hospital, Mom came with me and Tom and Suzanne to take her some flowers, and Mr. Tucker came too, with his arm in a sling, and he brought the ginger cat, which Mrs. Tucker had been looking after.

A nurse opened the door.

The Cat Lady was sitting in her front room, and she was looking at the wall. The nurse went into the kitchen to put the flowers in a vase.

And me and Tom and Suzanne and Mom and Mr. Tucker all sat down. On chairs. Because all the boxes and crates had gone.

The Cat Lady looked a bit scared. She was holding her hands tight under her chin. She looked around the room. And she saw her little bell, on the mantelpiece, and she rang it. And she looked up at the ceiling. And, very quietly, she said, "She's deaf as a post. One ought to replace her, but who else would take her, at her time of life?"

And then the nurse came in, and she said, "Can I help?"

The Cat Lady looked scared. "How did you get in here? Did Polly let you in?"

Mr. Tucker said to the nurse, "Prob'ly do with a brew up, I think."

And the nurse nodded her head and went to make some tea.

The Cat Lady looked worried. She put her hand on her forehead. "I was looking for something, just now," she said, "and I can't remember what it is."

She started looking around the room, and wringing her hands.

Tom opened the catch on the cat carrier. The ginger cat walked out, and it went over to the Cat Lady, and rubbed itself against the Cat Lady's legs, in the plaster casts. The Cat Lady picked the cat up, and closed her eyes, and held it tight.

Mom let me and Tom visit the Cat Lady after that. And for six weeks someone brought her meals on wheels and did all her cleaning, and looked after her while her legs were in plaster.

And then, when the Cat Lady got her casts off, the nurses and the helpers stopped coming. And the Cat Lady was pleased because she said, "Polly does everything I need in the house. And I'm quite capable of doing my own shopping."

And sometimes when we went, Mr. Tucker came with us, which the Cat Lady didn't like much, because she said, "How did you get in? Did Polly let you in?"

And Mr. Tucker said, "Spot on, Squadron Leader. Sit tight, shan't stop, quick shufti." And he picked up some rubbish from the corner and put it in his black trash bag.

And the Cat Lady said, "She had no business inviting any old Tom, Dick, or Harry in off the street," and she whispered to her cat, "The man is *quite mad*."

Mr. Tucker said, "That's it, tiggerty-boo, I shall get weaving. Chocks away." And he gave the Cat Lady a salute. And the Cat Lady looked at the wall. And Mr. Tucker went home.

Mr. Tucker came quite often, and picked up the litter in the Cat Lady's garden, and tried to keep things tidy in the house. And so did me and Suzanne. Because after the nurses and the helpers stopped coming, the Cat Lady started making a little pile of things at the bottom of the stairs, and leaving things in the sink, and once when we went, we couldn't see the kitchen table, and the time after that she had tipped cat food on the floor. And then, one day, we saw, behind the curtain, on the window ledge, there were three fruit boxes, with blankets in, and there was a sign next to them that said, "These cats are not forced to sit here. They do so of their own free will." And, slowly, after that, the cats started coming again.

The End